Ghost Bunny?

Twist dropped onto his stomach and stared at the rabbit. Slowly, he reached forward and his hand met no resistance as it passed over the line of blood. So he could cross it, but the rabbit was trapped inside.

The book had called it a containment circle. Well, that was pretty self-explanatory. And it worked! Twist had a hard time believing the dead witch's book was the real deal. It was all so bizarre.

He had to make sure, so he jumped to his feet again and ran around the circle, picked up some more gravel and tossed it at the rabbit. The animal jumped and scurried in a circle, clearly unable to penetrate the containment spell.

The rabbit raced another lap, then it veered into the center of the circle and dropped onto its side, convulsing.

"Uh-oh, Mr. Bunny. Did you get overexcited?"

The rabbit screamed. It sounded like a dying child.

"Well, that's creepy."

Then it exploded.

Twist leapt back, covering his face with his arms and raising one leg defensively, but the blood and gore sprayed against the invisible wall surrounding the rabbit, hanging in the air as if painted across a glass cylinder. Bits of rabbit fur and chunks of bone fell to the ground, but the blood hung suspended.

Twist stared for a moment, then jumped in the air. "Woo-hoo!" He danced around the carcass and did fist pumps. "I blew up Mr. Bunny!"

Containment circle? More like awesome explosive circle of death. Forcing himself to calm down, Twist glanced at the pile of bunny guts—

Wait. The rabbit sat in the middle of the circle again, staring calmly up at Twist as if nothing had happened.

"What the shit?" He crouched down.

The rabbit was grey, though, not brown, sort of silvery white, and. . . and the ground was clearly visible through its side.

"Whoa. Ghost bunny?" Twist scooted a bit closer. "Did I make a ghost bunny?"

The spell had said nothing about ghost bunnies.

This special edition includes:
Stretches
Step 1.5 in the Tango Triptych.

TANGO
with a twist

by

John Robert Mack

ZEN MONSTER PRESS

Tango with a Twist

This book is an original publication of Zen Monster Press.

Edited by Lauran Strait.
www.linkedin.com/in/lauranstrait

ISBN-13: 978-0692262146
visit the author at
www.johnrobertmack.com
email: john@johnrobertmack.com
www.facebook.com/johnrobertmack
Instagram: @johnrobertmack

Contact the author for information regarding volume discounts for classes, studios and other organizations. Bring the author to your live event, in person or online.

Jacket design by John Robert Mack.
Cover models Austin Tedder and anonymous woman.

For Chris and Andrew.

Take a deep breath.

One

Dead people. Everywhere.

The cemetery of my dad's hometown was the last freaking place I wanted to visit. I waited quietly in the Texas heat to give him a few minutes to pay his respects and to stretch my legs after the long drive from Austin. Was it wrong of me to avoid the reason we were there by recalling all the nights my girlfriend and I had sneaked into cemeteries to make out? Ex-girlfriend. Monika.

Grackles made that spooky sound grackles make while Dad stared at a rock. Cemeteries are weird. Not because of sparkly vampires or lacrosse-playing werewolves. They're just so damn. . . peaceful. I mean, if not for all the corpses, it would've been the perfect place for a family picnic.

"You can't park that there!" A loud South Texas accent hurried toward us, carefully avoiding the burial plots. He was built like a scarecrow and wore a police uniform two sizes too big. So much for peaceful.

Our moving van filled the dirt road, everything we had left in the world collected inside it. For a moving van, it was tiny. In the cemetery, it seemed like a Sam's Club hearse: *Bury Them in Bulk and Save!* The patrol car now facing it flashed red and blue lights.

"What the hell are you doing with a moving van in a cemetery?"

"Moving." Dad peered at the cop's name tag. "Palatino? As in old Sheriff Palatino? You his grandson?"

Oh, my God, small towns freaked me out.

Palatino adjusted his gun belt. "I'll ask the questions here." He couldn't have been more than a year or two older than me. Twenty at the outside. The acne made him younger. He nodded at the moving van. "Planning on loading up?"

"Loading what?" Dad waved at the nearest block of granite. "A lot of gravestones go missing around here?"

I chuckled.

Palatino squinted at me, then at Dad. I think the squint was meant to be intimidating, but Dad was a forty-something Conan the Barbarian. Except blonde and pale with a crew cut. He stared the guy down. "We're moving here from Austin. We stopped to pay our respects before heading over to my sister's place."

Again with the belt adjustment. "Who's your sister?" The dude reminded me of that Barney Fife guy on some old show my dad had made me watch.

"Macarena Davis." Like the cop would *happen* to know who she was.

The light of recognition sparked in Barney Fife's eyes. "You're the boxing coach?"

"Ex-boxing coach."

Oh, my God. This was *that* kind of town? Note to self: stay away from anyone named Bates. Everything about the cop's demeanor changed. He settled into one hip as if he'd channeled his inner Sheriff. "Had a little trouble with the law out there in the big city, didn't you?"

Dad took a breath. "It worked itself out."

Barney Fife squinted again, then turned his attention to me. "You're a dancer, right?" He looked me up and down. "Your aunt told me you were moving here. She told me a-a-all about you."

I pulled my shoulders back. Dad might've been willing to let this pissant twerp play big man, but I wouldn't.

"You a hot deal up there in Austin?" the cop asked.

I shrugged. I was a world champion. Well, ex-champion.

"You got a name?"

"Ethan Fox." Speaking through gritted teeth was a challenge.

More belt time. "Well, the family who runs the dance studio

hereabouts? They're close friends of mine, and if you do anything to mess with any of them, you will answer directly to me."

Dad's hand lifted as if he were about to take my arm, just in case, but then it fell to his side. Yeah. Dad had stopped touching people six months earlier, after he'd had his "trouble with the law."

"It's probably not much compared to those fancy Austin places," the cop said, "but Mrs. Montez throws a *heck* of a Saturday Social, and you need to treat her people with respect."

Kill me, now. Please. Barney Fife needed to be taken down a peg or two—

"Look, deputy. . ." Dad might have been adrift in a world of guilt, but he could still read my mind. "I'll get the van out of here in a few minutes. I wanted to say hello. . ." The sorrow and defeat in his voice pissed me off. "We don't want any trouble." He was a fighter, damn it. "I just wanted to say hello."

The people in the ground, at our feet, were strangers to me, but "Beloved-Wife-and-Mother" had been his sister and "Beloved-Husband-and-Father" had been his best friend.

Palatino pushed his hat back an inch and squinted down his nose at us. He nodded as if he were doing us the world's biggest favor by not running us in. He moseyed back to his car. "Welcome to Dumass, Texas, Ethan Fox."

No, really, that was its name. He'd tried to pronounce it *Doo-mahs*, but get a grip.

When the cop climbed into his car, Dad sighed. "You okay?"

I engaged my fake enthusiasm on supernova. "They throw a *helluva* Saturday Social!" Birds leapt into the air and flew off. "This place fucking sucks." If you notice the number of things in my life with the prefix "ex" you might have more sympathy for the attitude. A shrink would say it was a defense mechanism.

Dad returned to his silent contemplation of granite. He was so depressed he didn't even bitch me out for being rude.

Deep breath. It's a dance thing. If you're getting wound up, take a deep breath and it'll relax you. Deep breath.

The folks in the ground were my biological parents. Dad had adopted me after his sister and her husband died in a fire when I was only a few months old. I didn't remember them. At all. Well, Dad had told me tons of stories, but I had no actual memories, no flash of an angelic smile with an over-saturated sunny background. No mementos either. No baby blanket with my name on it.

To be honest, this visit was probably harder on Dad than it was on me. He'd been "Dad" for nearly all my seventeen years, so he was my *dad*, you know? What was I supposed to feel about these strangers who'd brought me into the world?

A concrete angel looked down on me disapprovingly. It was exactly like a statue in the cemetery where Monika and I used to make out.

I missed making out with Monika, and, just so we're perfectly clear, "making out" *is* a euphemism. Feel free to google "euphemism." Most of my friends were adults and anything lower than a B+ meant Dad kept me home from dance practice, so my vocabulary rocks.

I stared out across the trees. Dad wasn't going to say anything about my snide remark. "I'm sorry," I told him. "I'm a douchebag."

"I was going to say, 'little prick.'"

"Now you know *that's* just not true."

He chuckled. Good. He'd always been *that* dad.

A year earlier at the gym, this guy named Jimmy Russo knocked me out. When I'd come to, Dad was holding me. Paternal worry covered his face. "You okay, son?"

"Dad, I'm fine." With all the guys watching, I felt kinda dorky held in my dad's arms. "Let me up."

He tried to kiss my forehead.

"Dad! How old am I?"

"What? Too grown up to kiss the old man?" He pushed his face into mine. "That's it. I want a kiss on the mouth."

"Dad!"

I fought him off, much to the amusement of the guys watching. I fled to the locker room to check for a black eye. When I saw myself in the mirror, I groaned. A penis drawn in Sharpie decorated my cheek. Yeah. He was *that* dad.

Well, he *used* to be that dad. I missed it. A lot.

The call of a grackle brought me back to Dad. . . and the cemetery. . . in Dumass, Texas. The sun beat down on us like it wanted us dead. September in Texas? Fucking hot. He didn't throw a fatherly arm around me the way he would've six months before.

He'd killed a man. It was an accident, but he held himself responsible. That's how we lost everything and why we left Austin to move in with my Auntie Mac. It was the reason he didn't touch anyone anymore, and it was "that thing we didn't talk about." We used to talk about everything. Seriously. *Everything.* Certain people had called him a monster enough times he'd ended up believing them, I guess.

He stared at the rock for a long while. He laid down some flowers.

I tried to feel something and failed.

No, that's not true. I wanted my dad back, but I didn't mean the guy in the dirt. For the first time in my life, I felt like an orphan.

"You okay?" he asked again.

"I'm fine, Dad," I lied. "I'm fine."

David hunched over his tablet watching video of Katy and her best friend Gertrude, whom everyone called Juicy. They huddled together staring at Katy's cell phone. The camera set in the ceiling of the dance studio bathroom was perfectly placed to record both stalls and still see over Katy's shoulder at the vanity. The video had been recorded the day before. David had watched it a dozen times. What was he going to do?

"Oh. my. God." Katy squeezed Juicy, their breasts pressed together. "He can nail six, seven, eight. Eight! Eight turns he can nail."

"Don't bust a tit." Juicy grabbed the cell. "You are so hot for this guy."

"I have a boyfriend." Katy snatched her phone. "How many times do I have to tell you he's gay, anyway? Look at the way he dances. Straight guys do not move their hips like that."

"There is that."

Son of a bitch. Katy would never be interested in him now with this new, big city dancer in town. The son of a bitch was good looking, too, in that pretentious, pretty boy way Katy was sure to like. So what if he was gay? Girls always fell for the gay guys. What did they call it? Metrosexual?

David didn't have the luxury of waiting for her to dump the quarterback anymore. He had to make his move now. He glanced up. Photos of Katy watched over him from every wall of his bedroom, her face alive in the flickering candlelight.

God, she was beautiful. He would do anything, anything to make her love him. He'd even googled "how do i make a girl luv me?"

One site had grabbed his attention.

Simple instructions. Kind of whacked out, sure, but simple enough. Okay, fine, he'd give anything a try. The blogger was passionate. She'd been certain he would succeed, so certain she'd sent him naked pictures of herself dancing around a fire. So. . . dedicated, right?

He rushed to the small table in the corner and snatched up the cloth doll with Katy's face pinned to it. He slowly wound a cotton thread around and around the doll, muttering, "Katy and David. Katy and David. Katy and David."

After making sure I knew where Auntie Mac's house was, Dad dropped me off at the dance studio the cop had mentioned. "At least there's somewhere you can dance, right?"

Woot.

"I'll be at the house in a few to help you unpack," I said. The town was so small there was no reason I couldn't walk it.

As he drove off, I felt like a little kid on his first day of school. Don't forget I'd spent most of my life traveling the world on my own, so no big, right? The year before, I took second place at Blackpool, the most famous dance competition on the planet. I took first at World's too, which was almost as cool. All my friends, who were dancers and coaches, treated me like a king. Out here I was just Macarena Davis's nephew. Nobody.

Esmeralda's Tango Emporium lived at one end of a half-empty strip center that may have been posh a hundred years ago, but was now. . . well, the opposite of posh.

And "Emporium"?

I pulled out my cell and googled the word.

Thought so. Not a good name for a dance studio.

I snapped a photo for Instagram and was about to tweet. . . then I shoved the cell in my pocket. Who would read it?

With a deep breath to settle into my cheery dance champion persona, I opened the door and took one step into. . . the saddest, shabbiest studio I'd *ever* seen. A solitary old couple stumbled through something that might have been an ancient version of cha-cha and might have been the hokey-pokey. The music playing was "Sway." No, not the vaguely interesting remake with hot strippers who could sing. The original. And no one was being ironic. A dingy gold chandelier above needed so many bulbs replaced it actually managed to *darken* the room.

The little bell on the door behind me jingled.

"Out of the way, Ken Doll!"

Ken Doll? I glanced at my reflection in the hazy mirror: blond hair, blue eyes, nice teeth. Damn it, she was right. How had I never noticed that?

An elbow in the middle of my back propelled me into an imitation leather bar stool as a teenage cyclone in dance flats barreled past. I watched her from every angle in the studio mirrors as she stomped across the dingy parquet floor carrying more toilet paper than an army would use in a month. Latina, lots of leg in tight jeans, curvy under the t-shirt.

"Hey Tango, wait up." I trotted after her.

In the mirror, she smiled at the nickname. "Whatever you're selling, it can wait until I unload."

Man, she walked fast. "Let me give you a hand."

On the other end of the dance floor, she turned and stopped. "Do I look like I need help, Ken?" She did a double take so subtle nobody but a recently dumped guy like me could've noticed it. "I don't know you."

"I'm new."

Her face relaxed like she'd just recognized a long-lost friend. "You're the *dancer.*" She backed through the swinging door and vanished.

Was the town *that* small? I'd been there an hour. Tops.

Her voice called through the door. "Come on in."

Okay.

Smile: check.

Suave, masculine dance posture: check.

With a wink at the white hairs still dancing in the middle of the floor, I stepped through the swinging doors into the same storage room that's in pretty much every dance studio I'd ever seen: dark, cluttered and smelling vaguely of old shoes.

Nice. The first familiar thing in town.

Before you judge me for loving a stinky old closet, think of that ancient pair of shoes, the perfect pair that fits like skin and reminds you of every hike or race or ramble. This room was familiar like that to me.

"I guess I can't call you Ken Doll anymore." She stacked TP. "Didn't you win some kind of award at some contest somewhere?"

I hauled out my cell, tapped the screen and held it out to her. "Second at Blackpool." Here, at least, I was in my element. My titles always earned me instant cred at dance studios. "Ten-dance youth champion at World's. How do you know anything about me?"

She took the cell. "Get used to life in a small town. I talked to your aunt last week."

Hmm, small town creepy: check.

She watched the video and one hand went to her mouth.

Stellar. It *was* the best I'd ever danced, and. . .

She laughed out loud, killing my moment of pride. "You have an app of yourself on your home screen? That is so precious!" She held the phone out before the video was even done.

Precious? My masculinity whimpered and crawled away to die. I closed the app. I had to get used to it: out here everything I'd accomplished was irrelevant.

She pulled her t-shirt off and I sort of forgot about the cell. "Is she your BFF, the girl dancing with you in the video?"

Her bra was purple and. . .

Okay screw it, all I could think was, *omigod, tits!* Out of nowhere, a perfect valley of dark skin. I glanced around. Was somebody punking me? Don't get me wrong, I'd been backstage enough to see women in a quick change, but that was different. That was at a competition when I was more worried about forgetting my dance sequences. This was a shadowy storage closet, and internet porn had taught me what happens when hot girls undress in shadowy storage closets.

A heavy, boy's class ring dangled between the lovely hills. It forced me back to reality.

Wait. She was still talking?

". . .and the support group at school is great."

Support group?

"It's a small town, but you're perfectly safe here." She slid on a purple blouse and pulled her long, black hair out from under it. "Are you all right?" She didn't button it right away, which meant only one thing.

"I'm not gay."

She laughed again but this time with less gusto and she did up her blouse self-consciously. "What do you mean, you're not gay?"

I should've known what was up the moment she pulled off her shirt, but I was sort of distracted at the time. "*No. soy. mariposa.*" That's how to say it in South Texan. "Does your boyfriend know you strip in front of gay dudes?"

"How do you know I have a boyfriend?"

"Class ring on a string."

One hand went to the necklace. "Oh." Suddenly, her eyes grew huge and she spouted a litany of Spanish that went way beyond the phrases and obscenities I'd picked up at Austin High. She shoved me clear through the swinging door, where I stumbled a couple of steps and fell on my ass.

She finally reverted to English. "Why'd you let me take off my shirt in front of you, *culo!*"

"Like I could've stopped you."

"You could've turned around."

"I already told you I'm not gay, Tango." I got to my feet. "A hot girl strips in front of me, I'm only turning away if she asks me to."

"Tango's. . . racist. . ."

Ha. She was floundering, and the word "hot" threw her off track. Two points for me. "Then so's Ken Doll."

She planted her hands on hips cocked to one side in a very distracting manner. "You're a teenage ballroom champ with a gay dad and you expect me to believe you're straight?"

And there it was.

I'd learned how to cope: keep quiet and wait for her to figure it out on her own.

Having a gay boxing coach dad had its advantages: complete parental approval for the dancing hobby was at the top of the list. Insistence on boxing lessons to deal with the ramifications of the dance lessons was another. Why everyone assumed like father like son, I'd never understand.

Tango managed better than most. Rather than making it worse by babbling on about how many gay friends she had, blah, blah, blah, she stared at me for a few seconds while the old dancing couple watched the scene, probably wishing they had popcorn.

"Okay, Foxtrot, you get your first three Mexican stereotypes for free."

Several points for her.

"Hi there." I held out a hand. "My name's Foxtrot, and I'm new to town."

She smirked. It was a pretty smirk. Damn that class ring.

"Hey there, Foxtrot. My name's Tango."

We shook hands, and I tried to prolong the contact for an extra second or two, but she glanced past my shoulder and retracted her hand quickly. In the mirror, I watched several teenagers enter the studio. She stepped closer and whispered, "The banter is fun, but please don't tell anyone that you know I'm wearing a purple bra."

Understanding that she could get in trouble if someone suspected she wasn't doing her job, I inclined my head in a slow nod and stepped aside so she could greet the group, happy to keep the memory for my own enjoyment.

She strode across the floor and her bearing changed. She stood taller and pulled her shoulders down. Her hips rolled a little more and her steps hit softly. "*Oye chicos*, if you haven't practiced, I'm going to kick every single ass."

Holy crap. A coach? I figured she traded janitor service for classes.

There were four girls and five dudes. Oh wait, four dudes and one boyfriend. At least, from the way she latched onto him, I assumed it was his ring on her string. He was tall and shaped like a football player, not a dancer. He had dark hair and eyes and a face that grinned wa-a-ay too much. Seeing a hot chick you like kissing her boyfriend is like watching a

People of Walmart video. It's gross and makes you squirm, but you can't force yourself to look away.

Wow, was she *ever* going to come up for air?

My dance coaches never did that.

A very tall, white dude with Asian writing on his t-shirt blocked my view. "Hey there, I'm K-pop." His hair was tall too, black streaked with red, and cemented into fun angles like an anime character. Cool.

"K-pop?"

"I really like Korean pop music, so Katy calls me K-pop." He held out a hand.

I craned my neck to see around K-pop's hair.

Yep, she was still sucking face.

"Katy?" I asked, full of innocence. "She told me her name was Tango." I took the offered hand. "You can call me Foxtrot, by the way."

The girl, whose name was still open to debate, came up for air. The fact that she named all her friends was stellar because the names always meant something, like K-pop's. It made them easier to remember, but there were ten people on the crew, for God's sake, and who remembers the names of all seven dwarves?

She introduced them one by one and really fast: K-pop, Taco, Juicy, Shilling, Woody, Cosita, Mono, Ephraim and Boyfriend. Yeah, her boyfriend's name was "Boyfriend," which avoided confusion in the long run, I guess.

And "Juicy"? The girl must have noticed my unspoken question. "I really love Juicy Couture." Ironically, she actually *was* Korean, whereas K-pop was not.

Why did everyone let Katy name them when she herself had no nickname? No clue, but something told me that getting her to accept my suggestion would mean I had arrived.

She took center stage and clapped her hands. "Okay, Foxtrot, now you've met the gang, you can piss off. We have work to do."

Mutters of dismay communicated that the group felt she was being rude to the new guy. The new guy agreed.

"You don't want to sit here and watch." She spoke faster and she gestured more. "We're learning some new choreo. Bo-ring."

Hands in my pockets, I broke for cool. "I don't know. Maybe I can learn a new move?"

That's when it happened: the moment that changed the tone of the whole scene. I swear I heard the sound of a record scratch.

Juicy regarded me, full of wide-eyed curiosity. "Oh? You're a dancer, Foxtrot?"

If it'd been *Glee*, they'd all have turned to look at me simultaneously with a big whip-cracking sound effect. Except for Katy, who was already staring at me with a little extra salsa in her cheeks.

She hadn't told them.

And she knew.

She knew Blackpool.

She knew who I was, and not just from Auntie Mac.

She'd lied.

Closing in and holding her trapped in her subterfuge, I stared her down. "Well, I dance a *little*. I'd *love* to see what y'all can do."

A murmur of excitement at a chance to show off rumbled through the studio, cut off by a sharp whistle from Katy. "No offense, Foxtrot." All the bravado and teacher presence returned. "But you dance *ballroom*." She gestured at those around her. "We're a *crew*."

They fell out.

"Hells yeah," said Woody.

"Ballroom?" asked Ephraim.

Yeah. I had to cope with that shit a lot, too. Time to impress the freak out of them. Sure I danced ballroom, but I was more *So You Think You Can Dance* than *Dancing with the Stars*. I mean, I was seventeen, damn it. Back in *Austin*. . .

Well. . . I wasn't in Austin anymore.

Katy settled her shoulders, eyes blazing, all her Latina *La-tin-essss* daring me to ask for a showdown. A few months ago, I would have. Come on, this was my chance for the sexy face-off, right?

Something stopped me.

Deep in her eyes, she was afraid.

Of what? Of a hot, blond, Ken doll?

As I looked over her crew, a sick feeling hit my stomach, and I took a deep, deep breath, letting all the excitement bleed out of me. So *that's* why she didn't want me there. Why she lied about not knowing Blackpool. Why she made fun of my app.

I held up both hands. "My apologies, Katy. You're right. I should. . . go home and. . . unpack. . . things."

I shook a few hands and bumped a few fists. Everyone was friendly enough, but I saw it in their eyes: I danced ballroom. *Era ñoño.* I was lame. Not a good feeling, but if I was right about the crew, I had to let it go.

As I left, I watched Katy in the mirrors. When you're around mirrors long enough you learn to see the world almost 360 degrees at a time. She acted like everything was same old, same old, but she glanced at me out of the corner of her eye. She wore a mother's look, as if she knew her little kid had just avoided the neighborhood bully. Relief.

Outside, I hurried around the corner and waited. When the music started, I slunk to the glass door and peered inside. The music was faint, but it rocked. Katy's team, however, did not. Half of them were off beat. The choreography was what you saw in the first ten minutes of a movie about the downtrodden dance team who would rise to fame and glory by the end of it.

Okay, there's truly no way I can describe them without coming off as a complete douchebag. . . because they sucked. Utterly.

K-pop really wanted to be a pop-and-lock star, but all his moves reeked of five years ago. Juicy thought she was sexy but didn't realize that an ultra-flexible pelvis just made her look like a slut. It didn't mean she could dance. She couldn't have been worse if she'd been *trying* to look bad.

That's why Katy ejected me. She was smart enough to see the truth and didn't want her friends to know it: out here this crew probably rocked the planet, but anywhere else they were a bunch of wannabes in costumes. She didn't want me to laugh at them and force them to face how little they mattered to anyone outside their Dumass world.

So why stand down and leave when I saw that Katy was afraid? Why? Because that exact same haunted expression stared back at me every time I looked in a mirror. How could I make fun of that?

Six months ago, I probably would have.

Not anymore.

David sniffed the rose and adjusted the ribbon. He wiggled his fingers over the flower and muttered some nonsense from the naked chick's website. He placed it on the windshield of Katy's car and hid in the shrubs across the street. Red was her favorite color and she only liked roses with a strong scent. Unscented roses were a waste of time to her. She'd once told Juicy that a single rose was a romantic gesture, but an entire dozen smacked of desperation.

An hour passed.

Katy ran from the house and jumped into her car. She must've been late for the dance crew's performance. Would she notice the rose? Yes. She climbed out of the car and picked up the flower delicately. She glanced around with a smile that filled David with hot desire.

"Ethan Fox, you naughty, naughty boy." She sniffed the rose and her smile grew.

Son of a bitch! Nothing the naked chick told him to do worked!

Two

The morning after I met the dance crew, I struggled to hang a punching bag in the garage. *Mumford and Sons* played on the MP3 player that wasn't an iPod because I was too much of a leader to follow a trend. Someone blocked the light of the rising sun. Dad. He didn't offer to help. "How the hell did you sneak that past me?" With the sun behind him, he looked like a gangster in the cheap suit and tie Auntie Mac had bought him.

She'd picked it out too, thank God, so while it was cheap, at least it was stylin'. A little tight around the shoulders, but the shoulders in question were huge.

I managed to hook the bag. "You look good in the suit."

"Please answer the question."

I climbed down and propped one foot on the ladder channeling the emoticon of cool. All the boxing gear, apart from the bag and a pair of gloves, had been left behind in Austin. "You know how I snuck it past you. I paid Mario to do it for me."

"Sneaked," he auto-corrected. "How'd you pay him off?"

"Mario's getting married in a couple of months. He wanted to surprise Molly so I taught him a few waltz steps." I gestured at the heavy bag. "Ta-daa."

It was an argument bound to happen sooner or later, but, hopefully, the revelation about Mario's last-minute nuptials would distract him.

"Take it down." He spoke quietly, which was freakier than if he ran around yelling.

"No."

We stared at each other for about a gajillion years before he turned around and walked away. Up until the accident, Dad spent two hours a day, three days a week coaching me. Now, boxing was part of the thing we didn't talk about.

"Have fun jousting dragons, Dad." I called his job hunt "jousting dragons" because there were as many jobs to find as there were dragons.

Deep breath.

After setting *Mumford and Sons* to blast away on repeat, I pulled on the gloves and focused on beating the crap out of the bag. Hitting it hard helped me forget I was lonely and pissed off. It was pure and physical. I lost myself in it: constantly moving and hitting. Always keeping my guard up.

But my mind wandered: Monika's last words to me? You know, when she dumped me.

"After everything we've been through together and everything I've done for you, I just don't know how you can *do* this to me. I *hate* you, Ethan Fox! We're through!"

She'd stalked away and left me in the middle of a busy dance floor that'd fallen silent. About fifty people gawked at me, wondering what I'd do, a circle of vultures waiting to see if I'd break down and cry like a little girl.

"I told her the new make-up made her look like a whore," I lied. In my head, it was funny.

People had been a bit shocked, but they'd returned to their lessons.

I forced my attention to hitting the heavy bag in front of me. "One, four, three, two, three, three." It was a training drill. The numbers represented different punches. The drill was meant to clear my head.

Didn't work.

What had I really told Monika right before her tear-filled parting shot? "I'm sorry, Monika, but Dad lost *everything*, the gym, the house, the cars.

We're going to Auntie Mac's because we don't have anywhere else to go."
I'd worked hard to keep my voice low so all those people in the studio
wouldn't hear. "I can find a way up here on the weekends to practice, but
I can't afford the coaching anymore."

"What about the costumes? We can't use last year's costumes."

"There's no way I can afford new costumes now." I'd forced myself
to fake a smile. "You're the most beautiful girl out there no matter *what*
you're wearing."

Scroll back to her response, and maybe, just maybe, my stupid one-
liner won't sound quite so evil.

We'd met when we were eight. I was the only boy in class, and she was
the top girl, so our coach paired us up for a Fred and Ginger routine. We
were so darn cute, her parents begged Dad to pull me out of regular classes
so we could stay partners. And so it went. Monika usually got what she
wanted. We started dating officially the night she snuck into my hotel
room and introduced me to euphemisms at fifteen. It was the weekend we
won our first state comp, so two reasons to celebrate, right?

"One, four, three, two, three, three." I focused on beating the crap out
of the bag. My aunt's garage existed in a completely different universe. I'd
never see Monika again. Was that good or bad?

Something spattered across my shoulders and scared holy hell out of
me. I spun and blocked, ready with a powerhouse if I needed it.

The girl silhouetted in the garage door several feet away dropped the
extra pebbles onto the gravel drive. Monika? No, she cocked her hip in a
very recognizable manner. Katy.

I reached for the ear buds before remembering the gloves, so I
smacked myself upside the head at the same time I knocked the buds out
of my ears.

"Sorry, Foxtrot. I wasn't sure how else to get your attention."

"Hey." It was about all I could manage. No idea how long I'd been at
the bag, but it would be a few minutes before I caught my breath.

"Can I come in?"

I nodded. Wow, she was hot in the early morning light.

She looked me up and down. "Turnabout's fair play, I guess."

Oh yeah, I was shirtless and sweaty. Normally, no big deal. Dancer.

Boxer. Google "ethan fox shirtless" with your safesearch on and you'll find pix of me. But with Katy right there in my garage? Utterly different story.

By the way, without safesearch, you'll get an entirely different Ethan Fox.

I dove for snarky. "You stopped by for an eyeful?" Using my teeth, I ripped open the Velcro closures on my gloves. "Shouldn't you be in school?"

"Shouldn't you?"

I slipped into my discarded t-shirt. "Dad figured I'd be training all across the country this year, so I do school online." Had I managed to make that nonchalant? He'd paid in full before we went broke.

She hesitated, closed her eyes and shook her head microscopically. "You're from a completely different planet."

Was that a good thing or a bad thing?

She opened her eyes. "We had a dance gig this morning. The Starbucks' grand opening."

"Starbucks?"

She smirked. "It's a big deal around here."

Wow. I encircled the bag with one arm and leaned my head against it, trying for disarming cuteness while I let her get around to her reason for stopping by.

She raised one perfect eyebrow. "So. . . a boxing ballroom dancer?"

I shrugged. People get around to the point a lot faster if you let them talk.

"I'm sorry about the ballroom crack in front of the crew," she said, "but you took me by surprise. I figured it'd be a few days before you found the studio." She wandered around the garage, touching things and picking them up. It was cute. "I'm a tango dancer. Third gen. The whole dance crew thing is kinda new to me, but I'm the best dancer in town." Her tone wasn't egotistical, just stating a fact.

"Head cheerleader?" I asked.

She made a face as if she'd just sucked the mother of all lemons. "I said *dancer*."

So it was like that. I avoided smiling.

Cheerleaders and studio dancers? No love lost. Trust me.

"Anyway. . . your aunt told me about you because my mom owns the only dance studio in town, and she knew you'd make your way there eventually." She picked up a piece of newspaper, smoothed it out and folded it. "I saw your website and stuff." She glanced up. "It's not stalker or anything. I just thought maybe I could offer you a proposition."

Proposition? Now she had my complete interest.

She laughed. "I have a boyfriend, Foxtrot." She held the class ring up with one thumb. "I want to offer you a job."

"Coaching the team?"

She gave me the same face she'd made about cheerleaders. "I saw your coaching videos. You dance great, but your teaching sucks. I want you to show me choreography and *I'll* teach the team. While you've been running around the world dancing like a star, my mom's been training me how to teach."

"I'll do it."

"What? Just like that? No ego about how you're all world-famous and must know more than me about everything?"

"We need the money." Couldn't let her figure out the obvious reason why I'd rather work with her alone than with the whole crew. "Dad isn't going to find a job here any time soon. While it's great that we have a roof over our heads, sharing a bathroom with your dad isn't all it's cracked up to be."

"Too many hair care products?"

My turn to make a face. "Dude, he's a boxing coach. He thinks gel is something you use for a pulled muscle. I *so* get another Mexican joke, now."

Her face wandered from confused to amused. "Fine, but there isn't enough money for you to move out. I'll give you what I'm getting, but that's all I have."

"It's more than I'm making now." Score. Distracted her with the money angle.

The honk of a car horn startled me.

Katy spun around. "Shit, he's already done tearing down the stage?" She turned back to me. "If anyone asks, I walked here because you lost your wallet when I dropped you on your ass yesterday." She moved away slowly. "It's Corey, and I don't want the team to know you're coaching me."

"Corey?"

She lifted the ring again. "Boyfriend." She lowered her voice. "And while the rose was pretty, please don't do stuff like that, Foxtrot. I have a boyfriend."

"What rose?"

She blinked a few times. "The rose I found on my car this morning. Very sweet, but if we're going to work together—"

"Wasn't me. Perhaps Boyfriend?"

She chuckled. "We've been going out for a year. The roses dried up months ago." She settled into that hip thrust I liked so much. "It really wasn't you?"

"I don't know where you live."

Ha! She was disappointed. She *liked* thinking it was me, even if she had to tell me not to do it anymore.

Complicated.

Nice.

Boyfriend honked again. Katy jumped. "Whatever. Studio, ten o'clock tonight and I dropped off your wallet, right?"

I pulled it out of a pocket and waggled it in the air for all to see. "Thanks for the wallet, Katy," I said louder than necessary. "Sure am glad you found it. I was sick worried."

She tossed me a smirk before dashing down the drive to the waiting car. She didn't wave as they drove off, but I like to think she wanted to. She also didn't kiss Boyfriend hello, so that was nice.

He drove a new Dodge Challenger, which meant he had money but was compensating for a tiny dick. Good news and bad all rolled up in a shiny red package.

I missed my Roadster.

David adjusted his binoculars. In the garage, Fox stripped off his shirt, pulled on gloves and went at the punching bag again. Loud music destroyed the peaceful morning. Inconsiderate prick. The noise was helpful, though, as David slipped out of the bushes, across the street and around the side of the house. He hurried through the gate across the backyard and made his way into the kitchen. He'd been in the house a dozen times already. Macarena Davis was known to hand out leftovers from her restaurant to the local single men, as long as they returned her dishes promptly.

The room at the top of the stairs screamed teenage boy. Clothes littered the floor, half-unpacked boxes stacked up against one wall. A pile of gold trophies filled one corner. David slid one arm under the bed and attached a mic. He tucked a small cloth bag into the frame at the head: bladderwrack, anise, lemon verbena and mustard seed.

Ouch! A static spark hit him as he touched the metal frame.

The naked chick had promised *it would ruin the big city guy's mojo. Promised. And she sent him video of her with her toys, too.*

David didn't know if curses worked, but she'd guaranteed success and if the spell didn't work, she'd refund the money he'd spent on herbs. He'd try anything. Amazon had already shipped two books about witchcraft.

He stalled. Witchcraft? Seriously? Is that what he was doing?

Whatever. If it got Katy *to send him naked photos, who cared, right?*

He hurried from the room and down the stairs.

The sound of a patio door sliding caught him by surprise.

He froze. Was Fox coming in or going out?

Indie rock blared out from the backyard. David breathed again. He ran to the front door but slowed to a casual walk as he exited the house.

I arrived at the studio at eight o'clock rather than ten. Two advantages to a small town: everywhere is walking distance and it's easy to find out when the only dance practice starts.

Music filtered through the cracked glass. My look was a very carefully executed casual: sweatpants and a tank top that showed off my boxing shoulders. I checked to make sure everything was in place. How would I explain being early? *I just thought I'd stop by and practice my lame ballroom moves. What do you charge for floor fees?*

Okay. Showtime.

The studio was no better than the first time I'd seen it. Without sunlight filtering in, it was even shabbier, like something Liberace puked up in 1975. I've said there are advantages to having a gay dad. One downside is accidently dropping phrases like that. Google "liberace living room" and you'll get a good picture of the studio decor. Literally.

Practice was full-on. The "crew" was running—wait. Damn ironic quotation marks. I shouldn't let the sarcasm slip into my voice. Try again.

Practice was full-on. The crew ran a piece with K-pop and Juicy featured up front. They locked with a little popping and K-pop didn't completely suck, but Juicy was awkward. K-pop was more fluid, but slow. Juicy was faster, but she counted the moves out loud. Who did that?

The rest of the crew struggled through a time step in the background, a basic "step-touch, step-touch" thing white boys have danced for fifty years. Shilling moved pretty well, but her timing sucked. Woody had rhythm but moved his pelvis like a dick dancer. Put him with Juicy, upload the video to a porn site and they could raise some serious money. Ephraim and Mono stayed nearly invisible.

Taco was. . . Bless his heart, Taco just didn't belong on a dance team.

For those of you not familiar with the saying, "Bless his heart" is the greatest Texan contribution to the English language. You can say anything you want about someone as long as you precede it or follow it with "bless his/her heart." As in, "She is the biggest slut on the planet, bless her *heart*." Get the tone right and you have free rein.

The song ended, they struck a final pose and I applauded. "That was great, y'all. How long have you been working on that?"

Big grins all around.

K-pop answered. "Bro, that's our new piece. We started it today."

I excel at fake surprise. "Whoa. Today?"

Katy stomped over. "What are you doing here, Foxtrot?"

I raised my hands, warding her off. "I just thought I'd stop by and practice my lame ballroom moves. What do you charge for floor fees?" Rehearsal always pays off. The crew bought it.

Katy remained skeptical. "Take five, *chicos*."

I lowered my voice as she dragged me to the black leather bar. "I need to see what you have to work with, Katy. If I can't coach them directly, I need to know what they can do so I know what to show you." She wound up to get sarcastic with me, so I disarmed her with a compliment. "You're better than the rest of them. I can't choreograph based on what *you* can do."

She rolled her eyes. "You suck up." She squeezed my elbow really hard and I'd guess my growing excitement was the opposite of what she'd intended. "You can stay, but stop with the surprises and don't you *dare*. . ." The intense glare she fed me had a similarly opposite effect. "Don't you *dare* do anything to insult them."

I nodded. "I'd call first, but I don't have your number." Hopefully, the innocent face worked better than the compliment.

She released my arm and turned away. "Leave thirty bucks on the bar, Foxtrot. It'll cover you for the month."

K-pop wandered to my side. Fist bump. "Bro, you totally need to join the crew. Your shit on YouTube is beast." Big grin. "Total *Beast,* hai?"

Yeah, that wasn't a shocker. I had a routine on YouTube to a song from this Korean band called Beast, spelled B2ST for reasons undisclosed. Coming from one of their fans, it was a pretty big compliment. Those guys could dance.

I leaned closer. "Thanks, bro. But I don't think Katy likes me."

For the record, I'd never called anyone "bro" before.

He nodded sagely and the red streaks in his anime hair bobbed in the dusty light. "Let me work on the coach, bro." Another fist bump. Katy shouted his name and off he trotted.

He needed to be my new best friend. Everything about him screamed sidekick. Also, he was nicer to me than anyone else I'd met.

Speaking of which. . . a heavy arm fell across my shoulders. A deep voice said, "Hey, 'Foxtrot'," forcing me to check punctuation. See, that's why I rehearse. He didn't actually make the air quotes, but I heard them. It was Boyfriend, and I could tell he was working hard to keep his voice dark and menacing. "I see you staring at Katy, bro. I need you to stop."

Seriously? Do guys say "bro" anymore?

"Come on, Boyfriend." My response flew out of my mouth before I could stop. There was no lisping or mincing, but it was an Emmy-worthy performance. "Look at that outfit. And her hair? Perfection. How can I *not* look at her? OMG."

Lol.

I'm not proud of that moment, and if Dad ever found out. . . at least he'd likely touch me again. You know, to smack me. But I had to make sure this goon didn't see me as a threat or he'd *never* let Katy work with me alone.

"Wait a minute." His face ran the gamut from confused to stupid, back to confused and settled on stupid. Game show themes ran through my head. "Katy said you're straight."

My hip pushed out in a perfect copy of Katy's and I imitated her eye roll. To avoid an utter stereotype, I didn't put my hands on my hips. "I'm a teenage ballroom champ with a gay dad, how in the hell could I possibly be straight?"

Why did I do it? I can only guess I figured he might think I was funny and perhaps a little creepy and he'd want to leave me alone. Yeah. That didn't work.

Boyfriend's face lit up like I'd just offered him a free spoiler for his Challenger. "Bro!" He led me away from the group while I dealt with the whiplash from his change in attitude. "Next week is Katy's birthday, and I have no-o-o idea what to get her. You totally have to help me pick out something awesome so she doesn't break up with me."

I raised an inquiring eyebrow.

He grew sheepish. "We've been having a few problems."

In the mirrors, I saw Katy look around and spot us. From her expression, she was utterly perplexed as to why Boyfriend was suddenly my new BFF. She saw me watching her watching us and looked away abruptly.

My innocent face is my best. I have that open honest expression that helps me get away with murder. I gripped his arm with all the companionable *bon ami* I could manage. "Of course, I'll help you. We can't let Katy break up with you. . ." Wait for it. ". . . bro."

Fist bump.

Practice resumed. I had to remind myself that I'd promised not to insult the crew. Katy glanced at me a few times, obviously judging my reaction, but I'm so good at using the mirrors she couldn't have known when I was watching.

Their technique was shoddy. I mean, only one or two could smoothly pull off a double turn, which should've been easy after the first few months of dancing. Half of them had bad posture, and Taco, bless his heart, was never going to get the new bit. Then K-pop pulled him aside while Katy worked on something else. The skinny Korean wannabe drilled with Taco over a dozen times until he managed to—almost—nail it.

K-pop raised his arms and whooped. "You rock the world!"

Taco could barely dance through the move, but K-pop celebrated as if it were the most amazing accomplishment in the world. For Taco, maybe it was.

They rejoined the group. Everybody high-fived them and pushed ahead to the next section.

When Monika and I had practiced in Austin, we were *serious* about it. We were always preparing for the next comp or performance. Even with the other dancers at *our* studio there was competition. We never, ever laughed or joked with them. If another couple earned higher ranks, Monika wouldn't speak to me for a week.

The atmosphere at the Emporium was more like Dad's gym: a bunch of folks having fun. It was about spending time doing what they loved rather than being the best in the world. That was so not my norm. It wasn't even my occasional.

I wasn't there just to stalk Katy anymore. Watching the team practice was fun. But when it reminded me of the good times I used to have with my dad, I decided to head out. It was too confusing.

Everyone waved and said goodbye. K-pop and Boyfriend made a point of bumping my fist. Katy kept her back to me as I left, but she used the mirror to watch me all the way out the door.

Three

David watched the feeds from the studio. Fox made his way to the door—
"Excuse me?"

David snapped the tablet to his chest and looked out through the open car window where a hot blonde displayed her cleavage as she bent and smiled at him. "I'm looking for the dance studio."

He glanced across the motel parking lot. "Why?" A snazzy rental car was parked outside the office.

The blonde rose and her smile shifted to something more sarcastic. "I like to dance?" She giggled and leaned over again. "I'm looking for a young man named Ethan Fox. He'd be new to town. I figure he'll be at the studio." She held David's gaze seductively.

A hot slut looking for Fox? That was lucky. Hm. Had that spell worked?

The girl rose. "I can always ask at the motel and try tomorrow."

"No!" That was abrupt. Damn. "Sorry. He'll be there after ten tonight."

The girl raised one perfectly lined eyebrow as if curious how he knew that.

David shrugged. "It's a small town. And Katy's a friend." He pointed down the road. "Three blocks down and around the corner."

The girl's whole face showed her bemusement. "Katy?"

David smiled. "Well, shucks," he said in his best small-town voice. "Katy's darn near the best dancer we have in these parts." He smiled again. "She and Ethan Fox have already hit it off."

One eyebrow raised so high David was amazed it didn't break off. "Oh? Well, I've known him a long time," the slut said. "We'll have to see what happens, I guess."

"Yes, ma'am."

After she walked off, David tapped his tablet. There had to be a spell to ensure her success.

I killed time until my official meeting with Katy by exploring the town. Didn't take long. One exit off the highway direct to Main Street: three bars, two churches, one motel, a high school the size of Austin High's locker room, a drug store with—I swear to God—a soda fountain, and there I was at the other end of town. Okay, maybe it wasn't quite that small, but the streets were empty except for a cop car making its rounds and a couple of folks outside the motel. Most of the houses were already dark.

Ten o'clock found me back in the studio as appointed. "Hey, Katy."

Katy stretched at the barre to cool, downtempo, Middle Eastern music. "What happened to Tango?" She watched my approach in the mirror.

"You name people. We don't get to name you." I lifted a foot onto the barre.

"I don't know." Lifting her leg, she pulled it up until her foot was almost directly above her head. "I kind of liked Tango."

Wow, flexible. Distracting thoughts plagued me. With a dramatic sweep of one arm, I indicated the entire dance floor. "As you are a tango dancer," I said in my best goofy, Disney channel sit-com voice, "it was weirdly appropriate, was it not?"

After a final tug, she released her leg and bent to touch her nose to her knee. More distracting thoughts. "Okay, just say it," she demanded.

I refused to say what I was thinking as I watched her stretch. "Huh?"

She rose and looked at me without the mirror. "I could see what you were thinking the entire time you were 'practicing'." Air quotes and all.

"And what exactly was I thinking?"

She grabbed her towel from the barre. "No bullshit, Foxtrot. Just *say* it. You think we suck."

"Not at all." Of course, I did.

"No." The snap of her towel in my chest startled me. "If we're going to work together, do *not* lie to me. Do not try to make things nice because you're only here to flirt with me."

"Flirt with you?"

The balled-up towel hit me in the face. It smelled nice. Her perfume was spicy.

"You told Boyfriend you're *gay*?"

Yeah, that was bound to raise suspicions. "I wanted him to be comfortable about our professional relationship."

"He doesn't even know we're working together." She punched my shoulder. "It's a secret, remember?"

I smacked myself on the forehead. "D'oh."

"The Simpsons? Really? What are you, like, forty?" She unzipped her hoodie.

"I blame my father." Hoping for purple. Hoping for purple.

She wore perfectly respectable layered sports bras. Nothing girls didn't wear all the time in public and they didn't reveal a thing. . . but she pulled the hoodie off one shoulder and then the other. . . slowly. It dribbled down her arms and dropped into her hands. As she draped it over a chair, she stared at me with a smolder in her eyes and a pout on her lips. . . and broke down laughing. "You are so-o-o easy, Foxtrot."

Holy crap! She got me! "Dude! That is so not fair!"

"We have work to do. I'm paying you, remember?" She nabbed her towel from me and tossed it on a table. "Seriously. How bad are we?"

I stepped away for some breathing room after the last hormonal onslaught. "Okay. . . you know how girls ask guys if they look fat in a dress and the guy gets in trouble no matter what he says because guys are always wrong?"

She crossed her arms and pursed her lips. Very Mexican, but I chose to save up my freebie jokes.

"Is this one of those times?" I asked.

She raised an eyebrow.

Okay. She'd asked for honesty. Time to find out if she'd meant it. "They suck."

Wait for it.

Wait for it.

"Are we salvageable?" Her tone was calm and professional. Girl knew how to take a hit. Sexy.

"You're better than you think you are," I told her. "And I'm not saying that just to get into your pants. K-pop has potential, but you baby him. Juicy could be good if she stopped trying to be sexy." The list went on for several minutes. If she could take a hit, I didn't need to pull my punches.

When I was through, she processed for a couple of seconds. "Just?"

Try as I might, I had no idea what she meant. "Heh?"

"You said you weren't being nice *just* to get into my pants." She leaned against the barre. "So you *are* flirting with me?"

Was this a boxing match? Should I duck or jab?

She broke out laughing again but this time it was with me, not at me, so one small step for man, yada, yada. "All right, Foxtrot. I told you to be honest and you were. I gotta give you that one." She picked up her iPhone. "You were pretty spot on too. I hate to admit it, but you were."

She played the song.

"So. . . now that we're all business," I asked as I joined her, "should I quit with the witty banter?"

She wore a funny smile. "The witty banter's the best part." She elbowed me. "You need to loosen up."

It was meant as a joke, and I don't think she realized how accurate she was. "You're right. I do."

She raised an eyebrow at me, apparently noticing the change in my tone.

"If I say something real do you promise not to use it against me?"

"Maybe. We'll see."

A guy can hope. "Your friends need a lot of work, but they have one thing I've never had in all my years of dancing."

"What's that?"

"Friends. There are people I worked with for years. I thought they were my friends. They're gone." I didn't want to go into details right then, but, well, it was true. My cell had stopped ringing after Monika dumped me, when it was obvious I was off the circuit.

Katy stared at me, apparently fighting between a snarky quip and whatever the opposite of that is. The opposite won. She scrolled her iPhone to the second chorus of the song. "We have the first minute, forty seconds choreographed."

I moved out to the middle of the floor, stretching my arms above my head. "I started the new material there."

She looked up quickly. "You have material for us?"

"Wasn't I supposed to?"

"Didn't say that." She paused the music. "Do I need to play the song so you can review?"

"I got it."

"You already knew the song?"

"Never heard it before tonight. It's stellar. I like it."

"How much material you have?"

"About two minutes. I need to work out the counting on the bridge at the end."

Again with the eyebrow. "*Only* two minutes?"

Totally lost. "Oh, sorry. I thought that would be enough for tonight."

"For the song you heard for the first time. . ." She glanced at her cell. "Two hours ago?"

Did I do good or bad? "I put some sequences together while I was 'practicing'." Air quotes back at her.

She heaved a huge sigh. "Okay, as much as I want to keep playing totally cool about this. . . you just came up with this tonight while we were practicing and you're not going to act all superior about it?"

I nodded and shrugged at the same time to demonstrate my confusion.

She rolled her shoulders and hit the middle of the floor. "This humble side is freaking me out, Foxtrot."

I waited for her to elaborate.

"Okay, two full minutes of choreo would take me, and most other people, at least a couple of days." First of all, really? Secondly, was there something new in her expression? Attraction? "The fact that you aren't all full of yourself about it is. . ."

"Sexy?" Blame my defense mechanisms.

A little scoffing laugh jumped out of her mouth. "And you're obnoxious again." She stretched her right arm across her chest, definitely returning to work mode. "I hope the choreo's good."

For a second there, though. . . it almost seemed like maybe I had a shot.

"Oh. It is. It is." I faced the mirrors and shook out my legs. "When the chorus starts, I see you and Juicy front and center for *fouettés*."

"Cool. I've seen them, but never done one." Her honesty was hot. "How do you do it?" How awesome. She was training with me to make sure no one else saw her limitations.

I showed her the *fouetté*. Hard to describe. Think repeating roundhouse kicks, I guess. With pointed toes. Wikipedia has a GIF.

She applauded sarcastically, which is kind of a trick. "You're a lovely dancer, Foxtrot. I'm all impressed and shit. But how. do. I. do. it?"

Moving slower, I spoke as I moved. "Prep. Spin. Kick. Close. Repeat."

She shook her head. "See, that's why you suck as a teacher." Huh. The disarming honesty wasn't as sexy when it drove on the other side of the road. "Mirrors." She turned me to face them. "Not everyone learns just by watching what you do. This move is going to kick Juicy's ass." She positioned me slightly in front and off to one side. "Okay, show me the prep. And hold it."

She could do it in less than five minutes but spent another twenty figuring out how to break it down and explain it. Teaching. is. really. tedious.

"Bored already?" she asked.

"I. . ." I wasn't supposed to lie. "I just don't understand why it takes people so long to get this shit."

It earned me one of those hand-on-her-thrust-out-hip things I liked so much.

"You said to be honest," I reminded her.

"Do you know Argentine tango?"

"No."

Her arched eyebrows told me she must have seen her own "cheerleader" expression all over my face. "Something. . . *wrong*. . . with Argentine?"

"No. It's just a different world, and I've never had time for it." Thank God I recover quickly.

"Mmhm." She sauntered to the sound system and changed the music. She also dimmed the lights. Although it was something Argentine tango teachers liked to do, under the circumstances, I really wanted to read more into it than relax-the-student mood lighting.

Argentine is a specific kind of tango based on rhythm and movement that doesn't really have patterns and the music doesn't exactly have a beat. I mean. . . is that even a dance?

"I know you ballroom types look down on *tah-ngo*." Oops. And now she was pronouncing it Spanish-like. "Can you follow, or do you just lead?"

The question surprised me. "I can follow. Kinda."

"It's easier for me to teach you if I lead."

"Yeah. Sure. Stellar." I sucked at following but was hardly going to cop to it. Dancing *tah-ngo* meant I'd be able to touch her. A lot. "All right." I pulled her into dance position and gave her my best dramatic tango face.

She rolled her eyes. "I'm leading, remember?" She changed our frame so I was following. She shook me gently with her arms. "Relax." She shook me again. "Really relax."

"I am relaxed."

She thought a moment. "You're a boxer, right?" She broke away from me and adjusted her posture, shifted forward to the balls of her feet, brought her hands up and danced from foot to foot in a bad imitation of a boxer. It did very cool things to her chest. "Give me boxer posture."

It would bring me closer to her bouncing breasts, so yeah, whatever. I switched gears and hunched. She stopped shifting weight and took me into dance position. "Much better." She directed my face to look the same direction as hers. It was the exact opposite of what I'd been taught. "Let me shift your weight."

She'd touched my chin. I could feel the spot. . .

We shifted from foot to foot for a long time. "Close your eyes." We shifted some more. She smelled like cinnamon. "Let me move you."

Deep breath. I forced myself to relax. Dad used to do stuff like this to get me out of ballroom mode, too, so it wasn't completely foreign. I focused on my breathing and the smell of cinnamon. Her hand shifted on my back, drawing me closer. I looked into her face.

"Close your eyes."

But she'd been staring at me. Good sign!

My heart beat faster, and, behind my closed eyelids, little spots of light flared. Wow. Even considering two years of hot sex with Monika, I'd never felt so. . . alive.

She started with walking.

No. Really. Walking. To the beat.

Yeah. My thought, too, but I didn't care about learning Argentine tango. I cared about letting Tango teach me and dancing with her, one hand on my back, our hands curled together in a way that actually felt intimate. The clasp was almost worthless for connection, it seemed, but it felt. . . tender.

Wow, she smelled nice.

Wow, she felt nice.

Wow, I wished she was wearing the purple bra.

Damn, I stepped on her foot.

She was patient and, after half an hour or so, I could follow some of the basic stuff and she stopped laughing at my tendency to turn everything into ballroom tango, which is totally different.

Every few minutes, she'd make me let go and shadow box to reboot the boxer mode. She was an amazing teacher. Damp with sweat, we moved across the floor and the music played gentle and sexy.

"Ballroom tango is for the audience, for the people watching," she whispered. "It's flashy and exaggerated and the couple doesn't even look at each other." The music slowed and we followed the rhythm. "*Tah-ngo* is for the couple. It doesn't care who's watching."

She held me so close her breath felt warm on my cheek. "It's more intimate." Our cheeks touched. Err. . . I had to move my hips away a bit. I pretended it was for balance.

She led me through some swivels and pulled me forward so I leaned above her. It was creepy to give up control. . . but sexy to let her call the shots. "It's about communication and connection. . . not showing off."

She drew me closer. We stared into each other's eyes.

My heart beat like a motherfucker.

I wanted to kiss her. . . but she had a boyfriend. She'd made that clear—

She kissed me! Everything about this girl was a role reversal.

Okay, enough with the following.

I grabbed her, dipped her and planted a hot one on her meant to shake her to her toes. She responded by wrapping her arms around my neck and holding on tight. She tasted like raspberries. Bent backward, she weighed nothing in my arms, which meant she had wicked control of her center. It gave me ideas. Über sexy.

Loud, slow applause startled me so much I almost let go, certain Boyfriend was about to coldcock me. Not him, but the girl at the edge of the floor didn't need to touch me to lay me flat.

Brain. too. juiced. to. think. good.

Perfect. moment. ruined.

"Monika?"

"Bravo, Ethan." Clack, clack, clack, clack went her five-inch spikes. "Not even a week here and you've already moved on, I see." She stopped a few feet away and crossed her arms. "Congratulations."

As always, she was stunning: blonde hair pulled up in a ballroom bun, bright red, full lips and cleavage for days and days. I actually felt guilty at being caught with Katy. But damn it, Monika had dumped *me*.

Katy appeared guilty for her own reasons, but she clearly recognized my former partner and girlfriend and chose to stay out of it.

"What are you doing here?" I glanced at a clock. "At eleven o'clock?"

Monika seemed surprised. "This is when you and I usually practiced," she said. "I asked a colorful local where I might find the only studio in this one-horse town." She held out her hands in a ta-daa pose. "Where else would you be?" Pulling a bag off her shoulder, she moved closer to a table near the dance floor. She dropped a folder onto it. "I got us a sponsor."

Wait. . . what? She acted as if we'd just seen each other at the studio yesterday, as if this appearance out of the blue was the most normal thing on the planet.

"Eight months in New York. A time share, personal chef, tutors and all the. . . *coaching* you can stand."

She stood near the table with her feet wide enough to pull her short skirt tight across her thighs. The way she emphasized the word "coaching" with her feet spread like that assured me she meant the word to be both literal and euphemistic.

"Last time we took second. . . this time we win." She glanced around the studio as if seeing it for the first time, even though I knew she'd been scrutinizing it from the moment she walked through the door. "Holy pathetic shit, Batman." Always the lady. "Is it just me or did Liberace puke up 1978 in this funeral home?" One perfectly manicured hand slipped to her mouth. "I'm sorry, *senorita*. Was that rude?"

Deep breath.

You know what? She might have had me.

A full sponsorship to train in New York? Hell yeah.

A real shot at the full championship? Utterly.

All the rowdy sex I could stand? Duh.

But she slammed Katy's studio. Not cool. She slammed Katy. Even less cool.

Katy herself? Über cool. She turned off the music. "You took second at Blackpool? Wow."

Monika smiled.

Katy leaned against the barre. "Isn't there a saying? Second place winner is just first place loser."

Ouch.

Monika managed to hold the smile, and I only noticed the pause because I'd known her so long. "And what have you ever won?" She looked around at the shabby studio before returning her attention to Katy and raising an eyebrow.

Katy's gaze shifted between Monika and me. Okay, I'm not psychic, but this is exactly what ran through her mind: *I'm smarter than her. I could take her if I wanted to. But she's just not worth the trouble.* She lifted both hands in the air in a gesture of submission. "Feel free to use my studio to proposition Mr. Fox, Ms. Sterling. I have no claim to him." She turned away from us and started stuffing stuff into her duffle bag.

Monika smirked and slunk her way to me. "Foxxy?" God, I hated that nickname. "If you get packed tonight, we can be in New York tomorrow and we can pick up right where we left off." She stopped a foot away and placed a hand on my chest. "Before your dad ruined everything for us."

In the mirror, Katy glanced at me.

The word epiphany is a cliché. I won't say angels started singing or a holy light shone down from heaven. . . but standing in that crappy dance studio where I'd had more fun in one day, one lousy *day* than in all the years I'd trained for competition, I knew just how shallow I'd been.

How could I blame Dad for what'd happened to us?

Sure the studio was dingy, but they had *fun* here.

That one moment Katy had looked into my eyes before she kissed me meant more to me than the entire two years with Monika.

Retreating from Monika's hand, I softly declared, "I am a douchebag."

In the mirror, Katy smirked. She did it so much better than Monika.

"Well, yes you are, sweetie," Monika said, "but I'd still like to win Blackpool with you." Her hands slipped behind her back, which was her way to feign little girl innocence.

Why did she want me, specifically? It was eight months to Blackpool, and no matter how many dancers in movies and TV shows can pull off a World Championship in one motivational montage, it takes a helluva lot longer in real life. Even if she found another dude at our level without a partner, dance competitions are like sex: you never get it right the first time.

"Do it."

We both turned to Katy.

"Do it," she repeated and slung her duffle bag onto one shoulder.

"You want me to go?" I asked, more than a bit surprised.

Katy strode across the floor with the same determination she'd had the first time we met. . . was it just yesterday? "Don't be an ass, Foxtrot." Her nickname was much better than Monika's. "You will never have another opportunity like this."

She stopped beside Monika, facing me as if they fought on the same team. "Once you turn eighteen, it's a completely different playing field and you start from scratch. Turn this down and you will live the rest of your life with regret." She shoved a hundred-dollar bill into my hand. "Don't spend the next fifty years playing the 'what if' game."

Across the floor and away from me. "Thanks for the choreography. Make sure the door catches on the way out."

"Katy."

"I have a boyfriend." She waved a hand over her head once. "Good luck in Blackpool."

The door creaked open then slammed shut.

To her credit, Monika didn't say something snotty. "Apparently, you have good taste in girls, Foxxy. She seems intelligent." She turned to me and rubbed her hands together. "Alone at last."

I shook my head. I'd known her for nine years. After one month away and a single day in this podunk town, she'd reappeared and was suddenly someone I never really knew.

She wasn't there because she loved me. She was there because she wanted to win.

Was she even jealous at seeing me with another girl?

What the hell had I been thinking all that time?

My hesitations must have been obvious. "Foxxy, I know we had our problems."

"You dumped me because I couldn't afford coaching."

She opened her hands and smiled. "And now you can. Problem solved." She rolled closer with that pouty look she knew got me going. "Foxxy. . . I said bad things. You said bad things." Her hands found my chest again. They crept up to my shoulders. "The past is dead. It's time to move forward." She leaned in, wearing the perfume that gave me instant wood. "Don't you want to win?" She brushed my nose with the tip of hers. "It's a chance for your dad to make up for everything he did to you. To us."

"What does my dad have to do with it?" I moved away from the powerful spell of her scent.

She rubbed her hands together again. "If he hadn't lost his business, we wouldn't have lost each other." She shrugged. "Your dad screwed up and killed a man, Ethan. Why should you have to pay the price for his mistake?"

All the blood rushed to my face. I had to work to catch my breath. For the second time that night, I'd heard my own words out of her mouth.

Hearing them from her showed me how evil and self-centered they sounded.

She must have realized she was losing me. "All right, Ethan. If I can't seduce you, listen to what the girl said. You give up this opportunity you will regret it the rest of your life." She waved at the folder on the table. "The contract's there. Read it. I assume you still know my number?" She clacked her way off the dance floor. "Think about it and call me."

Apparently, it was my day to watch hot girls walk away from me.

I looked at the money in my hand and thought about Katy. . . and about tango. That short time dancing with her had felt more real, more intimate than nine years of dancing and two years of sex with Monika. How was that even possible?

The competitions. The titles. I'd worked so damn hard for them. It was *always* work.

I thought about K-pop helping Taco. About Tango teaching me. . . the faces of the crew as they helped each other get a new step.

There was this feeling I'd get standing in front of a crowd of thousands, when they handed me a trophy. It was all adrenaline and excitement, and for a few minutes I was the king of the fucking world. And championship sex was the *best*.

But the next day, it was back to work because there was always another competition. The crowd went home. My friends only called me when they wanted to show me off to their new dance partner. "This is my friend Ethan Fox," they'd say. "He's a champion." It usually got them laid. I never knew why.

I wandered off the dance floor, staring into every nook and cranny of that old place, hoping there was some secret there, some way to explain why all of a sudden all those years of hard work and success seemed like pointless bullshit. I sat cross-legged on that ugly, ugly carpet and stared at the mirrors and the lights and the old-fashioned parquet floor.

I shook my head. Tiny, tiny movements.

That old studio was home to memories that would last forever. Three generations, for Christ's sake. And the crew, they helped each other. Their passion was for each other, not just a bunch of stupid trophies.

I had to swallow hard. I stared at Katy's money. Her studio needed it, but she gave it to me so she could do her job better, so she could help her friends. It meant she was coaching the crew for free.

Monika would never do that.

Six months ago? Me neither. I rose to my feet and spotted the folder Monika had left. Someone was willing to give us shit-tons of money so they could say they helped us win. Because somehow, in some way or other, it would get them laid.

Did I want to win?

Fuck yeah, I wanted to win. I'd spent every waking moment for nine years building toward Blackpool, so fuck yeah, I wanted to win.

But. . . But it just didn't *matter* anymore. How could it? Watching someone die, seeing the look on my dad's face. . . it'd changed everything.

Four

David threw a kitchen chair across his living room. Fox had kissed her! That son of a bitch kissed her! The coffee table was over David's head when he stopped himself. If he threw it through the window, someone would notice. He sucked in ragged air.

The apartment was a wreck. Everything glowed with a red aura. He didn't remember throwing anything but the kitchen chair. Damn it. He set the table down. How had it all been destroyed? He hugged himself to keep from breaking something else. He'd need hours to put everything back in place. The disorder crawled across his skin like a cockroach.

He yanked a cell from his pocket. It was one of twenty disposables he'd bought in Austin. Texting was hard because his hands shook so badly. He needed to make Katy like him, to agree to meet before things with Fox went too far. Did you like the rose? *he typed.* You're so pretty like a rose.

The naked chick wasn't helping. At all. He needed something more serious.

I was back at the heavy bag around midnight. This time the garage door was closed and my pissed-off-at-the-world station on Spotify played on the speakers, not my ear buds. I ran through practice sequences, but the more I thought about Monika's visit, the more I just punched the shit out of the bag.

"Nice shorts." Hadn't heard Dad come in. He cut the volume on the music, but let it play.

One more really, really hard upper cut that hurt all the way to my shoulder and I turned around, forcing myself to joke. "Are you just getting in now, young man?"

He still wore the cheap suit, but now it was rumpled, and the tie hung out of a pocket. He grinned a lopsided grin. "Dragon jousting took longer than expected."

Wait a minute. He meant it. "You're out job hunting at midnight?" Without even thinking about it, I walked over with my hands extended so he could unfasten the gloves.

He stared at the gloves as if they might bite him.

I froze. "Dad, I'm sorry. I didn't mean. . ." It was something I'd done a million times. A total reflex. I turned away and grabbed the end of the Velcro in my teeth.

His hand on my shoulder turned me to face him. We stood like that for a few seconds. Normally, no big deal, but Dad hadn't touched me, or anyone else, since the accident.

We stared into each other's eyes.

The moment passed without anyone dying.

As if to make light of it, he cuffed me upside the head before taking a glove and yanking the Velcro strap. "I checked out a couple of bars to see if they need security." That explained his late arrival. "I'll find something." He undid the other glove, directed me to sit on a box and threw a towel around my bare shoulders, wiping me down.

There's that cliché about a lump in your throat?

Really hard to talk around.

He knelt in front of me and started at the tapes on my hands.

I cleared my throat and picked up my jeans. "Front pocket." I shook them at him. "I made some money for us. Here."

"How'd you do that?" He pulled out the hundred-dollar bill.

"Local dance team. I did some coaching."

"That's great, Ethan. Really. But that's your money." He tossed the jeans to the side and went to work on the tapes again, forcing a smile. He didn't fake those as well as I did. "I hear there's a Starbucks now. That should buy you a coffee, right?"

He moved through the old cool down routine of working out the cramps in my hands and shaking out my arms. The contact started to feel normal again.

Deep breath.

He pulled the towel onto my head, dried my hair and wiped the sweat off my face. "Tell me about your day." The towel fell around my neck as he stepped behind me to work out the knots in my shoulders.

I cleared my throat again and a water bottle appeared in my face. I took it and drank. With Dad finally starting to act like his old self, the news that'd brought me back to the punching bag was even harder to tell him. "Monika's in town."

The rubdown stopped. "What? Why?"

"She found a sponsor. Full ride out to New York for eight months to train for Blackpool."

I imagined what his face looked like: shock and trying really hard to be supportive. "That's great," he lied a little too enthusiastically. "Where will you live?"

"Timeshare. She has the whole thing figured out."

"She always does. Who's the sponsor?"

"I didn't look." I waved at the folder lying a few feet away.

"So. . . why aren't you jumping up and down doing fist pumps?" He picked up the folder and sat on a box in front of me. "This fixes everything, doesn't it?"

A couple months ago there'd been shouting matches about how much he'd fucked up my life. Good times.

"Ethan?"

How long had I been silent? Deep breath.

He grinned. "Ah. . . there's a *new* girl."

My cheeks felt hot. Damn Nordic genes. "Kinda. . . maybe. . . I don't know." I wiped my face with the towel. "And what about you? I can't just leave you."

He examined the papers. "You do not pass up a chance like this for. . .

me. . ." All the emotion drained from his face. He looked up at me. "You really don't know who the sponsor is?"

I shook my head.

He seemed to consider his options but knew I'd figure it out sooner or later. He handed me a single sheet of paper with a header I immediately recognized: Dad's gym.

"Wait. . . *you*?" I read further. It wasn't Dad's gym, anymore, but it was still up and running.

The new owners were offering *me* six figures to train?

What the hell?

Then I made the leap: the new owners were the same people who'd sued Dad and ruined our lives. They couldn't be trying to help me out. They were paying me to move across the country, away from my dad. They had to be doing it expressly to hurt him and Monika *had* to know what it would do to him. I was all he had left.

"That bitch." I crumpled up the paper. "That fucking bitch!"

Instantly on my feet, I slammed a fist into the bag as hard as I could. Everything Monika'd said suddenly made sense. I snatched the contract out of Dad's hands and threw it into one of the garbage boxes. "No way."

"Ethan. . ."

"No!"

He rose to his feet, rumpled and sad in his cheap suit that didn't fit well because they don't make off-the-rack cheap suits for guys that big. He'd always been the strongest guy I knew, until they went for his throat and he'd just rolled over out of guilt.

I wouldn't roll. "No."

How could we talk about *this* when we never talked about *that*?

He crossed his arms, which is probably how the suit got wrinkled in the first place. "Okay. . . you were already in a mood before you knew who was making the offer. What the hell happened?"

So I told him. Some of it was hard to say. "The crap she said about Katy. . . and about the studio." I stared at the floor. "And about you." I had to take a couple of breaths. "It's all shit I've thought, too." I felt his eyes on me and couldn't look up. "But I was wrong about all of it." I forced myself to meet his gaze. "Maybe it *is* a crappy studio and maybe they *can't* dance for shit. . . but Katy's a better *person* than Monika." I looked away. "They're all better *people* than me."

When he finally spoke, his voice was quiet. "Ethan. . ."

I looked at him.

The garage door opener jumped to life. I nearly wet myself. It had to be Auntie Mac just getting home from a late shift closing her restaurant.

Dad took my elbow and lifted me to my feet. "Sleep on it, Ethan. We'll talk more tomorrow." He gave me a gentle push toward the kitchen door as the headlights of Auntie Mac's car flared at the bottom of the rising garage door. "You better get inside. You know she hates the way we run around the house in our underwear."

I grabbed him in a quick hug. "I'm sorry I was such a douchebag about losing the money, Dad."

He returned the squeeze, thank God.

I hurried inside.

Five

What was the worst thing that could've happened to me the next morning? No. . . worse than that.

Worse than that, too.

How about hearing Boyfriend shout my name at the top of his lungs while he ripped the sheet off my bed? "I have a bone to pick with you, Foxtrot!"

That would be the worst.

I rolled to my feet on the opposite side of the bed, fists up, fighting my way to consciousness under the assumption the big goon had heard about the kiss I shared with Katy.

"What the hell?" I shouted.

He stood by the bed with a goofy grin. "Bro. . . birthday present? You promised?"

I relaxed. So. . . he wasn't there to beat the shit out of me? What time was it?

His hands came up quickly, and I dropped into a fighter stance, but he was actually shielding his face. "Speaking of bones, bro. Put that thing away before you put out somebody's eye. Geez."

Shitstix. I grabbed a pillow and turned my back to him. Give me a break. Seventeen. Nearly every morning was greeted with a salute.

"Ha-a-a, just messing with ya."

Asshat. I threw the pillow at Boyfriend. "How the hell did you get into my room?"

He tossed the pillow on the bed. "Front door's open, bro." He fell heavily into a chair in the corner. "You said you'd help me get the perfect birthday present for Katy, remember?"

Rubbing one hand across my face to wake up, I picked up a pair of sweatpants. "I don't recall saying eight o'clock in the freakin' a.m. on a Saturday."

He laughed and banged on the arms of the chair. "That is *so* big city." He lifted his face and tried to sound snooty. "I don't recall saying. . ." He laughed and banged the arms again. "Bro, I was milking cows, like, three hours ago. I sat outside on the porch for, like, an hour."

I pulled on a t-shirt. "Did my dad, *like*, notice you?"

"Uh-huh." I swear he bounced up and down in the chair like a coke addict, the powdered kind not the liquid. "He said to give you until eight and then knock myself out if you were still in bed."

Nice. Dad was a dead man walking. Time to dig up the Mardi Gras coming out pictures from his college days and introduce them to Facebook.

"Okay, bro. . . I had the best f-ing idea."

No. He really said "f-ing." He really talked like that.

And he just kept talking. "So at first I was going to take you to the Mall and have you pick out some lame jewelry or something?"

"Really, Boyfriend?" I amped up the fake enthusiasm. "The Mall?" There was only one mall. It deserved a capital letter.

He waved a hand and made a face disturbingly similar to Katy's cheerleader face. "Yeah, I knew you'd probably get a charge out of it, but it's not my thing." He stopped waving and looked like a puppy caught pissing in his master's favorite shoes. "Nothing wrong with shopping, bro. Just not my thing."

That's right. He thought I was gay. Could this morning get any worse?

"But I know Katy would go batshit *crazy* if you taught me how to do that tango thing she does."

I froze.

He'd managed to think of something that would actually work. Aaaargh!

When you're lost in the woods, never. ever. say, "Could be worse. Could be raining."

He pumped a fist. "Booyah! Nailed it, right?" He jumped out of the chair and ran closer to me.

I flinched. If he hugged me, I'd have to coldcock him unconscious.

He held out a fist to bump. "I. . . am the perfect boyfriend."

Reluctantly, I bumped his fist.

He winked. "I bet I get her to blow me on *her* birthday, knowwhatimean?"

My fist connected with his jaw before I even knew it was moving. Bam. Actually hurt my hand, too. I was used to gloves and tape.

"What the hell, bro?"

Quick. What Would Dad Do? "I'm sorry, bro, but I just can't let you talk about women that way. This isn't a locker room."

Wait for it.

Wait for it.

His confusion changed into an oh-yeah-gay-dudes-are-practically-chicks expression. "Hey bro, I am so sorry. I didn't mean. . . I didn't mean a *real* blow job. . . it was. . . a metaphor."

I held a finger to my lips and shushed him. "I can forgive you. Just remember that Katy is a lady, and I expect you to discuss her as such."

I read fantasy novels. I got the lingo.

His hands came up and he nodded more than anyone should. "Lady Katy. Got it, bro."

The bruise welling up on his cheek delighted me more than it should have.

Okay. . . teaching Boyfriend tango. There had to be a way to turn this to my advantage.

"Go down and get some coffee." I needed a few minutes to myself to piss. Something told me he was the kind of guy who'd talk to me through the door. We weren't that close. We'd *never* be that close.

David hovered near the edge of the crowd, gaping at Katy's car in the early morning light. What had happened? He remembered the paint and the roses. They were a grand romantic gesture. Right? But the rest? Did he do all that? He didn't remember doing all that. It wasn't romantic. It was fucking creepy.

"What sort of twisted. . ." Katy stormed past. "When I find the sick little twist that did this. . ." She stomped up to Mrs. Crawley's house and banged on the door.

David breathed out. The way she emphasized the word "twist," it almost sounded like one of her nicknames. Twist. Wasn't that a kind of dance, too? She liked dance stuff. "Twist," he said quietly to see how it sounded. He liked it more than what everyone called him now. And anything was better than David. David was quiet and. . . lame.

He'd have to keep it a secret though, until he figured out what to do about trashing her car.

How had that happened? He didn't remember. . .

Twist pushed through the growing crowd. He had as much right to be there as anyone. More even. He pushed through for a better look.

Boyfriend and I walked into the garage. We shoved all the boxes to the edges and stacked them higher than I could have done by myself. Dude was built like an ox.

I scrolled through my playlists and hooked the player to the speakers. "After careful consideration," I said in my best gay-but-not-nellie voice, "I believe *tah-ngo* is the wrong choice." I turned and held up one hand to silence him.

Yeah, he wasn't about to protest the way I'd assumed. Okay.

"While learning a dance is inspired logic, *tah-ngo* is the wrong dance for you."

His enormous brow furrowed. "But it's her thing."

"Exactly the problem, bro. *Latina* women want men to be strong. . . in charge. No offence, but you'll never be better than her at *tah-ngo*. You'll never come close. If you want to impress her with your masculine. . . *machismo*. You need *salsa*." I hit play and the room filled with salsa. "It's *muy caliente* and speaks to her *Latina* heritage, but you can be the man in charge."

For the record, Katy hated salsa.

She also hated macho.

"Yeah?" he asked. "In charge of Katy?"

"Of course," I forced myself to throw an arm around him all cozy-like. "She wants a man who's a real man."

"Yeah?"

"Strong. Forceful. Sexy. It's what all *Latina* girls want."

"Really?"

I patted his shoulder. "Really." I moved through a few salsa moves, going for Latin macho not Swishing with the Stars. "With *tah-ngo*, she'll always be in charge. With *salsa*, she'll be putty in your hands."

I swear he shivered. "Yeah?" Drool dribbled from his mouth. "Putty?"

I patted him again and moved away. "Putty."

Grinning, he looked around the garage. He jabbed a meaty thumb at the heavy bag. "Whazzup wit dat, yo?"

What was up with the way he talked? Was he trying to be "street" or something?

"My dad's a boxing coach. . . was a boxing coach."

Another big grin. "Awesome. That is so post-queer."

Okay, I almost popped him again. "What the fuck?"

Again the hands out in submission. "Dude, what?"

"Post-queer? Is that like ex-gay?"

He shook his head with the most confusion I'd seen on his face to date, and that was saying a hell of a lot. "Post-queer as in who gives a shit who you screw anymore, let's just get on with life." He shrugged. "It's a small town but we have, like, a huge number of gay kids in school." A shadow crossed his face. "Some of them say it's the water fountain on the third floor." He shook it off. "They all talk about how everything is post-queer, like lesbian supermodels and gay rugby players. Like all the stereotypes just don't matter now." He gestured at the heavy bag as if it were a game show prize. "Like a gay boxing coach is super awesome." His eyes lit up. "Hey, I would totally pay him for lessons."

Holy—wait for it—fuck. This Dumass, football-playing *dude* had just out-liberaled me. I couldn't even speak for a minute. I mean, he was the enemy, right? I had to teach him a lesson and prove to Katy just how much more "awesome" I was.

Right?

Without a word, I started moving to the music, demonstrating the basic.

He floundered along beside me.

After a couple of minutes, I gave up and stopped. "Do you even like to dance?"

He shrugged sheepishly.

"Why are you on the crew?"

"I thought I was the stupid one."

This big ox wanted boxing lessons from my gay dad, and if there was any way to talk Dad into it, those simple lessons would do more to help him than any midnight gab fest with me. Shitstix.

Maybe his problem was more the teacher than the student. Katy took the moves I did and broke them down so the crew could learn them. Could I do that?

I turned off the music and stood next to Boyfriend, taking his elbow. I shook my left foot. "Left foot."

He shook his foot.

"It's like the hokey-pokey. You put your left foot in."

We stepped forward on our left feet.

"You put your right foot out."

We stepped back on our right feet.

"You put your left foot in. You put your right foot out."

He repeated my rhythm. "Left foot in. Right foot out."

I played the music and took him into normal dance position. "Left foot in. Right foot out."

We danced the basic for half the song and he gave me a huge grin. "And you do the hokey-pokey and you shake it all about."

And, yes, he shook it all about. Foot-f-ing-loose, eat your heart out.

After an hour, we were sweaty, and I was tired. He'd learned three moves. Teaching Katy's way was hard.

"Break for drinks," I said.

"Beers?"

I stopped in the doorway that led to the kitchen. "Isn't it a little early for beer?"

He shrugged. "Not in China."

Wow. Compared to him, I *was* gay.

Standing in the kitchen with the fridge open I checked my options. What the hell. I grabbed a couple of Shiners and slammed the door. As I walked into the garage, he was still counting to himself. "You put your *left* foot in. You put your *right* foot out."

I took a slug of beer.

He looked up, saw me watching and grinned like a little kid whose dad caught him riding a bike by himself for the first time. Big thumbs up. "Left foot in. Right foot out."

I handed him a beer. "Corey?"

He deflated. "What happened to Boyfriend?"

"I can't call you Boyfriend."

"Everyone calls me Boyfriend."

The wheels on the bus go round and round.

"If I call you Boyfriend and a hot guy hears me, I might lose my chance with him."

Realization dawned. "Oh right!" Big smile. "Corey's my real name, anyway."

I was a douchebag. I was *still* a douchebag.

This poor guy was working his ass off to impress Katy, and I hadn't decided whether I was going to stay in town or ride off to the competition circuit with my bitch of an ex. What right did I have to sabotage his plans?

"Bro, why are you working so hard to keep her?"

"She's amazing."

"Okay, she's hot, I get that, but—"

"No, no, no." He shook his head a lot and held my shoulder with a meaty hand. After an hour of dancing with the guy, it didn't bother me, anymore. "Yeah, she's hot, but look at all *this*." He struck a pose. "I can get *hot* any day of the week."

He sat on a box. "Katy's smart. She's smarter than me." He smiled. "She's smarter than you, too. And that is *ho-o-ot*." He shook a hand as if he'd burned it. "I know I'm not smart, Foxtrot. I know if I lose Katy, I'll date a bunch of really hot stupid chicks, but I'll never find another Katy. Not in this lifetime." He winked at me. "I may be dumb. . . but I'm not stupid."

He rose and started moving through the basic. "Left foot in. Right foot out. Left foot in. Right foot out."

He looked at me with that big, goofy grin. "What else you got?"

His cell rang. Katy's ring tone was a tango.

His grin exploded across his face in a giant goofy mess. "Katy-pop!" The smile slid off so fast I'm surprised he didn't get whiplash. "Sorry, Katy. Guess what—"

I chuckled. She obviously didn't approve of his pet name.

His eyes narrowed and he met my gaze. "*What* happened?"

He hit speaker so I could hear her voice: "Someone trashed my fucking car."

Three minutes later, Corey and I jumped out of his Challenger at Katy's house. A crowd had gathered, including two skinny cops who seemed more like boy scouts than officers of the law. We ran to the scene, Corey calling Katy's name all the way. He threw his arms around her, but she didn't look like she needed a hug. More like a shotgun.

The car was totaled. Utterly. Anything glass had been shattered. The side mirrors were gone. The tires were slashed. It was really fucking creepy. Someone had taken a metal baseball bat to it and had wailed on it for a long time.

There was only one person I knew evil enough to do something like this. "Monika."

Katy furrowed her brow. "What?"

"It had to be Monika."

She pulled away from Corey. "Why in the world would Monika trash my car?"

"She's a jealous bitch?"

Katy's expression reminded me that no one knew about our little indiscretion except Monika and that Katy would like to keep it that way, thank you very much. Before I had time for a sterling recovery, the clack of heels on concrete distracted me.

"Why in the world would I be jealous, Foxtrot?" Monika brushed past me carrying a tray and two cups of coffee without so much as glancing my way. "Katy agrees you should go with me to New York." She handed a coffee to Katy, who accepted it with obvious gratitude.

Corey was pushed to my side while the girls sorted out cream and sugar.

"What the hell are you doing here?" I demanded.

"I liked Katy last night. She's spunky." Monika gave me her best innocent look. "I knew I'd be bored here while you made up your mind, so I stopped by." She waved her coffee in the general direction of the car. "I'm the one who noticed the damage." She glanced at the crowd. "Looks like the whole town's turned out." While she sipped coffee, she raised her eyebrows in this amazing way she has that's horribly judgmental, while not being obvious enough for anyone to call her on it.

"It's a small town," Katy muttered. Embarrassed?

Corey nudged me. His face asked me who the girl was.

Monika clacked over to him, hand extended. "Monika Sterling, and yes, that's my real name. Monika with a 'K' or I kill you." Corey took her hand. "You must be the Boyfriend I've heard so much about this morning." Monika glanced pointedly at Corey's crotch and smiled. "You get chilly at night?"

What the fuck? Had she always acted like a cartoon villain?

How had I missed that?

She acknowledged me as if seeing me for the first time. "Hello, Foxtrot." She smiled at Corey. "I'm Foxtrot's dance partner." She rolled a hand. "Well, hopefully I am."

So there we were, Monika and Katy facing Corey and me.

Keep your friends close and your enemies closer, right?

When, exactly, had my life turned into an episode of *Glee*?

Reality assaulted me in the form of a scrawny uniformed cop who pushed between us, forcing me away. "Is there any possibility to the accusation, Katy?" His name tag read Warren but call him "Officer

Friendly" for fun. He was anything but. Like the cop I'd met at the cemetery, he couldn't have been more than nineteen or twenty.

Katy shook her head. "I already told you, Warren, this started before Monika arrived."

The cop turned to me, hovering near Katy as if she were his personal responsibility. "And who are you, anyway?"

"Ethan Fox. I just moved in with my Auntie Mac. . . Macarena Davis."

He looked me up and down like I had a big sign around my neck that said, *Guilty as shit.* "You the boxer's son?"

Oh joy. "Yes."

He didn't say anything. He didn't need to.

The other cop joined us, the guy from the cemetery. Palatino, right? They formed bookend scarecrows on either side of me. "Is there a problem here?"

"It's the boxer's son," Officer Friendly said.

"We've met." Palatino looked down his nose at me, his squint in full force. "He causing a problem?"

"He has nothing to do with it," Katy insisted.

Officer Friendly nodded, made a few notes and kept glancing my way as he wandered off with Palatino. He might as well have done the two fingers to his eyes and then pointing at me thing since that's what his expression said: *You're the killer's son, and we all know the apple never falls far from the tree.*

Corey elbowed me again. "Chief of Police Olmos is in Houston for a case," he whispered, then leaned a little closer than was comfortable. "Rumor is he's actually in rehab." He used one hand to pretend he was drinking, you know, in case I somehow didn't understand rehab.

With one finger, I moved him away.

He jabbed a thumb at Officer Friendly. "Warren gets pretty full of himself when the chief's gone."

Stellar.

"And the other one?" I asked.

"Pal?" Corey chuckled. "He's harmless. Does what he's told and lets the pretty girls get by with a warning when it comes to speeding tickets."

He shrugged. "Probably whacks off to the Disney channel, know what I mean?"

I so did not, but Katy distracted me.

"Hot, hot, hot," she said. She sipped her coffee again. "There was a rose on my car yesterday morning." She glanced at me. "And then some texts."

"Texts?" Corey and I chorused.

She pointed at Pal. "Confiscated my phone as evidence as soon as they got here. The texts said things like 'Did you get the rose?' and 'You're so pretty like a rose.'" She glanced at Corey. "'A pretty rose deserves better than a big prick.'"

Corey raised a hand. "Hey, it must be someone on the football team."

Monika made a "bless his heart" face.

"Where did that come from?" I asked.

Corey tapped the side of his nose. "Whoever sent the texts knows I have a big prick, right? He must have seen me in the showers."

Monika clapped her hands in front of her mouth. "Tell me he has a twin brother."

So much for my theory about the Challenger.

Officer Friendly and his sidekick Pal asked everyone a million questions. Dumass hadn't seen this much excitement in months. Apparently, in a town this small, vandalism was a major event and Warren was going to milk it for all it was worth since he was top dog for the time being.

In Austin this kind of shit happened all the time. Piss off your baby-mama, she trashed your car. Out here? Out here it was spooky. I mean, how'd they total the car without anyone noticing? In a small town, someone heard a noise, they called the cops.

Officer Friendly twirled his handcuffs, apparently demonstrating the finesse with which he was going to arrest the culprit once apprehended. The cuffs flew off his finger and Warren whirled around to see where they landed. Idiot.

"I ignored the texts at first," Katy said. "I figured someone was just looking for attention."

Corey put his arm around her and held her close. I wished it was me, but he was genuinely concerned, not just making time.

Okay, maybe complicated *wasn't* so nice.

"When I got home last night, though," Katy continued, "they got creepier and more insistent."

"Like what?" I asked.

Her eyes travelled from Corey to me and back again. "'I know the secrets you don't want to tell.'" She hugged herself and Corey's grip tightened. "'No one knows the depths of your soul the way I do,' except. . ." Her face vacillated between worried and amused. "At first it came across as, 'No one knows the death of your soul,' but he blamed auto-correct."

Monika covered her mouth with one hand. "Bless his heart."

Katy studied the car, and I could see her trying to keep a brave face. "So I told him to get lost and leave me alone."

"Are you sure it's the same guy?" I asked.

She led the group closer to the car where Warren was bagging samples of the shredded remains of at least a dozen roses thrown across the interior. The side was spray painted in blood red: *every rose has its thron*

Holy. Fuck. Creepy as shit and kind of a loser, all at the same time.

"What's a thron?" Corey asked.

Katy took his hand. "Psycho needs auto-correct for his brain."

"Oh." He had no idea what she meant.

Warren slammed the car door. "Maybe he's dyslexic," he snapped, heading off to do whatever it is cops do.

"Someone's touchy," Monika said.

"I don't want to be the big city asshole," I said when the cop was gone, "but can't we bring in someone. . . else?" I looked around at the expectant faces. "My dad knows a great lawyer up in Austin. Ms. Delacroix has connections. She could get—"

Katy waved it away. "I'm not going to let this asshole freak me out." She even kicked the tire of the car. "It's what the sick little twist wants." She took a deep breath. It was sexy she knew my trick. "No, this is Dumass. Big, scary dramas don't happen here. Some deviant wants attention? Well, I'm not going to give it to him. I live my life like I always do."

Monika patted Katy's arm. What was *her* deal?

The rest of the dance crew arrived, and Corey took them aside so Katy wouldn't have to go through it again. Monika took advantage of the quiet moment. "So, have you given any thought to my offer?"

I glanced at Katy and shook my head. "Not the time or place."

Katy stared at her car. "I'm not a wreck or anything, mostly just pissed." She gave me her full attention. "Why *wouldn't* you go, Foxtrot?"

Did she want me to go? Was she happy with Corey? Or was she telling me to go but hoping I'd stay but not wanting me to stay for her unless I really wanted to. . .

Girls *are* complicated.

"Seriously, Foxtrot," Monika said, "why is it so difficult?"

So I let her have it. "Why? Because the people you got to sponsor us are the same assholes who sued my dad, stole his business, took our home and ruined his entire career because of an accident that was *not* his fault. It was horrible, but it wasn't Dad's fault."

Okay, when I got a head of steam up, sometimes it was hard to slow down.

"I'm all he has left, Monika, and you managed to find the one way they might also be able to take *me* away from him." I applauded. "Congratulations, Monika with a 'K,' you win bitch of the year award."

Was the shock on her face genuine? "Do you. . . do you *really* think I'd do something like that?" She made my acting skills look fifth grade class play.

Katy seemed shocked too.

"Yes." It was a statement, but now that I saw her face, I wasn't so sure.

Monika blinked and set her coffee down on the dented hood. "It never occurred to you that maybe, just maybe, I went to them specifically as a way to get a little revenge on *them*? To get a chunk of the money they took?" She deserved an Oscar. "They think they're sticking it to your dad one last time, and you go to Blackpool, laughing all the way to the bank."

She laid a hand on Katy's arm wearing her sad victim face. "I'm so sorry about your car, Katy, but I think I need to leave." She turned to me. "If you really believe I'm such a horrible person, I understand why you wouldn't want to dance with me."

Clack. Clack. Clack. Clack.

I waited for the explosion from Katy. The how-could-you-be-so-heartless speech. Or the way-to-make-her-cry speech. What she actually said surprised me. "*She* doesn't even know why she really did it, does she?"

I looked at Katy out of the corner of my eye to see if I'd heard her correctly.

"What? You think I'm going to take her side just because we're both chicks and she bought me a delicious mocha coffee thing?" She scoffed and turned toward her decimated vehicle. "I figured you knew me better than that."

I took Monika's coffee from the hood. Why waste it? "I've known you a day and a half. I try not to make assumptions."

She laughed. "Yes, you do. You make them all the time."

Damn it, she was right.

"Sorry about the car," I said. "Insurance?"

"Not for this."

"Ouch."

We stood in a companionable silence while the dance crew horsed around, and Officer Friendly took more statements.

Ephraim somehow miracled a baseball bat from thin air and held it over the hood singing, "I bust the windows out your car," while Woody took photos. Jesus Christ, really?

"Put your foot up on the wheel," Woody encouraged, crouching down as if he were a fashion photographer.

The moment Ephraim's foot touched the car, Pal appeared and pushed him away. "Have a little respect."

Ephraim instantly morphed into an expressionless statue, the baseball bat held to the ground as if it were an Englishman's cane. "Touch me again and your pathetic career is over," he said. "I'm Jewish and my father is the only lawyer in this town."

Without a word, Pal edged away.

When the cop's back was turned, Woody nudged Ephraim playfully.

The little guy didn't so much as crack a smile. "Same goes for you, Neanderthal."

Woody chuckled. "I will whip it out and pee on you right here, bubala."

Ephraim finally smiled, until he looked up and saw me watching, then his face turned to stone. I waited for the joke.

No joke. He just stared into my eyes like a pissed-off cat.

Until I looked away. Wow, creepy. They were acting like it was a carnival. Did people in tiny little towns think really bad things couldn't happen?

I returned my full attention to Tango. "You're *really* not freaked out about this?"

"A little," she said so quietly only I could hear her. She waved the coffee cup. "Shit like this doesn't happen here, Foxtrot. They have no frame of reference."

Wow. She *was* smarter than me. She settled into one hip and her smile told me she was deliberately changing the subject. "Why were you with Boyfriend at eight o'clock in the morning?"

I almost snorted. "It's a secret."

Her raised eyebrows told me she hoped I would elaborate.

"Birthday surprise."

More raised eyebrows. "You're helping my boyfriend shop for my birthday present?"

"Something like that," I said with a pronounced eyebrow waggle.

She chuckled, which made the whole morning worthwhile.

I nudged her. "And you're having coffee with my ex, plotting ways to convince me to move to New York?"

The tow truck arrived, and the seriousness of the moment returned. I nudged her again. "No dramatic bullshit this time, but I know a couple of boxers who can play bodyguard should the need arise."

Staring at her car, she finished the last of her mocha. "I'll keep that in mind." Her eyes met mine and for a moment she just stared. "Seriously."

"Foxtrot?" Corey's voice was hard to mistake. He dashed around his Challenger and ran up the walk toward me. "Bro, I'm sorry I didn't give you a ride home, but Katy. . ."

I dropped my duffle on Auntie Mac's front porch. "No worries, dude. She's priority number one, right now."

He nodded a lot. Then he stared at me. A lot.

"So. . . You just stopped by to apologize?"

He shook his head. A lot.

So I waited.

"Look," he said at last, "I don't want to drag you into anything."

I waved it off. "Drag away."

Fortunately, the unfortunate double entendre soared over his head. "You're new to town, and you're smart, so I figure you might help me figure out who's after Katy, you know, from a different angle." He made a number of cross-cutting motions with his hands, which, I presumed, were meant to illustrate his point.

It made sense. Someone new would have a more detached perspective. "It's all I can think about," I admitted. I led him over to a couple of wicker chairs on the porch. Jasmine wafted everywhere from the vines that spilled off the porch roof.

"Katy doesn't want to talk about what happened," he said. "She wants to pretend it's no big deal, but, bro, this doesn't *happen* out here." His face told me he was hurting over the whole thing. "I mean, some of the other little towns get the occasional beatdown on a bum or something, you know, assholes out joyriding? But here? In Dumass?" He pronounced it the way it was spelled. "This is once every five years stuff, and with Sheriff Olmos out of town—"

I patted the air with both hands to slow him down. "Okay, so let's think about who it could be." I rubbed my face. I watched reality TV. "Think of the quiet guys. Guys who don't date much, who stick to themselves."

He laughed. "That's K-pop."

"What?" The fact the Korean boyband wannabe was the first name out of his mouth surprised me.

He shrugged. "Quiet. Keeps to himself. Kind of a loner."

"He's on the dance team."

He waved his hands around. "I know. But. . . he keeps to himself." His brow furrowed. "Plus, he's been kinda weird the last couple of days. I tried talking to him and he kinda blew me off."

The skinny kid with Vash the Stampede hair didn't seem to fit the profile. He called attention to himself with the way he dressed, but I was here to keep an open mind. "Okay. So K-pop maybe."

"Except. . ."

I waited.

"Well, Juicy's convinced he's gay."

My whole body rattled. "What?"

He sighed. "The way he ran over to you when you showed up yesterday. She thought he was totally crushing on you."

I thought back. "No," I said, "I've had guys totally crush on me and it's different. He was just glad to see someone. . . new."

His face scrunched up a moment, then he chuckled. "Well, you'd know better than me."

Oh yeah. I was gay. Deep breath. "Who else?"

"Well, I *still* think it has to be someone on the football team."

Because of the dick comment. Hm. How to say it. "Corey, I think when he said, 'a big prick,' he meant more like a big jerk than a compliment about your. . ." For some reason, I couldn't say it. I gestured at his crotch with both hands.

The brow furrowed, then the eyes opened wide. "Ohhhhhh." Then they furrowed again. "Well, that's just mean."

Poor thing. "Well, we are talking about someone who trashed Katy's car."

He nodded and dropped his head in his hands. "Ff-frm." That's what it sounded like.

"Huh?"

He looked up. "Ephraim," he said. "Quiet. Shy. No girls. As far as I know, his only friend is Woody." His face lit up. "*And* he's on the football team."

Utter shock. "He's. . . kinda small for the football team."

Corey shrugged and looked around as if Ephraim might be lurking behind the Jasmine. "He doesn't play much, but he really works hard. It means a lot to him, being on the team." Bless his heart. I heard it.

I opened my hands wide in submission. "I'm sorry, Corey, I just don't know any of these guys well enough, yet."

"But you'll help?"

"Well, fuck yeah."

He grinned at my enthusiasm, then jumped to his feet. He actually shook my hand. "You are the *best* thing to happen to this town in a long time."

Oh. crap. Could he have said *anything* to make me feel worse?

Six

Twist propped his book open with a couple of rubber bands and laid it on the kitchen counter. Black candles lit the room with a flickering, shadowy glow. . . which made reading nearly impossible, so he turned on the light over the sink. Better.

In a stone bowl, he mixed bay leaves, marjoram and verbena leaves. He added oil to the mix and ignited it with a candle. While the herbs burned, he twisted a lock of Katy's hair that he'd stolen from a brush in her bedroom. He'd been so tempted to steal clothes from her laundry basket because they smelled like her sweat, but she'd have noticed that. It would have put her on her guard.

After checking the book, he chanted Fox's name while tying a knot in the hair.

Tying a knot in a girl's hair was harder than the book made it seem. He had to add more bay leaves to keep the fire burning. When the hair was knotted, he dropped it into the fire. "Shiva, destroy the power of my rival."

Christ that stank. No wonder he'd been told to light incense.

The fire burned itself out. According to the book, Fox's hold over Katy was null and void.

And Twist had plenty of Bay leaves and marjoram left over to bake a chicken.

He thought about the blonde slut from Austin. There had to be a way to use her, too. A way Fox couldn't refuse her. He dug through his bookmarked sites. Hm. Maybe a spell to ensure her good fortune? It would certainly help Twist if she got lucky.

That afternoon, the crew decided dance practice was the best way to pretend everything was normal while keeping Katy safe. Pal stationed himself outside her house to protect it from vandalism. Officer Friendly parked outside the studio. He glared at me like I was a serial killer when I walked by.

The crew worked on the new material I'd given Katy, and I stretched and pretended to practice my "skilz." I played at jazz isolations and some slow breakdancing exercises. Since I knew these guys made fun of ballroom, no way was I going to run through Cuban motion or rise and fall.

Corey jumped every time the door opened, which made some of his steps unique, but they were pretty one-of-a-kind anyway. Katy glanced in the mirrors every time. She caught me noticing her and smiled, jazzing me utterly. The mirror trick was our secret.

Ephraim never jumped though. He was cool as a cucumber. Hm.

I also used the mirrors to see if any of the guys were checking Katy out behind her back, but, well, she was the damn coach, so they *should* be watching her the whole time. I concentrated on Ephraim and K-pop, but I was a dancer, not Sherlock Holmes.

Katy demonstrated my combination for the really kick-ass bridge, and the whole crew went batshit crazy.

K-pop tried the moves immediately.

Juicy made an I'm-not-worthy mock bow.

Taco almost dropped his soda. His eyes opened huge and terrified.

Aww. . . he'd get it.

Eventually. . .

Er. . . Nope.

Half an hour later, he wasn't even close. He had the phrases before the bridge nailed so tight I could tell he'd been working his padded butt off, but the new part. . . my part? Nope. He was frustrated.

The crew was frustrated.

Even Katy was frustrated. She called a break and snatched up a towel.

K-pop kept practicing the moves, grinning like a kid with a new video game mod.

Taco sat off in a corner by himself eating a taco.

Man, he looked down. My fault. Call it "over-choreographing." I'd had so much fun impressing Katy with my mad moves, I completely forgot about the folks who had to learn them.

Watching the conversation between Juicy and Katy, I could tell Katy wanted to drop the material since Taco couldn't do it. Juicy wasn't happy. She loved the new stuff.

The rest of the crew would be pissed, too.

Duh.

Shitstix.

My mind raced.

I caught Taco's attention.

After stuffing the snack back in the pack, he jogged over.

I told him my idea.

His eyes popped open as if I'd just asked him to strip naked and whack off in front of us.

"Trust me," I assured him. "And if Katy's pissed, it's all on me."

"Tcha it is," he said, but he smiled as he slunk to his bag. He reached into his snack pack, glanced up at me and left the tacos where they were.

Next, I wandered to the water bottles, leaning close to Katy. "I screwed up."

She raised an eyebrow.

"That should have been a feature," I explained. "It's too much for the whole crew. Do me a solid and just run what you have from start to finish."

She leaned closer, pretending to rearrange the bottles. "They can't do it in pieces. How will they run it through?"

"You have speed control?"

She nodded.

"Tell them you're going to slow it down, but don't."

Now she looked at me like I was insane.

"You're a better teacher than me, but I'm a better bullshit artist, okay?"

She smiled at the compliment and rolled her eyes at the rest.

"Please?"

She smiled again. "Okay."

Without giving her a chance to change her mind, I hopped away from the bar and clapped my hands. "Hey, boy-zeds and gurl-zeds who are way too cool for ballroom. A breakin' coach I know in Houston heard I'm hanging out with a crew and wants to see what you got on deck." That had their interest. "If I send him a video, he'll give you some pointers and maybe send me a few moves for you." I pulled out my cell and held it up.

Katy moved forward on cue. "I don't know, Foxtrot. We just learned it. . ."

"If it were perfect would you need tips from a Houston coach who normally charges $200 an hour and produces music videos?"

Yeah, now they amped up.

Taco wandered past with his back to the crew. His eyes were desperate and his jaw wide open.

"Tell you what," I suggested. "Take it down like ten percent and just run it straight through, screw-ups and all. Don't stop for anything." I stood my cell up against a water bottle and set it to record. "And let's get *Tah-ngo* front and center."

The crew hooted and hollered, and Katy seemed to like the attention. Hey, if I pulled this off, she might even keep the nickname.

This was something my dad did with students who couldn't loosen up in the ring. Raise the stakes in a way that's perfectly safe and don't let them think about it. Just make them do it. Throwing an arm around Katy, I dragged her to the center of the group. She usually kept to the side to avoid overshadowing the others.

"Okay, killaz," I hollered in my worst oh-so-street voice. "Let's see how you tro down wit' da bad boyz-z-z." It was goofy enough for them to know it was a joke. With the morning we'd all had, we really needed a joke.

They took their places.

I hit the studio club lights, filling the space with red, blue and green. The lights flashed and spun across the floor.

The crew shouted.

"Are you freakin' ready?" I called.

More noise.

I killed the chandeliers so all we had were the club lights. "Are you freakin' *ready*?!!"

They filled the studio with their uproar. Even Katy joined in.

"Go!" I hit play after making sure the volume was so high the old farts who'd fill this place for a dance that night would complain because they'd hear the echoes.

They danced. They put everything into it and the energy was killer. Total *Glee*. Well, beginning of the first season when the actors were still pretending to suck. Oh, come on, a pep talk creates energy; it doesn't make magic.

I hooted and clapped and shouted.

They weren't half bad. Getting them to loosen up and just go balls out really did make a difference. Even Taco was kind of fun to watch.

Then they reached the bridge.

I held my breath.

While the rest of the crew managed a pretty passable job with the complicated new piece, Taco glanced my way and I gave him a thumbs up. The music dove into badass mode, a stellar dubstep bridge that utterly rocked. . . and Taco went cra-azy. He pulled a Running Man and a Roger Rabbit. . . every bad hip hop cliché he knew.

Katy stopped mid-step and glared at him with her hands on her hips and a look that should have destroyed him instantly, but the little guy kept going. He even broke out his Water the Lawn. It was total retro.

Everyone else kept dancing but watched the scene, not sure what to do. As soon as the bridge was done, Taco jumped right back into the choreography, glancing at Katy, as if he'd just been possessed by the ghost of hip hop past and couldn't stop himself.

When I killed the music, the crew fell *out*. They surrounded Taco to prevent Katy from destroying him, patting him on the shoulders and laughing.

K-pop looked down at me. "Tell me you got that, hai?"

I nodded and jabbed a thumb at the cell. He picked it up.

Juicy laughed so hard she could barely talk. "We have to do it just like that," she said. "You have to stop and give him that total pissed-off-mom look. And then. . . and then. . ."

"Then jump back in after the bridge," Cosita finished for her.

Fist bumps and high fives all around. Taco grinned so much I swear his face almost cracked. It could be his shtick. Once in a while he could break out the old school crap and go crazy. People would wait for it, wondering when it would start. Instead of the weakest link, he'd become the meme.

Then the world slowed down. Katy draped an arm around Taco's neck and drew him closer. She kissed his forehead to let him know she wasn't mad about the unauthorized deviation, and his face colored dark, beet red.

The kind of red that might mean a serious crush.

Wow. Was *anyone* above suspicion? Probably not. I moved away and shook off the heebie jeebies.

"Hey, Foxtrot."

Normal time resumed.

Katy stood close enough I had to swallow to keep from coughing.

She wore her snarky smile. "I'm impressed."

Unable to respond, I turned to watch the crew and pretended I was worldly and casual.

"That was stellar." She bumped my shoulder. "Maybe there is hope for you yet, Mr. Foxtrot."

I gave her a humble head bow. "We can only hope, Ms. Katy."

She backed away and waved her hands. "Katy? Who's this Katy?" She turned away with a wink. "I thought my name was Tango."

Score!

Yes!

Fucking *yes*!!

I pretended to be all cool and nonchalant while she got them under control. Corey worked with Taco trying to learn the Running Man, completely unaware that the move was older than he was and only good for comic effect. He couldn't do it, anyway. He noticed me watching and gave me a big thumbs up, which I returned.

Okay, K-pop should've been my best friend there, not the dude dating the girl I could *not* stop thinking about. Corey draped an arm over Katy's shoulders. She leaned into him, but I caught her glance at me in the mirror before pointedly looking away.

Three days in the new town and I found myself in the middle of some kind of love triangle best left to Shakespeare.

Deep breath.

K-pop ran up to me. "That was totally intense, hai. Wanna see it?"

He hovered over my shoulder while he played the video for me. He kind of bounced to the music. "So, you really know a breaker out of Houston?" Wow, he was trying so hard to be casual.

"Yep."

He bumped me with his shoulder. "You holdin' out, Foxtrot?"

"Maybe."

He watched the video and subtly went through his moves.

"Hey." I nudged him and he looked down at me from his very tallness. "You should come over some time. We have room to dance in the garage."

"Yeah?" He moved around in front of me and held out a fist for me to bump.

I bumped. "And bring some tunes."

He pulled back dramatically and eyed me with exaggerated suspicion. "Don't tease me, bro. I'm fragile."

"I'm a lot of things, K-pop, but I'm not a tease."

He offered the fist again. This time, he bumped me, pulled away and wiggled his fingers. "Swe-e-et."

So did I.

Okay, he was *way* two years ago, but maybe a guy didn't need to live life next year to be cool in the here and now. Especially when he didn't come with enough baggage to fill the taxi. I didn't want to think about him being a guy who could do that to Tango's car.

Seven

"Katy?" Twist hurried across the street to her, half a block from her house.

She spun at the sound of her name, then one hand went to her ample chest. "Oh, my God, I thought it was that sick little twist. You scared me."

"Sorry." He smiled. "No twists here. Just an old friend."

"What are you—" She glanced at his car halfway up the block. "Oh."

"I'm staying at my mom's for a few days to make sure you're safe."

She hugged him for two seconds. "That's very sweet. But I'm fine, really."

"Should you be going out this late?" He filed the scent of her spicy perfume away for when he was alone.

Katy put her hands on her waist and settled into one hip with determination in her eyes.

"Tell you what. Wherever you're going, let me walk you there and back."

A smile lit her face and she hugged him again. "That would be great." She broke away and headed down the street. "But you only need to walk me one way. Foxtrot can walk me back."

Twist stopped mid-step and almost stumbled. Son of a bitch.

What happened to "null and void"?

The tinkle of breaking glass woke me out of a sound sleep and dreams too randy to describe here. Instantly alert, I rolled away from the window and crouched behind the bed, images of supple female flesh exchanged for fear of the cold steel of a baseball bat.

Was the "sick little twist" after *me* now? I'd just moved there!

"Ethan?" Dad crouched in the doorway in his old-fashioned boxers. He knew about Tango's car and he wore his Protective Father face. He gestured to the other window, the one that didn't have glass sparkling beneath it.

Feeling very Sam and Dean Winchester, I nodded and we rolled over the bed to huddle under the window, peering into the night. He drew me close protectively, in case he had to throw me out of harm's way. Was it wrong for me to smile at that, even with the adrenaline rushing my brain?

The streetlight silhouetted a familiar shape.

"Tango?" I yanked the window open despite Dad's warning tug on my shoulders.

She looked sheepish, standing under the broken pane. When she saw me, she crept the few feet to stand directly under me and Dad. When she noticed my sidekick, her eyes opened wide. "Mr. Foxtrot, er, Mr. Fox," she stage-whispered. "I'm. so. sorry. I didn't mean to wake you."

Dad looked at me out of the corner of his eye, letting me take the inquisition.

"Are you okay? Is something wrong? Why are you out alone?"

"I told you I'm not letting anyone stop my life. I wanted to talk to you." She made a rather elaborate series of shrugs. "All my friends have rooms on the first floor. In the movies, people throw a rock to get someone's attention." She shrugged some more. "It seemed like a good idea at the time." She glanced at Dad. "I'm so sorry about the window, Mr. Fox. I'll pay to have it fixed."

Dad and I glanced at the fist sized rock lying on my carpet. "In the movies, they normally use pebbles," Dad whispered.

"She's never one to do things halfway," I told him. "I'll take care of it out of the money I'm getting from coaching her."

"I'm so-o-o-o sorry," drifted up to us.

He must have seen the pleading in my face. He rolled his eyes and shook his head. "Okay, Cyrano, go meet Roxane."

"Give me a minute," I called out the window.

She smiled.

Goosebumps.

Dad grabbed my shoulders. "You meet her outside." He glanced down. "Wearing pants." He held a finger at my nose. "Do not bring her up here."

"Dad."

"Please." He gave me his how-Disney-do-you-think-I-am look while I pulled on my clothes. "I'm perfectly aware my little boy's already been deflowered."

Really?

"This girl has a stalker. For all we know Officer Warren already has an Amber alert on her."

Okay. . . creepy, but logical.

"Also, for being Cool Dad, I earn the right to have you come tell me what happens." He grinned.

That got him another, "Dad!"

He chucked my shoulder.

"Dad?"

He stopped in the doorway.

"Thanks for being Cool Dad. . . and for coming to my rescue in the middle of the night."

He smiled one of the first genuine smiles I'd seen on him in a while. "Can't let my sidekick get hurt, can I?"

"Hey, you're the sidekick." I stopped with one leg out the window. "I have someone waiting for me outside. That's hero stuff."

"I thought the hero was the one throwing stones up at the girl's window."

"Dad, that is so-o-o twentieth century and sexist. We're living in a post-queer world, after all." Thanks, Corey.

He barked one short laugh. "Sometimes, Ethan, you're gayer than I am." He stood with one hand on the door jamb. "Stand in a streetlight. Wait for this to get cleared up before you go for the serious wooing."

"Wooing? Should I serenade her with *On the Street Where You Live?*"

He froze in confusion. Ha! Totally Kirked him with the musical theater reference.

I raised a hand. "That was ironic, Dad. Go to bed."

Without giving him time to razz me, I climbed out, scrambled down the tree and dropped lightly on the grass beside Tango. "'Sup?" The casual, agile hero had landed. I could've just gone out the front door since I had Cool Dad's permission, but where's the panache in that?

She smiled at my blatant attempt at suave. "Hi." God, she was pretty in the moonlight. "I'm *really* sorry about the window." She shifted all her weight to one foot.

"It's cool."

She fidgeted. "I figured you're from Austin and you're a dancer, so late nights are the norm."

I chuckled. "Even with a psycho stalker out there somewhere?" I maneuvered us under a streetlight.

"Don't be an ass." She punched me in the arm. "In a town this small, the worst he'll do is. . . trash my car." She held up a hand. "You know what? I don't want to talk about that piece of shit."

Okay. The fact that she was out alone at night meant she had something important on her mind. I gave her time to say her piece.

"This is going to sound stupid, but I can't stop thinking about what you did for Taco." She shoved her hands into her pockets, which made her jeans tighter. Too bad I wasn't standing behind her. "It was brilliant and totally different from your training videos." She paused. "You know. . . from the tiny bits I've watched."

Score. She'd definitely watched every one of them.

"Where'd that come from?" she asked.

"You."

She started, but she smiled. "Me?"

"And my dad. The way you break stuff down reminded me of the way my dad coaches." I crossed my arms. "For years it's been all about winning when I dance. Win this trophy. Win that comp." I shrugged. "So that's how I taught. If they couldn't get it, it was their problem, not mine. But when I was in Dad's gym, it was stress release and fun. If the guys got too macho for their own good, he'd have costume days, like pirates or military stuff. . . or ninjas. It kept things from getting too intense." I chuckled. "He got away with it 'cause he's gay and he made sure the games were still kind of. . . dude."

"No princess costumes?"

"No princess costumes." I shrugged again. "When you and I were working together? It was fun. You kept slowing me down and cracking jokes and. . . it showed me that *dance* can be fun, too."

"Dance wasn't fun?"

I sort of chuckled and shook my head. "Believe it or not, I never even thought about it that way." So many thoughts I wanted to share. "I met Monika when we started performing together at eight. Once we were competing? It wasn't about fun, it was about winning."

All those trophies and awards seemed so pointless now. "But Dad's gym was fun. He knew I was never going to focus on it enough to be a great boxer, so it was just about spending time with him and hanging out with the guys." Deep breath. "It was like that when you were teaching me tango, too. You didn't care if I got good at it. It was just nice to dance together." More than "nice," but, hey, why throw all the cards down at once?

Her face was happy and. . . happy is enough, I guess.

"So," I said, "when I realized Taco wasn't going to make it, I asked myself what Dad would do. Breaking out the old school hip hop? That's what Dad would do."

She bit her lip as her expression turned more concerned than happy. It was sexy as hell, but what was her visit really about? She shook her head and looked away.

Then it all made sense: Corey would never have thought of a way to fix everything. He was a good guy. Sincere, devoted. . . but that's not what she really wanted, was it?

A couple of months ago, I would've swept her into my manly arms and kissed her before she had time to think about it. Tonight was different. Tonight was post-douchebag. "Sooner or later, Tango, you're going to break his heart."

She sucked in a breath, as if I'd read her mind. Then she sighed. "I don't want to do that." She paced. "He's a great guy, Foxtrot. Sincere. Kind. Thoughtful, in his own weird way."

Okay, it wasn't bizarre that she chose *me* for this conversation?

She stopped pacing. "You taught him salsa?"

How'd she find out?

"Please." She made a face. "You told me there was a birthday surprise and it took me all of thirty seconds to wheedle it out of him." She hung her head. "That's the whole problem in a nutshell." She looked up at me. "He doesn't even realize he told me the secret."

I couldn't stop the words that came out of my mouth. "Don't break up with him for me."

I sort of expected some crack about not flattering myself, but she was too smart for lame pretense. "It didn't matter before. None of the guys in this town are rocket scientists. . ." She paused. "Well, except for the guys who will actually *be* rocket scientists, but they have issues of their own." She rubbed her hands over her face. "Damn it, Foxtrot, why did I come out here at two o'clock and throw a rock at your window?"

I kept my silence, which earned me her attractive hip jut.

I couldn't move.

So she rushed through the space between us and kissed me.

Strawberries.

My heart beat faster and sent blood surging to all sorts of interesting places. My hands went around her waist and pulled her closer so I felt the warmth of her body against mine. She fit perfectly there, like she belonged.

But it was wrong.

Fully aware that I was the girl in this situation, I moved my hands from her waist to her arms and gently pushed her away. "I won't do this to Corey," I whispered. I couldn't make myself let go of her arms. "I'm not a douchebag, anymore." It took every ounce of willpower to pry my fingers from her soft skin. "Don't break up with him for me."

I wanted to tell her, "Hell yeah, break up with him." I wanted to tell her how much I wanted to be with her, how I finally understood that lame cliché about butterflies in my stomach, something I'd never experienced before.

But I was *not* a self-centered douchebag anymore. I released her arms, folding mine across my chest to restrain them. I hated the pain in her face and that I had caused it.

She stuffed her hands into her pockets. There were dozens of clichéd, crappy things either of us could've said. We even could've gone for clever or snarky. The better part of wisdom, a wise man once said, is knowing when to keep your mouth shut. Or something like that.

A brief siren blast and flash of red and blue police lights ensured that neither of us said anything stupid or unnecessary. A spotlight hit us, blinding me. "Hold it right there," Officer Friendly shouted as he jumped out of the car.

"For crying out loud, Warren, turn off the spot," Tango called. "We're standing under a streetlight." She gestured at the nearby houses. "Or do you really want everyone in the neighborhood to wake up and find out you've apprehended nothing more than two people engaged in a perfectly innocent conversation?"

He reached in and killed the spot. "Your mom's freaking out."

Tango pulled her cell out of a pocket. "Oh, crap. I had the ringer off." Her fingers flashed across the screen. "Double crap." She gave Officer Friendly an acidic glare. "You called Boyfriend, too?"

The cop tried to puff up and look dignified, but he was only a couple of years older than us and skinny as a rail. "There was a crime committed against you today. When your mother discovered you weren't in your bed. . ."

"Don't pull that South Park *Respect my Authori-tay* crap, Warren. You went out with my best friend." She held the cell out to him. "Great. Now every person I know is awake and worried, thank you very much."

Warren tried to recover his dignity, but she cut him off with a wave of the cell. He deflated. "Sorry, Tango. I'm just trying to help. You really shouldn't be out like this when some maniac just trashed your car."

Hmmm. . . the nickname had already caught on outside the crew.

Sweet.

She slid the cell into a pocket. "I needed Foxtrot's advice. He's new to town and I wanted him to keep an eye out, you know, for anyone who might be acting weird around me." Her eyes met mine. Nice.

Officer Friendly eyed me suspiciously. "I think you should leave the investigation to the professionals, Tango." Wow, he really seemed to hate me. What the hell?

She scoffed. "No offense, Warren, but without Sheriff Olmos in town, we have you and Pal. You've been cops for, what? A week?"

"All right, Tango," he blustered. "I may have dated your best friend—briefly—but I am an officer of the law, and at least a *little* bit of respect would be nice."

Juicy dated *him*? Seriously? Did she hate herself?

Tango scoffed again and headed toward his car. "Please. Just give me a ride home." She glanced at me. "Keep your eyes open?"

"Absolutely."

Officer Friendly stared at me for a second with squinty eyes. Was that something they taught in Dumass cop school? I guessed he wanted me to remember that he'd never dated *my* best friend and so I still had to respect the badge. He actually tapped it and pointed at me before stalking off to the car.

Thank God he turned as quickly as he did, because there was no way I could've stifled my laugh for a second longer. No point in pissing off the local law enforcement. Especially with Dad's recent troubles. With the actual man in charge out of town, this pissant deputy *really* seemed to need to throw his weight around.

As they drove off, she didn't look at me or wave. Once again, I convinced myself she'd wanted to but feared giving Warren the wrong impression. Or the right one, actually.

Shitstix.

And now, Dad expected me to wake him up and tell him all the juicy details.

Like what? An amazing girl came to me in the middle of the night to pour her heart out, in spite of the potential dangers. She gave me a hot, wood-producing kiss. And I sent her off to her boyfriend because I'm too much of a gentleman and I respect the dude too much to hurt him. Which pretty much meant I *was* more gay than Dad. Except, you know, for the wood part.

Deep breath.

I ambled into the house. As I opened the front door, Dad whispered my name. What was he doing in the dark? He lit a lamp so I could spot him near the front window. He twitched the curtains closed.

"Were you spying on me?" I asked, not pissed off, but utterly surprised, because he'd never, ever been *that* dad.

He held up a hand. "After you went out the window, I couldn't stop thinking that if the stalker would completely trash her car, what might he do to the guy she was meeting in the middle of the night?" He peeked out between the curtains. "I'm sorry. I couldn't stop myself."

"No. I appreciate it." I dropped into a chair. "I guess I should start being more careful." Weird. Small towns were supposed to be safer.

He sat on the edge of the couch closest to me and nudged my knee with one hand. "So? You promised to tell Cool Dad everything." God, it was good to see him smile again. Almost made it worth it that he'd seen Tango kiss me.

"You saw everything. What's to tell?"

He leaned back with his hands behind his head. "Well, I couldn't *hear* anything." He grinned. "When you stopped the extraordinarily hot chick from kissing you, I couldn't tell if you were being a gentleman or if you'd finally decided to prove the homophobes right by turning gay because of my corrupting influence."

Now do you see where I get it?

Eight

Son of a bitch, bitch, bitch! Everything had failed, had sent Katy running to Fox. Magic was bullshit. If only he could get her alone. That was it. He needed to take her somewhere he could be alone with her until she saw how much she loved him and realized how perfect they would be together. Alone.

He ran a fingertip over a photo of her face on his wall. He leaned close and sniffed the sweater pinned below the photo, but it'd been thrown out. It didn't smell like her. The sweater, and the skirt below it, was arranged in a dancer pose. A figure four, Katy called it. Similar icons of her danced across every wall of his bedroom, watching over him. He lit a cinnamon candle and lay back on the bed, already naked, already aroused as his love looked down at him from every direction. The flickering flame radiated her scent.

How could he get her alone?

"All right, Foxtrot, you piece of shit, where is she?" The bellow shocked me awake, but not alert. Someone grabbed an arm, hauled me out of bed like a rag doll and threw me against my bedroom wall before punching me in the face twice. "Where is she?" He pulled me from the wall, then banged me against it again. "Where?"

I was too dazed and confused to respond.

Corey? What the hell?

My clock said it was 8:15 in the fucking a.m. When would Dad learn to lock the fucking door on his way out?

"All right, Boyfriend," a familiar male voice said. "Let's not jump to conclusions." Officer Friendly pulled him off me. "Even if he was the last person seen with her last night."

I slumped against the wall wishing for a gallon of coffee fed to me intravenously. "What the *fuck* is going on?" I wiped my bleeding lip with one bare arm and glared at Corey. "I thought we were friends, you asshat."

"There's no need for name calling," Officer Friendly interjected.

"No? What about names like *assault?* Or *battery?*" Okay, those weren't names, but I was still waking up. I reached for a pair of jeans and nearly wet myself when Officer Friendly pulled his gun and aimed it straight at my chest.

"No fast moves, kid."

I threw myself against the wall with my arms straight out at my sides, heart beating faster than the drums in an insane techno remix. I'd never looked down the business end of a pistol before. Shitstix!

Even Corey stepped back.

"Really. . . wanting. . . pants."

Officer Friendly nodded. "Just take it slow there, kid."

Kid? Could this guy even drink legally?

Slowly, I reached for the jeans again. He didn't blow me away, so I pulled them on with a mental note *never* to sleep naked in this town. Maybe it was time to invest in pajamas.

"Where'd you go after I left last night?" the cop asked.

"Nowhere. I was here." Shit. Button fly hard to handle with shaking hands. Should've grabbed sweats. "May I please put on a shirt?" I pointed at the t-shirt at my feet.

He nodded and lowered the gun but didn't put it away. "You have any witnesses?"

"Well, there was no one sharing my bed, so no—wait, I talked to my dad for a while."

Warren scoffed. "Your dad, eh. *That's* convenient."

Maintaining any sort of calm required a pretty huge effort. "Who else would be home with me at two in the morning?"

Corey shifted from foot to foot like a caged animal. "Where's Tango?"

His insane behavior finally registered, and a chill rippled across my skin. "She's missing?" I remembered Dad's warning about the stalker and the car.

"I'll ask the questions, here, kid."

"For crying out loud," I snapped, "stop calling me 'kid.' Have you even gotten *laid* yet?"

In a surreal moment, Corey actually chuckled and raised a hand for a fist bump. I glared at him, and he retreated behind Officer Friendly.

The gun flashed up and the snarky comment didn't seem so clever anymore.

Thank God I have a strong bladder.

Corey seemed to remember our male bonding moments. "Uh, Warren? Maybe you should put the gun away?" He touched Warren's arm for some idiotic, unfathomable reason.

The cop yelped in surprise. . . and pulled the trigger.

I closed my eyes and time stopped.

The sound of gunfire is the loudest noise in the universe when the gun is pointed at you.

Behind me, glass shattered.

I opened my eyes. Both windows needed replacing now.

Officer Friendly's face drained of color. "I pulled the trigger."

I moved faster than I have ever moved in my life. If Corey hadn't restrained me, we would've added "assaulting an asshole of the law" to my family's list of crimes, only this one would have been very, very deserved.

"You pulled the fucking trigger?!" The string of curses and profanity from my mouth would've made any of the boxers at Dad's gym proud.

Officer Friendly slowly returned the gun to its holster and sat on the bed, quietly muttering, "I fired it. I fired it. I fired it."

Corey held me to the wall and needed the full weight of his body to keep me from beating the unholy tar out of the bastard. "Foxtrot. Get it together." His face hovered close to mine. "He didn't hit you and Tango's really missing."

My blood ran cold. "I thought *I* was suspect number one," I snapped. Give me a break; there was still a lot of adrenaline in my system.

His face clouded with that pissed-in-his-master's-shoe expression. "I'm sorry. When Warren said it, it made sense to me." He eased up. "I'm really, really sorry." We faced each other, catching our breath. "The rose was sent right after you met her. The texts happened that day." His face took a detour into confused. "And you lied to me about being gay." His massive brow furrowed. "Why'd you do that?"

I swallowed and decided against the truth. "What makes you think I lied?"

"Monika."

Which made sense for two seconds and then confused me even more. "When did you talk to Monika about me?"

He shrugged. "After we—" He literally clamped a hand over his mouth.

Wow.

Just. . . wow. Didn't even know how to process that. I finished the sentence for him: "Had cookies and milk together?"

He grinned that big goofy, grin for a second but must've realized it wasn't going to fly. He drooped and stared at the floor. "No. It wasn't cookies and milk."

Officer Friendly didn't seem to be keeping up. "We still have a missing girl to think about, gentlemen." At least he wasn't calling us kids, anymore.

I grabbed shoes. "No, we don't." No reason to worry, even. Not when I thought about it.

"So you *do* know where she is?" His voice hovered between question and accusation.

"I have a pretty good idea." Pushing past them, I made my way downstairs to the cop car. Good thing Dad was out jousting dragons. Not sure what would've happened to Corey. Or Warren.

What kind of a worthless cop couldn't hit someone in the chest from ten feet away? Damn it! Twist had been certain all his problems were over when he'd heard the gun shot.

And his "good fortune" spell had completely backfired! How the hell was screwing the quarterback lucky for her?

Oh, wait.

Maybe he'd misunderstood how she was supposed to "get lucky." He began to suspect those damn spells were purposely enigmatic.

Hm. Maybe it'd worked, after all.

He flipped through his bookmarks. "Aha." Green candles, amber incense, bay leaves, yada, yada, yada. He made a screenshot of the slut on his tablet and stood it up behind the bowl. "Success for her is guaranteed on all the branches of a tree. Money and fame will grow there-on and as I say so mote it be."

Whoever made these spells needed a new writer. What the hell was a "mote"?

A few minutes later, the three of us walked into the dance studio. Officer Friendly's petulant persona returned. "You think we didn't try the studio? It was locked and empty."

"Did you check the whole thing or just the ballroom?" I crossed the floor to the storage closet. "Tango?" I opened the door to her inner sanctum.

She sat on the floor with a mountain of toilet paper rolls stacked around her like a castle. She saw me and her face lit up. She jumped to her feet but stopped when Officer Friendly poked his head through the doorway. The distinct lack of red eyes and running mascara told me she hadn't been crying. She was pissed.

"Tango?" Corey called from behind me.

Ever hear the saying about Hell and a woman scorned?

Yeah. Not even close.

She exploded past me, planted her hands on Corey's chest and shoved him. "You son of a bitch," she shouted, and that was the nicest thing she called him. "I saw you fucking Monika through your bedroom window!" She shoved him again. "You don't ever step foot in my studio ever again!"

Warren made a move like he was going to intervene.

"Really?" I asked quietly. "You really think getting in the middle of *that* is a good idea?" She wasn't hitting him or anything, just yelling a lot and shoving. I almost felt bad for Corey.

"How'd you know she was here?" Officer Friendly asked while Tango shouted.

I sighed. "Tango came to talk to me. I told her *not* to break up with Corey, which, in hindsight, almost guaranteed that she would. She is not someone to put things off, so she went directly to Corey's, where she looked through the window and saw Monika visiting. . ."

"For milk and cookies," the cop completed for me.

"For milk and cookies." I shrugged. "Once you get that far, it's only logical that she'd head for the one really safe space she knows."

"A broom closet?"

"You've never worked in a dance studio." I jabbed a thumb at the room. "Most studios don't have an actual break room, so the pros hide out in the storage closet when they need a quiet moment to detox."

Tango wound down finally. "And to think I felt guilty about one stupid *kiss* when you were screwing her brains out."

"Kiss?" he asked, glaring at me as if I were a traitor.

Oops.

"No!" Tango pulled the rug out from his anger with a very pointed finger. "You do not get to even think about resenting him for that."

Corey shrank.

"*I* kissed *Foxtrot*. I kissed him and he *stopped* me and told me *not* to break up with you." She glanced at me. "Still glad about *that*?"

My superpower is a blank expression.

Corey's brow squinched up. "So is he gay or not?"

She made a noise that defied spelling. It sounded something like "Argh" but went on a lot longer and had a Mexican accent. She shoved him out of the studio with a hearty, "And stay out."

As the door slammed, I swear Warren and I had the same idea: "Please God, let her not spew forth her fury at me!" How did we end up on the same team about *anything*?

Tango strode toward me and caught up after I'd only taken about three terrified steps backward. She threw her arms around me and latched on. "I am so glad you're a gentleman."

She kissed me.

Hard.

Ow, since I'd just been punched, but, oh well. . . no complaints.

She looked me square in the eyes. "Still glad you were loyal to him?"

Back to terrified. There was no right answer to that question.

Fortunately, she turned to Officer Friendly. "Why are you still here, Warren?" She did a double take. "Why were you here in the first place?"

He froze like a dancer his first time in front of the judges.

"Just go," I whispered.

He took off like a shot. Speaking of which, he stopped at the edge of the dance floor and turned to me briefly. "Sorry I almost killed you, Foxtrot." He dashed out.

Tango didn't say anything. Her eyes darted across my features as if seeing them for the first time and trying to take in every single detail.

I held her face in my hands and relaxed my body forward to hers.

We kissed.

My hands slid into her hair. It fell out of her ponytail in smooth, silky waves. My fingers travelled to the bottom edge of her blouse and ran across the skin of her waist, bringing a breathy little gasp. She pulled me even closer and chewed on my neck.

It sent chills all the way down to my toes.

That whole butterfly thing happened again.

Clack. Clack. Clack. Clack.

Seriously? Monika? Here? Now?

"Hope I'm not *interrupting* anything."

"Seriously, Monika?" I said. "Here? Now?"

Tango kept an arm around my waist. I had no idea how this was going to go down, but just how damned would I be if I thought a cat fight between them might be a tiny bit sexy?

"Why Corey?" I asked Monika. "You had to know that would leave a door open for me and Tango. Doesn't that actually hinder your plot for world domination?"

She played with a stray hair. "The best laid plans blah, blah, blah." She smiled at the innuendo. "Turns out he doesn't have a twin, and I really wanted to find out if what Tango told me was true." She winked and flashed Tango a thumbs up.

Tango covered her face with a hand but made no move to fulfill my cat fight fantasy.

I squeezed her. "Not going to lay into her?"

Tango rolled her eyes at the stupidity of all males. "*She* didn't do anything wrong."

Confused, I had to ask. "She slept with your boyfriend and that doesn't bother you?"

"Apparently, you don't know girls as well as you think you do," Monika interjected. "He cheated on her. I didn't cheat on anybody. . . last night, anyway. If it hadn't been me, it would've been someone else." She stopped in that feet-too-wide-apart stance. "It'd be stupid for her to get mad at me when Hung-like-a-horse made up his own mind, such as it is."

Girls. are. really. complicated.

Wait a minute. "What do you mean you didn't cheat on anyone *last* night?"

She waved away my concern as if it didn't matter. "The past is dead, Foxtrot. I'm here to talk about your future."

Not quite able to pretend I wasn't fuming about the idea that she might have cheated on me, I held Tango a tiny bit closer. "What do you want, Monika?"

She smiled like the cat who'd just eaten a pound of Alaskan Salmon. "There's been an. . . interesting development."

"Seriously? You screw Corey and think I give a shit about anything you have to say?"

She fiddled with her nails, way too nonchalant for my comfort. "I think you'll want to hear this, no matter who I fuck." That was her act when she was confident she could do anything and still win. "There's another deal on the table."

"I'm not interested," I shot back.

Her confident smile scared me. "Oh. . . I think you are." She drew an envelope out of a jacket pocket. "If we take first at Blackpool?" She extended the envelope. "We're both guaranteed spots on the next season of *Dancing with the Stars.*"

Tango squeezed me tighter, but that wasn't the reason I couldn't breathe.

How could I say no to *that?* The offer was too good to be true, but she wouldn't be here for a hoax. That wasn't her style. But she *must* have known about the deal last night. LA still slept at whatever stupid early hour it was. When she screwed Corey, she'd known it would free Tango and me to be together. She'd also known it would make my skin crawl every time I danced with her, with Monika, I mean. She knew all three of us, Tango, Corey and me, would be hurt tremendously.

And she'd done it, anyway.

Her eyes narrowed as she focused her complete attention on Tango while holding the envelope out to me. "Who's first place loser now, bitch?"

Holy shit. "You had sex with Corey to score points?" I asked. "This was a contest for you?"

She waved the envelope at me. "I like to win. You know that." When I didn't accept it, she placed it on a nearby table. "National television." She walked away. "It's worth thinking about."

Tango didn't speak until the door closed. "How does a real human being even get that evil? Has she always been like this?" What she really wanted to know was if I'd known my ex was an evil bitch while we were dating.

"She's the only girl I've ever dated, so what do I know from evil? I figured all relationships were like ours." I stared at the envelope. "She was always driven, competitive. But so was I." I wandered off the dance floor. "In hindsight, it's been worse the last year or so."

"What do you mean?"

"Do you really want to talk about my ex?"

"No. Not right now."

We stared down at the envelope that contained a letter of intent from a major TV network.

"Wow," Tango said. "*Dancing with the Stars.* That's like, the Holy Grail for ballroom."

"It is."

"How soon do you suppose you have to decide?"

"I don't know. I'm afraid to read the letter."

"Why?"

"I'm afraid it'll be too hard to turn down."

She took my hand. "It's sort of a damned if you do, damned if you don't thing, isn't it?"

"I do this, I lose all self-respect and probably my immortal soul along with it, so, yeah, damned if I do."

"But opportunities like this don't come along very often."

"So I turn it down, I likely live a life filled with regret."

She sighed. "Remember when Monika first showed up and I told you not to throw away something you'd later regret?"

"Yeah."

"That's my mom's life in a nutshell." She pulled me to chair. "She was a great dancer. Well, she still is, but when she was younger she was beautiful and sexy and she lucked out. This guy saw her dance. He owned a company producing a tango show in LA. He begged her to join the cast. It wasn't a huge part, but it was a foot in the door, right?" She sighed again. "But Nana got sick and couldn't run the studio on her own. Long story short, my mom turned him down. The show went to Broadway and they even made a DVD version."

She looked at me. "She would never show it, but I hear her crying sometimes, and I know what it is." She squeezed my hand. "I would hate to see you end up like my mom. . .especially if I'm part of the reason you'd give it up. I don't want to do that to anyone. . .ever." Her eyes grew moist. "So if I'm the reason you'd give this up, then, for my sake, you have to take it."

Okay. . .wrap your head around *that* shit.

Nine

Twist watched the feed from the camera on Fox's backyard privacy fence. Nothing he'd ever record. Seriously. That boy needed to learn how to wear a swimming suit. It was disgusting.

The entire alley that ran behind the house was fenced off, so he'd been able to work there completely undetected. He filed the information away for future reference and tapped over to another feed. He needed to find a girl's locker room before his eyes were permanently scarred.

The new offer from the slut was a bonus. It had to be the result of his green candle spell. It had to be. Maybe the magic was helping after all. He kept the women's locker room at the gym open in one window while researching a spell to force Fox to accept the TV deal.

Tango had church stuff that afternoon, so I floated in the backyard pool on a giant rainbow floatie with a two-liter of Mtn Dew at my side. What the hell should I do? Should I stay or should I go? Wasn't that some ancient song from Dad's time?

Ugh. Too hot outside.

I flopped down on the living room couch with my half-empty soda bottle. Time for some good, old-fashioned channel surfing. Headline news? Nope. Elephants banging? God, no. Seriously? Who watched that stuff?

Dancing with the Stars. Meh. Some has-been from a boy band that was popular for twenty seconds when I wore diapers sat cross-legged in the middle of a studio floor crying and flexing his pecs at the same time. Fuck. Really?

The routines had to be easy for the poor has-beens. All I'd have to do was flash my Ken doll smile and take off my shirt once in a while. I was guaranteed a million fans. The question was: could I spend the next eight months working with Monika every single day to have a shot at real fame, not just the kind that only ballroom dancers knew about?

I mean, half the country knew who was on DWTS. How many people knew who won Blackpool? Or even knew what Blackpool *was*? Could I be professional enough to put my feelings aside for eight months?

Did it mean that much to me?

Compared to a life in Dumass, Texas, it certainly had its appeal.

But what, when all was said and done, would it *matter*?

I left the rhinestones and glitter to hit the heavy bag for a while, which helped me get out of my head. Then I shoved the boxes out of the way and tried to dance. But every time I kicked, I broke a lamp. Every leap landed me in a cardboard box. After half an hour of that I felt pent up and twitchy.

I ate a pizza.

I played Dad's old video games from the Stone Age when he'd lived in the house as a teenager, but the low-res images pissed me off.

Ugh.

I walked. I didn't call Tango. It would be rude to lead her on if I decided to fly across the country, and I could hardly ask her to listen to me babble about it. If I left, I needed to make a clean break.

Late that night I found myself a block away from the studio. I had the pass code. No one would be there. I could kick and leap to my heart's desire without breaking anything. Maybe I'd find a revelation on the dance floor.

At the studio, music filtered through the glass door. No surprise. After learning that her boyfriend (note the lack of capital) cheated on her with the girl who wanted to take me off to New York, Tango must've had the same idea I had. The lights were on and she was most likely in there dancing the shit out of her system. It was dark outside and, as I reached for the keypad lock, I could see all the way to the dance floor.

Holy shit! Who was *that?*

A girl danced alone with the lights on low. It wasn't Tango. I could see the way she moved but couldn't make out her face. Juicy? She had the same slow, slutty walk, but when the music kicked into a faster rhythm, the mystery girl flat out nailed one of the hardest hip-hop sequences I had ever seen. She popped, she locked, she rolled so hard I thought she'd dislocate her entire body. Seriously, she moved as well as dancers in Houston. Shit, New York.

The song was something by Skream. It hit the inevitable slow break and the girl slid into lyrical dance as soft as the hip hop was edgy. She nailed Twyla Tharp's style in a way that would make a lot of dance majors need to go for the Google.

The music slammed into a heavy, techno bridge and this girl launched a gymnastic sequence across the floor that could take state. Who *was* she?

The song ended and she dropped into a full split with her back to me.

She finally stayed still long enough for me to read "Juicy" in pink across her ass.

Holy—and I really meant it—fuck.

This could *not* be the same girl Tango had to drill for an hour just to teach her a fouetté.

I yanked my cell out of my pocket because I couldn't remember the pass code anymore. I punched Juicy's icon and waited. Her cell jingled into the silence.

She popped out of her split much faster than anyone had the right to do and grabbed her cell. "Yo, I'm Juicy."

"Not to go all *Scary Movie* on you, Juicy, but turn around."

Slowly, she turned.

"Boo."

She dropped her cell and gave a little girly shriek. I knocked on the glass and waved her closer. She picked up her cell. "What are you doing here?"

"Just open the door. I don't want to do a scene from a Disney series." Wasn't that something they'd do? Two teenagers talking on their cells through the glass rather than just opening the door.

She opened the door.

"Holy—and I really mean it—fuck. You're amazing!"

She grabbed my arm. "You can*not* tell Tango what you saw."

"Why don't you want her to know you can dance?"

She released me and stared at me for a long time, like she was weighing me. Either she decided to trust me or she really needed to talk to *someone*. "It's all she has, Foxtrot. She's the town dancer. Her mom is a dancer. Her nana." She moved to the dance floor and dropped into splits. "I have gymnastics and cheer. I win crap all the time." She looked up at me. "She should get to keep the dancing."

"How did you get this good?" I joined her on the floor.

"Dance camps. Cheer camps." She shrugged. "YouTube. I know when the studio's empty and practice whenever I can."

"Okay. . . loyalty. . . I get it." I threw my hands up in a manly gesture of exasperation. "But if she's your friend, she'll want *you* to be happy, too."

Her cheeks flushed. "I'm happy, *chulo*." She started to rise. "She's happy, so I'm happy."

Ohmigod. It *all* made sense. Girls let guys think we're smarter all the time.

I took her hand and dragged her down again. "She doesn't know *that* either?"

She dropped cross-legged so close our knees touched. "You can*not* say a *word* to her, Foxtrot." Her eyes grew huge and desperate.

"So I'm upgraded from 'ass' to 'Foxtrot' when you need a secret kept?" I smiled so she'd know I was teasing. "And what's with the Spanglish, anyway, China Doll?"

"I'm Korean. Not Chinese," she corrected. "And this town is, like, eighty-five percent Mexican. Do you speak Norwegian, or whatever pasty white people you come from?"

"You're a phenomenal dancer."

Her whole face squinched up in confusion. "Are you being nice to the competition just to throw me off?"

"Sorry, girl, but you're not the competition. No offense." I meant it about the no offense. "I don't want to be all douche-y about it, but Tango doesn't swing on those monkey bars."

At first, she looked pissy, and I prepared for a clever snark, but she relaxed. "I know she doesn't. I'm pathetic."

I waited for her to get out the rest.

"I don't expect her to feel the same way, but my options are nada in this podunk, dumbass town." She stretched her legs out in front of her. "There are, like, three other lesbians my age and they could model for *Guns and Ammo*." She reached for her feet. "It's just to the end of the year and I can start over. I have a full ride at UT."

Wow. Impressive. University of Texas? Getting in was hard enough, let alone earning a full ride.

"Does anyone know?" I asked.

"About?"

"Take your pick."

She crossed her legs and ran a hand through her hair. "If I came out now, all three lesbutches would stalk me. Like I said, pickings are pretty slim." She snorted. "And this is a small town, Foxtrot. Everyone may be all liberal and twenty-first century in Austin, but there's still crap to deal with here." She looked down and picked at her t-shirt. "I can't tell Tango at this point. It's just easier to wait until I get to college." And the real question. "Are you going to tell her?"

I shook my head. "Not my place. Y'all have been friends for years. I'm so not getting in the middle of that." Deep breath. "Some folks at my old studio in Austin go to this group called OutYouth. I'll get you their e-mail addies."

She relaxed and took my hand again. "You come across as a total attention whore, Foxtrot, but you're good people."

Attention whore? Okay, maybe.

She released my hand and we sat in silence. I could tell she was giving me time to process her revelations. Wait a minute. I'd never even thought about a *girl* being Tango's stalker.

Juicy pointedly cleared her throat as if reading my mind. "If you're thinking what I think you're thinking, I will kick your ass. I had nothing to do with Tango's car, and I will end whoever did."

Okay, fine. She seemed pretty resigned to her situation. "Any theories?" Why pretend I hadn't wondered, though?

She shook her head. "None." She shrugged. "Or too many. She's pretty and popular and everyone likes her. Who wouldn't want to be with her?"

"Anyone stand out as particularly creepy?"

"Well. . ." She folded her arms and smiled with one half of her mouth. "There *is* this new guy who just moved to town and pops a boner every time she walks in the room. He's pretty creepy and full of himself."

I laughed. "Point taken." I rose and helped her up despite the fact that she didn't need it. Enough talking. I'd stopped by to dance. "Show me your Twyla Tharp. I wanna see if I can do it."

Her face lit up. "You got it? Ohmigod, I figured I was the only one under the age of, like, a hundred who knew the Tharp."

I danced some fans across the floor, my limbs loose and dangly, then popped a few shapes I'd copied from Baryshnikov. I crossed my feet and did a slow 360 offering my hands in a traditional "ta-daa."

She clapped. "How are you *not* gay?"

She jumped into a *pas de bourrée* and kept repeating until I joined her. *Assemblé, pirouette.* . . sorry, but there's no way to describe her shit without high-tech dance terms. Go check out every YouTube video on Twyla Tharp and you'll get the idea. No. Really, damn it. Go check her out.

Holy crap. It'd been a long time since I'd had to work so damn hard to keep up. She was better than me and I hated admitting that about anyone. It took me a while to learn the routine she'd been dancing when I arrived, but I didn't even try her across-the-floor gym sequence. Oh, and I never really nailed the slutty walk.

I was the one who finally called a halt. She smiled like she could have gone on for hours more. . . and I'd bet she could've. Damn, I hoped we could dance again.

"We could learn shit from each other," I said as she locked the door.

She raised an eyebrow in my direction. "What can I learn from you?"

Without another glance, I walked away. "Humility."

No idea what her reaction was. The whole night had been too perfect to ruin it by waiting for a response.

Twist entered the word "witch" into the almighty Google: About 46,800,000 results (0.21 seconds)

"Whoa."

He narrowed the search using words like "death spell" and "evil killer" but still ended up with searches in the millions of millions. There had to be a way to find someone who could teach him how to make the stupid spells work right. He spent hours researching. There were sites that offered love spells and spells to weaken an enemy. They accepted credit cards and cast the spells for you from the comfort of their homes. Would one of them cast a death spell for him?

What bullshit. He wanted to find an old woman with a crow on her head or something, an actual person he could meet face to face. Also, he doubted the logic of using a credit card to hire a supernatural hit man.

Hm. Maybe he should just try it the old-fashioned way.

He googled "hit man."

"Son of a bitch." Over a billion entries.

Wait. Maybe he needed to go local. He narrowed the parameters to places he could drive in a few hours. Huh. Okay. Better.

When something large and sturdy dropped onto the foot of my bed way too soon after sunrise, I didn't really need to hear the heavy sigh to know it was Corey, who was no longer known as Boyfriend. He lay there face down, kneeling beside the bed with his arms at his sides, face-planted on my blanket.

With a sigh of my own, I sat up and crossed my legs. "Hey, Corey."

"Hey, Foxtrot." His voice was muffled by the blanket, but he sounded pretty dead inside.

Dad hovered in the doorway. He wore the dragon jousting suit and an expression that told me he remembered what'd happened the last time Corey'd let himself into my room. I waved him off. He gave me a nod and left.

I sort of awkwardly dropped my hand onto Corey's head. He reminded me of a sad puppy, so I patted his hair. Dad did that kind of thing when I was depressed, but Corey's hair felt surprisingly soft, which made the moment weird. I shifted my hand to my lap. "You wanna talk about it, champ?"

"She dumped me." His voice sounded comical filtered through a comforter.

"Well, you did cheat on her."

"I know." He sat up abruptly, revealing a blotchy face and bloodshot, puffy eyes. No surprise he'd been crying his heart out. "I *am* stupid. I had the best girl I will ever know, and I fucked it up. I am *so* stupid." He hit himself upside the head, which was a little scary. "Stupid!" He looked at me directly. "Can I pretend you're still gay?"

"I was never actually gay. . . and. . . why?"

He looked down at his hands. "It's easier to talk to you if you're gay. My straight buddies just want details. . . and I really don't want to talk about that."

I ran a hand through my hair and patted the mattress. "I'll always be gay for you, Corey." In my head it was clever.

He took my comment at face value and sat on the edge of the bed. He heaved another big sigh.

"Dude, I know how much Tango means to you. What. the. hell?" I kept my voice as kind as I could, but it was a total bonehead maneuver what he did. He'd really hurt Tango.

"I didn't know. . ." He shook his head. "I'm just stupid, that's all."

There was something he wasn't saying. Well, there was a lot he wasn't saying, but there was something he was avoiding. But he'd almost said it, hadn't he? He didn't know. . . *what?*

I remembered looking down at Tango from my bedroom window. And she'd seen Corey and Monika through *his* window. Tango had a thing for late night visits and bedroom windows. And I knew Monika. What had she said to Corey that morning? "You must get chilly." Because she knew he left the window open in case Tango stopped by. If she were trying to score points, she'd dig up that kind of thing over, say, a delicious coffee beverage while commiserating about a vandalized car. Yeah, she thought like that.

"You didn't know it was Monika," I said.

His expression told me I was psychic. I had to be.

"Your room is on the first floor and you didn't even know it was Monika until. . . well, until after you'd already sampled the milk and cookies."

He looked at the floor. "Doesn't matter. I still did it."

I closed my eyes. Please let him *not* be more of a gentleman than me. "Did you stop her or decide, what the hell if it's too late. . ."

"What the hell?" He smacked my arm. "Of course, I stopped her, bro, seriously?"

I nudged him back. "Why didn't you tell Tango that part?"

He deflated like a spent balloon. "Yeah, because that would've sounded so much better." He addressed a pretend Tango in the doorway. "I know I screwed someone else, but it's not like it should count since I thought she was you." He looked at me. "I know enough to know that a girl ain't going to like *that* either."

Damned if he did, damned if he didn't

And he did. . . but, kinda. . . he didn't. I mean, how many red-blooded American guys would *not* have taken the oh-well-since-I-already-did-it-I-may-as-well-enjoy-the-moment route? I'm not entirely sure I would. Wouldn't. Whatever.

Monika had orchestrated the entire ugly scene.

What an unmitigated bitch.

And. . . he cried.

Scooching closer, I reached out and dropped a hand on his neck.

He didn't let out with the big-time sobs. His shoulders shook a little while he hung his head. I put an arm around him. He dropped his head on mine.

Good times.

K-pop appeared in my doorway. "Your dad said I could come up." He gestured down the hall. "I can go."

I shrugged. "It's a party."

With K-pop there, Corey started to pull himself together. "Hi, K-pop."

"Hey. . . Corey."

And there was the kicked puppy again since his name was no longer Boyfriend.

More tears.

I patted his head.

K-pop looked me up and down. "Nice skivvies."

Skivvies? "Thanks. People seem to see my underwear a lot since I moved here, so I put extra thought into my choices."

"Captain America's shield is very fortuitously placed."

Stellar. Not many people can find an opportunity to use a word like "fortuitously."

"That's why I bought them," I said.

We watched Corey weep. Periodically, I patted his neck.

"So, K-pop," I ventured, "what brings you to my bedroom at this ungodly hour of the morning?" I waved him into the chair. "Just hoping for awkward conversation?"

"No school today." He smiled sheepishly. "You said maybe we could dance in your garage?"

Oh, yeah. "Absolutely." Anything to distract the snuffle monster drooling on my shoulder. "You have some stuff you want to work on? A song?"

He grinned. "I'd love to throw down those moves you did to Beast." He crossed his feet at the ankle. "Why'd you pretend you just dance ballroom?"

Corey lifted his head. "He didn't want to blow Katy's cover."

"Cover?" K-pop asked.

"He's better than any of us, and she thought he'd be a dick about it." Corey wiped his face and blew his nose into sheets I would rip from my bed just as soon as he left. "She should know better by now." He blew his nose again. "Gay dudes aren't like that."

K-pop opened his mouth.

Not wanting to delve into the subtleties of Corey's self-delusions, I raised a hand and gave a quick little shake of my head.

Corey grabbed me in a bear hug so fast I couldn't duck and weave to avoid it. He held on tight and thanked me for being such a good friend.

K-pop's expression wandered from amused to slightly uncomfortable. Hug. way. too. long. "Really. . . wanting. . . pants."

K-pop laughed.

I extricated myself from Corey's grip and picked a pair of non-lethal sweats from the floor, shrugging into a t-shirt as well. Then I pulled off the shirt, used it to wipe Corey's slobber off my chest and chose a different one.

Ten

Twist sat in his car and listened to the mic in Fox's room. What did Katy see in either of those guys? They were worse than the boys in Teen Wolf, *the way they ran around weeping on each other's shoulders and acting as if the world was their locker room. Wait a minute. Locker rooms. The football team. He looked up. Sure enough, the entire starting lineup, minus Corey, was eating breakfast tacos across the street.*

He tapped over to the feed inside the diner. He listened for half an hour before hearing something important. "The bitch dumped him for that pretty boy from Austin."

"The fag?"

"The fag needs a beating, that's all I'm sayin'."

The others muttered their agreement.

Twist smiled. He climbed out of his car and hurried across the street. Sometimes local worked better than anything on the internet.

So three guys were in a garage dancing. . . it was the start of a joke my dad would've told once upon a time. I taught K-pop and Corey the first few moves from the Beast routine, trying my best to imitate Tango's ability to break down choreo. K-pop picked it up quickly, once I simplified a few parts.

Corey did better than expected. Channeling the way my dad taught, I physically pushed his body through the moves until he got them and then we ran it a hundred times for memorization.

"Dude, you're awesome," I told him.

"It's a guy thing," he explained after a high five. "Tango's stuff is great, but it's kinda girly."

K-pop confirmed Corey's assessment.

Corey held up his hands. "I'm not saying she isn't great. . . just. . . yours is more dude-like."

K-pop nodded.

It made sense. For the Beast routine, I'd incorporated a bunch of boxing moves. In some ways, we probably looked like we were fighting almost as much as dancing. We might be turning a pirouette, but we kept our arms close, our knees bent and our hands in fists. The guys' favorite part was a section of fake sparring. The punches were slowed down and all the moves smoothed out in time to the music.

I swung at Corey.

He leaned away and spun into K-pop, who ducked and threw a leaping kick at me.

I grabbed his ankle and he jumped up, turning and kicking his free leg right over my head. He planted his hands on the floor, and I threw him into a back tuck. He only landed on his ass three or four times before tucking at just the right moment.

Fist bumps all around the first time he nailed it.

As the sun climbed higher, so did the temperature in the garage. When it reached a hundred degrees, we lost the shirts. And yes, a hundred degrees is normal in Texas. We managed to work through the first half of the routine, which was pretty amazing considering my buddies' prior accomplishments.

I called a break for drinks but decided on water this time instead of beer.

Corey murmured his disappointment.

When I returned to the garage, he was showing K-pop his salsa moves. He grinned. "I got it, right?" He did. "Okay, boss. . . What's next?"

How could I say no to the big puppy dog? I took him into dance position and taught him a guy's turn, a simple about face. I only had to shove him through it a few times, and, when he got it, he whooped at K-pop. "Look, bro. *Soy salsero!*"

K-pop gave him a smack on the arm. "Hai."

We watched Corey practice his turn.

"You really need to join the team," K-pop said to me. "Tango's right. She *is* a better teacher than you, but you know more. No one's fooled, bro. The new mad moves came from you."

"We knew it right away." Corey kept practicing his salsa turn. "A-bout face, hai!"

"And you're not so bad a teacher." K-pop waved at Corey. "See? You figured out what he really needed was to get shoved around. With both of you there, we'll learn twice as fast and the choreo will be *sick* twisted, hai?" He looked to Corey for support. "Right?"

Corey stopped dancing. "Sure, bro, but I'll never be on the team again, anyway." He moved to the heavy bag and gave it a frustrated jab.

"Sorry," K-pop said. "I sorta forgot that part."

Corey gave the bag a serious punch and frowned at me, shaking his hand. He had power, but no control. His knuckles were already red, so I helped him into a pair of gloves. He threw a few more punches.

"Stop!" Dad called from the kitchen door.

We all jumped. Good thing we were drinking water instead of beer. He didn't mind my partaking once in a while but handing them out to my friends would've meant certain doom.

"Dad! Sorry. . . we were just. . ."

"Just messing around. I get it." He wore the dragon jousting suit and an expression of annoyance. Was he pissed? Teasing?

Corey fidgeted, perhaps remembering that his last punching bag had been me. "Hey there, Mr. Fox." He tried, unsuccessfully, to pull off the gloves. "Sorry."

Dad crossed his arms, still glaring at Corey. "K-pop."

"Sir."

Dad sighed a quick sharp, sigh and glanced at me. "He hits like *that* and managed to connect with you?"

I wanted to throw him a witty repartee, reminding him I'd been sound asleep at the time, but we were neck deep in dangerous waters and the scene could play out any number of shitty ways. Was he actually going to give Corey some pointers?

Dad turned his attention to Corey. "Hit the bag."

Corey glanced at me, but I wasn't getting a single piece of that, so he turned to the bag and sort of half-heartedly jabbed at it.

"For fuck's sake, Corey. It's not your grandmother. Hit it!"

I'm guessing the guys weren't used to parents who dropped the f-bomb. Corey grinned and gave the bag another jab.

K-pop nudged me, most likely curious why this was such a big deal.

I didn't dare move. I barely breathed. I hadn't heard my dad's teacher voice in months. If I moved, I'd upset the universe, a butterfly somewhere would croak and Dad would go back to being. . . not-Dad.

Dad rolled his eyes and tapped Corey's right foot. "Right-handed?"

Corey nodded.

"Then right foot back." He nudged Corey's shoulder. "Keep your shoulder over it. That's your strong arm." He grabbed the gloves and pulled Corey's hands up to cover his face. "Never. . . *never* let your guard down." He tapped Corey's head. "Now try."

Corey punched with his right but didn't move his body at all. I knew what came next and smiled.

Dad whistled. "That *almost* knocked down your grandmother." He stepped up behind Corey, taking his right elbow. "When you throw the punch, shift forward." He moved the arm as if Corey were a puppet and nudged him forward as the arm extended. "You're a big guy. Use that."

He led Corey through the move slowly a few times, then took two steps around the bag so he could demonstrate. He threw three punches in slow motion exaggerating the shift of weight so Corey could see it. Instinct kicked in and he attacked the bag in a flurry of blows that actually choked me up. It'd been so long since I'd seen him in action.

Corey whooped. "Whoa! Mr. Fox is da F-fuckin-bomb."

Dad stopped and gave him a stern look. "Watch your language in my gym, kid." He grinned. Then his face lost its color as he realized what he'd just said.

Corey didn't notice. He was already holding the gloves out to me and shaking them, so I ripped the Velcro.

Dad caught my eye, his face conflicted.

Suddenly, Corey held a credit card between us. "I need lessons, F-bomb, and I promise to watch my language, but you have *mad* skills." He shook the card. "I. must. learn. them!"

Dad stared at the card as if it were going to bite him. "I don't. . . "

I snatched the card. "Thirty-five an hour, three times a week, one month in advance."

Corey waved me off and gave his full attention to the bag. "You do the math. My mom takes golf lessons so she knows what it costs."

Knowing Dad, he was about to say he didn't have a credit card machine.

"I'll run it through Paypal," I said, shoving the card in my pocket, "and get this to you next time I see you."

Corey jumped up and down. "Awesome! Can we start tomorrow? Before school?"

Dad didn't move or speak, so I answered for him. "Six-thirty."

"Sweet."

I raised a finger in warning. "Do *not* wake me up." Corey kind of deflated, so I compromised. "Not before eight."

He jabbed my shoulder. "Okay, bro." He offered a hand to my dad.

Dad shook it.

"Thanks, F-bomb. I'm going to tell all the guys on the team, and I bet *they'll* all want lessons!" He bumped K-pop's fist then departed in a cloud of enthusiasm.

Dad and I stared at each other. There were a million things we could've said but didn't. Maybe because K-pop was there, but I doubt it.

Things had changed for the better. They weren't *that* good.

"F-bomb?" Dad asked at last.

I shrugged. "They do like their nicknames in this town."

Tons of conflicting emotions battled in his eyes, but he sort of, kinda actually smiled. He ruffled my hair before turning to go. "I'll let you boys play. I need to get out of this monkey suit."

After he left, K-pop broke the silence. "Wow. He really makes a guy rethink the stereotypes, don't he?"

I laughed so hard I coughed. "You have no idea, my friend." He seemed ready for more dance, but I was exhausted, hot and twitchy and wanted nothing more than to throw myself into Auntie Mac's pool. "I'm done, dude."

He nodded, but sort of hesitated. "Can we. . . talk a minute?"

"You mind talking in the pool? I need to hit that before I die."

He grinned. "Hai!"

So we made our way through the house, where I found a couple of towels before heading into the backyard. I dropped the towels on a chair, kicked off my shoes and untied my sweats.

K-pop hesitated. "Is your aunt around?" He slowly toed off his shoes, looking around.

"Nope." I gestured at the privacy fence. "And we don't need to worry about the neighbors." I pulled off my sweats. "You've already seen my Captain Americas, so I'm not worried." I dove in without waiting to see what my friend would decide.

That pool was a little slice of heaven in an otherwise imperfect South Texas hell. It wasn't big enough for laps, but it had a deep end, a diving board and an awning that covered it and kept it cooler. It was shaped like a paisley. As I reached the bottom, I heard the deep sound of K-pop hitting the water.

Nice.

I swam to the shallow end and over to the edge, wondering what K-pop wanted to discuss. After Juicy's big reveal, I'd stopped thinking of my new friends as small town simple. Hm. Friends. Interesting.

K-pop swam up next to me and leaned against the wall.

I gave him my full attention. "What's up?"

He seemed surprised. "I thought you might want to talk about whatever that was with your dad."

My turn for surprise. "What? I figured *you* had something going on."

He shook his head. "I'm pretty simple. I just figured you're new here. . . maybe you needed someone to talk to." He sort of froze for a second. "I'm sorry. Way too chick flick, right?" He moved away a foot or two. "I just figured, we're dancing together, we should get to know each other. I mean. . . that's what you do, hai?"

"Is it?" I stared at him like an idiot while a tornado of emotions whirled around inside and killed my snarky quip ability.

K-pop seemed to sense it. His face softened. "You're living with some demons, hai?"

I nodded, afraid to speak.

"Do me a favor?"

I nodded again.

"Duck under." He must've seen that I didn't understand. He dropped under the surface and came up streaming water. "Hai?"

I did as he asked and blinked the chlorine away.

He smiled. "Now all I see is pool water pouring down your face."

I had to swallow really hard.

He relaxed against the wall to let me know he was comfortable, and I could take my time.

"My dad's my only real friend, dude, and ever since the accident he won't talk about it. Until yesterday, he had this phobia about touching anyone. And today, watching him teach Corey. . ."

K-pop waited.

I swallowed again. "It's like maybe he's coming back. Like maybe I'll get my dad back." I couldn't talk for a while.

K-pop held out his hand palm down and lowered it into the water.

I choked out a laugh, ducked under and came up sputtering. "Sorry."

He shook his head with a don't-be-an-idiot face. "There's a lot more there, bro. I listen pretty good, you know."

"Yeah? Must be how you get the girls."

He chuckled. "Are you kidding? I thought it was my obsession with anime and Korean pop music. . . or maybe the fact that I spend all my time dancing and making animation." He turned toward the side of the pool. "Not a lot of ladies here share my interests."

So he'd never had a girlfriend. Although. . . Tango liked to dance. But I still had a hard time imagining K-pop as violent. "You have any ideas on the sick little twist?"

He started, then fought with himself.

"You do," I said.

He folded his arms over the edge of the pool. "I'm not supposed to tell anyone something."

"Which doesn't sound at all suspicious."

"I know, I know." He stared into my eyes as if judging whether he could trust me.

"If you know *anything.* . ."

He nodded. "Woody asked me to help him pick out some video cameras."

That sounded like stalker activity. "What kind?"

"Surveillance cameras," he admitted. "Inconspicuous. Four of them."

"Dude. Woody asked you to help him pick out inconspicuous surveillance cameras, and it never struck you as suspicious?"

His exasperation was obvious. "I know, I know, but he said it was for a sociology project. He needed to monitor kids in kindergarten and study how they worked in groups. The kids would be told the cameras were there, but if they didn't see them all the time, they'd sort of forget about them."

"Does he have a girlfriend?"

He laughed. "That's the thing, bro. He hasn't had a *steady* girlfriend for a while, but he 'goes out' with plenty." Jealousy rode shotgun with the words. "The only reason he'd be a secret admirer would be Boyfriend. They've been friends for years."

"But he told you not to tell anyone about the cameras?"

"Yeah, that's the sinister part." K-pop sighed.

An earlier comment he'd made finally registered. "You make animation?"

He laughed. "Non sequitur much?" Then embarrassment made an appearance. "I'm trying. There's a couple of online classes I took and some YouTube tutorials."

I filed away the info on Woody. "Dude! You have to let me see. Is there an iPad in your backpack?"

Of course there was.

"You really want to see my work?"

Duh! "You've seen my mad moves, bro. Time to return the favor."

He grinned, stoked that someone was interested.

We toweled off to avoid dripping on the iPad and stayed in the shade so we could see the screen better. I hunkered up next to him while he loaded some files and noticed that Naruto was kicking butt all over K-pop's ass. I laughed. "Dude, we're seventeen and we both have superheroes on our underwear."

He rolled his eyes. "Please don't ever share either that information or how you know it. I'd like to get laid *some* day, hai?"

His stuff was good. He had a couple of shorts in a series. They were pretty straightforward demons and cowboys stuff, but then he showed me an animated dance video that rocked the world.

"How'd you even do that? It looks like *Borderlands*."

His eyes lit up. "It does? That's what I was going for. That game is sick twisted." He pulled up another window that was just him dancing in front of a green screen. "I painted one wall of the garage so I can record myself and then layer on the animations and effects."

I whistled. "Seriously, bro. Tell me you're going to college for this."

I felt him tense up through my shoulder. "Yeah. . . sure."

He didn't have the money for it.

I didn't either, anymore, unless I sold my soul to Monika. "I bet you could get a scholarship for animation. . . or an internship or something."

"Really? For animation?" It was like he'd never thought of it. "It's that good?"

I gave him a shut-the-fuck-up look. "Austin has a whole film school for stuff like this."

"Okay, okay. . . I hoped it was that good. But you never really know until someone else says something, hai?"

Hai.

I prodded him to replay the dance video. "You're not quite Pixar material, yet, but you rock, bro. Why haven't you shown this to anyone?"

He shrugged. "No one ever asked."

I sighed. It was same reason I'd never talked to anyone about the accident.

"What?" He cringed as if he thought my sigh meant he'd said something wrong.

"You really want to know what's going on with my dad?"

He nodded and put the iPad in the pack. "But can I put on my sweats first? This is totally dudes-in-a-locker-room and all, but. . ."

I laughed. We hung our shorts out to dry, climbed into our sweats and t-shirts and dropped into chairs poolside.

I even brought out sweet tea.

Gay. All three of those losers were gay. Fox. Corey. K-pop, too, apparently.

Why didn't Fox ever invite girls over to swim? That would actually make sense and might even be worth recording. Ugh. Twist was tempted to pull the camera when he got back to town.

He closed the app and double-checked his email for the address from a guy named Mr. Magoo. The name had to be fake. The address was right, but the house was so boring. It didn't look like a place where forbidden magic hid. Unless that was the point.

He dropped his tablet on the passenger seat and walked up to the front door.

It opened before he could knock.

"Can I help you?" The man was ridiculously pale, like a fish. His eyes were big, too.

"Mr. Magoo?" Twist asked.

"Mr. Twist?" the pale man asked. "You need to control someone, and you have money?" When he smiled, his lips spread far too wide. "You have cash?"

Eleven

So here's what happened, the way I told it to K-pop.

There was a student, nineteen years old. He had a major fight coming up, a title match, and his parents were on my dad's case to make sure he was prepared. You know, work him harder, toughen him up for it, all that crap.

A week before the fight, the kid came in kinda banged up, but his parents told my dad he'd been sparring with some buddies. Dad chewed him out, told him never to do that outside the gym. Dad was a Nazi about safety. Which was ironic.

The kid wasn't sparring. He'd been in a car accident and had some pretty heavy head injuries and whiplash. The doctors had told his parents to keep him out of the ring until they knew if there was any brain damage or clotting or anything. His parents were all, "Yeah. Of course, we want to make sure our boy is safe."

Then they lied to my dad and kept on him to push the kid even more.

I was there that day. My dad and the kid sparred in the ring. The kid's parents yelled at them both to go harder and faster. "Knock him down, son. Get in there!"

The kid hesitated. Even I could see he was dizzy. Dad wanted to take a break, but the parents yelled even louder, so the kid danced forward and took a wild swing that Dad blocked and exchanged for a haymaker that landed solid.

The kid fell to his knees.

Dad dropped down to see if he was okay.

"I can't see," the kid said.

Dad grabbed his arms. "It's okay. You're just dizzy."

He shook his head. "No. I mean. . . blind. I mean. . . blind. . ."

He dropped forward like a sack of flour into my dad's arms and died. Right there.

His parents freaked. In front of the whole gym, they screamed that Dad was a killer, a violent sociopathic killer. Dad wanted to perform CPR, but they tore the kid out of his arms. "Don't touch him, you monster!"

It's amazing how truth can be created by a lie told with sufficient force. Even after the kid's doctors came forward and told the courts that the parents had known better, it was still too late.

Dad had built the gym up from nothing. He literally started it in our garage in Austin. At the time of the accident, he had several partners and a huge facility. His partners all suggested the business might be better off if he sold his shares.

So he did. He thought he was a monster, too.

We only found out much later it was the kid's parents who bought Dad's shares of the gym with their insurance settlement. Dad told me it was the partners' idea. With the grieving parents involved, most of the students felt they were doing some good staying in the gym. They felt less guilty about it.

What I wanted to know was how the kid's parents ever stepped foot in the building where their son died. Seriously. What the fuck was that about?

Charges were never filed against them. It was too vague to prove. Dad didn't want to ruin things for his students. His ex-students. As far as he was concerned, he deserved everything he got, so he didn't fight back. That's what'd caused the arguments with me. He hadn't fought back, so we both lost.

I kinda got it though, finally. It was like Corey. If he went to Tango and said, "It shouldn't count 'cause it wasn't my fault," he was an asshole.

There are times when you do shit, that you actually *do* the shit, but it still isn't your *fault*, and it's not fair that you get punished for it. If there's any moral to the day, that's it.

Which is why this story will never be on the Disney channel.

I leaned forward and refilled my glass, spilled a bunch because my hands shook. Talking about it for the first time had me unsteady. "You never see shit like that on Disney." The anger felt just as strong as the first day I found out the kid's parents had been warned. "The bad guys never win and the good guys never get screwed over." I took a long drink. "It's not that I think life should be fair or anything lame like that." I set the glass down carefully and shook out my arms. "I just wish something really, really bad would happen to his parents for what they did."

K-pop poured himself more tea. "So. . . you kinda do wish life was fair."

I managed a smile since he was trying so hard to cheer me up. "Does that make me a little girl?"

He shrugged. "I'd say fairy princess, but that would be rude to—"

He didn't get to finish his sentence because I grabbed him around the waist and threw him into the pool. He dragged me in with him. So we were soaking wet again, fully clothed this time, but what the hell, right? The action felt good. I needed something to work out all that anger. K-pop caught me in a playful headlock. Oh, yeah?

"Ethan?" It was Dad, in jeans and an old t-shirt.

K-pop released me quickly and jumped away.

Dad made his don't-worry-about-a-little-horseplay face and waved me out of the pool. "Can I talk to you a sec?"

His face worried me. It was his Untouchable Dad face. The one I hadn't seen in a few days. The one I first noticed after the accident.

Still riding an emotional wave, I slogged my way out of the shallow end and shook off like a dog. Dad had moved a few feet away, probably so K-pop wouldn't overhear. "What's up, F-bomb?" I asked, really, really hoping to keep this scene from going someplace ugly.

Dad frowned.

I tensed up. My hands closed into fists.

"That credit card?" he asked.

Damn it. "What about it?"

"Don't run it."

Fuck. "Why not?"

"You know why not."

"No, I don't," I lied.

He'd overheard my story and now he was going back to Untouchable Dad.

Anger rose up from the pit of my stomach. It probably wouldn't have been so explosive if I hadn't just relived the entire thing with K-pop. "I know what happened six *months* ago," I snapped, "but I don't know why you won't teach Corey." Adrenaline soaked through me and I wasn't going to stand down.

He glanced at K-pop who'd made his way to the pool steps and was wringing his shirt.

"You aren't getting out of this because K-pop's here." I crossed my arms. "He's my friend." I stared my dad square in the eye. "Which is more than I can say for you the past few months. Are you going back to *that* now, too?"

He closed his eyes for a few seconds.

Had I completely forgotten that things had improved the last day or so? Maybe. Or maybe that's why I pushed him. I'd seen a glimpse of the old Dad, the one from before the accident, and it infuriated me that I might lose him again because he overheard me spill my guts to K-pop.

"Why won't you coach him?" I demanded.

"Because I'm tired of teaching kids to beat each other up, all right?" He opened his eyes. "I heard what you told K-pop. That it wasn't my fault. That's bullshit."

I tried to interrupt, but when he had a head of steam up he was kinda hard to derail. The apple didn't fall far from the tree on that one.

"Don't give me the same old bullshit about it being his parents' fault, Ethan. Boxing is a dangerous sport. People get killed every year. No matter how safe I try to make things, kids get hurt. . . hell, that's the whole goddamned point, son. To *hurt* people." He moved closer, but I didn't flinch. He'd never swing at me. "I'm tired of teaching kids to hurt each other."

He glanced at K-pop before moving away. "Sorry, K-pop. Didn't mean for you to get caught in that." He gave me one last glare. "Do *not* run that card."

My throat hurt. My eyes burned and not from the chlorine.

It'd been better. He'd coached Corey, for Christ's sake. For one minute, he'd been my dad again. And I blew it all pouring my heart out to K-pop, letting myself get all worked up. If I'd just kept my mouth shut. . . if K-pop hadn't asked. . .

"Hai?"

Ah, fuck, I did *not* want to deal with his cutesy Korean bullshit. "What the fuck does that even mean? Hai?" I'd had my dad again. For half an hour, I'd thought maybe. . . "Hai? Hai?!" My hands clenched, I stomped closer and the fear in his face pissed me off even more. Did he think I'd actually hit him? "You aren't even Korean, for Christ's sake!"

The embarrassment in his face made me angrier because I'd caused it. I turned away so he wouldn't see my eyes. . . or maybe so I couldn't see his.

"Ethan. . ." He was *still* being nice.

It was too much to deal with. I swung around to face him. "Fuck off, K-pop." I stamped one foot in his direction, and he jumped. I stamped again. "Fuck off, hai?!"

He fucked off.

My throat was raw. "Hai." My eyes burned.

Naruto scowled at me from the arm of a patio chair.

Five minutes later, I stalked out the front door.

Twist crept through shadows and kept to cover while he followed Fox. If the jerk stopped in one place long enough, he could call on the football players. They just needed one tiny prod and they'd take Fox out. They already hated him. If the spell he bought from Magoo worked, Twist wouldn't have to lift a finger, just sit back and enjoy the show.

Wait. The cemetery? That place gave Twist the willies.

He hunkered down behind a mausoleum where he could watch Fox without being seen. Seemed liked the dick was stopping finally. Twist hauled out his cell.

Wait. A branch cracked nearby. Was someone else following Fox?

Twist crouched lower and waited.

I don't know why I walked to the cemetery, but I did. It was much farther away by foot than it'd seemed in a car, so maybe the town wasn't as small as I'd thought. After the tenth text from Dad, I turned off my cell. The whole point of walking away was to avoid confrontation. Thank God he was too old to think about GPS.

The sun was setting by the time I reached my destination, but it was still blazing hot. Beloved-Wife-and-Mother and Beloved-Husband-and-Father hadn't moved. A few grackles made those weird noises they make.

Why was I even here? "There's no one else to talk to," I told my parents, but that seemed rude. "Not that you're my last choice, but, really. . . face it. . . you're dead. The communication options are a little limited."

The cemetery lay empty but for me and lots of corpses. "It's me. Ethan. Your son. I'm taller than the last time you saw me. . . and I have hair now. And I don't shit myself anymore. . . well, unless I'm really sick. Oh. . . and I say things like shit, now. And fuck."

Deep breath.

"So I have this really big decision to make and sometimes saying shit out loud helps me decide if it sounds stupid or not." I shoved my hands in my pockets. "Although I already know what I said to Dad and to K-pop was really fucking stupid."

Everything had an orange-pink glow from the sunset. It was way too cheery for my mood.

"I shouldn't have made fun of K-pop. If he never talks to me again, I will utterly understand." I stared at the block of granite, trying to avoid the word tombstone. "I can't talk to Dad 'cause he'll tell me to go to New York because he won't want to be the one to say no. I can't talk to Tango, er, her real name's Katy and she's smokin' hot, but I've only known her a couple of days and she doesn't want to be the one to hold me back, either." I dug into the grass with a shoe. "Although. . ." I dug further. "I don't know. She's stellar. I've never felt like this before. All. . . stupid."

The grackles fell silent. A nice breeze started up, so it wasn't as godawful hot.

"Then there's Corey. He's a great guy. My best friend here, really." More toe digging. "But, really. . . bless his heart, he's. . . not the sharpest tool in the shed. And after what Monika did to him, he'd tell me to keep as far away from her as I could." I pulled my hands out of my pockets and wiped my face. "After what she did to him. . . I really. . . really. . . really should."

I stared at the granite. If Dad was going back to Untouchable Dad anyway, why stay in Dumass? Competition was what I knew. It was who I'd been my whole life. It made me feel good. Better, anyway. Better than this.

"Fucking bitch."

"Ethan?"

I jumped about a mile into the air and nearly wet myself, despite my protestations to my parents that I was potty trained.

"Sorry. I probably shouldn't have done that with a psycho running around loose." Tango regarded me from a few feet away. "But I couldn't resist." She could've smirked, but she didn't.

"What the hell?" I asked. "How did you even know I was here?"

"Your dad lojacked your phone. He told me you were here." She glanced at the granite. "Your other dad, I guess."

"My dad."

She nodded.

"You called me 'Ethan.'"

"If I'd said 'Foxtrot' you'd have known it wasn't your parents and you wouldn't have jumped so high."

In spite of everything, I smiled and waved from the granite to Tango. "Parents, this is Tango. Tango, my parents." I leaned closer to her. "They don't talk much."

Her face told me she wasn't sure if she should be amused or disturbed.

"This is probably the last question you want to hear right now, but. . . what do you mean what Monika did to Corey?" She crossed herself and bobbed down to one knee as she moved closer. "Sorry, but that stuck out for me."

Yeah. Not exactly the conversation I was expecting there. Deep breath. I couldn't discuss it directly. I was too attracted to Tango to think about it in real terms, so I opted for hypothetical. "Let me play psychic for a moment."

"Okay."

"You and Monika bonded over the whole stalker thing, right?"

She nodded.

"You got to talking about cute, weird things boyfriends did, and I never want to know what she told you about me." I waited for the smirk. "Right. So you told her how Corey leaves the window open every night, in case you decide to climb in. He's on the first floor, right?"

She needed a second, then she gasped. "Oh, my God. . . that evil bitch. That's. . ." She searched for the right word. "That's practically rape."

I let her have the silence while she processed a complicated set of emotions.

"Why didn't he tell me?" she asked.

"Because he would've just sounded like he was making excuses." I shifted weight uncomfortably. "He takes full responsibility for what happened, Tango. That's the kind of guy he is."

The sun finally dropped below the horizon.

"Why tell me this?" she asked. "Why tell me something that. . . holy shit, Foxtrot. I don't think I can blame Corey for any of this, anymore. Why tell me that?"

"Because Corey is a genuinely good human being and there are precious few of those left in the world." I thought about it. "Besides which, if something does happen with you and me. . . and then you find out I lied to you about this. . . about *this*. You'd never trust me again."

The sky cooled to gray.

"He should press charges," she said.

I managed to avoid chuckling. "Because the cops are going to listen to a seventeen-year-old guy who complains that a smoking hot girl crawled through his bedroom window and mounted him in the middle of the night."

She made her cheerleader face.

"Just sayin'."

"Oh, my God, Foxtrot." She took a deep, deep breath. "Is life always this complicated in the big city?"

I laughed. "Austin, Texas is hardly a big city."

"Ethan?"

I turned to her.

"You know I'm sorry about what happened to Corey." She stepped closer. "But. . ."

"But the two of you were bound to break up sooner or later."

"If it happens like this. . . does that make me a horrible person?"

"Monika's counting on you to feel that way."

"I really like you," she said. "I really think we could have a shot."

I waited for a few seconds. "But?"

"No buts, really." She finally met my gaze. "Well, one but. But are you planning to leave?"

Throwing away my only shot to recapture my old life suddenly became the easiest thing in the world. "After what Monika did to Corey, I couldn't work with her again." I moved closer to Tango, until we were almost touching. "She was a total bitch to you and I hate her for that, but Corey. . . He's this big innocent puppy. And what she did to him? If it isn't illegal, it should be."

The inches that separated us felt like more miles than I'd walked that day.

"If he hadn't stopped after he realized who she was," I said. "I'd have a lot less sympathy, but as soon as he actually woke up he kicked her out of his room. He. . ." I touched her shoulder and she shuddered. I pulled away. Why did she do that? "He loves you that much," I said.

It physically hurt to be so close to her without holding her in my arms.

She chuckled. "Sounds like you have a crush on him."

"No, but he's been nothing but good to me. I can't hurt him."

The gathering darkness felt more intimate. God, I wanted to hold her.

"I'm sorry. I shouldn't have made a joke," she whispered. Her arm bumped against mine.

I wrapped my arm around her shoulders.

Her arm wound around my waist.

We fit perfectly.

"Is this fair to him?" she asked.

"Is pretending you're in love with him fair?"

She almost pulled her arm away from my waist. . . but she didn't. "No. I guess it's not."

I exhaled a deep sigh. "Can I even presume to give advice?"

"Mmhm."

"Let him know you forgive him but tell him it's over."

In the last light of the sky, a tear rolled down her face. "How do you kick the puppy?"

"I have absolutely no idea."

She took a deep, deep breath. "You wanna go see a movie?"

"What?"

She smiled. "It's what normal people do, Foxtrot. They go see movies."

"There's a movie theater in this town?"

She punched my shoulder. "We have two, and if you act all surprised I will take you out."

"As long as it's not some gay chick flick," I said, "you're on."

She scrunched her face in confusion, then smiled. "It's so not fair you get to say shit like that and it's not offensive."

"Hey. . . gay dad. Membership has its privileges."

I took her free hand to see what she would do. She looked down at our clasped hands and then up at me. She smiled. Nice.

See, that's why I came to the cemetery in the first place: to figure out what I really wanted. Turns out what I really wanted was to hold Tango's hand.

We walked to Tango's house to borrow her mom's car. Apparently, the "movie house" was too far to walk. Before I could make a joke about her words for theater, red and blue flashing lights caught my eye.

"What now?" she breathed, then broke into a dead run.

Pal prowled around outside the house, but she blew right past him. "Mama? Papi?"

I followed her inside. Holy giant family, Batman. As an only child, huge families always kinda freaked me out. All those people in one house. Wow.

Her mom grabbed her tight and they talked in Spanish.

Officer Friendly planted himself nearby and made a big show of brandishing his tablet, fingers poised to type. "And what do you know about this, Fox?"

"About what?"

"In my room?" Tango shouted, grabbed my hand and dragged me to an addition at the back of the house. The entire family was agitated as we passed them. Then we made it to the bedroom.

Wow. There were about ten dozen roses in vases around the room. Tango stopped in the doorway and wrapped both arms around me. "*Dios Mio.*"

Her mother joined us and handed her an envelope, already opened. "We have no idea how he got in here with no one noticing," Mrs. Tango's-Mom said. "There's been someone home all day and a police officer outside."

Tango ripped a letter out of the envelope. Crisp bills cascaded to the floor. "I'm truly sorry about the car?" she read. "It was an accident? What the hell?" She held it out to me with *mucho* disgust in her face. "He signed it: *Twist, like the dance.*" She threw the paper away and stormed into the room, turning and taking in all the flowers. "Jesus."

I bent down to pick up the money and the letter for her.

"It's five thousand dollars, *mija,*" her mother said. "What *boy* has that kind of money?"

Corey did. Woody drove a beemer. Taco drove a fairly new Mustang. Ephraim rode with Woody. I notice cars. But for all we knew the stalker was the bank manager or a doctor. Or the mailman.

Tango ran her hands through her hair. "He was in my room, Mama. In my *room*, in my *house*." She reached to grab a vase, but I held her back.

"They need them for evidence," I said.

She struggled.

"He's right, Tango," Officer Friendly said. "We might be able to trace where he bought the flowers. He might have left fingerprints."

Tango grew still in my arms.

"They were all bought at different places." A heavy-set, bald man approached. He ran a hand over Tango's hair. Her dad?

"How can you tell?" I asked.

He smiled. "I own the cemetery and the funeral home. I know my flowers." He extended a hand. "Sonny Montez."

I disengaged one hand from Tango to shake the hand. "Ethan Fox, sir. If there's anything I can do."

He smiled and glanced at his wife. "He's just like his father." He gave my hand a hard squeeze before releasing it. "I played football with your dad," he said. He lost the smile as he surveyed the room. "When I find this *pinche pendejo. . .*"

"Get in line," Tango said. She led me out of the room.

Officer Friendly blocked the hallway, pointing at the letter and cash in my hands. "We need that for evidence."

As I handed it over, Tango grabbed a couple of twenties. "You don't need every bill," she declared, her stony expression daring Warren to challenge her. She dragged me past him. "Movie's on me," she said. "Please get rid of this shit by the time I get home."

The look on her face made it clear no one should bother trying to stop her.

She had no fucking gratitude. Five grand was nearly Twist's entire savings. She should've accepted his apology. And she planned to spend his money on Fox?

No. That was too far. That was not going to happen.

He knocked on the linebacker's door.

Gunner answered the door himself. "Yeah?"

"Guess who's going to see a movie with her new boyfriend."

The huge guy looked down and shook his head. "The same day? The same fucking day?" He joined Twist on the porch and closed the door.

"Yeah, and they were laughing about Corey, how he was over at Fox's crying his eyes out."

"That bitch."

Twist offered the beer Magoo had spiked with magic. "The weirdest thing is, I saw Corey over there this morning, in the garage. . . dancing salsa with Fox." *Twist's heart pounded. He had to take the bottle!*

"The hell *you say?"*

"How messed up is that?"

The linebacker took the beer. "That pretty boy needs to go down." He gestured to a bench with the bottle. "What the fuck did you see?" He drank.

Twist sat with him and sipped his own beer. It tasted normal, but Magoo promised that the bottles were linked, that Twist could control Gunner.

Twelve

The movie was a sensational idea: a superhero flick with lots of explosions. Watching things blow up in movies? Stellar, especially to avoid thinking and feeling anything about reality. So, superhero movie: check.

We sat near the back and held hands, sharing a popcorn and soda, just like a real date. I'd never had many of those. Monika and I spent nearly all of our time together practicing. We rarely had "dates." In hindsight, that seemed odd. So, holding hands in the dark: check.

Everything was amazing and perfect until halfway through the movie. The doors opened with a bang and a group of guys, all wearing letter jackets, stumbled into the theater. I smelled alcohol.

"Oh shit," Tango muttered and scooched down into the seat. "Corey's buddies from the team."

Joy. Corey wasn't with them. Was that a good thing or bad?

Maybe they'd go down front and not notice us.

Nope. When one of them spotted us, they elbowed each other and muttered and snickered like freaking eighth graders. They took the seats just two down from ours and kept up the noise, ejecting an elderly couple so they could have the entire row. No one seemed likely to tell them to cool it.

Every once in a while, one of them would mutter, "Fag Trot," or

"Slut," and cover it with a cough, which must have equaled the full extent of their comic repertoire since they laughed and fist-bumped the cougher each time as if he were Jeff Dunham.

"They must have heard I broke up with Corey," Tango whispered. "Maybe this was a bad idea."

"You know," I said, "maybe, but as far as those guys know, you broke up with him for screwing Monika. None of them knows what really went down."

"Be that as it may," she whispered. "I don't think explaining the details when they're drunk will help our cause."

"I'm not afraid of them," I lied.

Their coughing fit graduated to "fucking slut," and that was all I could take. Tango grabbed my arm before I rose more than an inch out of my seat.

"The chivalry is appreciated," she said, "but I can take these assholes myself."

"Whoa there!" I held her arm tight when she tried to jump up. "Maybe we should just leave."

Her arm shook. "No. We paid our money. We should get to enjoy the movie."

I did not enjoy the movie, but leaving might have been a bad idea, anyway. They may have followed us out if they saw they'd rattled us.

As soon as the credits rolled, they hopped up and filed past, every single one of them staring at me with drunken hatred. "You're dead," more than one of them muttered. "Dead meat."

"Okay," Tango whispered. "Please tell me you're at least a little bit scared, now."

"I am," I admitted. "Should we call someone?"

She shook her head. "If a posse of dancers meets us outside, it's guaranteed to explode and, other than Juicy, we're a bunch of pussies compared to those goons." She grabbed my hand and rose. "Tell you what, they have a Pump it Up in the arcade. We can kill time. They'll get bored and leave."

"Pump it up?" I asked as we crept out of the theater and into the lobby. No goons, so that was good at least.

She stopped and stared at me as if I were broken. "You've never played Pump it Up?"

I shook my head.

"It's a dance game." She hauled me into the arcade. "How can any dancer not know how to play Pump it Up?"

Maybe because arcade dance games were lame and boring?

"You'll love it."

I didn't. But we did kill almost an hour, an hour of my life I will never get back, but Tango enjoyed the game so much her enthusiasm was infectious. I forgot to be nervous about the football team. By the time we left the theater, I was certain they'd have gone home bored.

Tango took my arm with both hands as we walked out to her mom's car. "I so would have beaten you that last game if you hadn't—"

"Hey, Fag Trot."

Four of them appeared from behind a Ford Super Duty pickup with a camper top.

My whole body went cold. I mean, sure I was a boxer, but there were four of these guys and what about Tango? What the hell might they do to her once I was unconscious or dead? I pushed her behind me, and strangely enough, she let me. That's how much they scared her.

A bottle hit the ground and shattered behind us. We spun.

Four more sauntered toward us from that side.

Fuck. "If you get an opening," I muttered, "make a fucking run for it."

"I'm not leaving you."

"You know what these bastards will do to you once I'm out of the way," I hissed. "Promise me."

"I'm dialing 911," she shouted at the top of her lungs. "So you better—"

It's like that was their signal. Two guys grabbed her and ripped her purse out of her hands before she even reached her cell.

For once in my life I couldn't find a single smartass thing to say. All that witty banter in movie fight scenes is bullshit. The only thing I could think as I jumped one of the guys who'd grabbed Tango was, "Please don't let us die. Please don't let us die."

I punched the guy and he released Tango, but two more goons grabbed her and threw her into the back of the pickup. "No!" I screamed. "No!" If they trapped her in there, they could do anything.

A huge fucking guy threw me against the pickup. A fist hit my head at least six times, then the blacktop flew up and smashed me in the face. I sprawled on the ground while the Earth spun.

"He's a pussy *dancer*," someone laughed. "This'll be easy."

"Bro, his dad fucking killed someone with his bare hands."

"No shit?" Dark laughter. "Better not take any chances then."

A foot landed in my side, forcing all the air out of my lungs.

I struggled to look up, to see Tango. She shouted bloody murder, and the only consolation was that her screams were filled with anger, not. . . not what they'd sound like. . . if. . .

Heavy weights held my arms and legs. Through a blood red haze, I spotted Tango at last. She smashed the rear window of the camper top, and a couple of guys hauled her out and held her against the pickup. She kicked one guy solidly in the balls.

Nice.

That's the last thing I remember.

Holy shit! It was like riding a roller coaster! It fucking worked!

Twist rode that huge linebacker, looking out through his eyes, directing every move, punching Fox, kicking him in the balls. Holy shit!

He leaned in close to Fox's ear. "I won't let you take her from me."

Gunner hadn't needed much prompting, mind you. He wanted to beat the shit out of Fox all on his own. Most of the trip, Twist was a tourist, watching the show. But the linebacker didn't want to kill. Something held the son of a bitch back.

Twist tried to push him, to make the big goon kill.

He had to do it. He had to make it work.

He pushed as hard as he could, one last try. . .

Whuff! It was like Gunner physically shoved him out.

He opened his eyes, back in his apartment, gasping, laying on his bed.

"Fuck!" he shouted. "You fucking wimp!"

The next thing I remember? The hospital, someone cutting my clothes off so they could examine me. Lots of lights and noise. Everything in between, every moment of the actual beating plunged into a deep dark hole, never to return.

Dad was there, holding my hand. I kept begging him not to go away and he assured me that he wasn't going anywhere. I asked about Tango a million times, but Dad knew concussions well enough to know repetition was normal.

"She's fine, Ethan," he told me. "Bumps and bruises, but she's fine."

"They didn't. . .?"

"No, son, she's fine."

I asked it a million times, and never once could I finish that sentence. Dad told me the rest of the story.

After Tango smashed the rear window of the camper top, they just held her against the pickup and made her watch my beat down. Thank God they were from the school of thought that guys didn't hit girls. Seriously, thank God. To her credit, two of them ended up needing treatment.

The theater managers came out and broke it up, eventually.

As I lay in the hospital crushing Dad's hand, everything hurt. Even my balls were bruised. That was my least favorite part of the exam. Dr. Cherkasky was just doing his job, I guess, but he could've gone a little easier on the ol' family jewels.

Dad wore his coach face throughout. He'd held the hands of much older, tougher guys who'd been scrambled in the ring. He knew I needed him to be Strong Dad. While he must have been thinking murderous thoughts, he wouldn't show any of that until I lay safe at home in my own bed.

Not one broken bone. Lots of cuts and abrasions. Some bruised ribs. Concussion. A total of about a hundred stitches. While Dr. Cherkasky wrapped my chest to protect my ribs, Dad asked me if he could leave for a minute to tell everyone I was going to be all right.

"Everyone?"

"Katy and the dancers are out there. Auntie Mac, of course."

Not Corey. I didn't know what to make of that.

After Dad left, the doctor helped me into a gown, but I had to leave it down around my waist while I sat on the table and he wrapped me up.

Ow.

Voices in the hallway outside the room drew my attention. Dad was using his pissed-off voice and it wasn't the Pissed-Off Coach voice. It was his Pissed-Off Dad voice.

The door flew open and banged loudly against the wall. Dad marched into the room hauling Officer Friendly by the arm. He dragged the poor cop to my side and pointed at me with his free hand. I had never—ever—seen that much anger on my dad's face. On a guy that big, it scared even me. "Is this what you call 'youthful high spirits,' Warren?" He shook the skinny cop. "Is it?"

"I think you need to calm down, Mr. Fox," Officer Friendly said, obviously intimidated and trying to pretend he maintained some sort of control. "I know you're upset about your boy, but throwing accusations against this town's star football players isn't going to help anyone, is it?"

"Accusations?" Dad roared. "There are multiple witnesses. My son's blood is all over that pickup."

A suit at the door videotaped the scene with his cell. Tall and broad. Hispanic. About Dad's age. Expensive suit. Not sure who he was, but Officer Friendly didn't notice him.

"That may be true, Mr. Fox, but—" The cop refused to look at me. "But homecoming's a month away and that would put most of the starting lineup behind bars."

Dad shook him again. "Look at my boy and tell me those animals don't belong there." He hauled Officer Friendly closer. "A homecoming game is more important than punishing the violent criminals who did this?"

Warren made a mistake. He threatened my father. "A man with *your* record doesn't want to get violent, does he, Mr. Fox?"

Dad released his arm and grew very still. When he spoke again, his voice dropped so low it was nearly a whisper. "A man with my record?" Since he was a professional boxer and coach, he controlled his emotions pretty well in volatile situations. "What record would that be, Warren?"

Officer Friendly shrank a bit.

Dad spoke again in that scary quiet voice. "The record of a man who was accused of wrongdoing but was cleared by the court? Would you mean my one speeding ticket from five years ago?" His very lack of movement was somehow threatening. "Surely you don't mean the death that was declared an accident. If you took the time to look beyond the accusation and followed any of the actual court proceedings, you'd know I was found innocent. If you actually looked at the verdict of both the criminal and civil courts, you'd know I was cleared of any wrongdoing."

He jabbed a finger at me again.

Officer Friendly jumped.

"Unlike the cold, calculated and brutal assault perpetrated against my son. The boys who did this are animals, Warren. *Animals*." He touched my hair. "Do you have any idea how hard it is to beat someone to a bloody pulp without actually breaking a single bone?" He drilled Officer Friendly with his eyes. "It's really fucking hard, and it's only done because breaking bones can accidentally kill if the victim bleeds out and that's probably something the local law enforcement *won't* look past during game season."

Dad's breath escaped in soft huffs. "I accidently killed a man, Warren, but these sons of bitches carefully calculated how to beat the shit out of Ethan *without* killing him. . . not because they give a damn about human life, but because they want to play their motherfucking homecoming game next month." He sucked a deep breath. "You tell me who belongs behind bars."

Did he really believe what he'd said? Did he? I wouldn't let that cop see me cry, but the effort to keep from sobbing hurt so much I could barely breathe.

Dad kissed my forehead. "You get the part about not filing charges because of the football game, Mike?"

Officer Friendly jumped and spun around.

The suit named Mike waggled his cell in the air and slid it into a pocket. "Got it and it's already on my cloud, so it doesn't matter if he takes the cell." His smile was malevolent and fun. "You want I should upload it to YouTube right away?"

Dad took a deep breath. "Nah. As long as Warren does his job to the best of his ability, we won't need to report him to the state and have him prosecuted as an accessory after the fact." He loomed over the cop. "You don't go through what I went through, Officer Warren, without learning a hell of a lot about the way the law works in this state."

Dad looked into my face for the first time really, and he must've seen that I was about to completely lose it. His expression softened. "Get lost, Warren. Go do your job." He touched Dr. Cherkasky's shoulder. "Can I have a few minutes alone with my son?"

"Of course." He patted my knee. "I'm done here. I'll let the discharge nurse know you're set." He left.

Dad turned to the mysterious stranger in a much better suit than his. "Thanks, Mike. I owe ya."

Mike smiled. "You already owed me. Now you owe me two."

Dad inclined his head with a strange smile, like he knew this guy somehow. Maybe he was one of his Austin lawyers?

Mike looked me over. "Give 'em hell, kid." He left.

Dad wrapped his arms around me as gently as he could, and the sobs took control. I wept into his chest and couldn't stop for God knows how long.

"I'm sorry, Ethan," Dad sputtered. "I'm sorry I brought you to this town. I'm sorry I wasn't there for you." Tears ran down his face, too, but he held it together for me as best he could.

I pulled away and hit him in the chest. "Shut the fuck up, Dad. That's not. . . that's not why I'm crying." I grabbed his suit with both fists and smeared blood on it. "What you said to the cop. You meant it?"

"What?"

"About the accident," I sobbed. "About how it wasn't your fault and you don't belong in jail? Do you really believe that now? That it wasn't your fault?"

He got it, and it hit him square in the heart. His eyes watered up and he almost lost it. Almost. He swallowed. Twice. Then he could talk. "What they did to you, Ethan. When I saw you. . ." He wiped his face. "What I did? It doesn't even compare."

"I just wanted my dad back. And if this is what it took. . ."

He pulled me close, making shushing noises like he did when I was little and scared of the dark or a thunderstorm. "I'm back, Ethan. I promise I'm back."

I wept some more. We both did.

That thing we didn't talk about?

Maybe we could finally talk about it.

I wiped an arm across my face, which hurt. "Ow."

He handed me something to blow my nose, which hurt, too. "Ow." Somehow, it seemed funny and I chuckled, which hurt. "Ow." Which made me chuckle some more. "Ow. . . ow. . . ow."

"Goofball." He ruffled my hair. "Some of your friends are still out there. They want to see you before they'll leave."

I shook my head. "Holy shit, Dad, not like this."

He wiped off his own wet face. "I'll be right back."

A few minutes later, he sat on a stool in front of me. He dropped a sack on the table and opened a small zippered bag. "K-pop brought you some clothes."

"K-pop?" Really? After I was such an asshole? I dumped the sack: sweatpants and a Naruto t-shirt that obviously belonged to him because they were way too big for me. The socks and underwear had tags on them so I'd know they were new. The socks had the Trigun logo and the underwear was briefs with a smiling Captain America on the crotch and the words "Cap Dat Ass" on the reverse. "Ow." I laughed some more. "Ow." I did *not* deserve a friend like him.

Wait a minute. Dad was taking *make-up* out of the zippered bag. "First the Visine for your eyes." I let him tilt my head back and drop the drops into my eyes. "Look at me."

I did.

"Better."

I couldn't speak. My dad, the bruiser, knew how to apply make-up. Apparently, my astonishment was evident.

"There's a nurse close enough to your skin tone," he told me while he applied base. "There are two kinds of fighters," he added, "the kind who want their faces to look worse for the cameras and the kind who want to look better. Both kinds need a little help." He worked in silence a few seconds, turning my chin this way and that. "You'd be amazed what I've learned over the years as a boxing coach."

I chuckled. "Ow." He was so peacefully attentive while he worked. It was something I'd never seen on him before.

He noticed my stare. "What?"

"Do you realize this is the single-most gayest thing you have *ever* done?"

He smiled. "I assure you, son, I have done any number of things that are wa-a-a-y gayer than this, but I'm going to assume you don't want to hear the details about those."

I laughed. "Ow." I chuckled. "Ow. Quit it. Ow."

He tapped my nose with a make-up sponge. "The hardest part about make-up on guys is no one should be able to tell you're wearing it."

I noticed his suit, I mean, really noticed what it meant. "I suppose I kinda blew that interview for you, huh?"

"Interview?"

"The guy with the camera," I said. "Mike? You're wearing the dragon jousting suit. Second shift interview? Security or something?"

He blushed. My dad. . . blushed. "That wasn't an interview, Ethan."

"Oh, my God. . . it was a *date*?"

He grinned.

"You found someone to date out here the first *week*?"

His face burned red as hell. Where was my cell? "I knew Mike in high school. We were friends. . . and things got awkward." He shook his head. "Times were different then, this was B-WAG." Before *Will and Grace*, an old TV show and kind of a benchmark for gay acceptance. "I bumped into him at the Starbucks yesterday. He asked me out."

"Ah crap, that's worse! I ruined your first date!"

He winked and ruffled my hair. "I have an excuse to call him again, now he has that video for us." He sighed. "Besides, the most fun Mike and I had as kids was doing stupid shit to see how far we could push it without getting into trouble. This was probably a total thrill for him, sticking it to the man."

I said it before I even knew I was speaking: "Well, unless you go find him, he's sticking it to the wrong man, hai?"

An awkward silence descended.

Then we both fell out.

He had to help me dress. It reminded me of being a little kid. Every move hurt, so he even had to put my socks on for me. "I'm sorry, Dad. I'm pretty fucked up."

He scoffed. "Are you kidding? This is every dad's dream. Reliving all those corny baby moments when my son is seventeen?"

When I was dressed, he helped me into a wheelchair, because that cliché is true: they really make you leave in one. He crouched down in front of me with his hands on my knees, smiling more sincerely than I'd seen in too long. I really meant what I'd told him earlier: if getting this beat down meant getting my dad back? Utterly worth it.

"So can we agree that you say hi to your friends and then I kick them out and take you home?"

"Sure."

He smiled and kissed my forehead.

Fuck off. It's sweet.

I made the grand entrance. The only ones left were Tango, K-pop and Juicy. It was, like, three o'clock in the morning or something. Even Auntie Mac had gone home. Tango rushed to my side, then stopped, uncertain what to do. I held a hand out and pulled her close.

She knelt beside the chair. "Oh my God, Foxtrot, I don't even know what to say." Her eyes were red and puffy.

"Did you like the movie?"

She chuckled, and it almost made her cry again. "Honestly? I hate that macho superhero stuff." She had a few cuts on her face and arms, too. "I'm not going to ask if you're okay, but. . ." She shook her head.

I kissed her hand. "I'm okay." I couldn't remember what movie we'd seen.

Juicy took her turn. She ran a hand through my hair. "If you need me to beat the shit out of anyone, just let me know."

I nodded. "Word."

She snorted. "You are so white."

That left K-pop. There was a lot I wanted to say, but not in front of everyone.

He seemed to understand. He did the manly stand-back-and-nod thing, but he deserved a hell of a lot better than that. I held out my free hand and reeled him in. He dropped to one knee, and I grabbed him around the neck. "I'm so sorry, bro," I whispered in his ear. "That shit was off the scale. I am so-o-o sorry."

He hugged me. "Get out of jail free, hai?"

"Hai."

Fist bump.

The girls exchanged one of those boys-are-complicated looks that made me want to laugh, but it would have hurt too much. I tugged on Tango's hand and kissed her. After everything, I wanted a kiss damn it and she didn't seem to mind.

Dad broke us up. "Okay, kids, I'm taking him home now. Thank you for. . ." And he stopped.

We all looked at him to see what was up.

"Okay," he said. "I was going to lay a lame parental gratitude thing on you, but. . . it really means a lot that y'all are here. Ethan's new in town and the fact that he's already made such good friends? Well, a father can't ask for more. Seriously, thank y'all."

They weren't used to my dad, who talked to kids like people in a way most adults didn't. From the way they all pulled up a little bit and smiled though, they seemed to think it was cool.

Yeah. It was.

"Now get lost," Dad added, and they all laughed. "I need to get him home and into bed."

Three more quick hugs and a kiss from Tango and they took off. Dad ran the maze of hospital check out protocol and we were set free. He rolled me out the building and across the asphalt to Auntie Mac's car.

Clack. Clack. Clack. Clack.

Dad bristled. "What the hell are you doing here, Monika?"

She exuded innocence. "I just wanted to make sure Foxxy was all right, but those. . ." She nodded at the hospital. ". . .provincials wouldn't let me see him."

"Your call, Foxtrot," Dad said. His adoption of my nickname was stellar.

"Thank you for your concern, Monika," I told her. "Do you realize how this is your fault?"

Astonishment painted her face.

"You snuck into Corey's room, basically *raped* him in a way he couldn't—" Breathe. Breathe. Breathe. "In a way guaranteed to make Tango dump him." I waved my hands at my wrecked body. "And Corey's buddies decided to make hacky sacks out of my balls." I stared her down. "Thanks."

It killed me a little I could so easily see her maneuvering the best way to play me when I wouldn't have noticed it six months ago. She realized she'd lost. Utterly and finally lost.

Monika hated losing more than anything.

She clasped her hands together and extended her arms to crack all her knuckles. "All right, Ethan. Ruin our lives." She dared my dad to intervene. "But just so you know? Corey only fucked me for about ten seconds before wussing out, but when he was inside me, he filled me in ways you never. . . ever managed." She pretended she was about to go, then turned back for her parting shot. "And I did cheat on you. Of course, I did." She glanced down at my crotch, and I could tell she was about to denigrate my manhood further.

"So we all see that you're a fucking slut bitch, Monika," Dad said before she could open her mouth. "Big surprise. But before you regale Ethan with more made up bullshit about the adventures your nether ya-ya has enjoyed, remember I know your parents, and I know the conditions of your trust fund."

She froze. Deer. Headlights. All of it.

For the record? I'd never, *ever* seen Monika Sterling speechless.

Clack. Clack. Clack. Clack.

She was well and truly out of my life.

I grabbed Dad's hand. "Okay, my mistake. *That* was the gayest thing you've ever done."

He squeezed my hand and wheeled me to the car. "Okay, yeah. Got me there. Way gayer than all the blow jobs I've ever given. Combined."

Now this story will never. ever. be on the Disney channel.

I'm okay with that.

Thirteen

Twist knocked on an old, oak door.

He waited.

How could eight gigantic football players avoid killing the little bastard? What kind of pussies were they that the dancer was still able to walk? All to make sure they could still play their stupid homecoming game?

But it had worked! Twist had been there, riding the big guy, had felt all too soft flesh yield to his fists. What a rush! But Gunner was too good at the abuse, too good at hurting without killing, fucking sociopath. Twist hadn't been able to push him the final inch.

Twist would've just put a gun to Fox's head himself, but he enjoyed his life. He wanted to keep it, to share it with Katy, for their children to grow up in the same small town. Although, the question was if Twist could do the deed himself in the final moment. Could he kill Fox himself? He'd never killed. He didn't know.

But the son of a bitch was bound to get sympathy sex from Katy now. Damn it! There had to be a way to ruin him or to kill him, to destroy him without anyone uncovering Twist's identity. Juicy had pretty much glued herself to Katy's side since the attack, so it would be awhile before he found a way to get her alone.

Patience wasn't Twist's strong suit. He had to find someone to help.

The door opened. "Yes?" The woman was a nun, but she seemed to be one of those egg-rubbing Mexican nuns who also read tarot cards. Maybe she'd know someone more lethal.

Twist touched the brim of his hat. "Ma'am. Can I ask you a few questions?"
"About?"
Twist smiled. "Santa Muerte."

Believe it or not, I was disappointed when Corey didn't wake me up the next morning. I never thought he had anything to do with the attack, but I'd assumed he'd show up in the morning crying or something, asking forgiveness. I hadn't run the credit card, but I also hadn't cancelled his lesson with Dad. When he didn't show, either he supported his buddies or he was embarrassed. He didn't answer his cell. Direct to voicemail.

There was a knock on my open door, and I looked over quickly, thinking maybe it was him. Oops. Shouldn't have moved so fast. Stars are pretty. Dad leaned there in shorts and a t-shirt, drenched in sweat.

"Watcha been doing?" I asked.

He wandered in and plunked down next to my bed in the comfy chair that normally lived in the corner. "Hitting the bag."

"Leave any for me?" Just call me Mr. Cool. Inside, I did fist pumps.

He'd kept vigil, waking me every couple of hours, and every time I woke up on my own trying to roll over, which hurt like hell, he was always there sitting beside me.

At one point a TV had magically appeared while I was unconscious, and we watched *Glee*. Dad took great delight in teasing that we were a role-reversed version of Kurt and his dad. I reminded him of those Mardi Gras photos from his college days and he quickly dropped the jokes.

Ha. Ouch.

I liked having my dad back. Don't get me wrong, he still had a long way to go, but therapy and time would do wonders. Having a second date scheduled with Mike helped. Nurse-maiding me seemed to help.

Whatever it took.

Speaking of magical appearances, Tango materialized in the doorway as if afraid that stepping into the room would somehow hurt me. "The front door was wide open."

Dad jumped to his feet. "My pot roast!" Ever the bullshit artist. He slipped past Tango and gave her a gentle shove in my direction. "You two can watch a movie or something," he declared. "But the bedroom door stays open."

"Dad!"

He winked at me from the doorway. "I don't want you overexerting yourself and popping your stitches, son."

A pillow nailed him before he could escape.

I patted the bed beside me. "We have the old man's permission." Christ, it even hurt to waggle my eyebrows.

She slid onto the bed but remained hesitant. I knew how shitty I looked. Well, I knew how shitty I *felt*, too, but I didn't want her treating me like a fragile porcelain doll, so I drew her in. At first, her whole body stiffened, obviously afraid that anything we did was going to hurt me. Frankly, it would, but it would've hurt worse if we *didn't*.

She relaxed in my arms and lay back so I could rise up on one elbow and kiss her from above. Ow. No wincing. I couldn't let her see that every move was painful. She was warm and soft and no matter how much it hurt, holding her made me feel a thousand times better, so the pain was utterly worth it. Maybe you have to be guy to understand that.

"I don't hear a movie!" Dad yelled from downstairs.

Tango and I fell apart, laughing. He was yanking my chain, but Tango didn't know that. We streamed the original *Footloose*. Huh. Despite the godawful hair and clothes and the mediocre dancing, I liked it better.

"Oh, my God," Tango laughed. "That is *so* you and Corey!"

Okay. . . I couldn't just lay there and watch a dance movie. Before it ended, I felt twitchy and stir crazy. My feet followed the moves on the screen. My arms mirrored them in miniature.

Finally, Tango bounced out of the bed and turned off the TV. "Okay, Mr. ADHD, let's go down to the garage and work out some of those kinks."

A dozen jokes were available, but I let them go.

See how gallant I could be?

We spent an hour stretching and going through warm-ups, and I really did feel better as we continued. The garage made me think of Corey though. I knew. . . just *knew* he wasn't picking up his cell because he assumed we all hated him, that we blamed him for the beating. Add that to what happened with Monika and the poor guy had a heaping helping of guilt for stuff that wasn't his fault.

Tango lifted my foot for me, and I had to stop her when it was straight out. Crap. Normally, I could get it past my head.

"I still don't really understand why you're so loyal to Corey," she said. Before I could respond, she lifted the foot a little higher to shut me up. "Okay, maybe none of this was his fault, exactly. . . but you don't know he didn't teach those assholes how to put a smack down. He's the captain."

I gestured for her to lower the foot an inch. "That's just it. I don't know." I adjusted and relaxed my leg, then motioned her to lift the leg higher again. "I know he's not bright. *He* knows he's not bright. But he's a good guy. I mean, when you're dating someone, you only get to have that one person." I held up a hand. "That's the way *I* roll, anyway."

"You don't multitask well."

I grinned. "But I can have as many *friends* as I want." I motioned for her to lower that leg and lift the other. My left didn't want to go as high as the right. "I just think he really needs a friend right now."

"Total bromance, Foxtrot."

"Whatever."

"How are you going to get out to his place, anyway?" So she was not about to volunteer. "You can't drive."

"Dad told me he'd take me." I leaned into the leg to stretch it a bit more. "He wants to be there just in case, anyway."

She raised an eyebrow. "Is he worried Corey might be involved?"

"No, he's just concerned his parents might be a problem." I pulled my leg down. "Folks around here like their football almost as much as they like their guns, and those guys cost the entire city its homecoming victory."

"I'm not even sure there's going to be a homecoming *game* at this point." She shoved her hands into her hoodie pockets. "I really hope folks figure out who to blame for that."

"Me, too."

She motioned for me to kneel down with my hands behind my head so she could stretch my shoulders. "Corey's mom hosts an annual javelina shoot every year, by the way."

"Oh?"

"And she coaches at the local NRA." She pulled on my elbows from behind and pushed forward on my back with her chest, which felt nice.

When I faced her again, she was obviously waiting for more of a response.

"I have no idea what most of those words meant," I admitted, "but I assume the upshot is that Corey's mom is a badass with a gun and I should be scared."

Tango grinned and gave me her "bless his heart" face. "How am I supposed to tease you," she asked as she inched her lips closer, "when you're a poor, ignorant, city boy?"

Fortunately, the music was on already, so Dad couldn't comment on the ensuing silence.

She smelled like cinnamon and her skin felt like silk. She tasted like mint. After a few minutes, I didn't even feel the pain.

Dad drove me out to Corey's place. "I see your stitches are intact."

"Am I going to regret having you back to normal?"

He laughed.

Corey's place swung into view as we turned a corner. Tango had warned me what to expect, so I wasn't too shocked, but Dad whistled long and low as we pulled into the drive that led up to the main house.

Yeah: *main* house. And it was huge. Don't get me wrong, back in the day, Dad and I had been more than comfortable financially, but this was a whole nother category. It *looked* like a Texas ranch house. . . albeit a pretty new one: white with a wraparound porch that had to be twenty feet wide. Three stories. Tin roof to keep it from seeming pretentious. A number of red barns and outbuildings huddled around the main house and more stood out in the fields. The Ewing homestead seemed like a cheap knockoff.

The gate stood open, so we crunched over gravel, past the cattle who stared at us. We were probably the most exciting thing to happen all day. As we pulled into the parking lot, Dad whistled again. "Guess we should have asked more for the lessons."

He parked and we walked up to the house and across the enormous porch. A dog barked in the distance. The air smelled like fertilizer and the low murmur of cows and crickets was enough to let a blind man know he was on a farm.

Dad hovered a few feet behind as I rang the doorbell.

A pretty Mexican woman about Dad's age opened the door. She lost her happy, welcoming face when she saw me. Her eyes flashed wide in shock and her hand went to her mouth. "*Dios mio,*" she muttered. "And this is the next day." She moved closer until she noticed Dad lurking behind me. She put the door between us. "Why are you here? My boy had nothing to do with what happened. He feels horrible."

Corey's mom? I was only surprised because I hadn't realized Corey was Hispanic. He had dark eyes and hair, sure, but I knew more Spanish than him and, as dark as this woman was, Corey's dad had to be clear. I showed her my open hands to look unthreatening since Dad couldn't do so no matter how hard he tried. "No, no, no," I said. "I'm here 'cause no one's heard from Corey, and I was worried about him."

Her face changed again. She seemed confused. "You're worried about *him?*" Her eyes went a little moist as she looked past me, at Dad. "You've done a good job with this one."

Behind me, I knew Dad was nodding his acceptance. "From what I've seen, you did pretty well with yours, too, ma'am."

Mrs. Corey's-Mom relaxed with one hand on her hip, suddenly seeming much younger. "Don't you dare 'ma'am' me, Lucky Fox. I'm two years younger than you, and I haven't forgotten the sight of you drunk as a skunk at Veronica Porter's pool parties."

"I seem to recall a few times you had as much fun as I did."

Oh, yeah. . . Dad grew up here. Of course, they already knew each other. By the way, I was the only one who called him "Dad." To everyone else, he was Lucius "Lucky" Fox.

Mrs. Corey's-Mom looked at me. "If you've never heard the stories, I'd be happy to share."

I rolled my eyes. "Unfortunately, I've heard more details than a son should have to bear. I spent *way* too much time at Dad's gym, and those guys were always trying to outdo each other."

She opened the door completely and stepped out onto the porch. "Corey's in the horse barn." She pointed at a smaller structure in the field. "He's throwing hay." She must have noticed my double take. "I know we could have people do all that, but. . ." She seemed to consider her words carefully. "Corey's a *good* boy, but his best bet in life is running this farm one day. It's been in my family for generations, but if he doesn't learn it from the ground up, well. . ." She looked at the horse barn. "He's going to need people to run the business side of things for him, and if he doesn't know how to throw a bale of hay or milk a cow, those folks aren't going to show him any respect."

Wow. Really wise.

She turned her attention to Dad. "Why don't you stay here and tell me all about life in the big city while the boys work things out? I can get you a beer and show you my new shotguns." Her face said she'd just remembered he was gay. "Or a sweet tea?"

Dad stepped past me. "I'll take a beer, Maria, as long as it's not one of those sissy lo-cal piss-water beers. You got a Corona?"

"Always trying to shock us was this one." She hooked an arm through Dad's and led him into the house. "If you won't drink a good Texan beer like Shiner, you aren't welcome in my home."

Dad looked over his shoulder to make sure I was okay on my own. I shooed him away.

The porch gave a great view of the farm in all its massive glory. Okay, I wouldn't be a guy if I didn't think, "Jesus, everything this dude has is bigger than mine!" Hobble, hobble, hobble. That horse barn was a lot farther away than it would've been the day before.

Skrillex blasted the warm afternoon air. The doors stood open and Corey worked on the far side of the barn, grabbing bales of hay from a flatbed and chucking them into a stall. He wore bibs and a straw hat and, for the first time since I met him, he looked every inch the farmer.

As I watched him work, I realized why he was so strong. You have to put in hours every day at the gym to match that kind of work out. Also, he moved in perfect time to the music with a rhythmic grab-lift-heave-throw action. Hmmm. Interesting, since he had such a hard time keeping a beat on the dance floor.

He focused on his chore so much, he didn't notice me. The intensity in his face showed me he was working out his demons with the labor. The sound system sat on a nearby bench. It was worth more than Dad's old car and it lived in a horse barn. As I turned down the volume, Corey looked up in annoyance, probably expecting one of his parents. He held a bale of hay above his head like it was a helium balloon, then chucked it into the corner with its fellows.

I stepped closer so he could see me as more than just a silhouette.

He started. "Ah, Jesus. . ." He looked around as if he were embarrassed for someone to see him at work. He brushed off his bare arms, ripped the hat from his head and tossed it aside.

We stood in silence for a full minute. From his face, I could see he wasn't involved in any way with what had happened. "How much do you hate me?" he asked quietly.

"I'm not even mad at you, Corey. You had nothing to do with this."

"I'm gonna kill those guys."

"No."

"Foxtrot—"

"No. You'll get in trouble. I've caused you enough trouble as it is."

"You caused *me*?" His carefully trimmed brow furrowed. "You're the one looks rode hard and put away wet."

I moved closer. "So we agree: other people did this to both of us. None of this is you and me."

He closed the distance, still confused. "You're not mad at me?"

"Dude. No."

"You're the only one who's not." He sat down on a bale of hay, sniffled and wiped a massive arm across a face that was already wet with tears. "Bro, you're going to think I'm a little girl."

"Of course not." Of course, I did. A little.

"Tango and the crew hate me for screwing Monika and for what happened to you. The football team hates me because I didn't stand with them after what they did to you." He stared down at his feet. "I am so sorry they did that."

"Not your fault."

He still didn't look up. "I found out those guys've been doing it for a while, driving out to other towns to get their jollies. Jesus."

"I was in the wrong place, wrong time."

He glanced at me but had to look away again. "You're the only friend I have left, Foxtrot. I used to have tons. *Shit*-tons. Everyone else hates me now."

"No one should hate you." I sat beside him. "Tango doesn't hate you."

He made a dismissive noise I don't know how to spell.

I dropped a hand on his shoulder. "Okay, she should be the one saying this, but you won't answer your cell."

"I killed it." He pointed at the nearby wall and a little pile of plastic and circuitry. "Got mad at the texts." He looked at me again and didn't look away. "She should say what?"

"She's not mad at you. I told her what Monika did, that you pushed her off. So she's not mad at you."

He waited a moment. "But?" He wasn't stupid.

"She wants to be your friend, Corey, and she wants you on the crew. Everyone wants you back on the crew. . ."

"But. . ." He was so fucking brave.

"But she doesn't want to be your girlfriend, anymore."

"Because I'm stupid."

"No."

"Because she wants to be your girlfriend?"

I didn't know what to say.

He nodded.

"I'm sorry, Corey."

"We say that to each other a lot, bro."

"I'm still your bro?"

He actually chuckled. "Smart people live complicated lives, bro. I don't know how you do it." He thought about it. "You told her not to dump me. You stopped her from kissing you. I'm not so dumb I can't remember *that*. I got no beef with you." He dropped a hand on my knee. "It's gonna hurt, bro, but I still love Katy. I want her to be happy and I'm smart enough to see she'll be happier with you." He drew his hand into his lap. "You're the only one who's ever been able to give her a nickname."

I waited because there was more he wanted to say.

"I need to say something you're not going to like," he told me at last. "I'm saying it because I'm your friend even if it doesn't sound like it. . . but I gotta say it."

I waited.

"Katy and me had our problems. I knew all along it wasn't going to last past the end of the school year, but she was happy enough with me until you came along." He looked up at me. "All I can say is. . .watch your back." He stared at his hands as the tears poured down his face. "I'm just sayin'."

Again. Wow. Who'd want to think about his girlfriend that way, but I had to respect what it took for Corey to say it to me. I rose and stood in front of him. "You really want a hug, don't you, Princess?"

His shoulders shook a bit. "You have no idea."

I yanked him to his feet. "Okay, but be extra gentle. That one dude was a serious linebacker."

He wrapped his arms around me and held me as gently as if I were a porcelain doll. "We're okay?" he asked.

No idea why, but we were. "Stellar."

I felt him nod. We stood like that for a while.

"Foxtrot?"

"Yeah, bro?"

"Can my new nickname please *not* be 'Princess'?"

"No problem, *Farmer-C*. No worries there."

Fourteen

Twist banged on the old hovel's door. He knew the witch was in there; the nun had given him detailed directions and a telenovela *rioted away inside. He hadn't driven three hours into the middle of the fucking desert for nothing. He banged again.*

The door opened and an enormous red, gingham dress forced him several steps backward, to the edge of the stairs. "Get off my porch, ye foolish heathen, you stink of black magic." The old woman loomed huge, over six feet tall and almost as many around. Her white hair was pulled up in a rag. The broom in her hands meant business.

Twist stumbled onto the stairs and grabbed the railing. "I was told you're the strongest witch in the state."

Flattery seemed to work. "Some say so." She lowered the broom. "What do you want with magic, skinny cracker boy?" Confusion filled her face and she sniffed loudly. She leaned toward me and sniffed again.

What was her problem? Twist showered.

Her stony, brown face broke into a grin. "When a curse calls for a headless chicken, you kill the scrawny thing yourself, cracker boy. You don't buy it at Walmart and plan to cook it up in a stew later." She shook her head. "You'd be better off just buying rat poison if you want to kill someone."

How the hell did she know about the chicken?

Twist settled himself. "Then tell me how to do it right."

"No."

"What do you mean, no?" He slid his wallet from his jacket.

The old woman waved it off. "I don't want your money. I don't do what you want done."

Twist stared at her. "You're a witch, aren't you?" He pointed at the broom.

She looked down at the blue plastic in her hands and laughed. "You think this thing would get my butt in the air, cracker? I just use it to bash in the pointy heads of skinny white boys who think all witches practice black magic."

He did not drive that far for nothing. "Black, white, orange, whatever. I just need you to help me kill someone so no one can trace it back to me."

She planted the broom bristles-down on the porch and rested her chin on the end. "I am a God-fearing woman, skinny cracker boy. And I have power, the kind of power you can't buy on Amazon-dot-com." Her eyes narrowed. "And I am asking you nicely to leave my home while I will be able to clean the stink of you off my porch in less than a week."

"I drove three hours to get here."

"And you will drive three hours back, empty-handed."

Perhaps he'd been short with her because of the drive. He could make it right. He dug into his duffle bag and dragged out one of the books he'd bought. "Look, I'm sorry if I was rude." He held the book out to her. "Just tell me which of these spells will work. I'll do it myself."

The woman chuckled. "None of them."

He held out a different book. "What about one of these?"

"White boy, you can't buy magic on the internet." Her face scrunched up like a prune. "What do you want with all this dark evil, anyway?"

He shoved the book closer to her. "I need to get rid of someone, someone—"

She grabbed his wrist and twisted it so hard the book fell to the porch. He couldn't free himself. She yanked him closer and held his hand, palm open. She stared at his hand.

"Let go of me."

"Hush." The scowl left her face. She looked directly into his eyes for the first time since her grand entrance. Her face softened. "What you intend to do, boy, you mustn't do."

He tugged his hand. "Let go."

Her grip hardened. "You must trust me, boy. This is a dangerous path you follow. There will be consequences."

He yanked harder. "I said let go of me, you old witch."

Her face went slack. She chanted gibberish, and her eyes rolled up until all he saw was white, no, wait. . . her eyes were pale blue, he would swear to it, glowing.

Yes, her eyes glowed pale blue.

He trembled. Fuck! The trembling grew. He couldn't stop it. "What are you doing to me?"

Her chanting grew louder. The trembling grew to shaking, his whole body.

"Damn it, let go." It was a trick, like hypnosis. That's all it was, all this magic was bullshit and he knew it. He just felt so desperate. He wanted to believe anything.

Except, with the linebacker, it'd worked!

She squeezed his wrist so hard it hurt and she chanted louder.

The air around her sparkled.

Fuck, time to believe!

He drew his pistol and aimed it for the center of her face. "Stop it, you old bitch."

She shook his arm and screamed.

Bang!

The grip on his wrist released as the old woman fell backward and her brains splattered against the wall behind her. A flock of grackles, startled by the gunfire, leapt into the air.

Twist tumbled down the steps and lay on the ground shaking so hard he couldn't breathe.

He'd done it. He'd killed her. He could do it.

He sucked in a deep breath.

The shaking stopped.

He'd killed her. He was free.

Calmly, he rose.

Damn it, he was covered in bird shit from the startled grackles.

He used the old woman's apron to clean up and made his way into her house. There had to be real magic stuff in there somewhere. Might as well make the trip worth the three hours it'd taken to find her. Then he'd burn the old bitch's shack to the ground.

My life settled into a routine of rest, rehabilitation and recreation. My new three Rs. I spent a lot of time watching YouTube videos on Argentine tango. Once I turned off the sound, stopped trying to memorize all the Spanish names and focused on the way the leading and following worked, it made sense to me. It even reminded me of one of my favorite fun dances, west coast swing. When I discovered this sweet hybrid called swango, all the pieces fell into place. I even found a great, club remix of an old-school tango I knew Tango would love.

Her eighteenth birthday fell that week, but with everything that'd happened, she insisted she didn't want a party or anything.

There'd been no sign of the Sick Little Twist, so we all breathed easier on that front. Maybe after paying for the car, he'd decided to leave well enough alone. Maybe we'd never know who it was. Maybe that was all right, if it meant she never heard from him again. Just in case, a host of friends and family members stayed with her at all times.

But why *did* Woody have those cameras, anyway?

Whatever. Might as well let it go. The first string was out on bail pending trial, but Corey seemed to have that situation under control. One or two guys made some noise in support of the first stringers, and he kicked them off the team. He made it clear that if anyone came near me, they'd never play football again. In that town, it was a pretty major deterrent. He promoted the entire second string, who immediately adopted me as their mascot.

Dad broadcast the fact that if any of those guys came near me, they'd have to be carried home in a plastic bag, and my friends banded together to make sure I was never left alone in the house.

Now that Tango's birthday gift was *my* concern, I had to admit I didn't have the money to get her more than a couple MP3's of the swango music I knew she'd love. Hopefully, Farmer-C had nailed what she really wanted, anyway.

When she showed up after school for our daily stretch and make-out session, I met her in the garage and started up some traditional tango before I could chicken out. I hadn't been lying when I told Farmer-C it'd be difficult to impress Tango in her element. Hopefully, she'd cut me some slack and realize I was trying really hard.

When she noticed the violins, bandoneón and guitar in the music, she cocked her head with a furrowed brow. *"Qué es esto?"*

I offered her my left hand. "I was hoping you'd let me try some stuff I found on YouTube. See if you can help me make it work."

Her genuine smile told me she was happy I was trying. Sweet.

"Any chance I can lead this time?" I asked.

She grinned and took my outstretched hand with a simple nod, allowing me to bring her into dance position.

I adjusted my arms. "Is this okay?"

She kissed my cheek. "Just dance, *papi.*"

So I danced. I started easy, sort of leading her around and throwing in a few swivels that had some cute name in Spanish, but using my own words made them easier to remember. She responded smoothly and followed easily.

I tossed in a couple of other moves that I called a "grapevine" and a "sit-break" with a "flick." She smiled more and more as we danced, and the violins soared. I used the basic structure of the Argentine but threw in stuff I already knew from other dances, and Tango followed so well she could dance things she'd never done before as long as I kept it in Argentine tango mode.

The bandoneón played faster and faster and we danced closer and closer. . . and then everything but the violins cut out. The music turned soft and intimate. I stepped back and brought her close to me in something I called a "*corté.*" We stood nose to nose and she slowly wrapped one leg around mine. Not really sure how she managed that without falling down.

We kissed as the song ended, and my sweat dripped onto her cheek. Laughing, I moved away and picked at my damp shirt. "Sorry."

She smiled again, but this time with more in her eyes than mere happiness. "You don't need to apologize for a little sweat." She ran her hands across my chest. "Too hot in here?" She kissed me lightly and ran her fingers across my stomach.

I shivered as she pulled my shirt off over my head.

"Better." She ran her hands on my chest again, sending ripples across my abs.

I held her close and kissed her hard for a moment, until the music changed, and the club beat consumed the tango rhythm. She left me standing in mid-pucker as her face lit up at the bandoneón in the midst of the dub step rhythm. "This is awesome!" She nabbed my MP3 player. "You found this for me?"

"Happy birthday."

She smiled. "Thank you." Her face told me I'd landed the perfect gift.

Okay, stoked she liked it but feeling the tragedy of the fact that she'd stopped kissing me. I cocked my head to one side. "I was hoping you'd try an experiment with me. . . Game?"

She raised an eyebrow and stepped into dance position.

Wow. Every time I held her my whole body vibrated.

I led the traditional tango moves but adjusted to the club music.

She laughed like a delighted little girl.

I changed the rhythm.

She felt it. "Triple steps?"

Stellar. I nodded. Hadn't known what she knew besides Argentine.

"Kinda swingy?"

Über stellar. I nodded again and led her in a turn that was all swing, no tango. She followed perfectly. I switched to Argentine for a few measures, letting us get the rhythm settled, then threw in another swing turn. She nailed it.

I repeated the move but spun her six times.

She hit it flawlessly and dropped easily into a dip that only worked because she had perfect control of her body. Pain sliced through my hip, reminding me I was messed up, and I'd have dropped her if she hadn't caught herself in time.

Without missing a beat, we returned to the dance, moving easily between tango and swing, matching the music in this perfect way I'd never really felt before, as if the music danced us, not the other way around. The song fell into a slow violin chord progression, and I rolled Tango out, then in and held her facing away from me. I raised her arms while our hips kept beat, glued together. I nuzzled her neck and kissed it. Salty.

"Sorry about the sweat," she murmured.

"No worries."

She pulled our hands down to her waist and attached mine to the edge of her t-shirt in a way that meant only one thing. She raised her hands as I slid the t-shirt up.

She wore the infamous purple bra.

I had to chuckle. "Did you wear that just for me?"

She leaned against me, her back slick against my chest. "If you don't like it, I can always take it off."

Holy crap! "Well, you know I've always hated the darn thing."

She lifted her hair up, exposing the strap and clasp for me to undo. Which I did. . . er, undid. So. . . purple bra? *So* two weeks ago.

Tango has the softest skin on the planet.

I'm too much of a gentleman to say more.

But don't let your imagination go *too* crazy. We didn't get naked or anything.

Twist ran a hand across Katy's purple bath towel. It was still damp from her shower, water that had drizzled between her perfect breasts and down her lean thighs. He lifted the towel to his face and inhaled deeply. The scent was spicy and sweet. He rubbed his face against the damp fabric, then lifted his shirt and ran the towel across his stomach.

His face grew hot and his heart beat faster.

The doorknob rattled and Twist yelped.

"Sorry, didn't realize anyone was in there." Juicy lived at Katy's almost constantly since the attack. "Take your time."

Twist replaced the towel and hurried to the toilet to take care of business. Unfortunately, he'd need a few moments to be able to aim down. He snagged more hair from her brush while he waited. The witch's journal was definite about needing more of her body for the magic to work. Fortunately, it seemed to mean hair and finger clippings, and not fingers or toes. He doubted he could get chunks that big without her noticing, but the other stuff was easy.

If he could get his hand on Fox's bloody bandaging, he'd be set, but that huge monster of a father wouldn't leave the house.

He'd worked his way into Katy's "guard duty" schedule, but she was never alone with him. After the assault, it was like she and Fox both had twenty-four-hour protection. He needed to wait until the heat cooled off, until someone turned complacent.

Oh well, more time to study the old witch's journal. The internet had called it a "book of shadows," but the first page said, "My book of magic shit. Keep out." She wrote like a normal person without all the "blessed be" and "mote it be" shit he'd found in the books from Amazon. Her words made a certain amount of sense.

Twist had boxes of crap from the old witch. Bottles and jars and hand-written books, and he'd even taken the stuffed grackle because it seemed witchy and mean. He added some of the things to his room to intensify the shrine to Katy, maybe some of it would actually capture her essence or something.

Everyone took turns keeping me company and playing bodyguard. Most nights, K-pop came by after dinner. That Friday, we watched anime and worked on dance moves. After dark, we climbed onto the roof using the tree outside the window Tango broke. It was a great place to hang out, look up at the stars and talk.

"So how'd you get hooked into all the Korean stuff?" I asked.

He was quiet a moment. "How'd you get hooked into all the ballroom stuff?"

"Fair enough."

He glanced at me, then sighed and returned his gaze to the stars. "I'm not the most macho guy in the world," he said. "I like cartoons. . . I like *boy bands*, for Christ's sake." He lay silently for a while. "It's normal there. I mean, sometimes it's hard to tell the guys from the girls because all the roles are so different." He grunted. "Here?" He grunted again. "If you don't play football, collect guns and spit tobacco, you're a little girl."

After a full minute, he whispered something so quiet I scooted closer so our shoulders touched. "What was that?"

"Cosita is the prettiest girl I've ever seen." His eyes filled with stars. "She'd never be into a guy like me."

Maybe it's a guy thing, but that's all he needed to tell me.

I thought long and hard about the best way to give my friend hope. "It's different away from here. Ballroom's not the butchest pastime on the planet." I nudged him with an elbow. "In Austin, it wasn't a problem." I nudged him again and he looked at me. "They have anime clubs there. Huge."

He raised his eyebrows so much his eyes were practically exclamation points. "Hai?"

"Hai."

"Ethan?" Dad's voice reached us through the open window.

"Up here, Dad!" I scuttled to the edge of the roof.

He poked his head out the window, saw me there and I swear he threw up a little in his mouth. "What the hell are you doing on the roof in your condition?"

K-pop appeared at my shoulder. "I helped him, Mr. Fox."

"He practically carried me up here, over a shoulder."

Dad scowled. He always knew when I was lying.

"Seriously. . . carried. . . like a baby."

K-pop turned to me. "You only carry a baby over your shoulder if you're trying to get it to spit up or burp."

I glanced his way to express my utter disdain for his correction. "How do you even know that?"

"My little sister has a kid. He lives with us."

Interesting, but not especially germane to the conversation.

"Are you going to grow an ulcer with me up here?" I asked Dad.

He tried to say no but failed. "Just give it a couple of weeks for the old man, okay?"

We climbed down, and Dad will never know how close I came to falling and breaking my neck. He left for his second official date with Mike, so K-pop and I wandered out to sit by the pool instead. Since I was barred from the roof, I grabbed a few Shiners as way of compensation.

Well, a few *each*, which is how I decided we needed to go skinny-dipping a couple of hours later. Splash! The water was cool and soothed my battered body.

K-pop was rendered momentarily inhibited.

I splashed him. "Dude! Don't be an old man."

"When in Rome." K-pop chortled and left Vash the Stampede on the arm of a chair.

Cannonball!

He surfaced with a big grin and glanced around nervously. "Sweet."

I'd left Shiners at the side of the pool in the shallow end. "You never been skinny-dipping before?" I passed one to K-pop.

More grinning. "Nope."

I held up my bottle for him to clink. "Here's to first times."

He tapped my bottle with his. "First times." He drank and turned to watch the moon sparkle on the water. "You must think I'm a little kid." His speech was slurred.

"What?" I gave him my full, albeit fuzzy, attention. "Why?"

He scoffed. "Never had a girlfriend." He waved a hand across the pool. "Never swam naked." He looked at the beer bottle in his hand. "Never drank before." His face clouded a little bit. "Well, once before. . . that was different." He finally looked me in the eye. "It's like it's all normal to you."

I rejected the first ten things that came to mind. "Dude." I tapped his shoulder with my beer bottle. "This is one of those drunken late-night conversations, right? Where guys get to say emotional shit 'cause we can pretend we don't remember it in the morning?"

He chuckled. "Yeah. Kinda seems like."

I shrugged. "Never had one of those before. Well, maybe once with my dad, but that was different."

He held up his bottle. "First times?"

I clinked it. "First times."

He smiled. . . then he sputtered and broke out laughing. "Oh my God, did I really sound that pathetic?"

I went for sincere. "No, it was sweet. Really."

"Shut up." But he was smiling.

"No, really." I moved toward him. "Come here and give us a kiss."

He held me off with his free hand, still laughing.

One benefit of being both a dancer and a boxer is that even when drunk I can very quickly grab someone and throw him into the deep end of the pool.

Crap, that hurt! Forgot about the ribs!

K-pop came up sputtering. "Okay, that's it," he said with fake menace. "I still had beer in that bottle." He swam at me. "I have an older brother, dude. I know a thing or two."

Sam and Dean eat your hearts out.

Thank God the patio door is really loud, so when it slid open half an hour later, I heard it above the sound of our splashing. "Auntie Mac, no!" I called. "Don't turn on the light!"

K-pop squealed and ducked down so only his face was above water.

"Don't come out here, either," I added. "K-pop'll die of embarrassment."

"Dude, shut up!"

"He's naked and no girl but his mom ever saw his wiener!"

"Dude!" He pushed me under. Again.

Fortunately, Auntie Mac stayed inside. She would've had a few things to say about the beer. As the patio door slid closed, I registered K-pop's slightly unfocused eyes. "Auntie Mac?" I called. "Can you throw the air mattress and a coupla blankets into my room? K-pop's staying over."

K-pop grinned. "Sleepover? What are we, twelve?"

I splashed him. "Bro, you are not driving tonight."

"No worries." He fell quiet for a minute. "Never had a sleepover."

"Me neither."

Clink.

Farmer-C visited most mornings while I convalesced. We boxed a little and danced a bit. He showed me partner stretches from football. Dad started lessons with the two of us, and I talked him into taking Farmer-C's money since his parents were loaded and we weren't. Damn, it felt good to have Dad coaching me again.

Farmer-C *didn't* visit the morning after the sleepover because I'd texted him at some point in the middle of video games with K-pop at two in the morning. After K-pop left, I lay curled up in bed watching dance videos on my tablet.

Glass shattered, and I jumped.

What now?

The sound of muttered cursing from Dad's room pulled me out of bed. I ran through the bathroom and stopped in the doorway. He was alone and on his knees in the pants and shirt from the dragon jousting suit, sweeping up the remains of a lamp. An ugly lamp that had deserved to die, anyway.

"You okay?" I asked.

He looked up and went red. "Sorry." He sat back on his haunches, letting the hand broom drop. "Just having a moment."

"What's wrong?"

He pushed to his feet, glancing at me sheepishly. "Nothing."

"Dad," I warned him. "We've done our bonding, right? Don't get all distant on me."

He grinned, which had been the point. "I'm just going to sound whiny and stupid."

"Right, 'cause I never do that to you."

He regarded me for a moment and seemed inclined to experiment. "Mike arranged this lunch with some investors who might. . ."

I let him work it out.

"Okay. They might consider investing in a gym here." He held up one hand. "Don't get your hopes up, but. . ." He flailed at the closet. "Okay, it's not like I was ever a fashion plate. . ." The understatement of the century. He actually used the words "fashion plate," for Christ's sake. "But the few power suits I *had*, I sold before we moved." He wiped at the dragon jousting suit. "I stained the damn thing." He met my eyes levelly. "See? Whiny."

"Dad?" I asked. "How much do you trust me?"

Many responses to that question warred in his face but, considering everything we'd just been through, he had only one possible response: "With my life."

I nodded, pulled out my cell and hit Farmer-C on speed dial. "Then strip."

His brow wrinkled for a moment, then he chuckled and started unbuttoning his shirt.

"Hey, bro," Farmer-C said over the cell. "I thought you were nursing a hangover today."

Knowing he'd play along, I gave him my best secret agent voice. "Forget about that. We have a fashion emergency. Dad has a power lunch and nothing to wear."

There was a pause. "Local power or Austin?"

Dad stood awkwardly in paisley boxer shorts and a stained wife beater.

"Local investors or Austin?" I asked.

"They're from Austin," he admitted.

I nodded to Dad. "Austin powers," I said to Farmer-C.

There was a moment of silence.

"Can you help?" I asked.

"On my way," he assured me. "I got ya covered."

I flourished the cell and returned it to my pocket. "To the Batcave," I declared, leading Dad to my room.

After throwing a dozen t-shirts into a corner, I finally found what he needed: a white, v-neck with more Lycra than cotton. I held it out to him.

He pulled a face. "No way that's going to fit, son," he said. "No offence."

I brandished the shirt again. "With this much spandex, it'll fit the Hulk."

Skepticism all over his face, he pulled off the wife beater and managed to squeeze into the shirt, which now highlighted every muscle of his torso. "See? Way too tight."

I waited for him to realize that was the point.

He didn't.

"Are you even gay?" I demanded.

Farmer-C arrived with an armload of his best clothes, all of which would be tight on my dad, but that was the whole effect we wanted. If he was trying to get sponsors for a gym, he needed to show off the fact that he knew how to build a perfect body. Since he had one, he should flaunt it, not hide it.

When Farmer-C and I were done playing Ken doll, Dad worked black cowboy boots, stylishly ripped jeans, the white t-shirt, a black leather jacket and a rumpled Stetson with so many Xs, it had to be worth more than Farmer-C would pay for a month of boxing lessons. When it threatened to fall over Dad's eyes, Farmer-C slid in a spacer and plopped it back on Dad's head for a perfect fit.

We each took an arm and made him face the full-length mirror on my bathroom door. He stared at his image for a full minute.

"Eyebrows?" Farmer-C asked.

I nudged him. "One little step into the twenty-first century at a time." Farmer-C nodded.

Dad finally spoke. "I look like a gay cowboy."

"Well, Dad," I began with every ounce of mock seriousness I could call up, "I know this may come as a complete shock to you, but. . . well, you *are* gay."

Farmer-C fell out.

Dad smacked him on the shoulder, but Farmer-C kept laughing.

I threw an arm around Dad. "Be honest with me. What matters more to you, landing this deal or impressing Mike with how fucking great you look while trying to land this deal?"

He met my gaze evenly, and I could tell he was so going to lie through his teeth. "Mike's freakin' hot, Dad. Don't lie to me."

He smiled and stared at his reflection again. "I'm not trying way too hard in this getup?"

Farmer-C gave his arm a punch. "Dude, *I'd* almost do you. If you weren't, you know. . . Dumbledore old. . . and a dude." Another jab. "He'll be putty in your hands." A big wink for me.

Wow. It was hard not to break out in hysterical laughter.

Dad glanced from Farmer-C to me a few times before the motion turned into a general shaking of his head as he left us. "Wish me luck, guys."

"I wish you *get* lucky, F-bomb," Farmer-C called after him.

"Dude, he's my dad."

Farmer-C's face expressed confusion. "You don't want him to get lucky?"

Oh, my God, really? "I don't want to *think* about him getting lucky, okay?"

The rabbit sat in a scrubby patch of grass and stared at Twist. Its whiskers twitched and its little nose wiggled. Its coat was brown, and its long ears nearly doubled its furry height.

"Boo." Twist lay on his stomach, staring at the rabbit.

The rabbit didn't move.

"Boo!"

The rabbit stared at him. It seemed bored.

He snatched a handful of gravel and tossed it.

The rabbit jumped in surprise and scurried away, only to stop abruptly at the edge of the circle Twist had drawn on the ground with blood. It hopped backward and shook its head before leaping in another direction. That time, it stopped abruptly in mid-air as if hitting an invisible wall and dropped to the ground.

Twist jumped to his feet and whooped. It worked!

The rabbit scurried backward and huddled against the circle of blood as far away from Twist as it could.

Twist whooped again and was answered by the call of a hawk overhead.

He looked up to watch the hawk circle. "No way, bird," Twist called. "Mr. Bunny's all mine."

He dropped onto his stomach again and stared at the rabbit. Slowly, he reached forward and met no resistance as his hand passed over the line of blood. So he could cross it, but the rabbit was trapped inside.

The book had called it a containment circle. Well, that was pretty self-explanatory. And it worked! Twist still had a hard time believing the dead witch's book was the real deal. It was all so bizarre.

He had to make sure, so he jumped to his feet again and ran around the circle, picked up more gravel and tossed it at the rabbit. The animal jumped and scurried in a circle, clearly unable to penetrate the containment spell.

"Go Mr. Bunny!" Twist shouted, tossing pebbles one at a time and racing around the circle a few times for the sheer joy of seeing the spell work.

It was perfect. He could catch Fox and hold him. There was no way for him to get out.

Twist slowed to a stop, but the rabbit raced another lap, then it veered into the center of the circle and dropped onto its side, convulsing.

"Uh-oh, Mr. Bunny. Did you get overexcited?"

The rabbit screamed. It sounded just like a dying child.

"Well, that's creepy."

The convulsions shook the rabbit across the gravel. It vibrated and jiggled as if a dog had it in its teeth.

Then it exploded.

Twist leapt back, covering his face with his arms and raising one leg defensively, but the blood and gore sprayed against the invisible wall surrounding the rabbit, hanging in the air as if painted across a glass cylinder. Bits of rabbit fur and chunks of bone fell to the ground, but the blood hung suspended.

Twist stared for a moment, then jumped in the air. "Woo-hoo!" He danced around the carcass and did fist pumps. "I blew up Mr. Bunny!"

Containment circle? More like awesome explosive circle of death. It was perfect. There would be absolutely no way to trace a death like this back to Twist. Warren would be so freaked out by it, he'd probably wet his shorts.

Forcing himself to calm down, Twist looked at the pile of bunny guts—

Wait. The rabbit sat in the middle of the circle again, staring calmly up at Twist as if nothing had happened.

"What the shit?" He crouched down.

The rabbit was grey, though, not brown, sort of silvery white, and. . . and the ground was clearly visible through its side. "Whoa. Ghost bunny?" Twist scooted a bit closer. "Did I make a ghost bunny?"

The spell had said nothing about ghost bunnies.

The translucent rabbit twitched its nose at Twist and moved closer.

So he could blow Fox up and then have his ghost to torment forever? Welcome to the bonus round!

The rabbit inched forward. . . then its eyes flashed with a red, hot fire.

Its mouth opened to reveal huge, ravenous fangs.

It leapt at Twist, roaring in rage.

Twist fell back on his ass and scrabbled away in terror. "Devil bunny! Devil bunny!"

The ghost rabbit hit the containment wall and bounced back, then leapt at the wall again, screaming in rage. A third time it leapt at the wall, then stayed there, scrabbling at the wall, screaming in fury, its burning eyes locked onto Twist's.

He blew out a loud breath. Okay, so the ghost rabbit was insane and evil, but as long as it remained trapped in the circle, it still meant Twist could have fun with Fox's ghost. He rose to his feet and brushed the dirt off his butt. Since the damn thing was trapped in the circle, its hysterical thrashing was pretty funny.

The hawk cried overhead, as if answering the rabbit's wails.

The rabbit grew still. It looked up. It looked back at Twist. It smiled.

How the hell did a rabbit smile?

Then it stood up on its hind legs and stretched up and up, until it was stretched out like a cartoon. Then the stretched-out rabbit ghost left the ground and rose into the air, growing thinner and thinner all the time.

Twist shaded his eyes with one hand, but lost sight of the ghost rabbit against the bright blue sky.

"Off to rabbit heaven, Mr. Bunny?" Well, it wouldn't be nearly as much fun if he couldn't torment Fox's immortal soul, but he'd take what he could get. Blowing him to blood pudding would be good enough.

The hawk circled and circled. . . then it faltered. It dropped several feet, flailing its wings as if it'd suddenly forgotten how to use them. It righted itself. Swooped once—

And dove.

What the heck? The damn thing was headed directly for Twist.

Was it after the rabbit carcass?

The bird's eyes glowed red.

It screamed with the voice of a terrified child.

Twist dove for the ground as the bird's huge talons reached for him. "Devil bunny!" He rolled with his hands over his head protectively, but the possessed bird missed. It rose into the air, called out its unearthly hatred and dove a second time.

Laying on his back, Twist scrabbled for the gun at his waist.

He pulled it out, pointed it straight up overhead with both hands and pulled the trigger again and again. Every bullet struck home.

Twist rolled out of the way as the hawk's lifeless body pounded into the rocky ground. He leapt to his feet and fired round after round into the corpse until it was a pulpy mess.

He stepped back, gun at his side, breathing heavy. Creepiest son of a bitching thing he'd ever seen. He wiped one arm over his face before realizing he'd rolled into rabbit corpse. Gore covered his shirt and pants, and most likely his face, now, too.

"Damn it to hell. This is my favorite shirt."

He fired a couple of rounds into the matted rabbit fur at his feet. "Bad rabbit! Bad!"

He took a deep breath, glanced around. The ghost rabbit didn't reappear, and the hawk seemed equally unlikely to move. He took another deep breath.

So maybe using the containment circle on Fox wasn't such a good idea after all.

Juicy even stopped by once. For the most part, if Tango wasn't with me, she was with Juicy, who'd been vocal about her opinion of the local cops' ability to protect her friend. So it was a bit of a surprise to see her. "Hey there, Attention Whore," she said from the doorway to my room.

When I started to get out of bed, she closed her eyes and held a hand up between us. "Do not take off that sheet if Captain America is all you have on your lily-white ass." She turned away. "In fact, I'll just meet you down in the garage. I wanna show you some dance shit I found." She called up one last comment from the stairs. "Fully dressed, Foxtrot."

I was already wearing sweats, but I threw on a t-shirt and jazz flats. Since this was Juicy, chances were ballroom shoes wouldn't be flexible enough.

I was right. The sequence was filled with a lot of dropping to our knees and then rolling up to our feet. It was physically demanding, but none of the moves seemed tremendously complicated. The team was going to go *ballistic* for this stuff!

"Okay," she declared after I saw the video once. "I already figured it out, so why don't I just teach it to you?" She slipped her cell into a pocket and turned to me. For the first time since I'd met her, she hesitated. "You think it's cool, right?"

"Stellar."

She rolled her eyes and returned to her usual cockiness. "You *really* like that word." She shook out her legs and kicked one foot high enough to eat her own knee. "*And* you think it's cool." But she was teasing.

Okay, the stuff was harder than it'd looked. But it was still stellar.

By the time I had the moves down, we'd realized it would be twice as cool with the crew split down the middle and each half dancing as a mirror to the other. I figured with me to demonstrate and Tango to help break it down, everyone should be able to nail it. Juicy, for obvious reasons, would pretend she'd never seen it before.

Fifteen

Twist emptied Fox's painkillers into a plastic baggy of fine white powder. He shook the bag as if it were a soon-to-be-fried chicken then spread the mess on a paper towel on the bathroom counter. The old witch had given him the idea: just use poison. She might've claimed to be all goodness and light, but there was some badass juju in her book.

He waved a hand in a circle over the pills. "Confusion and mess, slide into death." He didn't feel anything. Oh well, the book said not to expect flashes of light or smoke because that was for the tourists.

He picked the pills out with a tweezers and dropped them into the bottle. He replaced the bottle into the medicine cabinet. Everyone on the crew was nervous about the practice that night, especially Fox. He'd never notice the difference.

Twist shoved everything into a plastic bag and into a pocket. He left the bathroom. Should he install a camera over the bed? The footage he had of Katy with Corey in the studio made him want to kill the dumb ox, but it was also the hottest stuff he had. No. No need. Fox would be out of the way too soon.

The house was deserted, but as Twist reached the front hall, a car drove up. He settled his shoulders, grasped the doorknob firmly and opened it just as Mr. Fox stomped up the porch. "Hey there, Mr. Fox. Fancy meeting you here."

The huge man froze a moment. "Everything okay?"

Twist hugged himself. "Everything's perfect, sir." He jabbed an elbow in the

direction of the house. "Just returning one of Mrs. Davis's pie plates." He rubbed his
stomach. "That sister of yours makes the world's best apple pie."

Mr. Fox beamed. "That she does."

"Okay then." Twist held the door as Mr. Fox passed inside. "You have yourself
a great day."

Ever since his first murder, Twist felt unstoppable.

After a week with the new girlfriend and lots of stellar bonding, reality
called, and it was time to get back in the game. Tango called dance practice,
and everyone planned to attend. Yep, everyone. I was officially co-
coaching with Tango, and Farmer-C was on the crew again. His nickname
had not been officially approved yet, but it was all I had.

"Hey, look who's here!" I shouted when he arrived. He was the last
one there, and I strongly suspected he'd sat out in the parking lot a good
long time before making his entrance. I wanted to make sure it was grand,
so he knew he was well and truly welcome. "Everyone tell Farmer-C how
glad we are to see him."

Of course, they'd been prepped. Everyone cheered and hugged him,
and fist bumps were had by all. Tango kissed his cheek and he smiled and
thanked her, but the look that hijacked his face when she turned away
made my heart bleed. When he saw me watching, he wedged his trademark
grin in place, but his eyes begged me for help.

I nodded once. I'd do what I could.

"Okay, *chicos*, party's over." Tango dove directly into professional
mode. "We have work to do." She played with her cell. "Foxtrot has some
secret moves for us to throw down. He'll show us the choreo, and I'll
teach it to you."

The music played and I threw down the new moves. The backbend at
the beginning was the only part that really hurt, but as I danced the
sequence, the body rolls and ribcage isolations were a bit of a bitch for my
not-quite-back-to-normal body. My pain pills didn't seem to be working
so well.

I hadn't shown any of it to Tango because I'd wanted to impress her with my ability to help with the teaching part. She'd learn the material quickly and would happily take the lead.

I finished the run through and looked up for my applause.

Crickets chirped in the silence.

Ten pairs of eyes stared at me, wide and afraid.

Well, nine pairs. Juicy stood off to one side with her arms crossed and one eyebrow cocked in an expression that could only mean, "I told you this was going to kick their asses."

Okay, eight pairs. Tango had *her* head cocked in an expression that told me some of that stuff was going to kick *her* ass, too. The look intensified as she walked to my side, letting me know I'd better be ready to take the lead on this one for a while. Then she turned to the crew with a big fakey smile and slung an arm around my neck, hauling me closer for a kiss. "What did I tell y'all? This is going to be *fun*!" She emphasized the word with another pointed glance.

I made the mistake of looking up to see how Farmer-C was handling the PDA.

Tango reeled me in for another kiss. "He's going to have to get used to it," she whispered.

"Well, yeah," I replied, "but does it have to be today?"

She muttered something under her breath about "bromances" and "missing the twentieth century," which was dumb since she was alive for, like, hardly any of it. I'd take her out for coffee afterward and make out with her in front of the Starbucks.

Farmer-C grabbed me in a bear hug and lifted me completely off the floor. "Is this guy great or what?"

Ow! My ribs creaked and a spasm of white-hot pain forced a curse from my lips. "Fuck, dude. Gently."

He lowered me to the floor. "I'm sorry." The pissed-in-his-master's-shoes face made a return appearance. "Bro, I forgot." I could tell he was trying to make up for the silence that had greeted my performance, much the same way I'd pumped everyone up when he'd arrived.

I plastered a smile on my face. "No worries, bro," I stretched the side that was seriously on fire. "Just a twinge." Since it was my first time as co-coach, I wanted to impress everyone. Hard to do as *Señor* Gimpy, so I sucked it up best I could. The whole goal for this practice was to prove we could all get along without hideous, unflinching awkwardness.

So I ignored the pain. You don't compete as long as I had without spending the occasional weekend in front of a huge crowd with a sprained ankle or a broken wrist. Injuries were there to be ignored. Right?

I snuck a couple of extra pain pills while Tango arranged the crew. She split them down the middle with each side acting as a mirror image for the other. I needed about ten minutes to show the stage left group their first couple of moves, and they sorta got it. Sorta.

In front of the stage right group I had to think for a minute. Okay, on the left I was facing the corner of the bar, so on the right. . . I'd be. . . facing the seating area. Crap. When Juicy taught me the moves, I learned it mostly on the left and not the right, so flipping it on the spot was a challenge. Normally not a problem, but the pain from Farmer-C's hug and the gentle fog from the pain meds made thinking harder than usual.

That made me nervous. Pain meds, good. Hard to think, bad.

I launched into the first rib cage isolation/body roll combo. . . which hurt like hell. The pain-filled gasp that escaped my lips despite my years of control brought a low "ouch" from the crowd. I shrugged it off. "Okay folks, follow along." What was wrong with the damn meds?

When I was in front of the stage right group, they could do it with me but the stage left folks floundered. When I switched sides, the stage left people could follow me but the stage right folks messed up. And it hurt. Every time I had to demo the moves, it hurt more.

Not sure what Farmer-C's hug had done, but it wasn't good.

Tango couldn't help much because I was an idiot and hadn't shown her the sequence ahead of time, so she was struggling, too. Well, of course. The moves kicked my ass the first time I saw them. So much for impressing Tango with how much I was learning as a teacher. Pretty much didn't work because we really needed two people up front to demonstrate both sides at the same time.

Crap. I sipped water and watched the crew completely unable to do the new moves. I mean, they could do the body rolls. . . kinda. But everything was out of sequence. Taco was getting frustrated with himself. Even K-pop was scowling.

Double crap. They could get this. I *knew* they could, but me trying to work double duty while getting dizzy from the old ribcage was not going to cut it.

Well, duh. Juicy was better at the moves than me, right? She showed them to me. I couldn't keep doing them much longer anyway because of the pain. "Juicy, just come down front and take the other side, all right?"

Brief silence.

Tango elbowed me and shook her head, letting me know it was just plain mean to tease Juicy like that.

Oops. Everyone else thought Juicy sucked. Stupid fog.

"But Foxtrot, why would you ask me to help you out?" Juicy asked. Okay, there aren't enough adverbs on the planet to describe just how pathetically phony that sounded. It was so bad everyone did another *Glee* whiplash and stared at her.

She turned bright red and shot horribly violent lasers of death at me from her eyes.

No. I mean that literally. I ducked so they'd miss. What the hell was wrong with me? I tried to cover. "Wow. I'm an asshole." I wrapped an arm around my ribs and grimaced. "Meds must be making me stupid."

"Stupid*er*," Tango muttered. She turned to Juicy. "What the hell is going on?"

"Nothing," Juicy insisted. "Nothing is going on. Let's just dance, okay?"

Tango crossed her arms and cocked that hip. It didn't look so sexy aimed at someone else. "I have known you your entire life. What the hell did Ethan do to you?"

"What?"

Blame it on what had just happened with Monika, but apparently Tango had a few trust issues. "What did he do? Why are you pissed at him?"

Juicy opened her mouth.

Tango stopped her. "And don't tell me it's just 'cause he forgot that you're. . ." Oh-fuck-don't-let-her-say-it! ". . .dance-challenged."

Fuck. She'd said it.

The temperature in the room dropped about three hundred degrees.

Blue frost covered everyone. I shook my head and the room reverted to normal. What. the. hell?

Juicy pulled up to the best dance posture I had seen on her. She gave me another blast of her death rays, then stared Tango directly in the eyes as she started the sequence. She eased the backbend all the way to the floor and popped up without any effort whatsoever.

Yeah. . . everything about her radiated how sick she was of taking Tango's shit. Anger flowed off her in red, fiery waves. Wow, what were those pain meds doing to me?

She danced the entire sequence, popping the isolations and adding triples to every spin. She hit it better than any of us could have. She spun to a halt in front of me after nailing six fouettés in a row. "'Asshole' is right." She turned to Tango, and if you google the word "confrontational," you'll see a photo of Juicy in that exact pose.

There was light applause and a few whistles of appreciation.

"Where the hell did *that* come from?" Tango demanded.

Juicy settled her hands on her hips. "Ten years of the cheer camps you make fun of all the time." She looked Tango up and down. "Maybe *you* should've gone, too."

Which started a fight. A loud fight. Most of it in Spanish.

From what I could tell, Juicy's dance secret came out completely and Tango was livid. Hard to decide the biggest issue. After all, her best friend, whom she'd known her whole life, had lied to her for years *and* she'd been holding back to keep Tango from getting jealous.

Which meant, you know, that she *needed* to do that. To keep Tango from getting jealous. Which meant Tango was the type to get jealous.

And suddenly we all knew that Tango wasn't the best dancer in town, after all.

That couldn't feel good either.

Sides formed up.

I stepped out of it, knowing that if I said a word or, even, like, breathed, they'd both turn on me. Since it *was* my fault. My ribs throbbed in pain and every object in the room gave off a faint golden glow. Something was seriously wrong, but I was so foggy. What should I do about it?

Farmer-C wandered over, to "sympathize" with me I'm sure, obviously stoked that he was no longer at the absolute bottom of the Christmas list. He looked about to throw an arm around my shoulders but stopped when I glared at him. Really? He was happy to benefit from my mistake? Dick.

"You look like shit, bro."

Fuck, my ribs hurt. I didn't want him to feel guilty about it, but. . . yeah, I kinda did. "Thanks for that, bro."

Back to the water bottles for a little alone time. Maybe I was dehydrated.

What could fix this fight? Something had to be possible. Didn't it? The argument grew louder and louder. I sucked down water. More meds? Bad idea. I was already half-baked from however many I'd taken.

Spanish rioted away behind me. I shook my head. Can you imagine what would've happened if I'd let it slip Juicy was a lesbian?

Go into slow motion.

A hand grabbed my arm.

K-pop stood there with an expression of ultimate shock on his face.

Had I said that last bit out loud?

K-pop opened his mouth.

Shit, I must have.

At that exact moment, a lull in the argument meant that whatever K-pop was about to say would be thrown out into a really unfortunate silence.

"Juicy's a *lesbian*?!"

Please note my use of an exclamation mark.

Normal time resumed with a painful popping sound.

"Oh, fuck me." K-pop whipped around to a wall of staring faces.

I am not qualified as a writer to adequately describe the chaos that ensued.

Juicy barreled into K-pop, shoving him.

He pointed at me to let her know I'd started it. What a little fucking kid.

I blasted him for not being able to keep his mouth shut.

Juicy blasted me for not keeping *my* mouth shut.

K-pop blasted me for dropping something like that on him without warning, making him look like a total prick.

Tango blasted me, too. "How could you know something like this and *not* tell me?"

"Why does it matter anyway?" Juicy demanded. "Is my being a lesbian a *problem* for you?"

"Don't be all politically correct, Juicy," Tango shot back. "You've been lying to us for *years*. I mean all those—" She didn't elaborate, but I'd seen this argument before. If she was like most folks, she was reeling through all the sleepovers, locker rooms and other intimate moments that suddenly may have meant something completely different.

"Come on, Tango," Cosita said. "It's not like she has a crush on *you* or anything, right, Juicy?" She turned to Juicy for corroboration.

Juicy turned a pathetic shade of red.

"No manches!" Cosita's hands flew to her mouth as she realized the truth. She shot K-pop a dark, hateful glance.

K-pop glared at me as if he'd caught me bludgeoning baby seals.

Okay, I'd pulled a total bonehead maneuver, but I wasn't the one keeping secrets for years. And *he'd* shot his mouth off like an idiot.

The pain from my ribs ripped at my insides. My stomach filled with acid. I took a deep breath to say something, but my side cramped hard and a slice of fire shot across my chest. Christ, it hurt.

My new friends shouted at each other, and it was my fault. Sooner or later they'd all realize it and turn their anger on me. An amazing week of friendship crashed down around my ears, and there wasn't a damn thing I could do to prevent it.

Farmer-C was the only one near me anymore. "Damn," he muttered. "I look like a freakin' saint, now, don't I?"

Could he be more fucking selfish? My ribs slashed at me again when I breathed, forcing me to gulp a few times. The shouting in the background was deafening. Farmer-C stood there smirking and oblivious, content that everyone's anger was pointed elsewhere. What a fucking jerk!

"Am I right?" he added.

Pain, anger and guilt blinded me. "Jesus Christ, how selfish can you be, you fucking retard?"

His smile cracked and died. All the color drained from his skin.

True, horrified silence filled the studio.

"Dude," someone muttered.

My stomach twisted hard. I covered my mouth with my hand.

Anger. Guilt. Frustration. Embarrassment.

All of the above.

Any sort of apology would've been hollow and lame.

Fuck.

I rushed out of the studio before anyone could speak. When you're used to seeing the world 360 degrees at a time, it's hard to cross a dance floor without looking in the mirrors, but I managed it.

I made it around the corner to a garbage can before puking everything I'd eaten in the last week as well as my lower intestine. My stomach convulsed over and over again, and, once it was empty, the spasms continued for a few minutes, until I was an exhausted sweating mess. Every twitch sliced my ribs with searing hot pain.

Good. I deserved it.

After an entire week of playing nursemaid to me, my new friends had just enjoyed the pleasure of me chopping off their heads and shitting down their throats. After everything I'd learned, I was still a douchebag.

What I'd said to Farmer-C wasn't something you said to *anyone*, but saying it to someone like Farmer-C, who knows he's not the brightest bulb on the tree, is the lowest form of evil imaginable.

I was worse than a douchebag. I was a supervillain.

The streets were deserted all the way home. Big shock.

Why hadn't I called a fifteen-minute break and worked through the sequence with Tango?

Damn it. I walked faster.

How the hell had I said Juicy's secret without even knowing it?

Faster.

And why the hell hadn't I just told Farmer-C to shut up instead of alienating every single friend I'd made since moving to Dumass?

I ran flat out.

If it hurt at all, I didn't feel it.

I didn't feel anything.

A short fence ran along the sidewalk. I jumped up onto it and fast-stepped along the cross beam. At the end, I jumped for the flagpole in someone's yard. Would've been a stellar descent if my entire body wasn't in need of traction. My side spasmed and my hands released the pole, flinging me onto the grass. Could've been worse. Could've been a driveway.

I rolled to my feet and sprinted. I still didn't feel the pain.

At Auntie Mac's house, Mike's car filled the driveway.

Stellar.

I couldn't even talk to Dad.

I ran around the side of the house, crashed through the gate and across the grass. I pounded over the diving board shouting bloody murder at the night sky and felt two seconds of absolute weightlessness before the cool water hit my shoes and sucked me down. Within moments, my lungs bitched me out.

Crap. It's hard to hold your breath with bruised ribs.

My feet found the bottom of the pool and pushed up at an angle so when I broke the surface gasping and cursing, I was already in the shallow end.

"Eight-point-five," someone behind me said.

I spun. Ow.

It was Mike. "Sorry to startle you, but I figured I should let you know I was here." He was stretched in a lounge chair, holding a glass of something.

I looked around, breathing hard. "Is my dad out here?"

Mike gestured with his glass toward the house. "He's on the phone. I came out here to give him a little privacy." He pushed up from the chair. "I can go out front."

"No. Sit." I slogged my way out of the pool holding my chest with one arm. "I should go in and change, anyway." Would my lungs ever slow the heck down? Ow.

"Here." He tossed me a towel from the nearby table. "Your dad and

I were going to swim. Mac'll have a fit if you walk through her house soaking wet."

"Thanks." I toweled off my head and started toward the house, but the awkwardness of the whole thing stopped me. "Mike?"

"Yeah?"

I took a deep breath. "Any chance you don't need to tell my dad about. . ." What? About my temper tantrum across the yard and into the pool fully dressed? How do you say that? How do you not say *something* about it?

He raised the glass to me. "Our secret, Ethan." He smiled. "Does that get me a point or two in the okay-to-date-my-dad column?"

His directness was cool.

"Maybe one."

He nodded.

"So. . . you're 'dating'?"

He laughed. "That's a question I'll let your dad field."

"Fair enough."

"Ethan?" He sat forward casually. "If I'm out of line, I get it, but you look like you could stand to talk about something, and I have a few minutes to kill." He waved at the house again, where Dad was on the phone.

Okay, maybe he just wanted to score more points, but he radiated this weird casual energy that made me want to talk to him. I needed to talk to *someone*. Deep breath. "I fucked up worse than I have ever fucked up in my life." I waited to see how he reacted to the f-bombs. Not at all.

He waited for me to talk, which I'd thought was *my* super power.

I wrapped the towel around my shoulders. "So I have these new friends who are better than any friends I've ever had except for Dad." Once I started, the waters kept rolling down the pipe as I told him what had happened at the studio.

"Wow." He saluted me with the glass when I finished. "You're like a supervillain."

"Dude." I dropped into a chair. "You kinda lost a few of those points with that one." Okay, yeah, I'd said the same thing, but that was totally different.

"We all do stupid stuff." The glass drifted to his chest. "I do." He waved it at the house. "Your dad? I could tell you stories about him."

He had my undivided attention. "Okay. Let's go with stories about Dad."

Another sip. "You know we were friends in high school, right?"

I nodded.

"We were best friends for a few years. Inseparable." He sipped again. "Then we both realized we weren't like the other boys, but we didn't know how the other felt and things got. . . awkward."

Dad had never told me this story. I thought I knew everything.

"I figured out the whole gay thing before he did." Mike chuckled. "Your dad was a little slow on the uptake about certain things." He stared at me for a second, as if deciding how to proceed. "So one day I kissed him. We were in the locker room, and I *thought* we were alone."

"Uh-oh."

"Indeed. He kissed me back and don't worry, I'm not going someplace gross. We heard someone shout, 'Holy shit,' behind us. He pushed me away and popped me in the mouth."

"Holy shit!"

Mike chuckled. "Yeah. Not his finest moment."

"No wonder I never heard this story."

He swirled the ice. "I'm not surprised." He looked at me. "So I was the queer one and he was just a guy I was queer for. This was all B-WAG, of course."

"Okay sure, times were different and all that, but, holy shit, what a douchebag. What did he do to make it right?"

"What do you mean?"

"Well, you're here in his lounge chair with a cocktail," I explained. "So he must have found a way to make it right."

Mike chuckled. "Well, I found out this week that he did keep the other guys from beating the crap out of me for hitting on him."

"But he apologized at least, right?"

He shook his head. "We didn't speak again until he spotted me in the Starbucks."

"But. . . but that's not my dad. He's all about personal responsibility.

What a hypocrite."

"Why?"

"Why? Because he popped his best friend and outed him and didn't even take the time to say he was sorry." I pulled the towel from around my shoulders and twisted it. "So what did you do when you saw him in Starbucks?"

"Well, I was buying a latte, and as I reached for my wallet, this big arm reached around me and dropped a twenty on the counter. It was your dad. He'd gotten so big over the years." Okay, the smile on Mike's face was a little creepy because it was my dad he was smiling about. "He said, 'I know this doesn't really do anything, Mike, but it's the only way I can think of to apologize for acting like a supervillain.'"

"Seriously? *He* said 'supervillain'?"

Mike nodded. "You and your dad are a lot alike." His face changed, became wistful, which isn't a word I'd have thought I'd use. "Both your dads."

"You knew my. . . my biological father?"

"We all grew up together."

He lapsed into silence.

"So what made you accept his apology after all those years?"

"Time." He answered quickly, as if he'd thought about it a lot already. "You hang out with adults, Ethan. That should give you a little more perspective than most folks your age. What happened was twenty years ago. Since then, I've done plenty of shitty things to other people way worse than panicking in a tight spot. If I held that one mistake against him, it'd make *me* a hypocrite."

He lowered his voice. "The thing is, your dad did what he did. It didn't make him a supervillain. If he'd have talked to me the next day, I'd have forgiven him. I wouldn't let years of friendship go down the drain for one stupid day."

"I've only known my friends two weeks."

"And a year from now, none of you will even remember this fight." He rose from the chair. "Beating yourself up and calling yourself a supervillain doesn't actually help the friends you hurt." He walked toward the house.

"Hey, Mike."

He stopped.

"What do you do for a living?"

He didn't answer.

"Psychiatrist or Psychologist?" I asked.

He acknowledged my guess with a nod. "Psychologist." He tossed the ice onto the grass. "I'll tell your dad I gave up that story. I think I know him well enough to say he's fine with anything I tell you as long as I'm trying to help."

"Mike? Is Auntie Mac around?"

He turned to me with question marks in his face. "No."

"Okay." I kicked off my shoes. "I was gonna swim for awhile, and she gets weird if anyone's out here without a suit."

He barked a laugh. "You are your father's son. If your dad and I want to sit outside, we'll hit the front porch. The pool's all yours."

Cool. He got my hint. "Thanks. And Mike? For the record, you can have a coupla bonus points."

He waved the glass above his head as he walked away.

Son of a bitch! Why'd the wuss have to freak out and puke? After that fiasco, everyone would've been certain he'd offed himself, completely to be expected. Twist worked so far behind the scenes, no one would've suspected foul play. That son of a bitch was way too lucky.

Huh. Was someone using magic to help Fox?

Whatever. It was time to stop working behind the scenes, time to take action.

Katy was still at the studio. And she was alone.

Sixteen

So I had this dream. . .

The music was creepy and weird. *Tiempo de Vals* or *Hijo de la Luna*. I wore a stellar black tux and Tango was dressed to kill in a dark red ball gown, her hair pulled up and her make-up competition perfect. We swept across an enormous, crowded dance floor, my friends the only people I could see in any detail. Farmer-C and Monika sailed past us, him in a cheetah-print caveman costume, her decked out exactly like Cruella De Vil.

Tango and I performed a faultless fleckerl, then swooped past K-pop and Cosita, who were drawn like actual anime characters. His hair was taller than usual and his eyes were literal exclamation points.

Dad and Mike spiraled by in matching white tuxes.

Juicy and Woody executed remarkable pivots. They wore g-strings and, for her, pasties. They stopped in the middle of the floor and kissed.

Boom! They exploded in a massive cloud of glitter!

Everyone glanced at the smoke rising from the dance floor, but we'd be next if we stopped, so none of my friends even slowed down. Tango back-led me into a series of twinkles to keep us moving. They carried us away as if we were dancing on a cloud.

Dad and Mike weren't so lucky: they paused briefly where Juicy and Woody had vanished.

Boom! More glitter.

The audience broke into mad applause. They surrounded the floor in rising tiers so high I couldn't see the top, thousands of people watching, all dressed in full-on Renaissance royal finery, white wigs and all.

In the weird logic of dreams, I had no reaction to Dad's explosion. I led Tango into a *developé* and flashed the crowd my biggest I'm-the-man-in-charge smile.

Farmer-C and Monika bore down on us from the edge of the floor, so I ended my pose a measure early and sailed off to another corner. That was the true test of a competitor. We all had our sequences, but how did we manage when we had to break choreo and wing it?

We swung around and trapped our pursuers.

Boom! Insane applause and glitter.

Tango laughed, and we floated off to the next victims. One by one, every couple made some sort of mistake that earned them an explosion. K-pop and Cosita were the easiest kill of all.

Eventually, Tango and I had the floor to ourselves. I spun her out so she could land and curtsy. I gave the deepest bow of my life as the applause rose to a deafening roar and confetti, balloons and flowers poured out of the ceiling.

I rose from my bow. Tango ignored the crowd, hands at her sides, staring at me. What the heck? She was going to offend the judges, and we'd end up glitter-bombed after all.

The tiers of seats slid away, leaving me adrift in the middle of an enormous, empty dance floor. Tango shook her head sadly and faded into smoke.

I called her name once. . . twice.

A vast, empty, parquet wasteland surrounded me.

I woke up with a spasm, which hurt more than it should have, but I'd fallen asleep on a deck chair which was dumb, dumb, dumb. My throat felt raw and every muscle hurt. Rain poured out of the sky. In a dream, it would've been the perfect symbol of my emptiness and sorrow. Except it was actually raining, and I was awake.

I hurried to the covered porch. Where was Dad?

Deep breath.

Probably sound asleep in his bed.

It's always weird to describe a nightmare that leaves you sweating in terror, because they're often lame in the telling, but the memory of standing alone on that horrible, empty floor left me shaking.

How had I ended up asleep in a deck chair?

Oh, yeah. After my talk with Dr. Mike, I'd jumped in the pool. At one point, Dad came out to check on me. I'd lied and told him I was great, which he bought, so Dr. Mike hadn't shared my tale of woe. Dad laid out sweats and a hoodie for me and reminded me that if I fell asleep in a deck chair in my condition, I'd have only myself to blame in the morning when my entire body ached.

After my swim, I'd dried off, dressed in fuzzy sweats and promptly fell asleep in a deck chair. Note to self: no whining to Dad about the aches and pains.

All caught up.

Rain drained off the roof.

I bounced like a bunny, shaking out my stiff muscles. I had to talk to Tango. I couldn't wait twenty years to make things right. Reaching into my damp jeans' pocket for my cell reminded me it had been with me when I jumped into the pool. Fuck. It was dead.

Oh well, Tango'd had no qualms about visiting me in the middle of the night. Turn-about was fair play. Rushing through the house, I found Dad's keys on the kitchen counter and ran out to Auntie Mac's car.

Mike's was parked on the street, now.

"Go, Dad," I muttered and sped off into the twilight.

The streets were deserted at Oh-my-God o'clock in the morning. Tango's driveway, too. Could only mean one thing, so I made a u-turn and drove to the studio. The rain had already stopped by the time I pulled into the parking lot. Success! Her mom's beat up Toyota idled by the door with the lights on.

Once I parked, I ran to her car and reached through the open window to kill the engine and steal the keys. If we were going to thrash through what I'd done, she shouldn't have a running car as an excuse to escape.

The studio was gloomy, the only light a slowly turning disco ball. It filled the space with thousands of white traveling dots. The quiet whir of the box that turned the ball was the only sound.

I stopped near the bar. "Tango?"

No answer.

"Katy?"

No answer.

"It's Foxtrot, Tango. I know you're mad at me, but I have your car keys and you're not leaving—"

Bam! Something hit the back of my head.

The disco ball blew up white hot. . . then everything went black.

Someone nudged my leg with a shoe.

"Ethan Fox?"

Male, and not a friend of mine because my friends called me Foxtrot.

Except that I had no friends now, because I was a supervillain.

"Wake up, Fox."

I gurgled. "Foxtrot."

"Are you drunk, too?"

Too? When I rolled to my stomach, pain split my skull and nausea filled my gut. "Ah, crap, again?" Who the hell hit me this time?

"You *are* drunk, you son of a bitch." He yanked me to my feet, which was not only mean, but foolish.

"Fuck me!" I yakked all over Officer Friendly's uniform.

He cursed, too.

"For Christ's sake, someone knocked me out." I stared at the puddle at my feet. "She's going to kill you when she finds out you made me throw up on her ugly carpet."

He pushed me against the bar. "How long you been passed out here, Fox?"

I gripped the rail and ignored the desire to repeat his words to him in my Cartman voice. "I don't know how long I've been *lying here unconscious*, Officer Warren."

He knocked my feet apart and commenced to frisk me. When he heard a rattle in my pocket, he shoved his hand into my sweats.

"Jesus, dude, don't you have a class in cop school that teaches you how to frisk a man without jingling his bells?"

"Shut up, Fox." He held a set of keys where I could see them. "You like Juicy Couture, Fox?"

I did my best to focus on the keys. "What? No, those are Tango's. Her mom's car is outside. The engine was running when I got here. What time is it anyway?"

"I'll ask the questions."

"What the hell's going on?" I demanded. "You can't arrest me for trespassing. I have the code to the lock. If you look right here on the log, I'm on the list—"

"I can arrest you for whatever I want, Fox. Don't play dumb. You know what's going on." He yanked one of my hands behind me. Cold metal clacked around my wrist and he reached for the other.

"What the hell?"

"You have the right to remain silent." The other cuff clicked into place tight and he jerked my arms.

"Fucking ow!" My ribs screamed at me, and I dropped to one knee. "You're arresting me? Seriously? I get knocked unconscious—*again*—and *I'm* the one in trouble?" I should've kept my mouth shut, but it'd been a really bad day. "What do you do for real criminals? Give'em a bubble bath and a happy ending?"

He forced me to my feet. "Explain how you got her keys."

"I told you, her car was running when I got here. I took her keys so she wouldn't waste gas."

He pushed me into the glass door and *then* opened it. "You're just a freakin' gentleman, aren't you?"

Notice he did not read my full Miranda rights? I noticed.

The cool morning air woke me up a little. Enough to see that Tango's car was no longer in front of the dance studio. "What the hell? It was right here. Where'd it go?"

Wait, did *she* hit me? No. No matter how mad she was, she wouldn't clock me from behind. She'd want to see my face when she smacked me. Also, how could she leave if I had her keys?

"Why don't you tell me, Fox?" Officer Friendly said in his small-town-smarmy voice. "Why don't you tell me down at the station?"

The lights from his car blazed and flashed in the early morning sun. A small crowd had gathered, and they all whispered and muttered when Warren stuffed me into the squad car. Most of them held Starbucks. The aroma of coffee, chocolate and butterscotch filled the air. I *really* wanted the caffeine in a mochachino. Trenté. Quadrenté.

Then the reality of the situation managed to crawl its way through my fuddled, most-likely-concussed brain: Tango was missing.

Again.

For real this time.

Son of a bitch! He'd only been away from the tablet for five minutes, but by the time he'd reached the studio, Katy was gone, and Fox lay there unconscious. Why hadn't he bashed the bastard's head in? He was so desperate to find Katy, he'd let the opportunity slip through his fingers.

What the hell? He hadn't been recording because, well, there was no sense in providing evidence of a kidnapping. Had someone else nabbed her? Had she finally had enough of the Austin pretty boy?

He sat in his car and flipped through the video feeds. There had to be an answer on one of his cameras, there had *to be.*

No. No. No. Not there. Not anywhere.

Fuck. Where the hell was Katy?

Fuck!

Officer Friendly and his trusty sidekick Pal shouted at me in a locked room with a big mirror. They performed an inept rendition of Bad Cop/Badass Cop with Warren hopelessly miscast as Badass Cop.

"Just where *were* you after the big fight at the dance studio?" Warren's nose was way too close to my face. "Where's Katy, now?!"

Again and again they asked the same stupid questions, as if the answers might change. Every half-hour, an annoying clock played the Big Ben chime out of tune and off time. It was torture.

"If not you, Fox," Pal shouted, "then who?"

Ratting out the guys on the team who might look guilty wouldn't help me with those two, so I refused to share any of my suspicions. Besides which, for all I knew the mailman had her.

"That's what I thought," Pal said after my silence.

Those two belonged in the cast of *Super Troopers*. The actual Sheriff or Chief, or whatever he was called, was still out of town "giving a deposition" in Houston. Remember Farmer-C's booze-guzzling gesture? I was stuck with two guys fresh out of the academy and eager to prove something. What the hell had happened to Tango, and who was out looking for her while the only two cops in town grilled *me*?

Piece by piece, I gathered the story from the questions Laurel and Hardy asked: no one had seen Tango since the explosion at the studio. She'd never made it home. In a surreal twist, Farmer-C was the last to leave. Were they together again because I'd been an asshat?

Farmer-C claimed Tango was closing the studio when she sent him home.

The last her mom had heard was a text saying she was going to spend the night at Juicy's, which Juicy flat-out denied. *She* hadn't seen Tango since the blowout.

No one had the least idea why her mom's car was at the studio with the engine running. Tweedledee and Tweedledum didn't believe my story about it, anyway. I was the guy with the only tie to her whereabouts. I had her keys.

Since I was already beat to shit, Officer Friendly didn't believe my knocked-on-the-head testimony, and there was really no way to prove it. "I say you got drunk and kidnapped Tango after your 'lover's quarrel'."

He said this with a straight face. "I say you dragged her out of the studio by force, you hid her car somewhere near the studio and walked back to lock up so no one would suspect. I say you passed out from the liquor." He gave Pal a knowing glance. "If you *do* have a new bump on your head, it's from the fall when you passed out."

The part that sucked the most was that his theory was only *half*-way insane.

"This all started right after you breezed into town, Fox," Warren shouted. "You can't tell me that's a coincidence."

He carefully avoided referencing Dad or Dad's issues with law enforcement. The whole thing made me crazy. Why was no one looking for Tango?!

A gentle knock on the door cut through a lull in the shouting. The cops' surprise was easy to read: how the heck had someone trespassed that deeply in the station? Pal yanked open the door.

I couldn't see who stood there, but I recognized her voice. "I'm so sorry to intrude, gentlemen," Saundra Delacroix said, in a regal African accent, "but there's nothing actually locked from the front door to this one. You have no privacy signs posted, either, so I naturally concluded that everything in your station is public."

Warren puffed up and pulled the door open all the way. "No one's supposed to be in here!"

"I'm Mr. Fox's attorney, and you can call me Ms. Delacroix, thank you for asking."

She was stellar. Absolute hell on four-inch stilettos: one of those amazing women who was drop dead gorgeous and smarter than everyone with no qualms about using both to her best advantage. To keep everyone off base, she wore her hair in four-foot-long braids and traded three-piece-suits for traditional African regalia. Okay, "regalia" isn't a common word, but if you saw her, I'd dare you to find a word that fit better.

From the looks on their faces, the cops had no idea what to do with her.

"Hello, Ethan." Her accent made my name sound way awesome.

"Hey, Ms. Delacroix. Really glad to see you."

She pushed past the Tweedles. "They treat you all right?"

"I could've used breakfast."

She studied everything from me to the cameras to the mirror. "Don't get cocky now, boy, just because your fancy, high-paid lawyer is here."

I loved, no, *worshipped* her fake, regal African accent.

She squared off with Warren. "Has my client been charged with a crime, officer?"

"Charged?" He and Pal exchanged a glance. "Not *formally*. . ."

She turned away from him abruptly. "Then let's be going, Ethan."

Before I could move, Officer Friendly put a hand on my shoulder. "He's being held for questioning, Ms. Della. . . Della. . ."

"Delacroix."

"He's being held. For questioning." Warren's feeble attempt to sound intimidating was sad. "I don't know how they do it in the big city—"

"Then I'd like a few minutes alone with my client, thank you," she declared without missing a beat. When he didn't move, mostly from confusion, she touched his arm gently. "I'm sorry if he's been a handful. I promise to get him under control."

"No, ma'am. No problem at all."

They scurried from the room.

"You laugh, and I walk out right now," she said in her real voice, which was somewhere between New Jersey and the Bronx. Sitting across from me, she appraised me critically. Her voice returned to the homeland. "Your father called me."

"Dad? Where is he?" He had to be going batshit crazy.

She held up one hand. "Don't forget we're being observed and recorded at all times." She glanced at the mirror behind me. "If you're alone in a cell, assume you're being recorded, so no whacking off, all right?"

"No, ma'am. No whacking off."

She leaned closer.

So did I. "How'd you get here so fast?"

"When your father called and asked how many years he might get for assaulting an officer of the law who needed a beating, I decided to risk the speeding tickets."

Sounded like Dad. "Is he okay?"

"This new man, Mike?" She patted my hand. "He seems to know how to handle your father." She glanced at the mirror. "There's a group of parents outside the station. He's with them. All the parents were perfectly happy to talk to me. . . a lot, and Ethan? This is the weirdest thing I have ever seen," she said quietly, drumming her immaculately manicured fingers on the table. Creating noise so the mics couldn't hear us well? "This girl is your girlfriend?"

I nodded.

"And you had a fight?"

I shrugged. "I said some stupid stuff."

"Don't say anything to the police. I hope you learned that much from your father's tragedy."

I'd learned a lot. "No Miranda," I whispered.

"Good to know, but in a small town it's your word against theirs. Not sure it'll help. But I'm glad you noticed. That means you're paying attention."

"What's going on?"

"Ethan, child, I wish I knew." She squeezed my hands. "You need to know the girl is well-and-truly missing. . . probably really kidnapped." She drilled me with her dark eyes. "I need you to keep it together. Don't say anything to anyone in here, even if he's your best friend."

My confusion must've been evident.

"There are twelve other suspects in the cells today. Ten boys and two girls." She shook her head. "All this time spent tilting at windmills and no one out searching for the poor missing girl." Anger smoldered in her eyes. "No Amber alert, either. The officer *in charge*," she added with more sarcasm than I can describe, "told the county and state that she's done this before and is perfectly fine." She turned her patient expression on me. "Which doesn't explain why he's also holding thirteen of you." Her face grew more concerned. "I hear you were hit again. Did you get medical treatment?"

"They don't believe it happened." Deep breath. "Ms. D. . ." There was no delicate way to put it. "*Why* are you here? I mean, I'm really grateful, but we don't have any money."

She patted my hands and released them. "I owe you, Ethan. I proved your father was innocent, but he still lost everything. That was my fault." She smiled. "Maybe I can do better this time."

I guess loyalty made sense. Those two had known each other since before I was born. Could I take it one step farther? "Can I ask a favor?"

"Anything."

"Go see what you can find out about Katy, where she might be, what the hell happened to her."

She frowned. "And leave you in here alone?"

I scoffed. "I'm not worried about those bozos." I fed her my most sincere pleading face. "I'm worried about Katy. Please."

She regarded me in silence for a long time before nodding once. "Your father is going to kill me for this, you realize."

A second later, she was gone, and I was alone.

Seventeen

Twist sat at the kitchen table with a pile of cards. Tarot cards. How the hell did they work? And why was there a "t" at the end no one pronounced? Black candles burned, and amber incense. He closed his eyes and placed a hand on the deck.

"Oh, mighty. . . Isis."

No, that was stupid.

"Oh, tarot deck, please show me where Katy has been taken."

The journal ridiculed the fancy spells and poetry of the other spellbooks. "Just say what you want," it advised.

He struck a match and dropped it into the stone bowl. An enormous fireball leapt up and scorched the ceiling.

Holy shit!

Dark blue sparks flew out of the bowl and Twist leapt from his chair, knocking it over. The table bounced.

He pressed against the wall while the fire died down. Wow. The old witch's herbs were a hell of a lot better than the crap he'd bought from the naked chick. It was a mix of stuff the journal called a "finding spell," which seemed pretty straightforward.

He sucked in his breath a few times to calm down. The flames settled into a bright blue fire that slowly consumed the black sticky mess in the stone bowl. The cards had scattered across the floor. How many were under the stove? Damn.

As he bent down, he noticed one card still lay on the table. It showed a tower, like a castle fortress, with two men falling out of it. A lightning bolt had struck.

A prison? Well, Fox was stuck in the jail, but Twist already knew that. He wanted to know where to find Katy. "Stupid cards."

I sat alone in that stupid room most of the day, not that I had any idea what time it was. The lousy clock chime was utterly random.

I paced. I sat.

I stood in front of the mirror and shouted. My ribs hurt, my head felt like a punching bag after an Olympic workout and my bladder threatened to explode.

Even my balls hurt again.

Guys: never take comfortable balls for granted.

While I was heavy into my seventh rant at the mirror, the door opened. "If I don't see a toilet in ten seconds, I will piss where I stand!"

Ms. D entered the room with a frown. "I'd rather you didn't. It'll have to wait a few more minutes."

"I'm really kinda desperate, ma'am," I said.

She took my wrist and led me out of the room. "Not one word, Ethan," she whispered. "Not one."

As she dragged me down the hall and past the bathroom, my bladder threatened to protest, but every time I'd shot off my mouth recently someone had gotten hurt, so I kept silent. She led me into the foyer, her hand still attached to my wrist. A mob of teenagers milled around.

Wait... I knew those guys. They were the football players who'd assaulted me. Weren't they out on bail? What were they doing here? Everyone seemed confused, Officer Friendly most of all.

We were suddenly outside.

Reporters. Oh, God, no.

Flashes exploded in my face. A couple of hands thrust voice recorders at me. In Austin, the press created a three-ring circus at everything Dad endured. There's one good thing about a small town, I guess: fewer reporters. They threw out a confused, overlapping mess of questions deflected on all sides by Ms. D's shielding litany. "No comment. No comment. No comment." She only broke the mantra once. "So sorry," she said to the man whose foot had the misfortune of landing under her four-inch heel. "No comment."

Our exit decelerated into an amazing Quentin Tarantino slow-mo where Ms. D dragged me through the reporters, flashes went off, and Skrillex played in the background. Yeah, that likely only makes sense to someone like me, with a parent who worships the man.

Looking over one shoulder, I found Farmer-C. He looked up, caught my eye. . . and looked away again as if I were a stranger.

No comment.

"Ethan!" Dad pushed through the crowd. He engulfed me in his arms, which would sound like hyperbole if you'd never been hugged by my dad. "Jesus Christ, son, what's going on?" He held me out and examined me.

"Dad, you just ruined the perfect Tarantino moment."

"You didn't hear the album scratch?" He ran a hand over my head. The anger on his face would've made the guy who knocked me out wish he was still No-Touching-Anyone Dad.

Ms. D interrupted his ministrations. "We talked about this, Lucius," she murmured in an annoyed sing-song voice. "We're making a getaway."

"Trust her, son," was all Dad managed to say before she shoved me into her hybrid.

She hauled ass away from the station. "First stop: restroom." Her East Coast accent made a comeback.

"What was all that?"

She drove past a perfectly viable mini-mart and a McDonald's. "They over-detained. They have one cell with a max capacity of four. They had ten boys in there, you in isolation in one interview room and the two girls in the other. With the reporters on hand, I made it clear I was going to call in the state to shut them down for overcrowding and have them all up on charges for cruel and unusual punishment." She smiled. "All bullshit, of course, but they didn't know it."

"So why the rush to get me out?"

"Just because they can't keep all thirteen of you for questioning, doesn't mean they can't keep five or six. I had to get you out before they realized that."

"Brilliant."

We pulled into a rest stop at the edge of town, and I sprinted to the restroom. I really, really, *really* needed a rest. I took a minute to wash my face before heading outside. Ms. D removed the last of her African costume, revealing trendy jeans, a blue Oxford and a nice figure. You know, for a forty-something woman.

She pointed at an enormous sandwich she'd miracled from thin air, and I dove into it headfirst. Yep. Dad had made it. Only he used that weird chipotle mustard stuff.

I nearly choked when she reached up and pulled the four-foot-long braids from her head. A wig? Holy crap! Under the wig, her hair was shaved in a crew cut. She was almost unrecognizable.

She smiled. "And people wonder why I keep my hand in the theater when I'm so busy as a lawyer." She scratched her head with both hands. "Okay, Ethan, what's going on? The whole story." She handed me a bottle with my painkillers. Score!

I told her everything. Well, I probably glossed past the making out and the beer while skinny-dipping, but the rest was there. She sat on the picnic table with her feet—now in converse high tops—on the seat, asking the occasional question.

"We need to get the state or county involved in a search," I said at last.

She shook her head. "I already told you, Warren contacted both to say everything was under control."

"What about John Walsh?"

She cocked her head at me. "Would you be serious?"

"I am. Someone knocked me unconscious and took Tango's car."

"No one but me believes you were attacked, so she's just a runaway girl—" She raised a finger. "Since she turned eighteen last week, as far as anyone outside Dumass is concerned, Katy's merely a young woman who had a fight with her friends and needed some alone time." She patted the table and I sat down. "My superpowers don't work as well on the outside world because people there actually know what they're doing. The guys here are idiots, and Warren is using this as an excuse to strut around like a cock."

I scoffed. "You got that right."

She rubbed her hands over her head. "Okay. I'm not sure where to go next. I'm a lawyer, not a cop. Wait." She looked at me. "What did you blow on the breathalyzer?"

"Breathalyzer? There was no breathalyzer."

"What? That makes no sense. His whole case against you relies on you being drunk and passed out in the studio. Why else would you take a nap there after kidnapping Katy?" She lapsed into silence as she thought things through. "Who do you think took her?"

"I have no idea," I lied.

She seemed to read me. "Ethan, even the vaguest suspicion might mean something."

So I laid out my thoughts about K-pop, Taco, Ephraim and Woody.

"Interesting. Nothing solid, though. We'll need to ask some questions." She opened her tablet. "Her best friend seems the most likely to me."

"What? Why?"

Her face told me I was stupid. "I talked to all the parents, Ethan. Katy's mom already has this girl convicted. She's carried a torch all these years. They had a huge blowout, and Tango may very likely never speak to her again. We know she can pull off a massive deception."

Wow. Put like that, it didn't sound good.

"If not her," she continued, "then the texts and car are a coincidence unless it's you. Next is the ex-boyfriend, who wouldn't have sent the texts or done the car." She made a funny noise in her throat. "After him is the entire group that assaulted you. . . and all of their friends or family members."

"Really?"

"Katy's the eyewitness who's likely to put those good ol' boys behind bars for a long time. Retaliation is a powerful motive."

"That's why the football players were in the police station," I said.

She stared at the tablet. "How well do you know the kids on the dance team?"

"I've only been here a few weeks," I admitted. "I don't see Juicy, Farmer-C or K-pop doing this, though."

"How *certain* are you?"

"I guess I'm not *certain*. . . but I'd bet the farm on it."

"And the other three?"

Lots of shrugging and shaking of my head. "I don't know them at all."

She thought about it. "I need to talk to everyone in that group. Would they talk to me?"

"More likely than they'd talk to me."

She handed me a cell. "From your dad." She gathered her things. "Hopefully they're more interested in helping Katy than in holding a grudge."

Amen to that.

How the hell did Fox land Tamara Taylor for a fairy fucking godmother?

As we drove, I sent a text: *dance cru @ studio. now. pls. Fxtrt.*

My phone didn't buzz once, but the studio was already bustling when we arrived. They must've already congregated.

So. . . there we were. . . Awk-ward.

Everyone shouted at me at the same time.

"Shut up," Ms. D yelled. "We all know Ethan's a piece of shit. Fine. Can we please move past that and try to help your friend?"

Murmurs of confusion told her some of them weren't sure who Ethan was. She rolled her eyes and pointed at me. "Foxtrot," she amended. "Man, you people are obsessive about nicknames." Hands in her pockets, she surveyed everyone there. "I'm Ethan's attorney, and I'm the best shot any of you have at staying out of jail and God help you all. Call me Saundra."

Now they were interested. While she spoke, I checked out the room. Not everyone was there.

"As we speak, my interns are compiling a class action suit on behalf of everyone you know for wrongful imprisonment, mental anguish and anything else they can make up a Latin name for."

Ephraim and Woody were missing, and we were short one girl. Mono, who was usually almost invisible, anyway.

"It's mostly meant to scare Officer Warren and his little friend and to keep them scurrying around chasing their tails while the twenty-four hours runs out and the real police can step in. We're going to e-mail a preliminary draft to get their attention." She looked at me. "They *have* internet out here, right?"

"Is she serious?" Juicy muttered.

"Of course, they do," I said.

No one would look at me. Cosita's elaborate shoulder shrug and turn made it obvious she was keeping her back to me on purpose.

"I see Ethan's father didn't exaggerate everyone's current disdain for his son," Saundra said. "Please understand I don't give a shit what you think about *him* right now. I'm here to help find this girl and her kidnapper."

"You can do that?" Taco asked.

She waved him off. "I'm not a cop, but I'm hoping to piece something together by the time the state police are involved." She looked at her tablet. "Which one of you is Gertrude?"

Snickers.

"My friends call me Juicy."

"So I've heard." Saundra pointed from Juicy to me. "You and Ethan are going to be suspects number one and two, with you at the top."

The crowd murmured and Juicy shrank. Cosita threw an arm around her. Hmm?

"The two of you are the only ones with a motive for the prior stalking." Saundra looked Juicy straight in the eye. "You actually *were* a secret admirer and have a history of lying. Also, the keys Ethan found had the Juicy Couture key tag." She stepped closer. "Could've been a gift to Katy from her best friend. Could *also* be that her best friend had a key to her mother's car. Katy was in the trunk and you left the engine running while you went into the studio to clean up after a struggle. When Ethan blundered in, you knocked him out, took Katy's keys from her purse and beat it."

Juicy turned pale. "You really think I could fucking do that?"

Saundra stared at her. "I don't know you well enough to have an opinion. But Ethan tells me you wouldn't."

Juicy looked my way, gratitude written across her face.

The lawyer towered over her. "The problem is you *look* guilty." She moved away. "I don't buy the football player theory, either. If this was just revenge, there are a lot of ways to get even with someone without committing a felony. Those guys had enough control to keep from killing Ethan. Why suddenly go postal before it even goes to trial?" She leaned against the barre. "Frankly, it could be any of you."

Murmurs ran through the group. Crap, that had come from out of the blue. I'd missed my chance to read anyone's reaction.

Saundra's sly smile told me she hadn't missed out. "I'm convinced the 'sick little twist' who trashed her car is the one who has her now."

Ring tones and vibrators went off across the room.

What the hell? Everyone grabbed their cells, including me.

I had a text. From the looks on everyone's faces, we all did. Mine read: *not evn clos*

K-pop said, "Not even close?"

For two seconds, everyone froze, then a flurry of fingers typed in a variation on: *who r u?*

One cell vibrated: mine.

Everyone looked at me.

I opened the message and read it out loud: "The sick little twist."

They crowded around me to get a look.

"Did he hear me?" Saundra asked the air.

My cell vibrated: *how do u no i'm a he?*

Murmured cursing surrounded me as the crew read the text on my cell.

Saundra shoved everyone away. "Read the texts out loud, Ethan. I hate that impoverished spelling shit." She looked around the room. "You can hear us?"

"Yep," I read off my cell.

Everyone looked around.

"The place must be bugged," K-pop offered.

Bngo, the txt on my cell began.

"Bingo," I read out loud. "Naughty, naughty boys and girls."

At least I wasn't the only one embarrassed. Apparently, most members of the crew had spent time in there doing more than dance.

Saundra took control again. "All right. All right. I don't care how many of you did the horizontal mambo in the studio." She addressed her questions to me as if I were the one on the other end of the texts. "You know where Katy is?"

"Yes," I read.

"Do you have her?"

"No."

"Did you see who took her?"

"Please tell me there aren't cameras, too," Farmer-C whispered.

"No. No cameras," I read. "Lol." K-pop and I exchanged a glance. Where was Woody?

Saundra glared at Farmer-C but spoke to the sick little twist on the other end of my cell. "But you heard something?"

"I hear everything," I read.

I had to ask my own question to the air up there: "Is she hurt?"

"No," I read. Thank God for that. "At least not when she was taken." What?

"Where is she?" Saundra asked.

The text read: *someplace safe*

"What the fuck?" I shouted. "Someplace *safe*? How the hell can she be *safe* if she was *abducted*?"

I read the screen and uttered another string of profanity.

"What'd he say?" Saundra asked.

"What an interesting question."

"This is a game to you?" Juicy called out. "Tango's been fucking abducted, and it's a *game* to you?"

"Okay, that's it," Saundra cut in harshly. "I am the only one to talk to this person. You're only going to make things worse."

My cell vibrated. "This person?" I read. "What happened to Sick Little Twist?"

"Oh, that is still on the table," Saundra admitted. "What do you want?"

"One date."

That brought a lot more noise until Saundra threatened to kick us out of the studio. "You want one date with Katy as payment for telling us where she is?"

"Guarantee it," I read. My spidey sense tingled.

"I can't guarantee anything," she said too fast for me to stop her. "It's up to Katy. I'll pass the request along. . ."

"No guarantee, no Katy," I read. I looked Saundra in the eye and mouthed the word, "Please?"

After a moment, she nodded.

"Look, Twist." I hoped that giving the sick little twist a nickname would endear him/her. "I will personally tell Katy you were the one to save her, and I will do everything I can to persuade her to go on that date with you."

Time passed.

The bell on the door rang and everyone jumped a mile. Shilling shrieked.

The girl in the doorway froze. It was Mono. K-pop ran over to her while we all fought to catch our breath and dry the pee running down our collective legs.

A message popped up on my screen: *fuk u fox. Ur a manpultiv bstrd.*

Fuck. I took a deep breath and only barely avoided throwing Dad's cell across the room. I read the message out loud.

Farmer-C's cell vibrated. His face turned bright red and he shot me a dark look.

"What's it say, Corey?" Saundra asked.

He stared me straight in the eye. "How about you, retard. You wanna try?"

I could only hope that my face expressed my self-loathing.

He waited for Saundra's permission before speaking. "Look, dude. . ." He glanced down at the vibrating cell and rolled his eyes. "Or *dudette*. You trashed her car. I can't make any promises. I'll do what I can, but what planet do you come from that you think—" He stopped when his cell vibrated again.

Saundra stepped closer. "What's it say?"

"Try," he read.

He shrugged. "I'll try."

He looked down at the cell.

"For a try," he read, "I'll give you a clue. 9-1-1."

"What's that mean?" Saundra asked.

Farmer-C stared at his cell but nothing happened.

"What do you mean?" the lawyer asked again, louder this time.

Time passed.

The crew fidgeted and muttered, but she waved them into silence.

When nothing seemed likely to happen, she headed for the door and encouraged us all to follow. While she walked, she placed a call. Outside, she led us far from the studio door.

Everything about her mannerisms changed. She stopped under a streetlight, one hand on her hip. "Sebastian Cawley," she drawled in a thick, Southern Belle accent. Her free hand drifted up to her collarbone as if she were touching a string of pearls. "As I live and breathe, however are you doing?"

We surrounded her in silence, and I, for one, was amazed at the transformation.

K-pop nudged me and asked me with his face if I'd ever seen this act before. I shook my head. This character was new to me. At least, I wasn't such a pariah he wouldn't touch me.

"Well, I'm doing just fine, Sebastian. I'm out here in Doo-mahs, Texas, and I need you to see if there were any 9-1-1 calls placed near here. We have a sweet little girl missing, and I do believe she may have placed a call."

She listened for a second and her face changed to stern and cold. She held up a finger, obviously warning us not to react to what she was about to say. Her voice never changed though. "Well, you know how folks are out here in the sticks, Sebastian, bless their simple little hearts. If we wait for the locals to figure this out, the poor thing'll die of old age." She listened. "Mm-hm." More listening. She smiled. "That's all I can ask, sweetness. Thank you ever so much and please do call me as soon as you know something. Buh-bye."

She ended the call and was greeted with a smattering of applause.

"We know one thing at least," she declared. "It's not anyone here."

"How can you be sure?" Juicy asked.

"Well, none of you can be the stalker anymore, obviously," she said. "And when the sick little twist revealed he knew who it was, you all reacted exactly the same, and I *know* none of you can act as well as I do."

Which narrowed it down to any of a couple thousand residents I'd never met. I still had my money on the mailman. Although Ephraim and Woody hadn't shown, yet, either.

"Do you have a way to find the bugs in the studio, ma'am?" Farmer-C asked.

She shook her head and scrolled through her cell. "What do I look like? *CSI: Dumass?*"

"It's pronounced *Doo-mahs*," Juicy muttered. Cosita put an arm around her shoulders. Maybe Juicy wasn't as alone as she'd thought?

"Sure it is, sweetie." Saundra tapped the cell and held it up to her ear. "I do have a guy who can do that sort of thing. Don't try it yourselves. Depending on what kind of bugs they are my guy may be able to trace them to Sick Little Twist. Max, sweetie, how *are* you?" Instantly Rastafarian, she gave her full attention to her cell and walked away. How many women was she, and how did she keep track of them all?

Turning around, I faced the dance crew. They stared at me, and I couldn't tell what any of them thought. I was so worried about Tango and guilty because of my own stupidity I didn't have a thing to say.

Fortunately, I didn't need to.

Juicy was the first to wrap her arms around me. "Thanks for telling the scary lawyer lady you knew it wasn't me." She squeezed me. "I'm pretty sure she wanted to throw me under the bus to save your ass."

I held her tight and choked out a laugh. One by one, the rest of the team joined us in a great big group hug. Thank God. Seriously.

"Looks like you're officially part of the crew, Foxtrot." K-pop reached over Shilling and held the back of my neck. He pressed his forehead to mine. "It's not official until you do something totally boneheaded and stupid to piss us off, hai?"

Everyone chuckled.

As grateful and relieved as I was for the gesture and the sentiments, they fell a little flat when the crew released me. Farmer-C wasn't a part of the huddle. He stood a few feet away with his hands in his pockets.

He nodded to the side, indicating I should follow him.

We walked around a corner and into the alley before he stopped and turned to me. He stared at me before speaking. "Don't ever call me that again." His voice was low and shaky with emotion, but I wasn't sure what the emotion was.

My stomach churned. "Never."

"I mean it."

"Me, too."

"Once is a bonehead accident. Twice says you think it's true."

I nodded. "Understood."

A single tear slid down his cheek. "I'm really scared. I know Tango dumped me, but I still really love her." He had to stop to swallow. "Really, *really* love her." He swallowed again. "And you're the only one. . . who doesn't laugh at me. . ." He had to take a breath. "Who doesn't laugh at me. . ."

I was the only one who didn't laugh at him when he cried. Jesus. I closed the distance between us and opened my arms. He held me tight and wept silently into my shoulder so no one around the corner would hear him.

When we finally rejoined the group, Ephraim had appeared.

"Where's Woody?" K-pop asked him.

Ephraim was the crowned king of scoffing. "Bitch didn't pick me up. Do you have any idea how much guilt a Jewish mother can lay down when you ask her for a ride at the last minute?" He looked around with disdain. "No, I don't suppose you do."

"You don't have your own car?" I asked, trying to make conversation.

The disgust on his face nearly crushed me. "You assume I'm rich because I'm Jewish? Wow. You are so fucking racist."

Picture me standing there with my mouth open, utterly unable to speak.

Eighteen

Twist hugged himself in the middle of his living room, trembling in anger. He'd had to get Fox to help. Fox. The enemy.

But he couldn't take Katy on his own. He'd tried and failed. He'd found her in the one room in that stupid building where he didn't have a camera. The sight of her bound and gagged in the flesh had overwhelmed him with desire. He'd been taken by surprise. His face and his ego both held the bruises to prove it.

He wanted to steal her away. He deserved her. She was his. But he'd tried the direct approach and failed. Fox was sure to run in like some stupid hero. Someone would get shot, killed. Maybe both of them, both Fox and the son of a bitch who'd beat Twist to Katy. Ha! And then Twist would be there for her, to hold her, console her after her ordeal, after the death of her gay boyfriend. That's what would happen.

Twist moved into the bedroom and leaned his forehead on the shoulder of his favorite Katy, the one in lingerie. He inhaled the scent of the candles and forced himself to calm down. Soon. It would all be over soon. His two greatest enemies would die in a bloody gun battle and he would watch on his tablet, just outside, so he could run in after it was over and hold Katy in his arms, and she'd offer herself to him. Gratefully.

A-a-a-and thirty minutes later, we were still waiting for the 9-1-1 transcript.

While the hugs and goodwill meant I was off the complete pariah list, Tango was missing and a lot needed to be resolved. No one seemed quite ready for small talk.

So, Juicy. . . lesbian, eh? How's that working out for you? Any other crushes you've kept secret for a decade we should know about?

Then Woody drove up. Before he even left his car, Ephraim materialized at the door. Their conversation was low enough I couldn't understand a word, but the gist was clear. Ephraim was pissed at getting "stood up." Woody seemed to believe his reason quite valid. They both kind of freaked me out, truth to tell. And neither of them had been in the room when Twist texted us about Tango's kidnapping. So. . .

Ephraim grabbed Woody's shirt, but Woody easily broke his grip.

Okay. I started over to slow things down, but Saundra's text alert alerted her. Buzz, buzz.

Everyone froze.

In total, the transcript read:

Operator: 9-1-1. Please state the nature of your emergency.

Female (?): 9-1-1? There's someone here. Oh, God, who is it? Wait. . . you?

[Ringtone (?) in background.]

Female (?): Shit.

[Call disconnects.]

Operator: Hello? Hello?

[End of transcript.]

"What the hell?" No matter how long I stared at the screen, the words made no sense to me. I handed the cell to Saundra. "This came from Tango's cell?"

"Yep." Saundra handed her phone around.

"And no one noticed it at the time?" Juicy asked.

Saundra sat on a table and crossed her legs. "They thought it was a prank. She isn't officially a missing person, since she's an adult and Warren told the state everything was under control. 9-1-1 wasn't notified they should be looking for potential calls. Out here they get more pranks than real ones. Kids assume they can't be traced on a cell."

"We can?" Farmer-C asked.

Saundra glared at him.

He blushed. "Why is there a question mark after 'female'?"

"I don't know," Saundra admitted. "Probably a lot of interference. I'd have to hear the actual recording."

"Can we do that?" K-pop asked. All eyes turned to him. "Can we get the actual recording?"

"To what purpose?" Saundra regarded him.

K-pop turned sheepish.

"Dude?" I asked. "You can do the same with audio you do with video?"

From sheep to wolf. "There's a difference?"

I turned to Saundra. "He's amazing. I know we're just meddling kids, but no one else around here seems to give a shit. He might be able to figure something out from the recording."

She considered me, then looked at K-pop. "You have an iPad or something? I'm not letting you take anything away from here."

He vibrated with excitement. "I do. . . but my laptop's at home. All the really good apps are on the laptop."

She pointed at the door. "Go."

He looked at me hopefully. "To the Batcave?"

Juicy and Cosita snickered despite the seriousness of the situation.

I didn't want to leave. What if news came through? But what good was I at the studio, really? And I still owed him. Something about the snickers bothered me, too. I turned to Saundra. "Anything happens, call me?"

"On the red phone," she said.

I pointed at the door. "To the Batcave." Batman wouldn't use an exclamation point. I was definitely Batman. K-pop was Robin.

He led the way out to his 1990-something Honda Civic. Red, of course. Before my door was even closed, he announced: "She's not into me."

"What?"

"I know we have more important things to worry about, but, Cosita? She's not into me."

"How do you know?"

"She said, 'You're a cutie, K-pop, but I'm not into you.'"

That took a second to process. It didn't leave a lot of wiggle room for optimism. "I have absolutely no response for that," I admitted. "Sorry, dude."

"That's just it, Foxtrot. Not your fault." He pulled into his driveway. Yeah, already there. "Blurting that out was a bonehead maneuver, dude, but it didn't hurt my chances." He jumped out of the car and grinned at me over the roof. "It actually made me work up the balls to ask her out."

"Hai?" I followed him into the house.

"After the drama scene, she was crying. I talked to her." He nabbed the laptop from his room and we ran back to the car. "Figured I didn't have anything to lose." He stopped on his side of the car and regarded me across the shiny red roof. "I don't know you all that well yet, bro," he said, "but we've had a few Sam and Dean moments, hai? Not many people in a small town like this understand a freak like me. You do. So you get to screw up once in a while. No harm, no foul." He smiled. "Life isn't a championship. Ain't no judges or scorecards."

Wow. "Have you given any thought to the possibility it might not be *you* she isn't into, but guys in general?"

His eyes opened into exclamation points.

"She's been touching Juicy a *lot* since the big reveal."

He glanced around as he thought through the last hour or so, then he nodded. "Bro, I am going to whack off to that possibility for a month." His face lit up. "You think—"

"Straight guys are the only ones with that fantasy. Lesbians never, *ever* have it."

He raised an eyebrow. "And how would you know?"

"I've asked." I ducked into the car before he could tell if I was yanking his chain.

He slipped in beside me with a dorky grin, which made the whole excursion worth every second. Two minutes later, we dashed into the studio.

Everyone gathered around as he warmed up the laptop and uploaded the 9-1-1 MP3 from Saundra's cell. I tagged Woody and led him off to a corner. "Where were you?"

He shrugged away from my hand. "What the fuck? Are you my mom?"

Okay, I might have sounded a bit hostile. "Sorry." I watched his eyes. "Tango's stalker texted us. We're jumpy."

"Juicy brought me up to speed while you were gone."

Oh yeah. Shit. No element of surprise then. No way to tell if he was conning us.

The 911 call played, stealing my full attention. I hurried to K-pop's side. The reason for the gender confusion was obvious. Static filled the line and the voice sounded like a girl's voice, but there was something weird about it.

Juicy spoke up first. "That's not Tango."

K-pop played the call again.

"You're certain?" Saundra asked.

Juicy threw her a look. "Are you that old? I've been on the phone with that girl a million hours, tired, drunk, sick and *whatever*. That's *not* her."

"So some girl kidnapped her and made a fake 9-1-1 call from her phone?" I asked. "What for?"

"It's not a girl," K-pop declared. He fiddled with the computer.

Saundra leaned over his shoulder. "How can you be certain?"

"It's been pitched up."

Saundra gave him an annoyed glance he didn't notice. "Pretend for the moment that not all of us are tech savvy."

"The caller used something to make his voice sound higher, like a girl's." His fingers flew across the keyboard and touchpad. "You can get a gadget at Spencer's and hold it between your mouth and the phone. That's why it sounds distorted. It's a cheap one."

He hit a key. The message played again, but this time much lower. Definitely a man's voice. And the ring tone at the end. . .

"What the fuck?" I dropped to one knee, reached past K-pop and rewound the file to just before the end.

Four tones chimed before the file cut off, but Farmer-C and I sang the end of the phrase. It was the off-key, tempo-challenged Big Ben tune from the police station clock.

The voice was easy to recognize, too.

"Officer Friendly," I said.

"Warren?" Farmer-C asked.

The crew headed for the door.

Saundra stopped them with a piercing whistle. "This man is a cop and he has guns."

Farmer-C scoffed. "My *mom* has guns."

Saundra blocked the door. "This is Texas. I'm sure you *all* have guns. The point is making sure Katy is safe, right?" Everyone agreed. "So let's not go off half-cocked and get her killed."

The seriousness of the situation prevented anyone from cracking a joke about being "half-cocked."

"Let's think this through," I tossed out. "Warren placed a 9-1-1 call from Tango's phone inside the station. Why?"

"Why would he even kidnap her?" Juicy asked.

"None of it makes sense," I admitted. Another thought hit me. "How did Sick Little Twist know about the call?" Murmurs all around. "Does he have the station bugged, too?"

"Maybe. Who cares?" Farmer-C paced like a caged wolf. "We need to go see if Tango's there."

"And do what?" Saundra asked. "We were in that station. It was standing room only. How could she be there and none of us knew it?"

No one had an answer.

"Just because he made the 9-1-1 call there," she said, "doesn't mean she's there now."

I touched Farmer-C's shoulder. "I agree with her, bro. Right now, we have an advantage because he doesn't know we heard the call. We go charging in and he knows we're onto him."

"At least now we know why he's keeping the state out," Saundra said.

"But how the hell could she be there without anyone knowing it?" Juicy asked.

"The hole," Farmer-C said out of nowhere.

Everyone glanced at him and then went on with the discussion. To be honest, it happened every so often. Farmer-C said random shit sometimes that no one understood.

But something in his face made me pay attention. "Wait a minute. What hole?"

"Whenever one of the guys started mouthing off or we started fighting, Warren threatened to throw us in 'the hole'." He used exaggerated air quotes and rolled his eyes to show his obvious disdain for all things hole-y. "Solitary confinement." He pointed at me and Juicy. "He could've put one of y'all in there, but he didn't. Says to me it was already being used."

"I was in that interrogation room a long time," I said. "Warren could've been using it to interrogate other people." I turned to Saundra. "What do you think?"

She contemplated Farmer-C for several seconds before answering. "I bitched about you and the girls being held in rooms that were not meant as housing," she said. "He told me there weren't any other rooms."

"He lied." K-pop drew everyone's attention to his laptop. "These are the blueprints for the building." He pointed at the screen. "Here's the solitary confinement room."

"And how in holy hell did you hack that?" Saundra asked.

K-pop blushed. "Not all of us spend our computer time posting selfies on Facebook, ma'am."

She shook her head. "Why does this shit always happen in small towns?"

"It's all the alien cow mutilations," Woody explained. "*Nos hacen loco.*"

He seemed a bit too amused by the whole thing. Too casual. I drew him aside again.

He rolled his eyes but followed me. "Look, Foxtrot, I get that I missed the big group hug and everybody loves you now, but who died and made you king?"

I stopped. "What? I never claimed—"

"Then why are you here asking me questions? You think I was off somewhere texting y'all? You think I'm the guy who trashed Tango's car just because I was off getting laid instead of sitting here accomplishing nothing with the rest of you?"

"You were. . . oh." Well, that would explain why he seemed so relaxed.

"You want to see the used condom in the back of my car?" He had a pretty intense stare when he chose.

Deep breath. "Not really."

He stepped closer and lowered his voice. "You've been here in this town all of half an hour, okay?" Hostility poured off him. "But Corey's been a friend my whole life, and what you said to him? He may forgive you just like that—" He snapped his fingers. "But I'm only easy for the pretty girls. And the fact that you took Katy from him? I'm not so happy about that either." He drilled me with his eyes. "So you want someone to ask me questions? Have the hot lady lawyer do your dirty work." He turned away.

What a douche. I snatched his arm. "What about the cameras K-pop helped you buy?"

His head snapped back the same moment he yanked his arm away. His eyes narrowed as he studied my face. Then he sighed. "I thought K-pop was my friend, too." He pointed two fingers in my face. "*Chinko me dinga, pendejo.*"

Er, that's South Texan for "None of your business, bro."

Saundra had a plan: wait for the county or state to make their move when the clock ran down. Once they arrived, we would present the audio, let their experts adjust it, blah fucking blah. . . You ever drive through Texas? It's big as hell. Tango could be dead by the time the cops made it to Dumass.

I agreed wholeheartedly with her lame-ass plan, then, while she was talking to the state police in one of her extraordinary personas, I gathered the irresponsible teenagers on the other side of the parking lot.

"What we need is a *distraction*." Juicy pursed her lips in a way that reminded me of Tango. "And I think *I* can handle that department." Remember? She was his ex-girlfriend.

"I'm going in to see if she's there." I said it so directly no one questioned me.

"Me too." Farmer-C tried to sound just as direct, but folks kind of hemmed and hawed. "What? Am I too dumb to help? If things go bad, you'll need a strong guy."

Woody shot me a wicked glance.

I smacked Farmer-C's arm. "Dude, let go of the dumb baggage. You were the one who figured out where she might be. That makes you smarter than all of us." I think I shocked him. "Me and Farmer-C go in while Juicy does stuff to distract Warren, stuff that I *never* want to know about."

Juicy did a fist bump with Cosita. "You know *that's* right."

Ew in thirty-one flavors. I mean. . . Officer Friendly?

Just. . . ew.

Ew.

Saundra had her plan. We had ours.

A short time later Farmer-C, Juicy and I parked in the town square. We hurried to the side of the station and a little-known door Juicy had used to (la, la, la my fingers in my ears) when she dated Warren.

Everyone at the station was so intent on the front doors, we slipped unnoticed across the grass. Juicy went in first, then waved us through. Farmer-C and I waited in the entryway while she slunk around the corner, into the main office. Her voice carried to us. "Hey there, Officer Warren."

"Gertie?" Officer Friendly asked. "What are you. . . Hwup!"

Their silence told me they were kissing.

"What are. . .?" Warren asked. "Why are. . .?"

"Shut up, Warren," Juicy demanded. "Where's Pal?"

"Sent. . . him. . . off. . ."

"Good. . . I can't get your fly open. This belt's in the way."

Our cue was the loud and pronounced clunk of a gun belt hitting the desk followed by the sound of chairs pushed out of the way while bodies fell to the floor together.

Corey and I peered around the corner secret agent style, him above, me below.

He looked down at me.

I nodded and pointed with two fingers at the door leading to the cells.

He scuttled to it, while I crept to the desk where the belt lay.

On the opposite side of the desk, Juicy made more noise than necessary, muttering loudly to cover any noises from Farmer-C and me.

My fingers were inches from Warren's belt.

"What?" Juicy cried out.

I abandoned the belt and dropped to my ass, back against the desk between us.

Farmer-C jumped behind a potted tree that wouldn't hide him at all if Officer Friendly looked that way.

In the reflection of a glass door, I watched Warren's back as he rose to his knees, dragging Juicy with him. "What's going on, Gertie?"

She pulled his shirt out of his pants. "I'm trying to have sex with you."

"Well, yeah. . . but we broke up."

Even with her, he couldn't admit she'd dumped him. Pathetic.

She oozed closer and wrapped her arms around him. "I know, but all this police work you've been doing? Sexy." She kissed him. "I don't know. . . I just can't keep off you now."

"Yeah?" His tone said he bought it hook, line, sinker and net. "See, I *knew* you'd come around if I. . ." He kissed her. "Everyone'll see I deserve some respect around here once I solve this case."

Before I knew what I was doing, I was on my feet, fists up. He'd all but admitted he did it, that he'd kidnapped Tango, knocked me unconscious, thrown my friends in jail. . . and all to have a chance to play the big, bad cop.

Juicy's eyes opened wide. She waved a hand to move me along, but Warren noticed. "What are you doing?"

The wave turned into a flutter fanning her face. "Ai, chu make me *sumamente caliente*, War-r-ren."

The *telenovela* accent was so hokey, Farmer-C clamped a hand over his mouth. Juicy opened her blouse a button or two, then pushed Warren's shirt off his shoulders. "Chu look so. . . *macho*."

"Yeah?"

She flashed me a face that told me to get on with my job before she had to take one for the team. She nodded in the direction of the keys on the belt, on the table, turning the movement into a nuzzle against Warren's neck and drawing him to the floor.

Deep breath.

I nabbed the keys and Farmer-C led the way deeper into the building to a heavy door with a small sliding window in it.

What if she wasn't there?

I opened the slide.

Tango looked up, but she was blindfolded. She was also gagged and tied to a chair. I kept quiet, afraid that if she heard me and called out in relief, she'd blow our cover. Farmer-C pushed his face close to mine, and I wrapped my hand over his mouth to keep him quiet. Once he nodded understanding, I released him and started working keys into the lock.

"Come on, come on," he murmured.

I elbowed him and kept trying keys.

Success! We hurried to Tango's side. Her hands were tied behind her and her feet duct-taped to the chair legs. I wanted to slam a fist into Warren's face again and again.

I knelt beside her. "Don't make a sound. It's Foxtrot. You're safe."

She sucked in a quick breath that set her coughing.

I pulled the gag from her mouth.

Farmer-C knelt behind her and worked on the ropes. "I'm here, too, Katy. We won't let anything happen to you."

When I pulled the blindfold off, she blinked a lot and focused. She kissed me hard. "Where are we?"

"We're at the police station." I started on the tape around her ankles. "It was Officer Friendly trying to make himself important."

Anger replaced the confusion.

"We just need to get outside," I explained. "There's folks out front."

I'd just finished with her legs when she threw her arms around me and held me tight. "Thank you."

I brought us to our feet. Everything felt right again.

"You, too," she told Farmer-C.

Farmer-C's smile was wistful.

A string of loud Spanish interrupted the moment and startled me so much I didn't move when Juicy stumbled into the cell, cursing.

The door slammed with a loud, definitive crash.

The lock clanked home.

Shit.

No . . . really . . . *shit!*

Warren glared at us through the sliding window. Anger, fear and frustration waged war in his eyes. Kinda scary. "You shouldn't be here."

Seriously? *That* was his definitive one-liner?

Deep breath.

"Warren," I said, "there are a dozen people outside."

"But they're not in here!"

"My dad and Ms. Delacroix both know we're in here," I lied. "And they know why." I let him process that. "They heard the 9-1-1 call. They know it was you."

He disappeared from the window. "Shit." He reappeared. "You shouldn't *be* here."

Tango started to say something, but I grabbed her arm. The goal was to get him to open the door before he realized that four hostages might get him out of town.

"No matter how this plays out you're in trouble," I said, "But if you let us out of here and give yourself up, I personally guarantee that Ms. Delacroix will take your case. She got my dad off a murder charge."

He hesitated a moment, then he moved away again and cursed some more.

While he was gone, I turned to my friends. "Please let me handle this. More than one of us and we'll lose him."

They nodded. Unbelievably, they trusted me.

Warren reappeared. "Why would she help me?"

"She owes me one. Long story. She will take the case."

"I don't have the money for a fancy lawyer."

"She will take the case."

Warren tapped his fingers on the door, and his eyes darted from face to face. "This wasn't supposed to go this way," he said. "I wasn't going to hurt you, Katy. I figured I'd take you out to Corey's barn and then find you there myself. I'd be a hero."

"My barn?"

"No one'd believe it was *you*," Warren whined. "Once I knew who the *stalker* was, I figured it'd be easy to pin it on *that* piece of shit. There was no way anyone'd believe he didn't kidnap Katy, too."

"Wait. . . you know who the stalker is?" I asked.

"Du-u-uh." All I could see was his eyes, but they glowed with smarmy self-importance. "You think you're so damn smart, Fox, and you didn't figure it out?" He opened the cell door, probably so I could see his smug face. "It's Palatino."

Pal? No way. Everyone crowded around Warren. From the muttered curses, they were just as surprised.

"Pal?" Tango shook her head. "I know he had a crush on me back in junior high, but. . ."

"Still does, freaky little shit." Suddenly, Warren acted all cozy with us, as if he thought we'd forget about the assaults and abduction. "When he found out I had Katy here, he *freaked* out, started spouting all this bullshit about magic spells and tarot cards. Said he had me on video grabbing her at the studio." He shook his head. "I told him if he was spying, no one'd believe he wasn't the kidnapper, too. He'd better get his freaky ass out of town before I arrested him myself." He puffed himself up. "No one would seriously believe *I'd* do something like this."

"Warren?" Tango went nose to nose with him. "You *did* do it."

She decked him. Knocked him out with one punch.

That's my girl.

Son of a bitch! No one Died!

Nineteen

We were mobbed outside the station. Everyone had a million questions. We would've been in a lot of trouble for taking the law into our own hands if we hadn't, you know, saved the day. Oh, and if there were any cops around who weren't also criminals.

Tango extricated herself from her mother and pulled me aside. "I need to know what Twist has," she whispered. "If he had cameras in the studio. . . who knows what he has on me. I don't want dozens of cops and lawyers and God knows who else examining that."

Since the only two cops in town were both wanted by the law now, she was in luck. It'd be a while before anyone made it out to Dumass to start the investigation.

I gave her a squeeze, then reeled in Dad and Saundra. "You need to cover for us."

"Where are you going?" Saundra asked.

Staring directly at Dad, I lied. "We're going to the cemetery to pay our respects to my parents."

Without hesitation, he hugged me. Out loud, he said, "Tell them hello for me." Much more quietly, so only I would hear, he added, "You'll tell me when you're done."

As my way of saying thank you, I kissed his cheek. Dads eat that shit up. He handed me the keys to Auntie Mac's car.

Mrs. Tango's-Mom chased us halfway down the block shouting a string of profanity her daughter refused to translate. "I can't tell her where we're going," Tango said. "She's a big part of the reason I need to do this."

Twist watched his apartment from the bushes. Fox and his lousy Scooby gang pulled up, just as expected. Well, he'd taken the boxes of magic with him, thrown clothes around the bedroom to make it look like he'd left town, which was the most logical thing to do.

He wasn't beaten, though. He had a plan.

One more day. Wait for the state cops to arrive, the big fucking know-it-alls. With them in town, everyone would feel safe.

Right. Because pushover Pal would just turn tail and run.

Pfft. He wasn't Pal anymore. He was Twist.

Twist, aka Pal, wasn't home. Hard to say where he was. Halfway to Mexico most likely. Farmer-C and K-pop met Tango and me there in case he showed up. He was a little guy. How much trouble could he be?

The front drapes were open and the four of us peered inside. Twist's living room was boring. A bit tidy for a nineteen-year-old dude's place, but harmless enough. Not a lot of furniture. K-pop "let us in" far more easily than I'd have expected.

Then Tango found Twist's bedroom. "Oh, my God."

Farmer-C, K-pop and I poked around the corner and peeked in. "Holy fucking shit," we chorused.

Photos of her stared at us from every inch of the room. Mobiles hung from the ceiling, along with what looked like trash and junk. Clothes she'd thrown out were pinned to the walls with photos of her face poking out of the necks of the blouses. In one corner, he'd made a bouquet of what looked, at first glance, like a bunch of little inflated balloons on sticks.

Tango gasped. "Holy fuck!" She pushed the three of us forcefully out of the room.

"What's the big deal about a bunch of balloons?" K-pop asked.

"Those aren't balloons." Farmer-C's face turned bright crimson.

"What the?" Realization dawned and K-pop's eyes grew as big as those annoying pet photos. "No. . ." He punched Farmer-C in the arm. "Dude!"

"Bro." Farmer-C flicked his gaze my way far too obviously.

Seriously? Could this day get any worse?

"Don't touch anything," I called out to Tango. "Come here first, please."

"What?"

"Please?"

She appeared. I held out a sack of rubber gloves I'd bought on a quick stop at Walgreens. She took it. "Thanks." She retreated into the room.

"I was wondering why we stopped," K-pop said. "I figured. . . You know. . ." He glanced in Tango's direction and nudged me. "Hai?"

I glanced at Farmer-C and then gave K-pop my expression of absolute blankness.

He looked from Farmer-C to me. "Okay guys, tough love time." He grabbed each of us by the front of our shirt and pushed us together down the hall.

"I'm not going to spend the rest of my life walking on eggshells for you two." He glared at me. "Foxtrot, Farmer-C did the Macarena with Tango and you need to deal with it." He punched Farmer-C in the arm. "If Foxtrot and Tango haven't done the hokey pokey, yet, it's only a matter of time." He opened his arms to us both. "Either you're friends and you deal with it and let the rest of us get back to worrying about whether we'll *ever* have sex, or just stop speaking to each other now and make life simpler for us all."

"K-pop?" Tango called from the bedroom.

"Yes?"

"Can you pull a hard drive out of his computer?"

"As if I was playing with Legos." He moved closer to Farmer-C and me with his arms open again. Group hug? When he was close enough, he smacked us both upside the head. "Deal with it."

He turned on his heel and strode away.

Farmer-C and I avoided eye contact. This was not a conversation for which I had experience. Deep breath. "I really care about her, Farmer-C, but you're, like, my new best friend all of a sudden." New? More like first ever. "I've never really had friends before," I told him. "I kind of like it."

He stared at his feet.

"Is there any way I can have both?" I asked.

"There's a saying about this," he said quietly. "For bros."

"Yeah." I chuckled. "One of the reasons I respect you so much is you'd *never* say it."

He smirked, and believe it or not, it worked on him. "Now, you just *know* that's not true." He grabbed me in a head lock and gave me a friendly noogie.

Why does spell check claim "noogie" isn't a word? It's in the *Urban Dictionary*.

"Oh, dear God," Tango said, passing us, "would you lesbians just find a room and get it over with?"

"Tango." I pushed Farmer-C away and hugged her. "You get what you need?" Before she could be snarky, I kissed her.

Farmer-C would have to deal with it.

She sighed. "Yeah."

I kissed her forehead. "Any chance you'll tell us what we might do time for destroying?"

"Yeah," she said. "Y'all deserve that much."

There was video.

Lots of it.

Nothing she ever wanted on the net.

There was a list of places cameras needed to be killed.

Doctor's offices.

Locker rooms.

Bathrooms.

Sick Little Twist wasn't even close to strong enough. As a cop, he'd had access to the entire city. And it wasn't just Tango. There were other girls, too.

We exited the house and gathered behind the car.

"Tampering with evidence is a felony." I held up the hard drive. "Which is fine by me, I just want to make sure we all know what we're doing."

"Those girls don't want this shit paraded in front of the entire planet." Tango crossed her arms. "Us girls." She looked down. "Me."

"Can you send him to jail without it?" K-pop asked.

I shrugged. "Saundra will just have to find a way."

"Someone had to ask."

Katie nodded.

I threw the hard drive on the ground as hard as I could. Metal and plastic sprayed the concrete. "And that's just the start."

Tango took a tire iron to it next. When she was done with it, it was dead. She loaded a garbage bag full of stuff into the trunk of Auntie Mac's car. When I reached her side, she was shaking. I wrapped her in my arms and held her tight.

"I'm pissed off," she told me.

"I know."

"Okay, good," she said. "I just want to make sure y'all know I'm pissed off, and I'm not going to cry like a little girl or anything like that."

"Pissed off. Got it. What do you want to do?"

"Blow something up. . . or pound the shit out of someone." Everything about her energy was direct out of a chicks-kick-ass movie. "Seriously, guys. Don't you want to beat the shit out of someone?" She regarded us one at a time. "Farmer-C: Monika practically raped you and screwed up things between us. Foxtrot: those bastards made you their personal punching bag, not to mention everything else that's happened to you in the past few months." She hit herself in the chest. "My shit's obvious." She looked at K-pop. "You have anything to make you want to beat on someone?"

"If I answer that question, bad things will happen to me." He waved the attention away. "I'm here to support my friends. You tell me who to smack down, I'm here for you."

I instantly loved the guy.

Tango shouted at the sky. "What the fuck is it with this town all of a sudden?" Pacing seemed to help. "For eighteen years, it's the most boring place on the planet, then out of nowhere we get stalkers and violence and whores."

"Oh m-y-y," K-pop added.

I was really glad he said it, because I'd wanted to, but was way too afraid of what Tango would do to me if I did.

She shouted again.

"We need a lock-in," K-pop said.

"A what?"

"A lock-in," he repeated. "It's something we do when shit just sucks."

It went like this: Farmer-C and K-pop made the calls while I drove us to the studio. The sun was already setting, but we covered all the windows with shades obviously made for just such a purpose.

Tango changed the codes on the security system so even her mom couldn't barge in. "I'll sleep in her bed tonight and she'll forgive me. She knows how much I need this."

The crew arrived one by one and in pairs. Woody and Ephraim arrived together, earlier conflict apparently resolved. If only I could be so fortunate. I met them at the door. "I am a complete and total douchebag and I'm sincerely sorry for all my douche-y behavior to both of you."

They stared at me for a moment, then exchanged a glance and Woody pointed at the dance floor with his chin. Ephraim nodded and walked away, muttering, "Racist."

I sighed. Really?

Woody, though, actually chuckled. "That's just his way of saying hello." He leaned with his elbows on the bar. I joined him. "What you did for Tango, the chances you took?" He stared at me, but his eyes didn't burn through my soul. "That was pretty stand up." Was he actually making peace? "I still don't like you, but I'm willing to give you a chance for the sake of the crew. Just don't try to hug me, okay?"

I nodded. "I appreciate the chance."

He stared at his hands a moment. Dude had the whole "brooding" thing nailed. "Look. Those cameras?"

"You don't need—"

"Shut up and let me talk."

I shut up and let him talk.

He moved closer. "Have you mentioned them to anyone?"

I shook my head and forced myself to avoid explaining why K-pop had told me about them.

"Good. I get why K-pop told you about them. I talked to him. We're cool." He looked me square in the eye. "Please don't tell anyone about them and don't ask why I have them. K-pop can vouch that I'm not a peeping Tom. I told him everything. I don't want to tell you because I still don't trust you."

"I won't say a word. I won't ask K-pop. I trust you."

His eyes flicked back and forth while he studied my eyes one at a time. He nodded and left.

Deep breath. Good times.

Tango played more of her Middle Eastern downtempo stuff. Once the whole crew arrived, we made a circle in the middle of the dance floor. I'd been told what to expect. Kinda. The details were fuzzy.

"We ready to throw down?" Tango asked.

Everyone responded affirmatively.

"Y'all okay with Foxtrot joining us?"

I held my breath.

More affirmative responses. Some were even enthusiastic, which really helped.

She held up her cell. The music stopped.

"Okay, then." She tapped the screen. "Dance."

Music assaulted the room, music to rattle the bones of the white hairs who would dance there years later. Decades. The overhead lights cut out and the club lights came on. The world devolved into a chaos of flashing, strobing images and spitting lasers.

The crew danced through the space, slowly at first but filled with the promise of much, much more. I tried out the rhythm, not accustomed to simply moving without the benefit of patterns or choreography. In my old world, we gave it a name: freestyling, as if the name somehow captured it and tamed it. But the crew, my new friends, they just moved to the music and filled the space with their bodies and their emotion.

I threw down my material, but it was too choreographed. Too controlled.

Tango danced up to me. "It's like *tahn-go*. Just do what the music tells you, what your heart tells you."

She spun away from me as the music changed.

Farmer-C appeared in front of me.

He didn't touch me, but he challenged me, rocking from foot to foot. His whole body beat an aggressive rhythm I matched. Then I switched so I was on the opposite beat, and he grinned. We danced facing each other, circling. Then he was gone.

In a flash of light, K-pop was there. He grabbed my hands and threw me into some of the swing moves I'd taught him, but more aggressive, more angry. We danced faster than the music. It felt off beat at first: spin one way, then the other, roll in, roll out, spin again about three times. Then I stopped listening and just followed so I could keep up. He spun me faster and faster, and by the time he released me, I was starting to let go.

Then Juicy took my hands. She placed them on her hips and ground us low and slow, chest to chest, her hands on my shoulders to control me. She forced me away from the music and completely out of rhythm. Slower. . . slower. . . It drove me insane, dancing off time. She grinned as I fought to lead her back on time. She shook her head and kept control.

Damn it! How do you dance to music if you're not dancing *to* the music? The whole *point* is to let the music move you.

Oh.

It all made sense.

The music. The lights. The anger.

I stopped fighting Juicy. She smiled as the tension drained away from my body. She found the rhythm again and we just rocked to the beat. No patterns. No choreography. Just moving to the beat. She pulled away from me, but held my arms, keeping me from doing anything other than rocking to the rhythm. With the flashing lights and trance-inducing, hardcore music it felt like meditation.

She released me. "Be the music, Ethan," she said, and I only knew it because I could read her lips. I found the music. I found the beat. . . just the beat.

I closed my eyes and followed the music, felt it in my heart and my gut and my spleen. Was the music louder now? Clearer? It was as if I'd opened my ears and heard rhythms I'd never noticed before. The music moved me, pushed me around the floor, made me jump and spin. I bounced up and down like a pogo stick.

And then I felt it. I felt the anger at that dead guy's parents, at my dad for rolling over for them. I spun like a dervish around the floor. I wanted to pound on Warren and Twist. The music threw me into a handspring that landed me on my ass. I shadow boxed, I twisted, I shouted at the top of my lungs and raged against the machine.

All around me, my friends thrashed to the music. All different, but moving in perfect rhythm with the music that filled us. Alone. . . but together, and the music danced us all.

Twenty

He had one last chance. Endgame. All the cards were on the table. One final gamble to have Katy to himself and get rid of Fox at the same time. He checked his gear: a gun in his belt and another strapped to his ankle, two sets of handcuffs at his waist with a few more in the car. He had a cooler of Katy's favorite foods, a picnic blanket and a bottle of wine.

He climbed behind the wheel and grabbed his tablet. After a second thought, he dropped the tablet onto the seat. He knew exactly where all the pieces were on the board. It would be his game this time. His rules. His victory. Magic was all well and good, but even the old witch couldn't stop a bullet to her brain.

"Today is a good day to kill."

I woke up to the sound of someone gently rapping on my bedroom door. "Foxtrot?" Farmer-C stood in the doorway, knuckles touching the frame. He wore a sweaty t-shirt and shorts. He was so polite, I wanted to chuckle.

"Hey, Farmer-C. Come on in."

"Awesome." Grinning, he dropped onto the bed beside me. "Your dad's awesome."

I sat up and crossed my legs, wiping my hands across my face to wake up. "Yeah, he is." I scratched my head. "You were working out with him?"

"He's an awesome coach."

Apparently, today's program was brought to you by the word "awesome."

"You ready for sparring yet?" I asked.

"Dude!" He punched my shoulder. "Utterly." He examined me. "Are you?"

Things still hurt all over. "Maybe in a couple of days."

He nodded a lot. "Awesome." He glanced at my bathroom. "Look, I really need a shower before school, and. . ." He gave me his sheepish face. "Some of the guys work out before school." More sheepish. "I really don't want to see them right now."

I waved at the bathroom. "Towels are in the cupboard just inside the door. Don't use all the hot water."

"Awesome." He jumped up, kicked off his shoes and shucked his shirt. "Are you ever going to go to school?"

"Someday." I leaned against the pillows. "No today." He didn't quite get the online high school program. But it was a thought. Maybe I should go to real school, after all.

"You doing all right?" he asked.

"What?" I looked up.

He was testing the water with one hand, a foot on the edge of tub. The question seemed sincere, not just polite conversation, so I gave it some thought.

"Yeah, I am," I told him. "All things considered."

He grinned. "You were awesome last night." Once behind the curtain, he raised his voice more than necessary. "I never figured a ballroom guy could throw down like that."

"I guess I had a lot of demons to work out."

"Amen to that, bro."

Tango likely had more demons to work out than me.

I grabbed my cell and switched to the comfy chair that sat, once again, in its corner.

U up? I texted.

After a minute, my cell vibrated: *Yup*

How u doin?

She sent a .

I sent her a ☺.

Can u talk? I typed.

State trooper

Oh.

The shower stopped.

Call me after? I typed.

"How's she doing?" Farmer-C asked, drying off in the doorway.

"Still breathing," I said, looking up. "She's with the state troopers right now."

Farmer-C froze. "What?"

"Giving a statement. Not arrested."

Relief covered his face. "Oh. . . yeah. Duh." He went back to work with the towel.

I looked around for a gym bag. Saw none. "You have clean clothes?"

He sucked in a quick breath. "Bag's in the garage."

I tossed him a pair of sweatpants. "Wear these. We don't have much of a dress code around here, but I don't want you giving Auntie Mac a heart attack." His grin made me hold up a hand. "She's my aunt, dude. No jokes."

He laughed, climbed into the sweats and ran out the door.

My cell rang. "Tango. How was it?"

She sighed. "They were nice about everything. They're on their way to your place, now."

"Crap. I need a shower."

"I figured. Your boyfriend there?"

I laughed. "Yeah, he was working out with Dad."

"Foxtrot?"

"Yeah?"

There was a long pause before she spoke. "Thanks." I could tell she wasn't done. "I never really said thanks last night, and not just for rescuing me. . . but for helping me. . . with the other stuff, too." She meant with the felony of destroying evidence.

"I'd say 'any time,' but I really hope there's never another time for something like that."

"Amen to that. Now go take a shower before the troopers get there." She chuckled. "And close the bathroom door if you don't want your boyfriend standing there talking to you the whole time."

I laughed. "I'll call you as soon as they're gone. You going to school?"

"Not today."

"Wanna get together?"

"Absolutely."

My shower lasted three minutes at most. As I was pulling on my shirt, Farmer-C poked his head around the corner. "Troopers are here, bro. You want I should stay or go?"

My first impulse was to tell him to go, because that's what I would've done most of my life. "Stay."

He smiled.

The meeting with the troopers was standard. We sat around the living room while they asked a bunch of questions. Saundra was in attendance, and the cops were obviously worried about massive unending lawsuits since the entire acting police force of the town, both of them, had gone rogue and committed dozens of felonies against me. Saundra made sure I stayed vague while I considered my options. I wasn't inclined to sue. It wasn't the city's fault. Saundra saw dollar signs.

My cell vibrated with a text from a blocked number: *I wud have gttn away w/ it if it wsn't fr u meddling kids*

My breath caught in my throat. It could only be one person, and he had to know the cops were there. Saundra was hassling the troopers, so I typed back: *Twst?*

U still o me a date w/ tango

What the hell? I looked around. Everyone was staring at me.

The cell vibrated again. *Tell them its me n someone dies*

Fuck.

"I'm really sorry, but I need to take this." I pointed at Farmer-C. "Can you ask him questions for a minute?" When a trooper opened his mouth to speak, I lied. "It's Tango. . . she's really upset. I'm afraid to put her off."

Nods and reassurances let me escape down the hall to the kitchen.

Wht th hell? I typed, standing at the kitchen sink.

U said u'd get me a date w/ her

Tried my best

"Try harder." That wasn't on the cell. Someone said it out loud behind me.

I froze. The reflection in the window above the sink showed me a skinny, acne-scarred face with an arm extended in my direction. "Hey there, Foxtrot," Twist said. "I'd turn around slowly, and I wouldn't try to get anyone to help because, unlike Officer Friendly, I know how to aim."

"What are you doing here?" How'd he know my nickname for Warren?

"I still want my date with Tango," he said as if I was simple. "And you're going to help me get it." When I didn't respond, he smiled. "You're going to walk out the back door right now, or I shoot you in the head."

Would he? Hard to say. He was a Sick Little Twist. I'd seen enough of his shrine to figure that out. In theory, he could shoot me, go out the door and disappear by the time the troopers got up and moving.

He waved the gun toward the door. "Okay, you've done the math. Move."

I moved.

"Leave the phone on the counter."

Shit. No GPS for me.

We walked out past the pool and through the gate that led to the alley where his car waited, rear door open and engine running. All the neighbors had privacy fences, so no one could possibly see us. He shoved me against the car and quickly cuffed me before tossing me into the back seat. As soon as I was down, he cuffed my ankles as well. It happened so fast, I couldn't do anything to stop him.

In moments, the car roared to life and carried me away.

My mind raced.

"Stay down," he warned me.

"Or what?"

"Or I shoot you in the head and drive out of town, change cars at a truck stop and cross the border into Mexico."

I stayed down.

We rode in silence for a few minutes.

"So you use me to force Tango to meet you," I said. "Then what?"

He didn't reply, which told me he was smart as well as twisted, which was even scarier. Damn it, the whole Barney Fife thing must've been an act.

Deep breath.

I rolled onto my side so I could at least see out the tops of the windows. Maybe signs or trees would tell me where we were headed.

"We're going to Farmer-C's farm," he told me. "So feel free to relax and enjoy the ride."

"Farmer-C's farm?"

"That's where Warren was going to take Katy," he said. "I like the symmetry."

"And it's out in the middle of nowhere."

He scoffed. "Everywhere's the middle of nowhere out here."

We rode the rest of the way in silence. Twenty minutes later, he parked in Farmer-C's horse barn. He opened the door nearest me. "Get out."

"I'm kinda handcuffed hand and foot."

"You're the fucking dance champ, douchebag. You should have good balance."

So I wriggled out of the car and carefully rose to my feet. I leaned against the car. "Now what?"

He grinned. "Now we make things interesting."

The gun moved so fast it was a nightmare.

Bang! It felt like a baseball bat hit my thigh.

I stumbled and fell onto my face on the straw-covered floor.

He shot me!

He fucking *shot* me!

A cell hit the ground near my head. A moment later, I felt him messing with my wrists and the handcuffs fell away.

Gunshots really fucking hurt. "What the shit?" It was hard to think.

"Call Katy and tell her to come here to meet me," he said calmly. "If she isn't quick, you bleed to death. If she brings help, I shoot you in the head while they're a half mile away. Feel free to play hero and offer to bleed out, which might be fun to watch. I can videotape your death, desecrate your body in ways that would've made Dahmer sick and then make sure she knows I'll do the same thing to the next person I kidnap. Juicy? K-pop? Her Mom?"

I lay on the ground, breathing straw and bleeding, wracking my brain to find some way this didn't end in utter tragedy for all of us. Nothing.

"Make the call."

I made the call.

"Hello?" Tango asked.

"It's me."

"What the hell? Your dad just called—"

"Tango, listen to me."

"Oh, now all of a sudden—"

"Twist just shot me."

Silence.

"I can tell her where I am?" I asked Twist.

He was silent for moment.

"Not much chance of her coming here if I don't."

He crouched beside me. "Make sure she's alone."

"Tango? You alone?"

Silence.

"You still there?" I asked, wondering how bad off she was.

"I'm here. I'm alone."

It was a lie.

I didn't care. "He wants a date with you."

"I have chicken parmesan and merlot," Twist threw in. "And put it on speaker."

I obeyed. I almost told him you can't do red wine with chicken, but that was probably the least important faux pas he would commit that day. "He has chicken parmesan and wine."

"With whole grain pasta."

My face must have informed him just how much his comment made me want to kill him.

He waved the gun. "Whole grains are important to her."

Her voice, when she spoke, sounded much stronger than I'd expected. "I have dinner with him, we get to leave and he goes away forever. Like Mexico forever?"

I'd sort of hoped she'd play him more, but what the hell. I looked up at Twist.

The gun dangled between his knees and his fingers tapped it in distraction. "I want her to go with me."

"To Mexico?"

He nodded.

"Dude, I promised you one date."

"I don't care. I want her to promise she'll go to Mexico with me."

Okay, this conversation was going from Tarantino to Fellini.

A gunshot echoed throughout the barn. My breath caught in my throat, but there was no pain. Twist's eyes went big and the gun fell from his hands.

Instinctively, I grabbed it and threw it as far away as I could.

"Foxtrot!" Tango's voice screamed from the cell. "Foxtrot!"

Twist fell to the ground beside me, and I scrambled away as best I could with hands and no feet.

I looked up.

A woman ran toward me, holding a shotgun. The sound of that gun chambering imbedded itself in my memory forever. The woman standing above me, with the business end of an enormous shotgun in my face, was Farmer-C's mom. "Foxtrot? What on Earth. . . Oh, my God, you've been shot!" She raised the shotgun's muzzle to the ceiling.

Tango shouted hysterically over the cell. "Ethan!"

I snatched up the phone, keeping my eyes on Twist, who had curled up in a ball, whimpering.

"Tango, I'm fine. I'm fine."

She sobbed. "You son of a bitch, why didn't you say so?"

"Shot in the leg, sweetie? Gun in my face?"

Mrs. Farmer-C's-Mom helped me move far away from Twist. "Is that Pal?" she asked. "He *shot* you?"

Tango was still talking, but I'm not sure what she said. To be honest, the world seemed a bit fuzzy.

Mrs. Farmer-C's-Mom took the cell. "Katy? Is that you?" She nabbed the keys from Twist's belt and freed my ankles. "Mmhm, well, I think that can be left to the past for now. I should probably get Foxtrot to stop bleeding so he doesn't die. Can you call the paramedics and the police. . .?" She regarded Twist's curled up form. "Oh, well, don't bother calling the police, I guess. Paramedics, though? And why not just bring everyone you know to the farm. Since the police seem to be worse than the criminals these days, we'll just handle this on our own." She was about to hang up but had a thought. "I have pies and ice cream. Just made the pies today."

She ended the call and dropped the cell. "You look like hell, boy."

I could not disagree.

"You really haven't seen our town at its best." She cinched her apron tight around my leg. "It's not all violent sociopaths and redneck beat downs."

She was awesome.

"I was inside cooking," she said, "when I heard a car crunching gravel up the drive. I came out to see who it was and heard the gunshot. Well, you know my first reaction was to load a handy shotgun so I could protect my own." Two things to notice there, right? "Handy shotgun" and she saw me as one of her own.

She looked around. "Now where'd that piece of shit get to?"

Twist was gone.

"What the hell?" She rushed to the rear door. "I shot him square."

A trail of blood led out of the barn.

He was nowhere to be found.

"Well, he won't be much to worry about tonight after the hole I put in him," she said. "Let's get you inside."

She helped me hobble to Farmer-C's room and onto the bed. "Now you just hold still while I get those jeans off you." She held up an enormous pair of sewing shears.

My hands came up. "Whoa, whoa, whoa there."

She raised an eyebrow at me. "Ethan Fox, I saw your father naked at more pool parties than I care to remember. I can handle seeing your boxers."

Not something I'd needed to know.

Also, not the issue. The jeans were DKNY and had cost almost two hundred bucks. A bullet hole would've just added to the badass quotient.

Maybe she'd sew them up for me?

Twenty-one

Twist stared at beams of dusty sunlight filtered through holes in the roof. He hadn't left the bed since a family of illegals found him and took him in. "La migra," he muttered from time to time to keep up the pretense he'd been shot by the border patrol while helping immigrants cross into Texas. "La migra." The mama kept him fed, and the daughter bathed him. The only thing they hadn't removed was the charm around his wrist meant to ensure that girls found him irresistible, fat lot of good it'd done him.

"You need to stay clean," the daughter told him with a mischievous smile, "or you will become infected." She drew up a bowl of hot water with a washcloth and tugged the sheets away. "Eres mi héroe."

Twist closed his eyes and saw Katy. The girl attending to his needs was lovely, but she wasn't Katy, could never be Katy. If only Katy would touch him that way, so tender, so sensuous. When he opened his eyes, she was Katy. Or maybe it was shock and blood loss. He'd lost a lot of blood. Too much?

He didn't know.

I lived. Obviously. The bullet didn't do any serious damage to my leg and Dad pushed me every day to get me in shape in time for the homecoming dance. I enrolled in Dumass High after all. Go Mules.

Officer Friendly went to jail, which also should not come as a great surprise.

Twist? Not really sure. Nothing in his car indicated what his plans might've been. Three weeks passed without a sign of him. Texas is a big fucking state and Dumass was a couple days' walk from the border. If we were lucky he'd bled out somewhere in the middle of the desert.

I didn't sue anyone.

The Dumass Rampaging Mules lost the homecoming game. Farmer-C did his best to amp up the second stringers who were suddenly the first string, but to no avail. Surprisingly, the entire town didn't hate me for it, and the new first string was stoked at their promotion.

Being the captain's buddy helped me, I suppose. Rescuing Tango and getting shot by Twist made me a bit of a local celebrity. My friends still called me Foxtrot, but to the rest of the town I became That Dance Guy, as in, "Oh, you're That Dance Guy, the one who helped save Tango."

From Ethan Fox, World Ten-Dance Champion. . . to That Dance Guy. Meh. I could live with it. After everything that'd happened, titles didn't seem so important.

The crew was set to debut the new routine at the homecoming dance the night the Mules got their asses kicked. It was a blend of Tango's choreo and mine with a section that was all Juicy.

The homecoming dance itself was more festive than I'd expected after a loss. Farmer-C did a great job of making the guys feel they'd held their own on their first game out. It was good to see him in his element, gave me a new level of respect for the goofball. He was good with his team. Seriously.

A salsa played, and he looked up at me with his big puppy dog eyes.

Tango and I were on the floor dancing at the time. She saw his look and laughed. "Oh, go ahead and dance with your Boyfriend." I heard the capital letter and laughed with her. I guess Corey would end up nicknamed Boyfriend after all, but with a much more ironic meaning.

So I held my hand out to him and he dashed over, reaching my side with a long, impressive slide. "Left foot in, right foot out," he whispered, grinning the whole time. He'd had a few more lessons and was picking it up pretty well. After the lock-in, I'd taught him to listen to the music the way he did when he was throwing bales of hay and he'd improved his rhythm tremendously.

"Sorry about the game," I told him.

He shrugged. "It's not about winning." He spun me. "Those new guys are awesome. . . and they're not going around beating the shit out of my friends." He leaned in close. "Okay, can you pretend I'm leading something really cool? I think Theresa Sanchez is checking me out."

I glanced at a pretty girl who was definitely watching.

"She's. . . *valedictorian*," he added with a lascivious chortle.

I snorted. He'd said "valedictorian" the way most guys would say, "She has really huge tits."

"Gotcha. Get ready to take my weight. Death drop."

He grinned. "Awesome."

I spun myself off to one side as if he'd led me there. Okay, try to picture it, I guess. It's called a roll-in. We stood side by side holding hands with arms fully stretched. I spun into him, wrapping myself up like a yo-yo. When I was tucked in close, he steadied me with his free hand.

"Lunge to your left," I whispered.

He lunged, and I leaned against him in a very swing pose.

"Here we go," I warned. I stepped across him, turned and let myself drop to the floor back first.

Everyone gasped when it looked as if I were about to crack my head, but Boyfriend caught my weight just in time, and my head stopped about a half-inch from the floor. Ordinarily, I can get myself back up, but he overbalanced me a bit and I *had* been shot in the leg, so I was kinda stuck there. "Bring me up, bro."

I'm going to guess I weigh less than a bale of hay. He yanked so hard, I shot up and caught air before landing lightly at his side, ignoring the flash of pain. . . just a couple of feet from Theresa.

The crowd went wild.

Still holding Boyfriend by one hand, I turned to Theresa. "Have you met my friend, Corey?" I offered her my free hand.

She smiled shyly and took it.

I passed her to Boyfriend, who gave me a big grin and punched me in the shoulder. I avoided rubbing my arm until after he'd turned away.

Guys: always remember that girls will overlook almost anything for a dude who can dance.

The music slowed and Tango found me. "That was pretty good for a guy who was laid out three times this month."

"Well, you've been *really* helping with the 'physical therapy'." I gave her my tacky eyebrow waggle.

She chuckled and punched me in the exact same spot as Boyfriend.

I managed to avoid wincing.

We did the boat. You know, typical slow dance hugging and swaying to the music. I always say if you're able to think enough to do fancy shit to a slow dance, you're obviously holding the wrong person. She felt perfect in my arms. Her body was warm against mine.

Deep breath. The good kind.

Boyfriend and Theresa boated nearby. He gave me a thumbs up.

I winked back.

Juicy and Cosita danced together, too, and I loved that no one hassled them. Seeing the two of them made me think of my dad, who was a chaperone. Where'd he get to?

He was dancing with Dr. Mike on the fringes of the floor. Most likely because they were chaperoning and not because they were both dudes. The happiness in Dad's face amazed me. Here he was, once again in his alma mater, finally celebrating at the homecoming dance he should've had over twenty years ago. I'd never seen him look at someone that way. He was utterly in love with Dr. Mike.

The way Mike stared into Dad's eyes, the feeling was mutual. Wow.

No, seriously. . . wow.

K-pop and Taco hovered by the food. K-pop watched Cosita with Juicy, and I hoped the surprise I'd planned for him would do some good.

Right on cue, the DJ announced the crew's performance.

We took our places at the end of the gym near the stage, and the crowd gave us room. The giant screen that'd cost me all my coaching money unrolled behind us from the ceiling. K-pop was understandably puzzled, especially when he saw that everyone else expected it.

As he took his place, I squeezed his shoulder and grinned. "This is for your own good, K-pop."

He raised an eyebrow. "What is?"

I patted the shoulder. "We're using your video for a backdrop."

His face turned whiter than usual and his eyes opened into total anime exclamation points.

"Dude, I'm telling you ahead of time so you don't freak out in the middle of the routine."

Some of the crew had wanted it to be a complete surprise, but Tango and I knew it'd be unfair to spring it on him that way.

"Your shit's sick wicked," I said. "The world deserves a chance to see it, hai?"

He didn't speak.

I grabbed both arms. "You gonna be okay?"

He looked around at the expectant faces of the crew and took a deep breath. "Hai."

"Hai." I gave his arms one last squeeze and moved into position.

Yep, I was dancing, too. The new pain meds were stellar.

I signaled the lighting crew.

The overhead fluorescents died and the spots flared up.

"Hit it!" I shouted at the top of my lungs.

We hit it.

The routine started with a jazzy section left over from the old way they danced, and the crowd settled in for the same old, same old. We did that for twenty seconds. . . then the music cut out for four beats while the entire crew screamed, "Five, six, seven, *eight!*"

The video flashed into life with a twenty-foot animated K-pop dancing behind us. The music screamed into the killer swango I'd given Tango for her birthday, in a K-pop-rendered mashup with a dubstep remix from one of the *Step Up*s.

The crew launched into a brand-new hip-hop sequence from my buddy in Houston.

The crowd practically came on the spot.

Tango and I performed a duet that earned spontaneous cheers.

K-pop, Farmer-C and I debuted the sparring material we'd lifted from my *Beast* video.

Juicy danced a solo for a few phrases where she finally let loose for the first time ever in her hometown, and the crowd went in-sane, but not nearly as wild as the moment Taco broke out his hip hop shtick. They went cra-*azy* for that.

By the way, the video of our performance went viral as: *retro hip hop dude goes cra-azy*. From that moment on, Taco's nickname was Retro.

It was, to quote one of my friends: "awesome." It wasn't the best choreo I'd ever danced, and I was still nursing bruised ribs and a gunshot leg, so I was off my game, but I'd never, *ever* experienced the euphoria I felt with those folks on that gym floor in tiny, little Dumass, Texas.

The routine ended.

The lights cut out.

The crowd exploded.

Well, not literally. I mean, with everything else that'd happened, who'd be surprised, right? They swarmed us, and it was hard to tell what impressed them more, the upgraded dance crew who'd never performed better or the amazing video backdrop. Everyone asked what movie we lifted the animation from and when they found out it was a K-pop original, they could *not* believe it.

Well, first we had to explain who K-pop was. Since he was so quiet, no one really knew him as anything other than That-Pop-And-Lock-Guy-On-The-Dance-Crew. Once we pointed him out, his new fans mobbed him.

However, the one girl in a Naruto t-shirt hesitated.

Okay, two shy people will *never* meet without the heavy hand of a true friend.

I snagged K-pop's arm. "Bro, I need to talk to you about—" I hauled him right into the girl. Bam!

"Oh wow," I said, "I am *so* sorry." I pointed at her t-shirt "Naruto?" I spoke in my horrible rendition of a fake, deep anime accent. "K-pop, she wears a Naruto t-shirt." I maneuvered him closer. "I have seen you wear Naruto underwear. You should show them to *her* some time, hai."

And off I dashed, back to Tango, who had seen me at work. "Do I need to start calling you Yenta, the matchmaker?"

I held her in my arms. Yeah, never going to stop mentioning how good that felt. "I just want my friends to be as happy as I am."

"So you have friends, now?" she asked, referring to our first dance session a lifetime ago, less than six weeks earlier.

"The best."

She kissed me. That was nice, too.

We danced some more.

We kissed some more.

A good time was had by all.

A couple of hours later, Dad and I lounged in the swimming pool with beers. A sign on the patio door read: "No aunts or sisters allowed."

I slugged my Shiner. "So. . . Dr. Mike, huh? Looking pretty serious. PDA and everything."

He splashed me. "We're hitting it off all right."

"I hear he has a nice couch in his office. Leather."

He raised an eyebrow. "Do you really want to go there?"

I thought about it. "I'm not sure. Maybe. In small doses." A beach ball floated past and I tossed it at him. "I mean, the jokes at the gym were one thing, you know? Ever since you dropped the bomb that you know I've been 'deflowered,' I've been thinking about that whole topic of conversation."

"And?" He tossed the beach ball at me.

So it was time to see where we stood.

"I really hated there was something we couldn't talk about." I let the beach ball drift and leaned against the side of the pool. "Everything in Austin was horrible enough as it was, but. . . you were my only friend then, and it was like I lost you the same time we lost everything else." I sipped beer. "I don't want that to happen again."

"You have other friends now."

I smiled. "I do, and it's cool. . . but you're my *dad*. I know you were trying to protect me from the shit you were going through, but it backfired. Hiding it from me just made everything worse."

Guilt wrote itself across his face.

"I get it," I told him. "I'm your kid, but I'm almost an adult now, too. I want you to be able to talk to me like an adult."

"I thought I did."

"Most of the time, yeah. But for six months, there was this huge thing we couldn't talk about because you thought I was too young to handle it." I shrugged. "Maybe I am. I don't know. I'd like to start trying. . . in small doses."

"Small doses, eh?" He grinned.

I prepared for the worst.

"So I shouldn't just haul off and tell you. . ."

Yeah. . . whatever he said, I blocked it forever from my memory.

I drank my beer. "Maybe we could start a little smaller than that."

His next response? Also eradicated.

"Well, you did bring Mike up," he told me.

"I thought that was your job."

He raised his beer bottle in salute. "Okay. . . that's a start."

So that thing we didn't talk about?

"I was the one who threw the punch, Ethan." He leaned against the side of the pool and took a swig of his beer. "I'll never really get past that." Another swig. "I ended his life before it'd begun. I get now it wasn't really my. . . fault, maybe. But he still died in my arms." He met my eyes. "And I wanted to fight it for your sake. I *did*." He looked at the water. "But I couldn't. They lost their son. I couldn't stop thinking how I'd feel if it'd been you who died. I wouldn't be able to work. Or *function*. I'd need that insurance money to get by."

I didn't say a word.

"But *now* I can't stop thinking about how I fucked everything up for you."

I started to speak but stopped myself.

He noticed. "It took me a while to figure out you were never mad at me about the accident. You were pissed I let them win." He took a deep breath. "I can't stop wondering what your life would be like this year. . ."

I wanted to tell him how much better my life was, but again kept my mouth shut.

"I even wondered if I should've let Mac have you to begin with." He sipped his beer. "If I should've let her take you when Megan died. . ."

"Why didn't you?" I whispered. We'd never talked about it.

"She was in the middle of a divorce." He shook his head in tiny movements. "She was already a wreck, and she took your mom's death really hard."

"There wasn't anyone else?"

We were so still the stars reflected in the water. He ran a hand across the surface and set the stars to dancing. "The truth?" He smiled. "You were this incredible, amazing thing. This. . . little guy." He looked at me. "You were only six months old, but you were already *you*. You were smart and you laughed and you were a sneaky little shit." He smiled. "I used to tell Karl, 'Look out for this one when he's a teenager. He's going to be smarter than you.'"

He looked me square in the eyes. "I took you because I wanted you, because I loved you from the day you were born, and I was convinced that I'd give you the best life anyone could." He spoke more quickly. "I took you away from here because it wasn't my home anymore and because I knew that's what Karl and Megan wanted for you, to have a better life than we'd had growing up." He looked away. "And I ruined it all by—"

"Dad. . ." I cupped my hands in the water and ran it over my face. Deep breath. "How many seventeen-year-old guys go swimming in the middle of the night and drink beer with their dad?" I chose my next words carefully. "I know my biological parents were great people, and I'm sure they'd have been great parents and maybe Auntie Mac or someone would've been fine, too. . . but I'll never know. . . and I don't care. I would never *ever* wish for anyone other than you for my dad. Please don't ever forget that."

He raised his bottle. "I am one lucky son of a bitch."

"Yes, you are." I clinked his bottle. "So am I."

Acknowledgements

A huge shout out to Ryan, Hope and the B-boys, Blake and Byron, for putting a roof over my head and adopting me into their family. Big kiss. Many thanks to my editor, Lauran Strait, who can spot the difference between an emdash and an endash at thirty paces. Any errors you find were not her fault but are the result of good advice foolishly rejected. Gratitude to Michael Khandelwal of the Muse writing center in Norfolk. Thanks for helping me into your workshops and for all the good advice. Thanks also to his many students and their valuable opinions. A massive *gracias* to the ladies of my morning critique group: Nancy, Jan, Mary, Donna, Lisa, Cecelia and Jean. Hugs to Candance, Glenn and Ramona for critiquing the entire thing. Extra hugs to Amber Dawn Bell for helping me work through the early stages of brainstorming. (I finally snuck a witch in there!) A special nod goes to Caren Bevil (C.L. Bevil) for her sage advice regarding mysteries and to Alma Katsu for taking time out of her busy schedule to read my story. A firm handshake to Jeff Andrews and Dawn Dowdle for time and advice. Kudos to the Hampton Roads Writers, a wonderful and welcoming organization. Go to their annual conference. It rocks. Fist bumps forever to Kevin Maurer for doing me a solid. And thanks to Sarah and Dan for being awesome.

Mrs. Barbara Roloff: you taught me that the writing of a sixteen-year-old freak is just as valuable as any classic. I can't thank you enough.

Finally, serious freakin' gratitude to my beta-testers.
Seriously. Thanks.
Without y'all, this book would be lame.

About the Author

John Robert Mack grew up in Wisconsin, fled the snow to Texas and has moved to Virginia on a writing sabbatical where he lives with his adopted family, including a pair of ginger nine-year-olds and a husky. Yikes. He taught dance full time for twenty years, published the short story "Jonny Hates Jazz" and self-published the inspirational book *KEEP BREATHING: Zen and the Art of Social Dance* long before self-pubbing was trendy. For two years, he wrote the column "Dancing the Rainbow" in the Texas periodical *Dancer's Guide*. He's been mentioned in several magazines and local news programs. He has written twelve novel manuscripts as well as six full length plays (one on commission) and ten screenplays. He hopes to see them all published/produced. He has also led workshops on creativity and self-publishing for the Hampton Road Writers and the Muse writers' lab. By the time you read this, John could be living just about anywhere. (Hint, as of 2019, the release of the special edition, he's back in San Antonio.)

For more info, visit: johnrobertmack.com.
Stalk him at: facebook.com/johnrobertmack.

Stretches
Step 1.5 in the Tango Triptych

John Robert Mack

Lucky Me

Seventeen years ago.

Lucius hated cemeteries. They were nothing more than hideously expensive monuments to human folly. He stared down into two perfectly rectangular holes and waited for the next wave of nausea to hit. Two piles of dirt lay off to one side. A backhoe kept watch.

"Mr. Fox! I'm so sorry we haven't had a chance to clear things away, yet." Sonny Montez's voice was easy to recognize. He seemed to have inherited both his father's business and his professional manners.

Lucius held up a hand. "You saw me puke out a burrito bare-ass naked after every homecoming game, Sonny. I think we can skip the 'mister.'"

"Sorry, Lucky. It's the business."

Lucius closed his eyes against that wave of nausea he'd been expecting. "No, Sonny, I'm the one should be sorry. You're just doing your job."

No one had called him Lucky since he'd escaped Dumass, Texas and gone off to Austin for college ten years earlier. Even his family had understood that he'd needed a change and stopped using the nickname.

His family.

Mom and Dad's year-old granite block stood a few feet away from where the new one would stand. All Lucius had left was his older sister, Macarena.

And Megan's baby, Ethan. His godson.

Lucius finally focused on his old friend. Wow. If he hadn't recognized the voice, he'd never have known who this man was. A decade after graduation and Sonny had lost all of his hair and most of his muscle. What he'd gained had to be, God, more than a hundred pounds.

The surprise must've shown. Sonny straightened the coat that strained against his protruding gut. "You look good, Lucky." He pointed at him. "Haven't changed a bit, you lucky dog." He glanced down at the twin holes. "Sorry about. . . I'm sorry."

Lucius swallowed hard to keep his lunch where it belonged. "Thanks for—" For what exactly? He couldn't say it out loud. "It must've been a bitch to get everything done so fast."

"I know you're trying to do everything from Austin, Lucky, and Barty owed me a favor. The stone'll be done lickety split." Everyone owed everyone a favor in a small town. "Megan was so young. Nothing could've been planned ahead of time."

"How's Sally?" Lucius asked abruptly.

"Ah, she's great, Lucky." The professional mode returned. It had its advantages. The change in subject didn't seem to give him whiplash.

"How many kids?"

"Three boys now and one girl who had her first birthday last week." He laughed. "We're hoping she'll take over Esme's studio, of course." Another shorter laugh. "And you? Some lucky girl must've stolen your heart out there. . . in the. . . big city."

For the first time in forty-eight hours, Lucius managed half a smile. "No, Sonny. No girls."

"Yeah, right. I mean. . . Jesus, Lucky, I'm sorry."

Lucius turned away from the twin holes where his sister and his best friend were going to be buried later that day. "Don't sweat it, Sonny." He patted his old teammate's shoulder as he passed. "I put this town behind me ten years ago. I'm impressed you even knew."

"Ah hell, Lucky. We were friends, right?"

"Sure were, Sonny." He hoped he'd make it to the car before he started bawling. "Good times."

"How can you possibly take care of a six-month-old baby, Lucius?" Macarena held Ethan and paced the living room, bouncing him so much it was a wonder the little guy's head didn't pop off. Such a tiny baby in the arms of a Valkyrie. He half-expected his sister to break out in operatic song.

"I assume the basics are the same as they've been for thousands of years." Would she ever stop bouncing him? "Put food in one end and clean shit off the other."

Well, it got her to stop pacing. She glared at him. "And how much experience do you have with either of those?"

"Not much, apart from a few visits."

"I've been the one here with him since he was born," she insisted.

Lucius couldn't bring himself to mention that the only reason Megan and Karl had stayed in Dumass was to help Mac deal with Mom and Dad's death a year ago. Otherwise *he'd* have been the one to see all of Ethan's firsts where they should have happened, in Austin.

Megan wouldn't have even had an apartment in Dumass. . .

Mac turned away and bounced Ethan again. "With your lifestyle, Lucius. Honestly, how would you take care of him?"

"My '*lifestyle*'?"

Mac stopped and turned to him with wide eyes. Oops, that must've been louder than he'd intended.

He took advantage of the pause to steal Ethan from his sister. Bright blue focused on Lucius' face. The boy seemed to remember his uncle. "Well, I *am* working pretty hard these days, but the gym'll let me set him up in a corner." He stared her down. "I know my apartment isn't as big as this place, but I keep it clean."

"Well, you know. . ." She straightened her skirt.

Lucius kissed the baby's forehead, and the little guy grabbed one of his uncle's ears. "No, Mac. Why don't you tell me which aspect of my 'lifestyle' renders me ineligible to raise my godson."

She blew out a heavy breath. "You're going to make me say it." She waved her hands. "The *gay* thing."

Huh. What was it about holding a baby that made a person *want* to bounce him a little? "I'm gay, Mac. I'm not a whore."

"Oh, come on, Lucius. I know what it's like in the big city."

"No, you don't." For the baby's sake, he modulated his voice as if he was telling the cutest, funniest joke on the planet. "You haven't once visited since I moved there. You never even visited Megan, so you have absolutely no idea what it's like."

Ethan gurgled.

"No, she doesn't, does she?" Lucius gave his head an exaggerated shake. "The mean old lady doesn't know *anything* about your Uncle Lucius *or* Austin, does she?"

The baby squealed.

"Now, that's uncalled for."

"But it's true." He turned to her.

Tears ran down her cheeks.

Damn it. "I'm sorry, Mac. The mean old lady part isn't true, and you're right. It was uncalled for."

She wiped her face.

"But you don't know anything about me, Mac. You really don't."

She was ten years older and had moved out of the house to get married by the time he was eight and Megan was six. She'd had her own life. As close as he and Megan had been, Mac had always looked down at them as if they were little kids.

Her eyes shown with tears. "The divorce is final next week."

Damn it again. He hadn't known.

She raised her chin. "Maybe you don't know anything about me either, Lucius."

He was bouncing the baby. He stopped. "Well, now I know *you're* certainly in no position to take care of him."

And no one would need to if Megan and Karl had returned to Austin after Mom and Dad's funeral. It was rude, but it was true.

Lucius sat in Megan's old bedroom. He held a pillow in both arms. It was soaked and rumpled from the hour he'd used it to stifle his sobs. His butt was sore from the hardwood floor. He leaned against the bed and stared up at the stars only barely visible on the ceiling.

He'd kept it together for the whole nightmare of a funeral, then escaped to the house and noticed the light on in Megan's old room. As soon as he flicked the light off, the stars had jumped into brilliant life.

Fuck.

The first sob caught him by surprise.

The stars had been a Christmas present for Megan a million years ago in a much happier time. "Should we find a star chart to make constellations?" he'd asked her.

"Oh no, Lucky. We can make up our own!"

Lucius rose to his knees and lit the bedside lamp so the stars would recharge. In the bright light, he regarded the stuffed animals who lived on her bed. Mom had never changed the rooms so the kids would always know they were welcome.

Mac had left everything, too. Technically, the house belonged to all three of them, but Mac was the one who lived there.

He tried to turn off the lamp, but his hands shook so much, he couldn't make the switch work. He turned it harder, and the lamp wobbled and crashed to the floor in pieces. As darkness enveloped him, the stars leapt to life.

He'd seen stars just like them in a head shop in Austin. With Karl. It was while they were roommates and shortly before Megan had started at UT. There was a black light room filled with glowing posters and toys.

"Hey! The stars are just like Megan's," Karl had said.

Lucius had elbowed his friend as a joke. "And what are you doing in Megan's bedroom in the dark, dude?"

Karl hadn't answered. He'd turned a very embarrassed red.

"Dude?"

That was how Lucius had discovered that his best friend and his sister were in love.

"Both dead and gone."

There. He'd said it.

He cried some more.

A lot more.

He woke up in the morning with the momentary panic that comes from regaining consciousness in unfamiliar surroundings. He was alone in the bed, which was a good sign. He wasn't a whore, but he wasn't a saint, either.

Oh yeah, he was in his old room in Dumass, Texas.

And Megan and Karl were dead.

Heaviness dropped onto his chest like a concrete block.

Ethan babbled across the hall. The sound was so happy, and the kid seemed to know what he was talking about. Lucius listened to the non-stop barrage. Man, that little guy liked the sound of his own voice.

The concrete block lifted.

Lucius pushed out of bed and padded through the open door and across the hall into the makeshift nursery. Ethan stood in the crib they'd borrowed, hanging onto the railing. As soon as he saw Lucius, he squealed and stamped his feet in a clumsy dance.

"Gonna be the next Kevin Bacon?" Lucius picked up the baby and held him close. He sniffed, too, but the kid seemed clean. Baby smell. It was a cliché, but it was true: something about baby smell told him all was right with the world. "Should we go downstairs and see what we have for you to eat?"

He stopped at the top step when he heard voices below. Decidedly unhappy voices. Well, *one* voice sounded unhappy. He stayed put while he considered whether he needed pants.

". . .the car, too, Ms. Davis," a male voice said. "They thought of everything."

Uh-oh. That was lawyer-speak. Probably had to do with the divorce.

"Both life insurance policies," the voice continued, "the renter's policy *and* the house in Austin. Everything. It's not like he's going to be rich or anything, especially with the baby, but he'll have plenty for at least the next couple of years while he adjusts to life as a father."

The baby wriggled in Lucius' arms and he relaxed his hold a little. He hadn't even thought about the insurance. He'd been so afraid he wouldn't be able to take care of Ethan the way he should. He made enough at a couple of boxing gyms for a single guy in a shitty apartment on the East side, but it would never be enough for a single dad.

But if he had a few years' worth of diapers and formula. . . maybe he could do it!

He stared into Ethan's bright eyes. He'd been in love with the kid since the minute he was born, all squishy and slimy and deformed. The baby patted Lucius' face and gabbled.

"Whose fucking lawyer are you, Milton?" Mac was obviously trying to keep her voice down and not succeeding very well. "You're here to find a way to *keep* him from taking that baby."

A cold vise squeezed Lucius' stomach. He couldn't breathe.

"I don't care about the house or the money," she insisted. "He can have all that, but I'm not letting him. . ." She lowered her voice. ". . .not letting him take that baby to a parade of orgies and naked men and. . ."

"And what, Ms. Davis?"

"What? Orgies and naked men aren't enough?"

Lucius lurched away from the stairs. His knees wobbled and he dropped into the chair outside his room.

"This is Texas, Milton." Her voice reached him. "If you can't keep a gay man from adopting a baby in *this* state, you should be disbarred."

"The will is very clear, Ms. Davis."

"Fuck the will. I answer to a higher authority."

He couldn't listen anymore. He brought Ethan to the nursery and settled him in the playpen. The keys to Megan's minivan lay on the changing table. The minivan had a car seat. Lucius' Fiat was too small to fit one.

Mac had never seemed judgmental. But then, she'd never been willing to talk about it, either. It was the card Megan had always played when she wanted to get rid of the older sister: "Say, Lucius, how's the new boyfriend?"

Suddenly, Mac had always had somewhere else to be. It'd never felt like a big deal before. . . before she'd hired a lawyer to rip Ethan out of his life.

Megan had done her homework. She'd known the battles he'd face, and she'd done what she needed to protect them. To protect Ethan.

Lucius dressed.

He threw his things into a duffle bag.

In Megan's old room, he stared down at a bed full of stuffed animals Megan hadn't touched in years. Now they were ruined. The whole house was ruined. Burn it down like the apartment that'd killed Megan and Karl. He wouldn't care.

He dropped the keys to his Fiat on the changing table and snatched the minivan keys. Karl had always called it the baby wagon. Lucius lifted Ethan and balanced him in one arm, hoisting the diaper bag and duffle onto the other shoulder.

"Da!" the boy laughed. "Da da da da da da da da!"

Ah, hell. Lucius's vision misted over. He dropped the bags on the floor and held the baby close. He pressed the little face to his own and had to swallow hard.

Ethan grabbed an ear and yanked on it.

It was a coincidence. Had to be. The kid was just making noises.

Lucius left the bags on the floor.

His stuff could be replaced.

Lucius hated cemeteries. Tacky fake grass carpeted the freshly filled graves. The backhoe was gone. A granite block had replaced it.

Beloved Wife and Mother.

Beloved Husband and Father.

"That's your mommy and daddy, Ethan," he said quietly. "They were about to come home to Austin. They moved to Dumass when your grandpa and grandma died last year." He sat in the grass and let the boy crawl around. "Your Auntie Mac was so upset they decided to stick around awhile after the funeral."

The baby patted the Astroturf and laughed and laughed.

Lucius ran a hand across the artificial grass. It *did* tickle.

Ethan made a break for it and Lucius scooped him up, then rolled onto his back and snuggled the boy against his chest. Ethan squealed in delight.

"Do you want to escape to Austin with your Uncle Lucius?" He kissed the boy. "I think we could live in your mommy and daddy's house."

Oh fuck. Could he even do that?

"Da, da, da, da, da. . ."

For Ethan, he would do whatever it took. Anything.

"You want to live in Austin with me?"

The boy babbled and furrowed his eyebrows as if he were giving a very serious answer. Lucius chuckled. Probably time to buy some diapers.

Lucius' butt vibrated, and he called out in surprise. The cellular phone in his pocket vibrated again and he pulled it out. He'd never get used to carrying a telephone around wherever he went. He recognized the number. Thank God for caller ID. "Saundra? You got my message?"

"I did, *Mr.* Fox." She seemed irritated. "And you know damn well I passed the bar. I was first in my class as well, since you forgot to ask."

"I know, I know. Sorry. Just trying to make a joke." He carried Ethan to the baby wagon.

She sighed. "Okay, I'll grant you a stay of execution this once. Extenuating circumstances."

Ethan giggled and tried to grab the phone.

"Uh-uh, baby," Lucius muttered. "I'm talking to someone."

"Oh, you did *not* pick up the phone in the middle of a—"

"Saundra," he interrupted. "Really?" He worked Ethan into the car seat with the phone cradled between ear and shoulder. Man, car seats were like Chinese puzzles!

"Who is that then?"

"He's the reason I need a good lawyer." He closed the door and climbed into the driver's seat. "I have Ethan."

"Megan's Ethan?"

How many Ethans were there? "Yes, Megan's Ethan."

Lucius watched the baby in the rearview mirror while giving Saundra time to process. She was the smartest person he knew. Even though she was a new lawyer, if anyone could figure out how to beat Mac's attorney and the Texas legal system, she would do it.

He waited some more.

Ethan chewed on his fingers.

"You mean it, Lucius? You've thought it through?"

He started the car and turned on the AC. "You know I almost stole him away the day he was born, Saundra."

She chuckled.

He glanced out the window at the fake, plastic grass. "Nothing has changed." He forced a lump out of his throat. "They put it in the will, Saundra. They made me beneficiary to the insurance policies and left me the house. They knew. . . they knew what it would take."

He glanced at his godson again. "Mac thinks I'm evil, Sandy. She thinks I'm going to—" He couldn't even say out loud what she likely thought he'd do. "If I don't get away now, she'll. . . she'll. . ." He forced himself to say it. "She'll steal him from me. I'll never see him again"

"Okay, Lucius. I'll start the research. You have money for me to pull in assistance if I need it?"

Ethan found his toes. One foot in each hand. From the huge grin on the baby's face, it was the most exciting thing he'd ever done.

"I don't care if it takes every penny. Do what you need to do."

"I'll try to leave you a nickel or two."

"Thanks, Saundra." He put the car in gear. "Look, I need to put the phone down so I can drive. I want to get out of here before Mac has me arrested for kidnapping. Sheriff Palatino would love to nail me for *something* before he retires."

"Kidnapping we don't need. Where are you?"

Lucius turned and squeezed one of Ethan's little feet before answering. "We're coming home, Saundra. We're coming home."

What a Girl Wants

Two years ago.

That slut from Houston was trying to sink her claws into Monika's dance partner. Yeah. That was so-o-o not going to happen. She stomped across the dance floor while the Houston slut laughed and gently touched Ethan's arm.

He bought it.

Did he not see that she was just sucking up to him because everyone knew her partner was about to dump her for Bailey Thompson, whom everyone knew as Kegels?

Three steps before she reached them, she slowed down and shook her hair out of her face. "Ethan, sweetie." She took his arm. "I think we're just about ready for warm-ups." She turned to the Houston slut. "Bailey's already warming up, from what I hear."

"What? She doesn't have a partner." The Houston slut's eyes opened wide.

And off she ran.

Mission accomplished.

Monika turned to Ethan. Crap. From the look on his smooth, little-boy face as she flounced away, he already had a hard-on for the bitch. Keeping him focused was harder since he'd hit puberty and the more likely it was that he'd discover sex. He was an amazing dance partner, but part of the arrangement that made it work was that they were partners first, last and always. Anything romantic would just cause problems.

But he was a guy.

And he was fifteen.

She knew fifteen-year-old guys. There were several in her home-school group she knew intimately. They were all pigs. Which made them easy to manipulate.

He smiled at her with his puppy-dog eyes. "She seems nice."

"For a fifteen-year-old with herpes," Monika said.

Ethan jumped.

"Seriously? That skank's the kind of girl you go for?" Monika had relied on the fact that Ethan seemed to be a "late bloomer." While he'd been mooning over Hilary Duff, Monika had already plowed more than one field with the home-school group.

"Herpes?"

"Oh, sweetie, that's the least of her problems." She steered him out of the main ballroom and into the side room where warm-ups happened. "Is that really the kind of girl you're into?"

Ethan jumped again. "What? No."

What a liar. All guys knew that if a girl had an STD that meant she was a sure thing. How the fuck was she going to deal with the fact that her dance partner had finally discovered girls? She didn't want to date him. God no. But he was a phenomenal dancer, focused more than most guys his age and, well, he had a penis and boys without dance partners were a helluva lot harder to find than girls.

Damn. She had to figure out how to keep him focused. If he started fucking some slut, he'd follow his dick and Monika would lose her shot at World's, maybe even Blackpool. Well, perhaps it was time to re-negotiate the arrangement.

She pulled Ethan onto the floor and took her place a few feet away to set up for their chacha. She glanced around at the other men on the floor, all of them much older and sexier than her partner. Suddenly, Ethan's rhinestones seemed a bit too gay. She caught his gaze.

He tried to smolder as his hips moved to the beat, but he was such a little boy.

Hm. Well, why not see what happened. She shook her shoulders as if something were wrong with the costume and adjusted her halter top, making a point of nearly pulling one tit out of its secure place.

Ethan's eyes opened wide for an instant before he regained control. She waited for a moment. And, yes, he had to adjust, as well. Okay, maybe this wouldn't be so hard, after all.

Well, maybe it would. But that was the point.

Monika stood at the edge of the floor with Patricia Harris, one of the least annoying and stupid girls on the circuit. "Barry," Pat said. "Look at his eyes."

The man in question was tall, dark and more muscular than the average ballroom dancer. His shirt was completely sheer. Monika looked at his eyes. While the man was sex on the dance floor, his eyes weren't, in fact, glued to his partner as they seemed to be. They were looking past her. "I know for a fact he took it up the ass last night from Viktor."

Pat gasped and laughed. "Really?" She stared at the object of their discussion. "You just can't tell these days."

No, but the fact that he was gay didn't stop him from making every female heart skip a beat. That look he gave his partner, whatever long Slavic name she had this month, he knew how to act, and he knew all about sexy, how to make someone want him. It wasn't who he thought about. . . it was that he had someone *to* think about.

"You're sure Ethan's still a virgin?"

"Please," Monika said. "He's a child."

The girls turned to watch him. He sat on a table, curled over his cell phone texting away and grinning like a five-year-old. "His father's his best friend," Monika elaborated. "If he's not with me he's pounding away on a boxing bag at that gym of theirs. He doesn't have time to pound anything else."

Pat stroked her chin in that annoying affectation of hers. "The smile on his face says he's texting a girl."

Monika chuckled. "He looks that way about Daddy. He's a—"

Ethan suddenly covered his mouth with one hand and turned beet red. He also adjusted his pants again. Damn. Could the stupid girl be right?

Without a word to Pat, Monika hurried over to Ethan, slowing down just as she reached his table. She grabbed the phone. "I haven't said hello to your father all weekend."

"That's not. . ."

Cute brunette. The name read "hotkiss." Monika's recovery only took one second. "Silly me," she said, holding the phone out to Ethan. "That's not your father." She smiled. "Sorry."

Ethan's face burned hot red. "No. . . that's this girl. . . in my math class. I was asking about today's test."

Monika held her hands behind her back and pushed her chest a bit tighter as if she were just stretching. "It's important to keep things like *grades* up." It was time to take off the kid gloves. "Everyone can tell you have a boner, Ethan. Time to graduate to the big boy underwear."

Somehow, he managed to turn a brighter shade of red while he hunched over himself and looked around.

Sigh. Well, there may be no avoiding it. She glanced down at his lap. "Although all that might be hard to tuck." Without waiting for a reaction, she turned and walked away. "Next round in ten minutes, sweetie."

Lie to a boy about the size of his dick and you owned him.

Monika stood in her hotel room staring at herself in the mirror. Her hair was down, but brushed and smooth. Her oversized t-shirt covered enough to be legal but would allow her to take care of business without removing it.

They'd won semi-finals. Ethan's performance had been exemplary as always, but his expressions in the Latin just didn't cut it anymore. The other boys knew what they were doing. Ethan was still pretending.

Finals the next day.

Sigh.

In the mirror, her eyes were empty. What she was about to do didn't really matter. She needed that boy to win. With that boy she was guaranteed to win.

If.

If he knew what all the fuss was about.

She turned on her sparkle.

What a difference. Her eyes lit up and her chest rose. The smile was good enough for both the Disney channel and a porn site. Perfect.

Monika slipped through the door between their rooms. She'd made a point of flirting with a bellhop to get it unlocked from her side earlier that day. Ethan's breath was slow and steady. He used a night light. That was so cute.

Bleah.

"Ethan?"

He startled awake and sat up. "Huh? What?"

She pushed him down and slipped under the covers, straddling him. "Ethan, sweetie, it's Monika. Don't be scared." She held his shoulders and moved her hips.

His eyes were huge and bright. "Monika? What are. . .? Well, I guess. . ."

He wore boxers, and Monika could feel his instant enthusiasm as she rubbed against him. "Shh, Ethan." She kissed him briefly. "I've wanted you for so long, now. There aren't any words that could make it better." And if he spouted off on one of his smarmy tirades, she might just puke.

"But, Monika. . ."

She pulled him up to a sitting position, yanked her t-shirt off and pushed his face into her cleavage. "Shhhh." The shift nearly forced him inside her despite the boxers. Really? Boxers? The boy needed to invest in boxer briefs at the very least. She pressed him down onto the bed and tugged the boxers off.

It would be his first time.

Shouldn't take too long.

As soon as he finished, Monika jumped off. "What was that? Did you hear that? I think someone's coming." And it certainly wasn't her. She slipped into her t-shirt before leaving the bed. "I should get back to my room."

"Monika," he called after her.

She looked back.

He stood beside the bed, naked, juvenile. "Good night."

She'd probably have to get used to seeing him. But she'd never like it. "Good night," she said. Please, don't let him say it.

"I love you."

Damn. "Get back to bed, sweetie."

She slipped into her room and closed the door. She bundled up in her sweats and crawled into bed. She didn't need to worry about getting pregnant, and he was a virgin. No chance of STDs.

She hugged the hotel pillow close. She slowed her breathing. He was hers, now. She wouldn't have to worry about those sluts stealing him away. There was a saying: "Men are like floors. Lay them right the first time and you can walk all over them forever."

She shuddered and gripped the pillow closer

No. No memories.

Her hips convulsed once.

No.

She smelled tobacco. She tasted stale rum.

She forced her stomach down.

No. Not tonight. Tonight, she needed to sleep.

Her body shook.

No!

She pushed the memories away.

She'd thought maybe with Ethan, sweet, innocent Ethan, maybe this time would erase the memories. But, no. Maybe one day she'd find someone who could erase them, who could cover them up with new memories. Maybe one day, she'd have enough new moments to cover over and erase the past.

Maybe one day.

No today.

The next day, she and Ethan won State.

Hugs

Six months ago.

Saundra dropped the folder into Lucius's lap. "What the unmitigated fuck were you thinking?" She crossed her arms and glared. "Why the fuck did you do this without contacting your overpriced lawyer?"

Lucius sat in an old recliner wearing boxers and a dirty t-shirt. "Because you would've told me not to do it."

Pathetic. She had to work to keep from kicking him.

"And why do you pay me enough to afford that new car in your driveway right now," she yelled, "if it's not to prevent you from doing stupid shit like this?"

The way he sat there calmly pissed her off even more. He had no idea what his idiocy had caused. And the worst part was she should have seen it coming. That was also why he overpaid her. To keep him from *doing* stupid shit that would require her services to undo.

"Why the hell did I work so goddamned hard to prove your innocence," she yelled, "and waste my time protecting your assets, if you were going throw everything away afterward?"

His calm was infuriating in its ignorance. "Actually, I gave them the gym because you were so damn good at your job."

"What?" That made no sense.

"Since it was an accident and you proved it wasn't my fault. . ." His tone told her he believed the exact opposite of what he was saying. ". . .my insurance wouldn't pay out. They didn't have a life insurance policy on a nineteen-year-old kid, so they spent their life savings trying to sue me and now they're bankrupt." A crack in his wall finally showed around his mouth. "I couldn't let them go bankrupt."

Saundra pulled the wig from her head and threw it to the floor. "And why the hell not? They were perfectly fine trying to destroy you for something that wasn't your fault."

"They lost a son, Sandy." He swallowed hard. "If it'd been Ethan? If *my* son died? I wouldn't be able to work. I wouldn't be able to function. They need this more than I do."

"And what about Ethan? What do you suppose this will do to him?"

Lucius scoffed and crossed his feet at the ankles on the footrest. "Ethan's too worried about competing, coaching and banging Monika to even notice that I don't own the gym anymore. As long as I keep paying for his ridiculously expensive haircuts, he'll be fine."

Now she had him. "And how do you expect to pay for those haircuts, Mr. Fox?"

"Same as always." He shrugged. "What's the big deal? The gym's just there for retirement. I make most of my money running the gym, not owning it. My salary isn't going to change." He smiled. "They actually gave me a raise. I'll build a new retirement nest egg."

Was he really that stupid?

He frowned. "I don't want to own it anymore, anyway."

Okay, she had to calm down. "Why do you suppose they told me about this change in ownership today, Mr. Fox?" How had he not known what would happen?

He glanced down at the folder in his lap. "Good question. I signed the paperwork two weeks ago."

"Yes, you did," she said, "and now it's too late for you to tap into the unspoken seller's remorse clause implicit in every contract in the great state of Texas."

"I'm not going to change my mind."

"Well, they did."

He looked up at her, confusion obvious in his face.

She gestured at the folder in his lap. "They dropped this off about an hour ago. That's not only the contract you signed, Mr. Fox."

Lucius opened the folder and read. His expression changed from confusion to shock. "They. . . they can't do this. They promised."

They promised. If she had a buck for every client who'd said *that* she'd be even wealthier than she already was. "They lied."

"They can't fire me," he insisted. He pushed up from the chair and walked circles in the living room while he read. "We have a contract." He brandished the contract as if it meant something. "Right here."

"And there is a clause in there that says you can be fired without notice for 'conduct unbecoming' to the gym."

Lucius scoffed. "I hardly think sitting around the house in my underwear would warrant getting fired."

"No, Mr. Fox, but killing one of the students just might."

His brows knit together, and he examined the papers. The color drained from his face. He looked up at her with obvious dread. "But that happened before we made this contract."

She let him read. He'd figure it out himself.

He sat on the footstool, staring at the papers. "But the media coverage hasn't stopped, yet." He didn't seem to be reading anymore, just staring. She almost felt sorry for him. Almost. She'd been working on his guilt for months, forcing him to see how much it was hurting his relationship with Ethan. But this? This was stupid and reckless, and she should have seen it coming.

And now it was too late. There was nothing she could do about it.

There was a hole in the ground that would never become a swimming pool. The foundation for the pool house was laid and the framing was up, but that would likely just bring down the value of the house since there was no money to finish the project. Saundra had already talked to Lucius's accountant. The renovations completed the year before had tapped him out, and the pool was financed with the house as collateral. At least he hadn't used the gym for any of the loans. That could've landed him in jail.

He sipped a beer and stared at the hole.

She touched her wig to make sure it had completely settled in place.

The house was overdeveloped. No one willing to spend that much on a house wanted to live east of that stretch of I-35. "I never planned on selling this house," Lucius said as if reading her thoughts. "It was Megan and Karl's." He looked up at the sound of a car. "I was going to let Ethan have it when he got married or whatever. I would've bought a condo downtown."

A blast of chacha music and the slam of a car door announced Ethan's arrival.

Lucius sipped his beer. "I've completely fucked up my son's life."

Saundra couldn't disagree. But she wasn't blameless. She'd suspected he was up to something stupid but had convinced herself he'd talk to her first.

"Yo, Dad?" Ethan poked his head out the patio door.

"Out here with Ms. Delacroix," Lucius called.

"Hey, Ms. D." Ethan waved. "You making dinner or should I grab something after practice?" He grinned. "The question was for Dad, Ms. D. I wouldn't ask you to make dinner." He grinned more. "Couldn't afford you."

Saundra watched several emotions warring in Lucius's face. "You can't afford to eat take out anymore, Mr. Fox," she said very quietly.

He scowled at her. She probably shouldn't have used the formal, pissed-off name.

"Ethan, come out here a minute."

Was he going to tell his son right away? That would, in fact, be the most prudent action, but that's exactly why it surprised her.

"I'm running late, Dad."

Lucius scowled again. "One lousy minute, son."

Ethan trotted to them, rolling his eyes, but amused. "Dad, do I really need to hug you every time I. . ." He froze.

Apparently Lucius had invented an entirely new level to the word awkward. "I. . . I just wanted to know whether you wanted Chinese or

Indian," he lied badly. "I was hoping we could have take-out and movie night?"

Even Saundra could see that Ethan knew he was being bribed.

"You pick the movie." Lucius's desperation was pathetic. "No Tarantino."

That seemed to work. "You promise?" The young man crossed his arms. "I can have violence and explosions with no dark, arty expressionism?"

Lucius held up his beer. "I swear on Tecate."

"Chilantro's."

Lucius groaned, but it was obviously a put-on. "You're going to make me go chase down a food cart?"

Ethan started to make his getaway. "You want to bribe your son for some unknown reason, expect to work for it, Dad." He dashed away.

When the boy was gone, Lucius grew very still.

"You're going to tell him tonight, I presume?" If he didn't, she would.

"How do I tell him I just gave away his life?" He turned to her, and she could see his question wasn't rhetorical. "What the fuck am I going to do, Saundra? There has to be some way to fight this."

She was not going to give him false hope. "There isn't. Their lawyer is good. Almost as good as I am, and he's not as scrupulous, which makes it easier for him to win." She stared at the house, where Ethan was likely changing from expensive and stylish school clothes to expensive and stylish workout clothes. "No hugs?"

Lucius turned his head to glare at her so quickly she was shocked he didn't end up with every lawyer's best friend. "Not open to discussion."

All right then. File that in the column marked "things we don't talk about."

Valentino's Day

Today

Kenny Valentino held a handful of pills and a bottle of Jack Daniel's. He'd collected the pills for the past six months, one or two at a time. Everyone in his family was on something, and nobody missed a pill here or there.

His sister Nancy couldn't sleep because of the baby. She was fifteen and wasn't sure which guy was the daddy.

His brother Ed had PTSD, and the leg that wasn't there still hurt.

Mom thought her job was to fix everyone else's problems. She had nightmares.

Dad? Well, it wasn't nice to say, but Dad had to put up with Mom. That's why there was always a bottle of Jack Daniel's in the bar.

Kenny wasn't sure what his own deal was. He stared into the bathroom mirror at a moody teenager in Ed's old suit and one of Dad's ties. Straight hair fell almost to his shoulders. The suit was crap and hung on him like a sack. At least it was black.

At least he wouldn't have to sit in detention for skipping school.

What if school called Mom, though? She'd drop everything and run home to yell at him for skipping. He might survive. He might be left a vegetable.

He jiggled his sweaty hand, but some of the pills stuck to his skin, bleeding a bright, friendly rainbow. He snagged a cup from the counter. For some stupid reason, he didn't want to be found with a drug-stained hand. He wiped his palm on the suit and rattled the cup so the pills wouldn't stick together. "I suck at this." The guy in the mirror frowned. "I even suck at *this*."

The letter from the University of Texas lay in pieces on his bed. It was the only note he'd leave. He hadn't been certain about the scholarship. His grades were good, but he didn't play sports and he sure as hell wasn't class president. Unfortunately, no one gave out money for break dancing or "making cartoons," as his mom called his greatest passion.

"I hate to see you spending so much time making your little cartoons," she said at least once a week. "Get out there. Meet a girl."

He met girls. They laughed at him.

In Dumass, Texas, if you didn't play football you were laughable. Ed had been a football hero once upon a time. That didn't help. The fact that Kenny loved anime and Korean pop music made it worse. He was on the local dance crew. That should've helped, but even the girls there laughed at him.

The letter from UT had politely informed him he'd been rejected. Not just for the scholarship. For the school. He hadn't been prepared for that. Selection was very competitive— blah blah, blah, blah. One more rejection.

Well, unless the Devil kicked him out of Hell, it would be the last.

He swirled the pills in the cup. He grabbed the Jack Daniel's.

Why? Because he was sick to death of being alone. In a house full of family, in a school full of kids, he was alone. Even at the dance studio, he was alone. UT had been his last hope. Austin had anime clubs, a film school and girls who liked tall, skinny guys with streaks of red died into their hair and jacked up like Vash the Stampede in *Trigun*.

But Austin didn't want him.

No one did.

Okay. Time to do it.

He lifted the cup to his mouth. The pills rattled loudly.

He closed his eyes and ignored the tears streaming down his face.

"Do it."

The stupid website he'd found a few weeks ago popped into his mind. "Give it one more day. You can always change your mind tomorrow and do it anyway, but you can never take it back."

With a spastic movement, he pressed the cup onto the bathroom counter and the bottle of JD beside it. Air jumped into his lungs. He hadn't even known he was holding his breath. He wiped at his face before looking into the mirror.

His eyes were red.

"Stupid wuss."

Fine. The pills would still be there when he got home. The JD would wait for him in the bar downstairs. It made more sense to do it after everyone went to sleep, anyway. He didn't want his mom to come home in time for him to end up a vegetable.

His phone rang and he jumped.

It was Mom. "Kenny? Why aren't you in school?"

Yeah. One more day to prove to himself it was the right thing to do. One more day.

He reached Dumass High, home of the Rampaging Mules, just in time to hear the bell ending third period. The hallways filled. Joy. Every head turned to stare at him as he walked the hall. There were giggles and laughter.

"Get a load of asshat in the suit," someone said loudly.

More laughter.

"Hey, Valentino, what happened to the fag hair?"

Kenney stopped. Why the hell not? After today, nothing would matter. "I just came from my mom's funeral. Figured the fag hair would be over the top since she died from bleach poisoning at the salon."

Without waiting for a response, he strode down the hall toward class.

"Still a fag," someone called after him.

"Jesus, what if his mom really died?"

"Still a fag."

Yeah. Wearing a suit to school made you a fag. So did wearing your hair in anything other than a crew cut. Online, he'd seen photos from the Austin Comic Con where these losers would be the ones laughed at. Of course, he couldn't afford gas to that event, let alone tickets. Stuff like that happened out there, but he'd never see it. He'd be stuck in Dumass his whole life.

Might as well make it a short one.

He plopped into a desk in history class and dropped the backpack on the floor. American history. No one took it seriously this far south. The whole region had been Mexico more than Texas, and Texas was barely a part of the US, anyway.

Paunchy, middle-aged Mr. Gonzalez stopped beside Kenny with a wry grin. "Well, Mr. Valentino. We're rather formal today. To what do we owe the pleasure of your unusually traditional hair?"

Seriously? Even the teachers?

"I was planning on committing suicide this morning. Figured I should dress up for the occasion."

Gonzalez lost his smile and peered down at Kenny over the thick black frames of his glasses. "I'm going to let that slide, Valentino, because you normally don't cause trouble." He moved off. "But be warned."

The teacher was going to feel like hell the next day when Kenny's body was found. His juvenile crack would turn into one of those "cry for help" things people whined about after a suicide. Interesting.

"Freak," Diane Conner muttered behind him.

Yeah, he'd never heard that before.

At lunch, he sat by himself and read *manga*. There were stares and whispers, as usual. A couple of girls from the dance crew wandered past.

"Hey, K-pop," Katy said. She was the crew captain. "See you tonight?"

"Yeah. . . sure."

She nodded and returned to the conversation with her best friend.

Katy nicknamed everyone. As soon as she'd found him listening to Korean pop music, his was inevitable. It wasn't a tease, though. For Christ's sake, she called her best friend "Juicy" and her boyfriend was just "Boyfriend." As nicknames went, Kenny's was pretty cool.

But they didn't sit with him at lunch.

A bell rang. Damn it. Gym class.

Kenny snatched up his tray, threw out the trash and hurried to the locker room. Since gym was right after lunch, he tried to arrive early so he could change before the muscleheads made their entrance. Seniors didn't need to take gym, so the only guys in class were jocks who wanted an easy A and dorks like Kenny who'd thought it was smart to get kicked out of gym class halfway through second semester junior year. When he'd learned he wouldn't graduate without a full credit, he'd almost killed himself right then.

The locker room was busy. Great. Kenny kept his eyes down and did his best to avoid eye contact. In his head, he heard a documentary voiceover from Animal Planet: "It pays to be cautious when you encounter the musclehead athlete in his natural environment. Try not to draw attention to yourself and you might emerge unharmed."

"Where'd you get the gay shorts, Valentino? Toys-R-Us?" Gunner was the Platonic Form for the football linebacker.

Kenny looked down. Shit. He'd totally forgotten about the *Trigun* boxers. They'd have been ironic. His hair was slicked back and the suit was conservative, but the coroner would've had a view of Vash the Stampede when he stripped Kenny for the autopsy.

Gunner and his first-string buddies were all grinning and bumping fists. Yeah, that was the height of humor for them. Fuck irony and Plato.

Well. . . screw it. He stood up and looked Gunner in the eye. He wasn't taller than Kenny anymore, but he was three times bigger across. "Gay? I'm not the one checking out another dude's package."

There was a short silence while Gunner stared, apparently shocked that Kenny had actually mouthed off to him.

Someone said something like, "Ooooh, burn."

Then Gunner lunged across the bench at him.

Oh well, maybe he'd saved his dad a bottle of Jack Daniel's.

Totally worth it for the look on Gunner's face.

The linebacker only managed to land two or three punches to Kenny's gut before he was hauled off and a massive hulk appeared between them.

Boyfriend, otherwise known as Corey, looked down at Kenny. "You okay, K-pop?"

"No worries here."

Suddenly, the other guys had better things to do. Gunner held his hands in the air as if he were perfectly innocent. "Just horsing around. Right, Valentino?" He fixed Kenny with a look that told him, "Maybe not today, but one day. . . one day you are a dead man." He even did the two fingers to his eyes thing. He jabbed them at Kenny and stalked away. All of that behind Boyfriend's back.

Apparently, the captain of the football team didn't have as much control of his first string as he thought he did.

Boyfriend turned to Kenny with a grin. "Isn't it great when we all get along?"

Kenny faked a smile.

Boyfriend leaned closer. "I'd think twice about the cartoon skivvies on gym days, bro."

Of course. Cartoon underwear meant he was asking for a beat down, right?

When Kenny made it out to the gym he was horrified to learn that they were wrestling that day. Gunner cracked his knuckles and grinned.

God damn it.

Kenny made it to the studio that night with only a minor limp from the punishment generously provided by Gunner in gym class. Fuck it. He'd had worse horsing around with Ed before his brother's deployment.

After school, he'd run home, showered and changed. The suit would get in the way at practice and the crew should have a sincere chance to prove they gave a shit. No fair giving them a reason to tease him.

Katy was on the dance floor. . . with some blond guy. Who was he? Kenny had seen him before. He was positive.

"*Oye chicos*," Katy called, "if you haven't practiced, I'm going to kick every single ass." And then she and Boyfriend had their obligatory kiss and grope moment.

New guy seemed annoyed by that. Interesting. Competition for Boyfriend?

"Hey there, I'm K-Pop." Kenny held out a hand.

The new guy looked down at the extended hand, then at the *Black Butler* t-shirt Kenny wore. "Cool shirt." He looked into Kenny's face. . . then higher at his hair, which was once again jacked up and held in place with liquid cement, red streaks shining. He smiled and nodded approval. "K-pop?"

"I really like Korean pop music, so Katy calls me K-pop."

The new guy nodded again. He craned his neck to look around Kenny. Yep. Definitely hot for teacher. "Katy?" he asked. "She told me her name was Tango." He finally took the offered hand. "You can call me Foxtrot, by the way."

Kenny shook hands, still trying to place the guy. He didn't stay long, and after he left everyone asked a million questions because Dumass was a small town and a new dancer was almost as rare as an open-minded football player.

Foxtrot was really Ethan Fox, Macarena Davis's nephew. He was from Austin, which was just too awesome. It explained why, against all odds, he'd liked Kenny's t-shirt and hair. Where the hell had Kenny seen that guy before?

Practice was the usual. Dancing was always fun, but no one really talked to him. No one asked about the limp. No one really cared.

When he got home that night, the baby was screaming. Ed was yelling at the TV. His mom was on the phone shouting over everything. Dad was somewhere hiding. Like father like son, Kenny ran through the living room toward the stairs.

"Kenny?"

Fuck.

Kenny stopped with one hand on the railing. "Yeah, Mom?"

"What's this I hear about you mouthing off to your history teacher?" She still had the phone in one hand, so she expected a short conversation. God forbid she sit and listen to his side of the story.

"Sorry," Kenny said. "It won't happen again."

She smiled. "That's my good boy." The phone rose to her ear. "At least that one never causes trouble."

Nope. Never did. Never will.

Up in his room, Kenny sat on the edge of his bed and stared at the clock.

Dad went to bed first. Doors opened and closed in the bedroom downstairs.

Then Nancy and the baby. She sang to the poor little guy as they went into her room.

The TV downstairs fell silent, and Ed and Mom said goodnight at the bottom of the stairs before Ed tromped up to his room.

Kenny waited another half hour, just in case, then sneaked down for the Jack Daniel's, which was only marginally lighter than it had been that morning. He changed into the suit and stared into his dresser mirror, a cup full of pills in one hand and a bottle of booze in the other.

Had anything changed?

Not really.

He took a long, hard pull on the whisky. . . and nearly choked to death before he could kill himself. Holy crap! Dad drank that shit almost every night?

He listened. No sounds. Apparently, no one had heard his coughing fit.

He sipped. He closed his eyes and took a deep breath, but he didn't cough. Kenny wasn't much of a drinker. Guys his age were usually peer-pressured into it. A guy needed peers for that.

He sipped again.

Nothing.

He tapped his phone and played his favorite band. B2ST. Not too loud.

It'd been one more day of no one giving a shit. One more day getting pounded. With the rejection letter still in pieces across his bed, he knew for certain he would never get out. He'd even thrown the whole suicide thing out there in history for everyone to see. Did anyone care? No. He just got yelled at for causing trouble.

He rattled the pills in the cup.

What had one more day told him?

That no one would miss him.

That there was only one way out of this town.

In the mirror, Kenny's eyes were already dead.

He shot another swallow of the JD. There were no tears this time. He took a breath. The song did, too. It was one of his favorites. "Breath." The perfect send off.

He lifted the cup to his mouth. His hand didn't shake this time.

Suddenly, it was peaceful and easy to do.

Wait a minute—*That's* where he'd seen the new guy!

The bottle and the cup went to the dresser, and Kenny picked up his tablet. The video was up in a matter of seconds: the new guy danced to Kenny's favorite song. He'd bookmarked it because Foxtrot lived in Austin, and Kenny had vowed to look him up if he ever got there. Ethan Fox. The guy could freakin' dance.

Kenny clicked on the next video. Crazy ballroom stuff. Wow, he could dance that, too. Katy and the crew had given him crap about the ballroom thing, but, to Kenny, Foxtrot was someone who understood what it meant to have his passions insulted.

He looked up at the mirror and saw something he hadn't seen in months. Hope. What were the odds? He'd been rejected by Austin, told he wasn't good enough for them, either, then this tiny piece of Austin ended up stuck here in Dumass, Texas with him.

Replaying the video, he tried to copy Ethan's moves, but, when he spun, the room kept going around after his body stopped. So *that's* what booze did. Interesting.

He grabbed the bottle for another pull of whiskey and accidently knocked the pills off the dresser. They scattered across the floor. Oh well, he'd sweep them up in the morning.

He sat down to watch the next video.

What He Said

Last night.

Corey slept soundly, but rhythmic movement on his hips woke him. He opened his eyes. The bedside clock read 11:45 p.m. He looked up and smiled. "Hey, Katy."

She leaned forward and kissed him. She wasn't really one for small talk.

Corey kissed her hard. There was something awesome about a girlfriend who snuck into your bedroom in the middle of the night and woke you up. Totally worth the heat or cold from the open window. You know. . . just in case.

He rolled them over so he was on top.

She rolled them back so she was.

Okay. She was in one of those moods.

Corey relaxed and enjoyed the ride.

He liked the way her weight felt on his arm as they lay side by side breathing heavy and sweating. Some of the September heat had bled off in the night, and there was a breeze coming through the open window. He glanced at the clock: 1:30 a.m. He rolled the time around in his head.

Once, Katy had run up to him at school all smiling and perky. "How'd you sleep, Boyfriend?" She'd winked at him.

"Like a baby!"

The smile dropped off her face faster than shit out of a pigeon.

"Uh-oh." That was Juicy, who was always attached to Katy's hip at school. "He slept through it?"

That'd been a bad day. A very bad day.

Now, Corey always checked the time when he woke up and when they finished. For some reason, checking the time always helped him remember her visit the next morning.

Katy snuggled up next to him. "Any big plans this weekend?"

Uh-oh. Trick question. There must be plans she thought he'd forgotten.

He hadn't. Had he?

"Any shopping you might be doing?" Her voice was definitely different now. It was her annoyed voice.

Shopping? Think fast. Shopping meant presents. Presents meant anniversary or birthday. Wait! They'd started dating last September. He had it!

"Well, yeah, there's the *shopping*," he said, kissing the top of her head. "You didn't think I forgot our first big anniversary, did you?" Ha, nailed it.

She pushed away and sat up. "Anniversary?"

Uh-oh. It hit him. Crap. Her *birthday* was next week. The anniversary was *two* weeks away. "Well, yeah. . ." Think, think, think! "Because. . ." Think faster!! "Because I. . . already. . . *have* your birthday present, so I don't need to get you one of those." Would she buy it? "Since I already have one." Okay, he had to shut up now.

She looked over her shoulder at him.

For a really long time.

"You are so lying to me," she said at last.

"Katy!" He sat up fast and scooted closer. "I'm not lying."

"Yes, you are."

He didn't know what to say. Her hair falling across the one bare shoulder like that was really hot. Moonlight fell on her face and her eyes smoldered. He could see the intelligence in them, staring right through any lie he might think up.

She glanced down. "Really, Boyfriend?"

He couldn't stop the growing hard-on. "I can't help it, Katy. You're just so hot when your eyes get all smart like that, when you figure shit out."

She smiled. "So it's the intelligence in my eyes and not the naked breasts?" She turned and arched her back, which put her perfect boobs on display as well.

Holy crap. "Instead of fighting, can we have sex again?"

She reached for the condoms.

Corey's alarm woke him at precisely 5:00 a.m.

Katy'd left at 2:40 a.m.

Well, the animals wouldn't feed themselves.

He pushed out of bed and wandered into the bathroom to pee. He grabbed his work overalls from their hook. Socks. Boots. Hat.

Coffee. He needed coffee.

His dad was already dressed for work and reading the news on a tablet in the kitchen.

"Hola, Papa," Corey muttered. He'd called him Papi until the J-Lo song made it creepy.

Papa held up a mug of coffee. "Morning."

Corey took the mug in both hands and sipped. The temperature was perfect, so he gulped down half the mug. "Thanks," he said, reaching for the pot to top off the mug. Papa always poured the coffee a few minutes before Corey woke up so it'd be cool enough to drink.

"Yep." Papa's face was really red. It even showed through the thinning blond hair.

"Too much sun?" Corey asked.

Papa scowled at the tablet. "Be glad you have your mother's skin, Corey."

Corey sipped coffee, but his dad didn't seem likely to share how'd he'd gotten the sunburn. "Well," Corey said at last, "the animals won't feed themselves."

"Nope."

Corey liked the animals. He even enjoyed feeding them. Hauling bales of hay from the barn to the feeders in the field was good work. He could turn the tunes way up and lift things and throw them. The animals appreciated it. He started with the horses waiting around the feeder.

He had to watch for a while to make sure they got there in the right order. If one of the mares decided to butt in before her turn, they all got upset and fights could start. They were pretty, but kind of dumb when it came right down to it.

While the horses ate, he hauled the feed out to the cows. They weren't as skittish as the horses, but they weren't as pretty, either. More relaxed. Smarter. Less temperamental.

Once the cows were fed, he brushed out the horses and checked their hooves. He could tell a lot about a horse from her hooves.

"What're you doing out in the back forty?" he asked old Bella, who normally stayed close to the barn these days. "Feeling frisky again?" He scraped the clay out of her hooves.

He checked his tractor since he had a few minutes before he had to get ready for practice. He called her Bessie. Papa had bought her for him to help with the farm work, and she was cherry. At least once a month, he took something apart and put it back together so he could learn everything about how she worked. Thank God for YouTube videos.

And Harvé. He was the guy in charge of all the equipment on the farm. If Corey couldn't get something running, Harvé helped him figure it out. Good old Harvé.

Bessie was fine as usual, so Corey ran to the house for a shower before practice.

"Are you almost ready?" Papa asked from the doorway to Corey's room.

"Almost," Corey answered, digging in one ear with a Q-tip.

"You aren't even dressed?" Papa clapped his hands. "Chop, chop, Corey. I need you to drop me off downtown."

Corey looked at his dad in the dresser mirror. "What's wrong with the Beamer?"

"Harvé heard a noise," Papa explained, shaking his head. "You know how he gets when he hears a noise."

Corey dropped the Q-tip in the basket and opened the drawer for shorts and socks.

"What's the point of taking a shower before practice?" his dad asked. "You're just going to need another one after."

"I don't want to go to school smelling like cow shit, Papa."

His dad clapped his hands again. "Chop, chop." He left.

"Yes, sir." Corey scrambled into jeans and shoved everything he'd need for the day into his duffle bag: two-a-day practices plus dance crew after his after-school practice.

Every day he felt like he was packing for a weekend. It took too much time to drive out to the farm if he forgot something. He pulled on a t-shirt and counted on his fingers to make sure he had clothes for each part of the day.

With a final nod, he grabbed his boots, hoisted the duffle over a shoulder and headed for the door.

"Gunner!" He'd almost forgotten his promise to hit the weight room with his buddy during lunch. He snagged a t-shirt from the floor.

Ugh. Why had he promised the extra workout? After the exercise Katy'd given him that morning, he could use a rest during lunch. Grinning at the memory of Katy's visit, Corey ran out to his Challenger. Papa would be there with the engine running.

Katy and Juicy huddled together watching something on Katy's tablet when Corey found them after morning practice. Freshly showered and a bit tired, he stopped behind them and zoned out to wait for one of them to notice him. He'd learned the hard way not to interrupt best girlfriends when they were so intense.

"See?" Katy said in her absolute proof voice. "No straight man moves his hips like that."

Juicy made a Mexican noise, like an "M" long and drawn out that finally ended in, "*Mira!*" She pointed at the screen. "I see your point."

Juicy made no sense. She was Korean but had been adopted by Mexican parents when she was a little girl, so she knew more Spanish than Corey and, for that matter, was more Mexican than he was in spite of the fact that his grandpa was from Mexico City.

"And no straight man would wear that many rhinestones," Katy said, "even on *Dancing with the Stars*."

"And he's moving *here*?" Juicy sounded doubtful.

"Mm-hm." Katy's voice rose on the "hm" into a squeak. It was cute.

"Why is a world-class champion moving to Dumass, Texas?"

"It's a big mystery," Katy whispered. "He's Mrs. Davis's nephew. Moving here with his dad from Austin. Something bad happened, but I don't know what."

Gossip time. Corey settled in. This could go on forever. He let his eyes drop closed.

What should he give Katy? He had two presents to find now, and he hated the mall. Hey! Gay dudes liked to shop didn't they? Maybe the new dancing dude could help him find something. . . for. . . Katy. . .

The girls had fallen silent.

He opened his eyes.

They were staring at him, and Juicy had laser beams shooting out her eyes at him. "How long have you been standing there?" she demanded.

"What? I wasn't. I was just waiting. You always tell me not to interrupt."

She faced off with her hands on her hips. "That was a private conversation."

Corey's brain froze. "What? I wasn't. I was just waiting. You always tell me not to interrupt." His heart beat fast. Getting on Juicy's bad side was always the worst way to piss Katy off. There was nothing he could do to fix it.

"Slow down, Juicy." Katy looked deep into Corey's eyes. "He's half asleep."

Saved! "Yeah. . . half asleep." He slid his arm around Katy's waist and hugged her close. "All I heard was gay ballroom dancer with chacha hips." He looked down at Katy who smiled up at him with that grin that told him he'd done a damn good job with her last night. He smiled. "And you left at 2:40 a.m." He smiled. "We had sex twice." He grinned. "It was awesome."

Katy kissed him then pressed her hand to his mouth before he could say anything further. "I am so sorry I ever got mad at you for sleeping through that one time."

"Your anger was perfectly understandable," Corey mumbled through her fingers. He'd rehearsed that line with Gunner a million times.

Juicy giggled.

Katy took her hand away. "No, I mean I *regret* it, Boyfriend. It's not the same thing."

In a no win situation, Corey always punted. "You know, if he needs someone to show him around town, you know, like the mall and stuff? I'd be willing to help out." He added a smile. Katy always liked his smile.

"The mall?" Juicy asked.

"Gay dudes like to shop, right? That dude on *Glee* always has new stuff. He has to shop, like, all the time."

Katy gave him a big hug and a kiss. Okay. Cool. That must've been the right thing to say, even if Juicy giggled again.

The bell rang.

Katy released him. "See you at lunch, Boyfriend."

"Gunner asked me to help him work out at lunch," Corey said.

Katy walked away backward, holding the tablet to her boobs. "I didn't work you out enough last night?" Her hips rolled, and she wore her sexy half-smile that made Corey instantly hard.

"Love you!" he called out, wondering how obvious it would be if he adjusted his jeans right then.

She blew him a kiss and hurried off with Juicy.

He rushed into the bathroom.

Thank God Gunner didn't want a serious workout over lunch. Corey lay on one of the benches in the weight area off the boys' locker room. The equipment there was old, so most guys worked out in the new room. He and Gunner had the area to themselves.

"Bro, you fucked for how long?"

"From 11:45 p.m. until 2:40 a.m. with a short break so she could get mad at me."

Gunner was benching low weights since Corey wasn't pushing him.

"You're gonna rub it raw that way."

Corey smiled. "I got no complaints."

The weights crashed home and Corey opened his eyes in case Gunner was in the mood to wrestle. Nope. Just changing to bicep curls.

"Wish I had that kind of action," Gunner complained.

"What about that girl over Mercedes' way?"

"Mercedes?"

Corey laughed. "Aw, come on, you and the guys go out there every weekend, right?" He sat up. "And meet those girls you told me about?"

"Oh yeah. . . the girls." Gunner grinned. "But they don't climb into my bedroom window."

"Well, no, I don't suppose they do." Corey lay back down and drummed his heels on the floor. He would never say anything, but he was kind of jealous. Not about the girls. Katy was awesome, but ever since he'd started dating her things had changed with the guys on the team. They went out all the time and left him behind because it was all about chasing girls.

"You saying you want a piece of that action, bro?" Gunner asked.

Corey scoffed. "And ruin a great thing with Katy? Are you serious?"

"Just checking."

Corey was pulling up his pants when he heard Gunner's voice around the corner.

"Where'd you get the gay shorts, Valentino? Toys-R-Us?"

Corey's breath caught in his throat. K-pop was there? He must be in Gunner's gym class. "Walk away, K-pop," he whispered. "Walk away."

"Gay? I'm not the one checking out another dude's package."

Shit. Gunner wouldn't like that.

Corey buttoned up his fly as fast as he could. What the hell? K-pop *never* mouthed off.

Someone said something like, "Ooooh, burn."

Corey made it around the bank of lockers just as Gunner lunged across the bench at K-pop. His friend only managed to land two or three punches before Corey hauled him off and tossed him aside. "You okay, K-pop?"

"No worries here," K-pop said.

Really? No worries? Had Corey misunderstood the whole thing?

In nothing but his superhero underwear, K-pop looked skinny and vulnerable. He'd grown, like, six inches in the past year, but Corey'd never seen him in just his shorts. The new height made him look like a scarecrow. A bruise was already rising on one side.

Suddenly, the other guys had better things to do. Gunner held his hands in the air, like he was promising Corey he didn't want to hurt K-pop. "Just horsing around. Right, Valentino?"

Corey turned to K-pop, ready to defend him if need be. No matter how tight he and Gunner were, Corey wasn't going to sit still if K-pop felt assaulted. Papa hadn't raised a bully.

K-pop managed a smile. "All good. . . Corey. No worries. Just horsing around."

Corey grinned. How cool! He'd always been worried that his football team and his dance crew might not get along. K-pop was even smart enough not to call him Boyfriend in the locker room, which would've sounded weird. "Isn't it great when we all get along?"

Gunner was already gone.

K-pop smiled.

Corey leaned closer. "I'd think twice about the cartoon skivvies on gym days, bro." He gave his dancing friend a wink so he'd know he was just razzing him. The shorts were pretty cool. He patted K-pop's belly before heading to his own locker to finish dressing.

Maybe he should get to know K-pop better. He seemed really smart and kinda lonely. If the guys on the team were going to spend all their time out in Mercedes getting laid, maybe it was time for Corey to make more friends on the dance crew

"Jesus Christ!" Corey shouted. "My dead grandmother can throw better than that!!" He crossed his arms and watched the pass relay drill he'd thought up.

"Corey?" Coach stopped at Corey's side. "What are you doing?"

"Pass drills. The guys are finally passing more, but the completions totally suck ass, so who cares, right?"

"What do you mean the completions suck ass?"

Corey laughed. Coach had to be testing him. "Oh, like you don't already know the completions are at twenty-one percent."

"Of course, I do, Corey. How do you?"

"It's basic math, ain't it? If you look at the number of passes attempted, the numbers are off the scale, but they just keep missing." Corey's buddy Stanton missed again. "Dude! Get your head out of your ass and catch the fucking ball!" He glanced at Coach. "Sorry."

"No," Coach said, "no problems. Looks like a good drill you thought up."

Awesome. Conversations with Coach were about the only time Corey didn't feel stupid when he was away from the farm. Something about cows, machines and the football team always made sense to him.

"Where'd you get your stats?" Coach asked.

Corey elbowed him in the side and glanced down at Coach's tablet. "Is it different than what your program says?"

"No, no. . ." He waved the tablet in the air. "It's exactly the same thing."

Corey nodded. "Then I'll keep working the guys 'til they do better."

Corey liked showers. They made him feel clean, and, considering the number of times in a day he shoveled shit or worked himself to a ball-sweating fury, showers were awesome. He turned off the water and grabbed his towel. He swiped a few times to get rid of the main wetness then made his way to his locker.

Gunner and most of the first string were on their way out already, laughing and making noise.

"Bros," Corey called, "where you going?"

They were all dressed in black, as if they were on their way someplace fancy.

Stanton smiled. "There's these. . ."

"Girls," Gunner interrupted, smacking Stanton for some reason. Probably to keep him from lying. "You know. . . the girls in Mercedes I told you about?"

Corey dried his hair and dropped the towel on the bench. "Oh yeah. You going. . ." He wished he had something to say. Some reason to go with. He had nothing. "Well, y'all have fun, right?"

"Hell yeah," Gunner yelled. "We'll have fun!"

The other guys whooped and did fist bumps and high fives.

Man, Corey felt left out. But he was lucky. Katy was amazing. She was smart and pretty, and he wasn't about to mess that up. . . but he missed the guys.

"You really buy that?" Ephraim asked him. He was the only other football player on the dance team, too.

"Buy what?"

"That they're going off to bang Mercedes hos."

Corey scoffed. "That's what he said, right?"

Ephraim raised a hand. "That is indeed what he said." He shook his head and grabbed his pants out of his locker. "I wish I had your faith in humanity. It's a God damned blessing it is."

"I've known Gunner my whole life, bro. Why would he lie to me?"

Ephraim was so smart, he intimidated Corey, but he liked both Football and dance crew. He was another guy Corey should get to know better. "You need a ride to practice?"

"What? Wow, thanks for asking, but Woody's already waiting outside."

"Yeah, yeah, yeah. Of course. Duh." Corey had to check on the equipment, anyway.

Would it be totally weird if he asked whether they wanted to hang out after practice?

But that'd be the only time he had to spend with Katy.

"Another time?" Ephraim asked.

"Awesome."

They bumped fists and headed in separate directions.

By the time Corey reached the studio, he was dead tired. As he pulled into his usual parking spot, everyone else was rolling in, too. Bummer. He liked to get there first for alone time with Katy to catch up on the day. They were both so busy, it was hard to find time to just sit and talk. Oh well, hopefully after practice.

Corey grabbed his duffle out of the trunk, and K-pop zoomed past. Corey wanted to ask if he was doing okay, but the hip-hop dancer was already gone.

All distractions left his mind as he stepped into the studio. Katy crossed the floor with her sexy walk and wore his favorite purple blouse, the one that meant she was wearing the purple bra under it. The purple bra was *hot*. And easy to remove. Maybe catching up on the day wasn't so important. There were other ways to pass the time after practice.

"*Oye chicos*," she said in her hot teacher voice, "if you haven't practiced, I'm going to kick every single ass."

As soon as she stepped off the floor, Corey took her in his arms. Normally, she'd hold back at practice, but today she was on fire! Oh yeah, talking could wait. She snuggled close and gave him a taste of mint as her tongue slipped into his mouth. She pressed herself against him. Instant wood. Wow, he must've *really* hit all her buttons the night before!

"What'd I tell you?" Juicy asked after clearing her throat. She nudged Katy and pointed at the dance floor with her chin. "See how fast he went up to ChaCha Hips?"

He who? Oh. K-pop was talking to the new guy. "What about K-pop?" Corey asked as he stared at the two dudes talking.

"God, don't make it *obvious* or anything."

Katy kept her voice down. "Juicy has this *theory* about K-pop and why he never seems interested in the girls."

"He's really shy?" Corey suggested.

Juicy scoffed. "You are such a guy." She nodded at K-pop and the new dancer. "He's practically drooling."

Drooling? Corey figured he was just glad to meet someone from the big city, since he really wanted to move there. He wasn't going to say that, though. Juicy would make fun of him.

Katy clucked her tongue. "Well, for K-pop's sake, I hope you're wrong."

"Chacha Hips has a boyfriend?" Juicy asked.

"We can't call him Chacha Hips." Katy stared at K-pop and the new guy. "He's not gay."

Damn. So much for someone to help with the shopping. However, the intense look on Katy's face suddenly seemed to mean something much more complicated than her checking out a new dancer. Was she "checking-him-out" checking him out?

"Hm?" Juicy nudged her. "And how can you be so sure of *that*?"

Katy shot her a dark look. "He said so." She pushed away from Corey and headed out to the dance floor.

Juicy glanced at Corey. "Guys say a lot of things." She followed Katy.

He hated the way the girls could talk without saying anything he understood.

"Okay, gang, there's a new dancer in town," Katy called out. "Call him Foxtrot."

Corey hung back. If the new guy wasn't gay, what was he doing there alone with her before everyone else arrived? Katy hadn't mentioned an appointment. Why would she hide that? And Foxtrot might be talking to K-pop, but the way he looked at Katy the whole time wasn't comforting. Like he was hungry.

Damn it. Corey felt even more tired. Exhausted. If the new guy was a champion dancer, how could he compete with that? He could hardly do a jazzy box, or whatever the fuck it was called. What was worse, maybe that awesome hello from her wasn't because he'd hit all her buttons the night before. Maybe she was trying to convince him not to worry.

Even worse, maybe she was trying to convince herself.

Slow Down Your Heart

Last night.

Juicy opened the studio door and closed her eyes as a wonderful breath of cold air washed over her and the bell jingled. Cinnamon. The studio—and Katy—always smelled of cinnamon. An old-fashioned tango played. Juicy breathed it in as she made her way past the bar with her eyes still closed. She'd walked that path so many times she didn't need—

Oof.

Why the hell was there a chair where she was walking? Oh. Katy was cleaning. With the music, she probably hadn't heard the door open. She scrubbed the tables with gusto, her back to Juicy. The view was nice. Katy's ass filled out her sweats and jiggled with every swipe of the sponge across the table.

Juicy sighed. Damn, why did that girl have to be so fine? Juicy shook her head to clear it and pulled out her phone, moving close enough to the sound system to Bluetooth to Katy's phone. She tapped her screen and the music cut out.

Katy looked up. Smiled. "Hey *chica*, what's the big idea killing my tango?"

Juicy waved her phone like a magic wand while it uploaded the new music to Katy's cell. "Happy Birthdanukah," she said, tapping the screen. Violins screeched to life.

"Birthdaukah" was the girls' tradition since their friend Ephraim had told them about Chanukah. They exchanged presents for the entire week before a birthday. Nothing big, but something every day.

Katy dropped her cleaning supplies onto the table while she assessed the music. It was funny. Katy assessed everything. She couldn't take anything at face value. She'd been that way out of the womb. Juicy should know. She'd known her almost that long.

Katy made her way to her phone where it lay near the sound system. "Piazzolla?" she asked. "But who's the band—"

A techno drumbeat kicked in and a harsh, buzzing backbeat followed. A smooth, electronic chord sailed in over the violins and a dubstep break took over.

Katy's eyes opened wide and she froze.

Aces. Juicy'd nailed it. She'd heard of a new wave of tango at cheer camp that summer, but had saved the news for Katy's birthday. From Katy's reaction, she hadn't heard of the band.

Katy grabbed her phone. "Bajofondo?" She scrolled through the albums. There were three of them. "How have I not heard of this?"

Juicy repressed the urge to tell her it was because she stayed in Dumbass and never travelled for coaching or camps the way Juicy did. All Katy's training came from her mom and Nana. They were great, but, well, they were her mom and her nana.

"We're out in the sticks, girl," she said instead. "I'm lucky I stumbled onto it all."

Katy skipped to the next song, grinning like a kid with a new toy. Her smile gave Juicy a warm tingle in her stomach. She loved making her friend so happy. The girl really was sort of trapped in their home town with all her studio work. Juicy felt bad for her and tried to find ways to bring little slices of the outside world back to her without letting on how much her own horizon had expanded in the last couple of years. While

Katy was training to be a teacher and run a business, Juicy was learning to dance like a star.

The next song kicked in. "Oh, hell yeah," Katy said, sliding her phone onto the counter and running over to Juicy and dragging her to the dance floor. They slid into dance position and started the tango with the ease of two friends who had danced together for years. Katy's lead was strong, and the *ochos* and *sacadas* were effortless. They moved across the floor, foreheads close and breasts touching.

Once upon a time that hadn't been a problem, but now, as the music slowed down, Juicy felt Katy's chest pressing against hers. She smelled cinnamon. Her heart beat faster. Katy had to feel that pounding in her chest. They held a quiet pose while everything but the violin dropped out. Juicy felt dizzy.

Then the drums kicked back in and Katy swept her across the floor. They shifted apart for *la calecita*. Katy stepped lightly around Juicy, supporting her and balancing her perfectly on one foot so Juicy could spin and flick and kick her free foot. Lightheaded, she laughed and kicked as high as she could.

Katy laughed, too. "Damn, *chica*, you've been *working* that stretch!"

Reality rushed back as a grim reminder that Juicy was supposed to suck. Carefully, she rolled off her foot. Enough to fake a stumble, but not enough to hurt anything. Katy caught her before she fell all the way to the floor.

Juicy limped a little, rubbing the thigh of the leg she'd let Katy see over her head. "Ah crap, what was I thinking?"

Katy helped her to a chair. She clicked her tongue. "I keep telling you to stretch more."

A fake wince helped Juicy cover her annoyance. "I know."

Since she'd been going to every dance and cheer camp she could squeeze into her schedule, Juicy was now twice the dancer her friend was. The deception was getting harder and harder to maintain—

Katy pulled Juicy's hands away and worked on the supposedly strained thigh herself, kneading the muscle expertly.

Juicy's pulse raced.

She caught a glimpse of smooth brown cleavage while Katy bent to work her magic. If only her hands would knead higher. Just a little higher. . .

"All better." Juicy pushed her chair back abruptly. "Thanks."

"Thanks for the music." Katy hurried back to her player. "I love it."

Juicy sucked in a few deep breaths to slow down her heart.

She closed her eyes a moment. If only it were that easy.

This morning.

Juicy stopped in the hallway when she heard Ephraim Miller trying his best to butch up around a corner. Her back hit the wall near the intersection, and she held her book bag to her chest. She'd sworn to let her friend fight his own battles, but she was there with her Krav Maga if need be.

"I'm sorry Gunner, I need to study tonight." He always forced his voice down half an octave when he was with the other football players.

Why Ephraim was on the football team in the first place baffled Juicy. He insisted that being gay didn't mean he couldn't like football.

She always said it just meant he liked football *players*. Naked. In the locker room.

"You don't need to study every night, you pussy." Gunner voice made Juicy's skin crawl. "You wanna be a part of this team, you need to be a part of the team."

Juicy knew Ephraim well enough to picture the way he was waffling. He was on the dance crew, and they'd known each other almost as long as she'd known Katy.

"What are y'all doing out in Mercedes?" His voice was so obviously fake, now. Way too low. "Meeting girls?"

Juicy winced. If the Neanderthal Committee was off picking up girls, Ephraim would have a hell of a time pretending he liked them. Juicy was about to hurry around the corner with some made up bullshit about a project, when Gunner's chuckle stopped her. Something about it scared her.

"Well, yeah." His words were low and gravelly. "There'll be girls later, but the best part is with the bums."

"Bums?"

Gunner must've leaned closer, because his voice dropped so low Juicy couldn't make out a word. Bums? Mercedes had bums?

Ephraim's voice broke out much louder. "You're assaulting bums?"

Juicy winced. He'd been way too loud, and what straight boy said "assaulting"?

Wait. What the hell? She shifted closer.

"Jesus, douchenozzle, why not announce it to the whole fucking school?"

The smack was audible around the corner. Juicy winced again.

"It's hysterical." In his obvious excitement, Gunner wasn't much quieter than Ephraim had been. "We find some homeless asshole fresh from the border. . ."

Holy *shit*.

She moved away. She didn't want to hear more.

If she knew what they were doing, she'd *have* to tell someone and then she'd likely get pounded, too. Immigrants? They were pounding Mexicans? How many guys on the team were Mexican?

Corey was Mexican, on his mom's side. Was he involved? Had to be. He was the damn captain. How could something like that happen *without* him knowing? Even *he* wasn't that oblivious.

There was a tug on her book bag, and she spun to see who'd grabbed her.

A locker had snagged it.

The bag yanked her and she lost her footing. "Fuck!" She was so freaked out, she slipped and fell on her ass.

When she pushed back to her feet, way too many pairs of eyes stared at her. It seemed like the whole team had appeared around the corner.

She snatched her bag from where it had caught on the lockers.

"Fucking lockers," she muttered, then pretended to notice Ephraim for the first time. "*There* you are." She cocked her hip and tried to be casual. "If we don't finish that stupid project, we're dead, Miller."

"What project?" Gunner demanded. His voice and face dripped suspicion.

Juicy was used to making shit up. "Ten-minute presentation on Stephen Austin due tomorrow, and Miller here has been so busy practicing his pass drills with the Montez *familia* he hasn't had time for his fair share."

Gunner seemed happy to hear his weakest link was practicing. Man, he acted like he was Captain instead of Katy's asshole boyfriend.

Screw it. Hopefully the bitch card would work on these goons. "You make me fail this project, Miller, I will wind your balls up so tight they won't be good for anything but Christmas Eve tamales."

The guys made stupid guy noises, but when Ephraim acted all whipped, Juicy realized she could drag him away safely. There were times when it was just easier to play the bitch. Nice girls finished last.

She dragged him away.

"Christmas Eve tamales?" Ephraim whispered.

"Chanukah. Whatever," she whispered back.

She only realized how fast her heart was beating when they were safely in a chemistry room with the door closed.

"What the freestyle flying *fuck* was that?" Her hands shook. She'd known those guys were bad news but hadn't a clue just how bad.

Ephraim shook his head. "You heard?"

"Yeah, I heard. Smacking down bums?"

Ephraim clenched his fists and shook them. "Damn. 'Smacking down' sounds so much cooler than 'assaulting.'" He shook his head. "I am such a fag."

Juicy punched his shoulder. "If I think, for one minute, that you are even considering tonight's little field trip you will never find out whether you like to give head because I will kill you right here right now."

He held up his hands to block her. "What the hell? You even think that?" He crossed his arms. "Bitch."

She paced and dropped her bag on a table. "Okay, okay. Sorry. Kinda freaking the hell out here."

She paced and rolled it around in her head.

Ephraim seemed to do the same thing.

They spoke at the exact same time: "Do we tell anyone?"

As soon as the words were out of her mouth, Juicy was already shaking her head. "No. Gunner's a sociopath. We nark him out, we die."

"True."

"It's just one more secret we keep." She held up a hand with a pinky out.

Ephraim raised an eyebrow. "Pinky swear? Really? How old are you?"

"Old enough to kick your ass and tell Katy you want to blow her boyfriend."

Ephraim Miller held his hand out to meet Juicy's, pinky extended. "I'd rather blow Sam."

"Granted."

They shook on it.

If Juicy lived past lunch without getting assaulted, chances were the football goons didn't suspect she'd overheard them.

Wait. She gripped Ephraim's finger. "Was Boyfriend there?"

Ephraim seemed genuinely surprised. "What? Of course not. You think that teddy bear would go around smacking bums down?"

Juicy released Ephraim's pinky. "Smacking down bums." She shook her head. "Smacking bums is far more *your* thing."

He grinned. "I hear that."

She grabbed his wrist. "Don't snap."

"I wasn't going to."

"You were, too." She released his arm and grabbed her pack. "Ephraim, why is the lesbian teaching the gay boy how to stay with the times? Your people had a show for this kind of thing."

"When I was five." He followed her out of the room.

"True." The bustle of the halls calmed Juicy. It was normal.

If she could just make it past lunch, she'd feel safe.

Katydid

This morning.

"Ohmigod, ohmigod, ohmigod." Katy rushed through the hall to her locker. If Juicy wasn't there, she was going to scream, which would be embarrassing since Katy was not a little girl. Not even remotely. But this? Scream-worthy.

She seized Juicy by the strap of her backpack and spun her. An elbow shot out defensively, but Katy evaded it. Her best friend had taken too much Krav Maga for her own good.

"Down girl," Katy said. "You need to see this."

"What's wrong?"

"Nothing." Katy held out her iPad. "Watch this video."

Juicy shoved her backpack into her locker. "You're freaking me out, *mija*. You never get excited unless someone's dying."

Seriously? She needed to hurry up before Katy exploded.

She shook the iPad. "Watch. Now."

Juicy regarded her for way too long with that affected you-did-not-just-order-me-around-outside-dance-practice face. Pursed lips, cocked hip. When her hands folded into fists at her hips, Katy surrendered. She let the tablet drop to her side.

"A world champion dancer," she explained, "is moving to Dumass, Texas."

The only thing the most exciting news of the year managed to do was lift one of Juicy's overly manicured eyebrows.

"Seriously, Juicy. This guy can freakin' dance."

Her friend relaxed. "Wait a minute. You told me about some dancer moving to town, but you didn't say *nada* about 'world champion.'"

"I know, I know, I know." Katy held up the iPad again. "I just saw his videos this morning. Mrs. Davis never said, 'world champion.' She just said, 'He dances.'"

Juicy's expression told Katy she was finally interested. "Romantic possibilities that would let you unload the linebacker?"

What was her beef with Boyfriend? "Boyfriend's a quarterback and. . ." This one needed a huge pause for emphasis. "N-n-n-no."

Finally taking the iPad, Juicy raised an eyebrow.

"Gay," Katy said.

Juicy's second eyebrow joined the first.

"*Gay* gay," Katy insisted. "And not just kinda."

Juicy smirked and hit play.

Wait for it. Wait for it.

Juicy chuckled and rolled her eyes.

"See?" Katy said. "No straight man moves his hips like that."

"*Mm-m-m-m-mira!*" She pointed at the screen. "I see your point."

"And no straight man would wear that many rhinestones," Katy added, "even on *Dancing with the Stars*."

"And he's moving *here*?" Juicy asked.

"Mm-hm."

"Why is a world class champion moving to Dumass, Texas?"

"It's a big mystery," Katy whispered. She sidled up next to Juicy so they could watch the video together. "He's Mrs. Davis's *nephew*. Moving here with his dad from Austin. Something bad happened, but I don't know what."

"Bad?"

Katy shrugged. "I think someone died or something." The guy could dance, though.

"Or something?"

What was she, a parrot? "What part of 'I don't know' is hard to understand? *No sé.*"

Katy tapped the screen to the next video. It was full on hip hop. And it was good. No, holy shit, it was a-ma-zing.

"Holy shit," Juicy said.

"You read my mind." Seventeen years as best friends did that. She'd known Juicy her entire life. Their moms were best friends, too, and Juicy was more like a sister than Katy's own sisters, all five of them.

The new guy was *too* good. Way too good. There was no way he'd be interested in her dance crew. There was so much she could learn from him, but he'd never be interested in a small town crew like hers. Katy sighed.

"I know that sound," Juicy said. "I know exactly what you're—why the hell is Boyfriend eavesdropping?"

After recovering from mental whiplash, Katy turned.

Boyfriend stood dozing a few feet away.

He opened his eyes.

Juicy pounced on him. "How long have you been standing there?"

"What? I wasn't." His eyes opened wide. "I was just waiting. You always tell me not to interrupt."

She faced off with her hands on her hips. "That was a private conversation."

"What? I wasn't," he repeated. "I was just waiting. You always tell me not to interrupt."

"Slow down, Juicy." Katy looked deep into Corey's eyes. "He's half asleep."

His eyes lit up. "Yeah. . . half asleep." His arm slid around Katy's waist and he hugged her close. "All I heard was gay ballroom dancer with chacha hips."

Katy smiled up at him. He wasn't the brightest bulb on the tree or much of a dancer, but he was one of the sweetest guys she'd met. And his smile always made her feel special. As one of ten kids, special was a plus.

"And you left at 2:40 a.m. We had sex twice." He grinned. "It was awesome."

He was like a kid giving a book report. If she let him, he'd probably start listing their positions. Katy kissed him, then pressed her hand to his mouth. "I am so sorry I ever got mad at you for sleeping through that one time."

"Your anger was perfectly understandable." Corey mumbled behind her fingers. His words were so well prepared, he must've rehearsed them a million times with Gunner. Ugh. Gunner was a friend he could do without, but Katy kept that to herself. If Boyfriend ever tried to get between her and Juicy, he'd have to carry his balls around in his duffle bag.

Katy took her hand away. "No, I mean I *regret* it, Boyfriend. It's not the same thing." No point in explaining.

"You know," Boyfriend said. "If he needs someone to show him around town, you know, like the mall and stuff, I'd be willing to help out." He added a smile. The smile and his tone of voice told Katy there was more going on than Boyfriend trying to get on her good side.

She and Juicy exchanged a look.

"The mall?" Juicy asked.

"Gay dudes like to shop, right?" Corey asked. "That dude on *Glee* always has new stuff. He has to shop, like, all the time."

Katy almost laughed out loud. He was hoping for help picking out her presents, bless his heart. Katy gave him a big hug and a kiss. Sometimes simple was an advantage.

The bell rang.

Lunch time.

Katy's grapes were warm. She hated warm grapes.

Juicy picked at her tuna. "So what was all that weirdness I saw right before we noticed tall, dark and bless his heart standing behind us?"

"What weirdness?" Katy asked. She also sometimes hated that Juicy could read her so well. "I recall no weirdness."

"Pfft." Juicy had a vast array of sounds she used to express herself. "You think Chacha Hips is too good for us."

She should've known she wasn't going to sneak that past her best friend. "Okay, fine." She gave up on the grapes and drank her Diet Coke. "I know we're hot shit around here."

"You know that's right."

"But Chacha Hips is in an entirely different league." Fine. Might as well tell her the whole thing. "What if we scrounge up some money to bring someone in from Houston?" She'd been thinking about it all morning instead of paying attention to her stupid classes. What did a dancer need to know about history, anyway?

Juicy froze with a forkful of tuna at her lips. "And?"

"And have them coach us before Chacha Hips gets here." What else?

"And?"

"Are you stuck?" She and Juicy loved listening to the old vinyl records from when Katy's nana owned the studio. "Should I smack you?"

The fork hit the tray. "You want to pay someone to come coach us so Chacha Hips thinks we're good enough to dance with him?"

Well, when she said it like that, it sounded bad.

Katy sighed. The thing was they *weren't* good enough. Well, not all of them. Certainly not Juicy, but if they improved, she might be able to get him on their team. Katy was good enough, and if she could land Chacha Hips, she might be able to do something with her dancing better than owning Esmeralda's Dance Emporium in Dumass, Texas.

As always, Juicy must have known her every thought. She picked up the tray and dumped its contents into the nearest can. Crap. She was so sensitive about her own dancing. If she'd practice more. . .

Katy dropped her Coke can into the trash and hurried after Juicy. "Don't get pissy with me."

Juicy didn't look at her. "I'm a little tired of you always thinking you're so damn much better than the rest of us."

Well? She was.

"See?" Juicy snapped. "That's just what I mean."

"I did not say a word."

Juicy made another of her many sounds. "You don't need to. I know you. I know how you think better than *you* do. . ." Her voice trailed off as they passed K-pop. He was cute in a sensitive emo kind of way, but was painfully shy when he wasn't dancing, bless his heart. He was one of her best dancers.

"Hey, K-pop," Katy said. "See you tonight?"

He looked up from his comic book as they passed. "Yeah. . . sure." He wore a dark suit and his hair was down instead of jacked up to Jesus as usual. She would never figure that boy out.

When they were past him, she gave Juicy her best get-off-my-ass glare. "I do not think I'm better than everyone."

Juicy scoffed. "You want to land the big fish?" She slid sideways through the crowd and hauled Katy along so they were hidden but facing the cafeteria. "There's your jail bait." She was staring at K-pop.

"Him?"

Juicy rolled her eyes. "One: gay. Two: the best guy we have on the team." She pulled out her phone. "Didn't Chacha Hips dance to one of those Korean songs he loves?"

Katy grabbed her friend's wrist. "You still think K-pop's gay?"

Okay, if Juicy rolled her eyes one more damn time. "Have you ever seen him talk to a girl?" She examined K-pop as if considering how best to sell him to the new guy. "Remember when you, me and Cosita sat with him last year at lunch?" She looked at Katy with her most superior expression. "Didn't say one word." She must really think she had it all figured out. "Awk-ward."

"Maybe we aren't his type," Katy said.

Another sound from Juicy. "Have you *looked* at Cosita? She's everyone's type."

It *had* been pretty awkward. He'd just kept reading his comic book as if he didn't want them around. They'd never tried to sit with him again.

"Maybe he's just painfully shy."

"Gay," Juicy insisted.

The bell rang, and K-pop looked up in a panic. He threw his tray so hard it bounced and fell to the floor. Katy and Juicy shrank into the corner as he dashed past.

"What straight guy would come to school dressed like that?" Juicy said.

It was Katy's turn to roll her eyes. "I think he looks good in the suit." He disappeared around the corner. "He's actually pretty cute with his hair down and normal."

Juicy nudged her. "No shit. What straight guy could pull off *either* look at school?" She nudged her again. "What straight guy would try?"

Katy led the way out of the corner and headed to Chemistry. "So you're saying we pimp out K-pop to Chacha Hips to get him on the crew?" It actually made a certain amount of sense. There wouldn't be many options for a cute gay dancer in Dumass High.

"You say 'pimp out' like it's a bad thing." Juicy led the way to the lab table they shared. "You know that tall, skinny white boy needs to get himself some-some one of these days." She dropped her books on the table. "Might as well take one for the team. Then Chacha Hips can teach us his stuff."

Katy made one of Juicy's sounds. "I've seen his teaching videos. Boy can dance, but he can't teach."

Juicy leaned away with both eyebrows so high they disappeared under her bangs. "Stalker much?"

Katy moved beakers around for something to do. "It was my duty to the crew to find out about this guy."

"Mm-hm. And the fact that he's cute had nothing to do with it."

"Cute and gay."

Juicy sighed. "Which is where K-pop comes in."

"What if he's not Chacha Hips' type?"

"Pfft. In Dumass, gay beggars can't be choosers."

The bell rang.

When Katy reached the studio after school, Mr. and Mrs. Tijerina were already dancing. They'd sunk so much money into the studio, they had the passcode.

"*Hola,* Mr. T," she called out, "Mrs. T."

Mr. T waved, but the music was starting up, so he had to focus. The retired couple was rehearsing for a show that weekend. They were performing a history of Latin dance for the Fiesta Latina. When the music started, Katy smiled. It was an old-fashioned chacha so ancient, it always made her laugh.

The Tijerina's were local legends. They travelled to Houston to compete and always placed well, so seeing them dance something even older than they were was hysterical. They were sure to get a good laugh at the festival.

Letting them practice, Katy wandered around the studio picking up trash and straightening chairs. Since she was the oldest daughter, her mom assumed she'd be the one to take the studio. Her sisters danced, but none of them as well as Katy. None of them had the passion, either.

Katy did.

Dancing was her life. Both performing and teaching, and she was *good* at both. *Damn* good. Not Chacha Hips good, but better than someone who wanted to run a small town studio in the armpit of the state.

She snatched a rag from behind the bar and spot-cleaned the mirrors. They were getting smoky with age. In the mirrors, she examined the rest of the studio. With Chacha Heels on his way, Katy saw the studio with new eyes. It was dark. It was dingy. It was old.

She'd never noticed before. Until today, it'd always been a place to dance. Who cared what it looked like? It had a hardwood floor. It had mirrors. The sound system was killer since her mom had actually taken Katy's advice when she'd had to replace the whole thing a year earlier.

The crew had even used the money from a couple of local shows to buy some serious club lights, just for the hell of it. K-pop knew a guy who'd nailed a great deal.

She sighed. Great lights and sound, but would she even get a chance to show them off? Would Chacha Hips hang out long enough, or would he take one look at this place and walk out? There had to be a way to get him to hear her out.

He might be her ticket out of this town. If she trained with him, if she met people through him. . . Her mom would *have* to understand. She *had* to. Mom knew all about regret. She'd never let her daughter lose an opportunity to dance on a world stage just to stay here and run the Emporium. There had to be a way to make it work.

Maybe pimping out K-pop wasn't such a bad idea.

And if Boyfriend really wanted to show him around town. . . that'd be good. Boyfriend was popular, captain of the football team and all. Everyone liked Boyfriend, and since Chacha Hips was gay, it's not like her boyfriend had a reason to get jealous.

The door opened with a ring.

Good old Juicy, right on time. Not much of a dancer, but always on time. Well, except when she danced. Katy suppressed a smirk. If only she could get Juicy to focus more on her dancing and less on that stupid cheerleading crap, she could make a dancer out of her.

Whatever. She was tired of banging her head against that wall.

"Hola chica." Juicy made a beeline for the bathroom. "Gotta pee."

And she was gone.

Katy chuckled and watched the Tijerina's work on their turns. Mrs. T wasn't connecting.

"Slow down, Mrs. T," she called out. "If you wait for him, he can help you more."

"Thank you, dear," Mrs. T called back.

Katy heard a string of creative Spanglish profanity from the bathroom above the sound of the music. She rushed through the swinging door. "What's wrong?"

"You're out of TP," Juicy said, "again."

Oh yeah, there'd been a dance the night before. Must've been more folks than usual. Katy snatched a box of Kleenex from the vanity and dropped it over the stall door.

"Incoming."

"Thanks."

At the door, she stopped for a second. "I need to run to the store, Juicy. We'll need TP for practice."

"Go ahead," Juicy told her as the toilet flushed. "I'll steal some Cokes from home." As Katy left the room, Juicy called after her. "Get enough TP so you won't run out any time soon, okay?"

Katy let the door swing shut. Enough? She smiled and waved at the Tijerinas as she left. How much TP could she fit in her car?

Gunner

Tonight.

Gunner smelled smoke. He opened his eyes for no real good reason. It was fucking pitch black in the shed and that wouldn't change, but the smell scared him. What if the old bitch passed out smoking? Or his asshole father forgot the smoker was lit and threw something over it again?

Shit.

He breathed in. The smoke smelled clean, like wood, no plastic or anything chemical. Maybe the old man was just cooking up some meat. Maybe Gunner wasn't about to burn to death or get himself smoked like jerky.

He leaned against the wall and closed his eyes. He'd tensed up, so he relaxed his legs as much as he could with them pulled up against his chest. He let his arms drop around them looser. The chains rattled when he moved.

His folks were smart enough to make sure the cuffs were leather so he wouldn't get scratched up no matter how long they left him in the shed, and the old man, especially, was good at hurting him without leaving any marks.

Back in sixth grade, when he'd found out he'd be showering for gym class, Gunner'd prayed long and hard that someone would notice the cuts and bruises. But his parents just got more creative. The electricity was the worst.

When the leather cuffs showed up, he'd known there was no reason to pray. The God they used as an excuse to torture him wasn't listening. So there were no bruises for the other boys to see in the locker room, and the showers just created problems of their own.

He slammed his head against the wall.

The old man liked that he was a football player. He spent most of his time bruised up. No one really paid close enough attention to see that not all of them happened in the game. He was good at football, too, since he knew how to ignore the pain.

He slammed his head against the wall.

Corey'd been wiped out at practice. Too tired from fucking his girlfriend all night long to give Gunner a good workout. He just lay there the whole time on a bench, head back, eyes closed, feet wide apart and legs loose while Gunner pumped iron.

He slammed his head against the wall harder.

The stars came out.

And then that. . . *freak*, that fucking cunt of a pretty boy had to go and mouth off. And he'd lost it. Just. . . *lost* it right there in school. And Corey took the pretty boy's side like he was Corey's bitch girlfriend or something.

He'd seen the look in Corey's eyes. If the freak had ratted him out, Gunner would've had to beat the shit out of his best friend.

Well, maybe Corey wasn't really his best friend, anymore.

He slammed his head one last time.

A blinding light woke him up fast, and he curled in on himself as best he could. He actually liked the blast of cold water after a night in the hot, smelly shed but didn't want his folks to know that. And the power hose washed away the piss. He'd stopped bothering to hold it years ago. He wasn't positive, but he was pretty sure they wouldn't let him out until he pissed himself, anyway, so why hold it?

A shadow crossed him. "You have heard that it was said, 'an eye for an eye and a tooth for a tooth.'" The old man's voice prompted Gunner to cup his hands over his junk. "But I say to you, do not resist an evil person. Whoever slaps you on your right cheek, turn the other to him also."

Yeah, Jesus didn't have an old man who sprayed a power hose directly at his balls just 'cause he thought it was funny to hear the screams.

"Have you seen the error of your ways?" the old man asked.

"Yes, sir. When Valentino mouthed off to me, I should have let it go. I should not have punched him." Next time, he'd slit his fucking throat.

The keys landed in a puddle at Gunner's feet. He waited.

"Have a blessed day."

When the old man was gone, Gunner snatched up the keys and undid the shackles with shaking hands. He wanted to hit someone, kick something, hurt someone. Didn't matter who.

He stalked across the field to the back door of the house. When he'd been little, he'd run as fast as he could, afraid someone would see him. The closest neighbor was almost a mile away, though, and Gunner's folks made him strip off on purpose to embarrass him, to make him feel ashamed at crossing the field naked and smelling of his own piss, shit or puke, depending on what they'd done to him. Eventually, he'd stopped being embarrassed. Being naked just meant the hose cleaned him off that much better.

Inside the kitchen, the old lady was making coffee. "Sleep well?"

Gunner stopped and turned to her. "Like a baby, ma'am."

The bitch asked that every time, like nothing had happened. He watched her eyes as her smile faded. Ever since his balls had sprouted hair, she'd been more and more awkward around him. Being naked was a weapon, now.

She looked away and fluttered a towel at him. "Well, don't stand there dripping on my kitchen floor. Go get some pants on and come back in here and clean up this mess."

"Yes, ma'am." He didn't let himself smile until his back was turned. As victories went, it was pathetic as fuck, but Gunner took them where he could.

Practice after school was intense. Good. Gunner was happy to hit hard. They'd cancelled practice before school because Corey's dance crew was performing for the Starbuck's opening. Lame.

But Corey was in peak form that afternoon. He kept everyone running plays for real. They scrimmaged like it was the homecoming game. Corey was a demon, and when they worked together it was almost like old times, like maybe Corey was still his friend. By the end of practice, Gunner was beat, bruised and sore, but for all the right reasons for a change.

As they jogged into the locker room, the whole team shouted and banged on the lockers. Man, if Corey could keep it that intense all the time, they were guaranteed to kick ass every game.

"You're like a demon, today, bro," Gunner said as they pulled off their pads. "It's awesome."

Corey grinned that goofy grin Gunner hadn't seen in a while. "We gotta be ready for homecoming, right?" In about two seconds he was naked.

No one Gunner knew was as comfortable naked as Corey. Of course, if he had as much hanging as Corey did, he'd probably want to show it off, too.

"Come on, bro. There's gotta be something more going on." Gunner grabbed for his shorts.

"Dude," Corey said. He looked confused. "Take a shower. You stink."

Shit. "I gotta get home." He hated showering at school.

Corey looked disappointed. "I was hoping we could hang for a while, you know, before I have to go dance." He rolled his eyes. Was he finally getting over the stupid dance thing?

It'd been a long time since Corey had asked to hang out.

"All right, all right." Gunner dropped the shorts and followed Corey to the showers. "But if you grab my ass again, you fag, I swear I'll fucking deck you."

Corey laughed. "Oh dude, you should be so lucky."

They joked back and forth while they showered, just like the old days. Gunner turned off his water and grabbed a towel. "Dude, you take longer showers than a girl."

Corey didn't take the hint. "You say that like it's news, bro. You've known me how long?"

Pretty much since birth.

When the last of the other guys left the room, Corey looked around. "So you really wanna know what's up?"

"Here we go." Gunner wrapped a towel around his waist. "Bro, you know you can always pour out your girly heart to me."

Corey grinned and let the water run down his back. "Why am I your friend, again?"

Yeah, Gunner really didn't want to get all sentimental. "So what's up?" He grabbed a clean towel and tossed it. "And turn off the fucking water. We live in a desert."

Corey looked around. "I don't want anyone to hear."

"For crying out loud, Oprah." He padded closer and turned off the water himself. "Just spill already. No one's listening."

Corey grabbed Gunner's arm and twisted it behind him, putting him in a head lock. "Hah! Got you."

Gunner tried to twist free, but he'd been so surprised Corey'd been able to lock him in. "Okay bro, no naked wrestling. It's not horseplay. It's just gay."

Corey didn't let go. He laughed.

Gunner's towel started to slip. "Seriously, asshat. Let me the fuck go."

The hold vanished. Gunner moved away and secured his towel.

They stared at each other.

Maybe too much had changed. Maybe they weren't friends anymore.

"There's this new guy in town making moves on Katy," Corey said. He wrapped the towel around his waist and sat on a bench. "He's a fucking champion dancer, and he's hot in a snooty, big city way that chicks dig."

"Chicks 'dig' that, do they?" Gunner leaned against the wall just close enough that the guys around the corner wouldn't overhear. "You seriously need to lay off the thirty-year-old sitcoms on Netflix, bro."

"Hah!" Corey grinned. "Dude, I found some new shows. You totally need to come over some time and watch with me."

"New guy sounds like a fag. Why worry?"

Corey sighed. "Katy says he's not gay."

"Do I need to take him out for you?"

Corey eyes nearly popped out of his wussy head.

"Kidding!" Gunner was tired of Corey's pussy side. "I'm kidding." Corey was like the brother he'd never had, but his whole kindness to strangers thing? Lame. Okay, he had to think like Corey to get this whiny talk over and done. He sat on the other end of the bench. "Dude, either she loves you or she doesn't. If this new guy can take her from you, I say you're better off."

Corey shrank a little. "Maybe if I can find the perfect birthday present for her." He looked up expectantly.

Gunner rose. "I am not helping you shop for a birthday present, and I officially need pants covering my junk now just because you even wanted to ask me." He headed to his locker. "I may be willing to watch sitcoms from the dark ages, but I don't have a snatch, bro."

"Oh yeah?" Corey grabbed the towel from Gunner's waist and ran between the lockers with it, laughing. "I guess not!"

Gunner shook his head.

Well, if the new guy caused any problems, Gunner had Corey's back.

He pounded some stupid son of a bitch they'd found hitchhiking. Anyone dumb enough to do that in the twenty-first century deserved to get his ass kicked. Gunner punched his ugly face a few times then let him fall to his hands and knees. He kicked the son of a bitch.

Stanton did too, from the other side. He picked the guy up and held him.

Gunner took a few free shots to the guy's kidneys. He punched the guy in the balls.

That's when the guy started screaming. Not shouting. Screaming. Full-on horror movie screaming that just went on and on and on. Jesus fuck, how did the guy have that much air?

Gunner knew that sound.

He'd made it himself.

It had to stop.

"Shut up!" he shouted, but the guy kept screaming. "Shut up!" Gunner couldn't breathe. He felt acid in his throat. "Shut up!"

Then he was pounding the guy and kicking him and shouting at him, and when he fell down, Gunner yanked him to his feet and forced him into Stanton's hands so he could pound him some more. "Shut up!"

By the time the guy shut up, Gunner was covered in blood and his hands hurt like hell. He was gasping for breath, even though he could normally run 10K easy.

His buddies all stood a few feet away. No one said a word.

"What?" Gunner spat blood. Whose was it? "At least he shut up."

An hour later, he lay on a bare mattress in an old, abandoned nursing home. Some girl was sucking his dick. Her name was Tiffani or Jesse or something. He didn't care as long as she gave good head. She wasn't bad.

The other guys all had girls of their own and rooms of their own along one wing. The faint moans and grunts were a turn-on, along with the rhythmic pounding and springs squeaking. He didn't want to fuck this girl. He just wanted her to suck him off so he could close his eyes and pretend she was someone else.

He was freaking amped when they rolled back into town. The guys were loud and half-drunk still, and everyone in the back seat was wrestling. Without taking his eyes off the road, Gunner reached over the seat and got in a few good punches of his own. Marty tried to climb over the seat after him, but Stanton shoved him back.

"No fucking with the driver, asshat."

After he'd dropped off the last of them, he was still wired. He tapped the steering wheel and bounced in his seat, but nothing worked. He still had enough energy to beat down the entire Mercedes football team with enough to spare for all the cheerleaders. He felt that hitchhiker's face, felt ribs creak, felt his wad blow in that bitch's mouth.

Katy's piece of shit car was parked in front of her house. As soon as he passed it, he slowed down. Then stopped. Tap-tap-tap-a-tap went his fingers. See, she was a bitch to play Corey the way she was. So what if Corey sucked ass as a dancer? Only fags could dance, anyway. Corey was captain of the fucking football team, fucking *captain*. Most girls would get wet just for that, but he was rich, too and the dude could take an engine apart and put it back together blindfolded.

Tap-tap-tap-a-tap. Okay, girls probably didn't care about the engine thing, but Corey was hot too, and girls liked that. He saw the way girls looked at Corey. And he got all worked up to make sure she had nice presents.

Tap-tap-tap-a-tap. But fucking *Katy* was too good for him. She wanted some pretty boy dancer from the big city, and she was going to break Corey's heart. The dude was like a great big puppy dog and she was going to step on his tail and make him squeal.

Bitch.

Okay, maybe he and Corey hadn't been so tight the last year, but why was that? Because he spent all his time with her and her stupid dance crew. He'd known Corey since they could talk. She'd only dated him a year. Corey was his brother. His best friend. Hanging out with him reminded Gunner just how much he missed the big wuss.

Tap-tap-tap-a-tap.

And the bitch was already breaking his heart.

That did it. He had Corey's back, even if no one could ever know about it. He jammed his car in reverse and backed up to Katy's tiny foreign piece of shit.

Attaching the chains took less than a minute, and if she was stupid enough to leave her car unlocked so he could put it in neutral then she was practically asking him to trash it.

He towed it downtown to an empty warehouse.

He pulled an aluminum bat out of his trunk.

He wailed on that fucking car for half an hour.

Corey was his friend. His brother. There'd been a time when he would've done fucking anything for Corey. Anything. He wiped his sleeve over his sweating face. Anything. . .

Towing the car back took longer. Whenever he tried to speed up, the damn thing rattled. He knew no one was awake, but if he made any noise at all, someone would wake up.

At Katie's, he unhooked the car, piled the chain in his trunk and drove home.

He slept like a baby.

His phone woke him up way too early the next morning.

It was a text from Corey. *Some mthrfkr killd Katies car cum ovr?*

His heart pounded in his chest. It was hard to breathe.

Maybe trashing her car hadn't been such a great idea.

The phone rang again. It was a photo. Katie's car, beat to shit the way he'd left it, but someone had painted writing on the side: *Every rose has its thron*

What the hell was a thron?

Another ring and another photo: the interior of Katie's car covered with rose petals.

Holy shit. Had it been like that when he jacked it?

He didn't know. He hadn't looked that carefully and it'd been dark.

What the fuck? Did someone else have it in for the bitch, too?

My Friends Call Me K-pop

Sometime after Twist was shot.

Kenny Valentino woke up in the middle of the night. He lay still, then realized the room smelled wrong. And it was too quiet. Where was he?

He sniffed, panic rising in his chest, and sat up. The mattress under him squeaked.

Oh yeah. He was at Ethan's on an air mattress.

What was that noise?

Ethan breathing and the sound of water running.

Mr. Fox must be having a wiz.

Flush.

Yep. Okay. He lay down and listened to the sound of Ethan's breath. It calmed him. The air smelled of cologne and maybe a little bit of old socks, but not in a disgusting way, just faint, so he could tell it was a dude's room. His friend. Ethan Fox.

The sound of the flushing toilet faded to a stop.

And now Kenny really had to wiz.

Every move squeaked the mattress and made him wince. Once he was free of the mattress of squeaky annoyance, he padded barefoot to the bathroom. Thank God for the little light Ethan had lit for just such an eventuality.

In the bathroom, Kenny closed the door and made sure the door to Mr. Fox's room was closed as well. He took a deep breath and turned on the light. His face jumped out in the bright overhead light. Huh. He looked different. He was smiling.

Best. night. ever.

He took care of the wizzing issue, then returned to the mirror.

He ran his hands through his hair to tame the wild waves. They'd been swimming. Skinny-dipping, for Christ's sake! He'd never done that before.

He wore a bathrobe to and from the shower in his own house for Christ's sake. Here, the entire house was practically a locker room when Ms. Davis was gone.

Kenny grinned. Locker rooms had never been a good place for him before. Bad connotations: insults over his tall, scrawny body and inability to give a fuck about sports, trying not to make eye contact, hoping he could sneak out without having to take a shower.

Here? They laughed and danced naked by the pool and wrestled in the water like fucking jocks for Christ's sake.

The smile vanished.

Kenny and his brother Ed used to wrestle and horse around. They used to talk late at night and make forts when Kenny was little, and Ed was the big brother who knew everything. Then Ed left for years and years, and then he came back last year minus a leg and plus horrible night terrors.

Since Kenny's room was across the hall, and because his sister had the baby to cope with, Kenny woke up when Ed screamed. He crossed the hall to Ed's room, and he talked him down. It was freaking scary. Ed lashed out a lot. He'd never, *never once* hit Kenny. But it was fucking scary the way he shouted.

And then in the morning they'd all pretend it'd never happened.

They always pretended everything was okay.

Ethan's home was so different. Here they talked about things. Sure, there'd been some bad times, but Ethan and his dad were talking again. Ethan told him so. And Ethan talked to him, told him the bad shit going on in his life. He didn't pretend everything was fine.

Hell, he'd seen Ethan cry, even. Nobody cried in Kenny's house. Nobody but Kenny. And he never let anyone see it.

And Ethan had given him a couple beers. That'd been cool, too. That's what friends did.

He smiled again. They'd drunk beers and horsed around and talked about girls and played video games. . . that'd been sick wicked. It was just like normal kids, like he saw everyone else at school and on TV. His breath caught in his throat.

While he and Ethan played video games, Ms. Davis, who insisted he call her Auntie Mac, had brought out pie and ice cream, just like on a freaking Facebook meme.

And when Mr. Fox came home and went up to bed, he made K-pop get up and hug him.

He'd almost lost it. His own dad hadn't hugged him in years.

"Dude, I am so sorry about that," Ethan had said. "It's a gay dad thing, I think. All the hugging."

Kenny had played it casual. "No worries, hai? I'm chill."

Kenny hiccoughed and couldn't stop a few tears from leaking out. He covered his face in his hands, but he couldn't block the pain. It shook his shoulders and cramped his gut.

The people in this house didn't even know him, yet they acted like they loved him. More than his family, more than anyone in that fucking town he'd lived in all his life.

Oh, shit, he couldn't stop the sobs. He covered his face with both hands to stifle the sound. What if someone woke up?

"Kenny?"

Fuck. He gasped and wiped at his face. A single sob choked out. "A-okay, F-bomb." Should he call him that? "Mr. Fox." Shit. He had to get it under control. "I'm fine." He sucked in a ragged breath. "I am so sorry I woke you."

"What's wrong?"

"Nothing." He wiped at his face again, then glanced in the mirror. Ah, fuck. His eyes were bloodshot, and his hair all fucked up. He straightened his hair.

Mr. Fox leaned in the doorway in sweats and a bathrobe. He seemed genuinely concerned.

"Nothing. I'm sorry." Suck it up. Suck it in.

"Come here, Kenny." He moved away into his own room and flicked on a lamp.

Kenny followed obediently.

The room was neat, but the furniture was old. He guessed it was what'd been in the house when Ethan and his dad moved in.

"Did Ethan do something?"

"What?" Ah shit, he couldn't get Ethan in trouble! "No, no. I'm fine, Mr. Fox. Ethan is. . . he's my friend. He's a good friend. He didn't do anything." Damn it, he was going to screw it all up, ruin it. "I had a great time tonight. He's the first person who ever talked to me. We had beers—" Oh shit. "I mean. . ." This huge ball of yuck filled his chest.

And then he felt ten years old again, with this huge hulking man who reminded him of the man his own father had been when Kenny was ten and who'd stopped existing a year or two later.

"I just never had a friend before." Oh, Christ on a stick, that sounded pathetic. It *was* pathetic, and then Kenny sobbed, and Mr. Fox wrapped him in strong arms, arms that promised everything would be okay, even though Kenny was almost an adult and shouldn't need a father to hug him and kiss him goodnight. And Ethan had those arms to hold him every day.

The sobs wouldn't stop. Not for a long time.

Mr. Fox held him and said nothing, just stroked his hair from time to time.

A million years later, Kenny made himself stop crying. He drew away from Mr. Fox, wiping his face with the short sleeves of his shirt, with the bottom edge of it as best he could reach, since most stupid shirts were barely long enough for him.

"I'm so sorry, Mr. Fox." He noticed the great wet blob on the tattered bathrobe. "Oh, Jesus Christ, I soaked you. I am such a little kid."

"Kenny, don't." He met Kenny's gaze evenly and calmly. "Don't be embarrassed."

Kenny had nothing to say.

"When Ethan was attacked," Mr. Fox said quietly, so very quietly, "I freaked out. I was a complete wreck and I had to keep it together because he was the one who'd been beat to shit." He waited until Kenny met his eyes. "You were the one who thought to bring him clothes. Shit, I have no idea where the hell you found those shorts and socks that late at night." He guided Kenny to a chair and crouched beside it. "I will never, *ever* as long as I live, be able to repay you for that kindness and thoughtfulness. That's something his father should have thought to do, and I didn't." He smiled. "You did." He shrugged. "You had my back."

Kenny's face burned. No one had ever said. . . his eyes burned.

"I tried to kill myself." The words were out before he could reel them in.

Mr. Fox's eyes widened. Not so much it looked like shock, but they opened wider.

"I was going to kill myself." He gulped. "The day Ethan moved here. I was going to take pills and whiskey." He'd said the words out loud, and he had to follow them all the way down the path. "Then Ethan showed up at the studio, and he liked my hair and he liked my Black Butler shirt. And I knew I recognized him from somewhere, and when I went home to kill myself, I remembered that he danced in a video to my favorite band." The sobs hit him out of nowhere. He forced himself to say it all. "And no one I'd ever known, no one ever. . ." He couldn't say it. He'd lose it again if he said it, but this man deserved to know. "No one ever liked me."

And then he lost it again. And Mr. Fox held him while he sobbed, and this time it was okay for some reason.

"I get it, Kenny," Mr. Fox said. "I get it. I grew up in this town, Kenny. I know what it's like."

This time, when the sobs subsided, Kenny felt calm. He took a deep, deep breath.

After a long time, Mr. Fox finally spoke. "Does Ethan know any of this?"

Kenny shook his head. "No. He has so much crap to deal with. He almost died. Tango has this stalker." He didn't mention all the crap with Mr. Fox's issues. "He doesn't need to deal with my shit. I'm just. . . I'm just lonely, or something." He was just a loser.

Mr. Fox brought them to their feet. He held Kenny by his shoulders. "I'm not going to say anything to Ethan about what you told me tonight. And if you ever need to talk to someone, I still owe you, okay?"

He waited until Kenny nodded.

He squeezed Kenny's shoulders, then released him and moved to the bedside table. He grabbed a cell phone and held it out to Kenny. "Here's my info, Kenny. I want you to make me a promise." He handed the phone over. "Put it in your cell."

Kenny drew his cell out of a pocket and transferred the data.

"A promise," he repeated. "If you ever, at any time of the day or night, *ever* think about hurting yourself again, I want you to call me first, give me a chance to talk you out of it. If I can't, okay fine, I tried. But I want you to promise to give me that chance, then I won't feel guilty if you do it."

Kenny handed back the phone. "I wouldn't. . ."

"I've been there, Kenny. I tried it twice."

Kenny couldn't breathe.

"Pills once." He held out a wrist. "Then this." The scar was still visible, lengthwise down his wrist. That way said he'd meant it, too. "So I'm not bullshitting you when I say I understand." He drew his hand back. "And that's something Ethan doesn't know, so if you tell him, he will be surprised."

"I won't tell him."

He shook his head. "I would never ask you to keep a secret. I just don't want you to get blindsided if he freaks out." He shrugged. "Probably about time I told him."

Jesus fucking Christ.

"I will not share a word of this with Ethan until you tell me he knows it already." Mr. Fox was so serious.

"Oh, I couldn't. . ."

"Why not?"

Kenny sucked in a ragged breath. "I don't know."

Mr. Fox gripped Kenny's shoulder. "I think Ethan can handle it." He smiled. "I think he'll actually be pretty flattered." He lost the smile. "Ethan knows how much he owes you, Kenny. He didn't have *any* real friends before he moved here, either, just a bunch of sycophants who leached off his fame. He's damned lucky to have you."

Holy shit. His dad knew that?

"Don't be so surprised, Kenny." He grinned. "I'm gay. We have special mutant powers."

Kenny grinned. "I really hope Ethan knows how lucky he is, Mr. Fox. You're sick wicked."

He laughed. "Fortunately, I'm hip enough to know that's a good thing." He grimaced. "Hip was a horrible old guy slip, wasn't it?"

Kenny sucked in a breath. "I'll let it pass this time."

Mr. Fox opened his arms and Kenny hugged him tight. "I'm sorry to be such a little kid tonight," Kenny said.

Mr. Fox scoffed. "More people need to hang onto their inner child, Kenny."

Kenny held him out at arms' length. "My friends call me K-pop."

He smiled. "All right, K-pop it is."

Kenny made his way to the bathroom.

"K-pop?"

He turned.

"Does this need to be a secret from Ethan?"

Kenny considered. "Can it be for now? All this sharing crap is new to me."

Mr. Fox nodded.

"I'll tell him as soon as I can, okay?" He moved through the bathroom.

"K-pop?"

Kenny stopped again.

"I think he'll surprise you. He really does love you, although he might not be so great at showing it." He raised a hand. "Sleep."

Kenny nodded, crept back into Ethan's room and settled onto the air mattress as quietly as he could. How anyone slept as soundly as Ethan amazed him. He lay back and listened to the sound of Ethan's breath. He'd never fallen asleep to that sound before.

Call Me Twist

Some days later.

Twist slipped out of bed as quietly as possible, but the damn woman woke up and took his hand. "Aw, sweetie, don't you have time for just one more?"

"Benny's on his way home," Twist reminded her. They'd done it three times already.

She smiled up at him as if she hadn't heard. Likely, she hadn't. He needed to tone down the damn attraction bracelet. He touched her forehead with one finger and closed his eyes. "Sleep."

She drifted onto the bed and lay still.

It was weird. All the words and herbs and candles hardly seemed necessary anymore. After he'd practiced one of the desert witch's spell three or four times, all he had to do was focus and abracadabra, it worked. It didn't make sense.

Oh well, no point looking a gift horse in the mouth.

He padded through the messy living room and grabbed his jeans where he'd left them neatly folded on the arm of the couch. He was still packing away and zipping when Benny opened the door to the single-wide, flooding the cheap furniture with unflattering light.

"Hey, Benny." Twist buttoned his jeans and slipped into his sandals.

"Twist, buddy!" Benny beamed and extended a grease-stained hand.

Twist forced himself to take it without hesitation. "Good to see you."

Benny's eyes unfocused for a split second. "The little lady sleeping?"

"Like a baby."

Benny squeezed Twist's hand and released it. "You are a miracle worker. I swear she didn't have a single night's rest until you breezed into town. And now? With a baby on the way? Well, we sure are grateful to you."

"Always glad to help." Of course, he was glad to help. The brat was his. "The pleasure is all mine." He moved to the door. "Well, I should be on my way."

A hand touched his shoulder. "You know. . . you don't need to leave right away, do you?"

Twist bristled and quickly slid the bracelet off. He shoved it into a pocket.

He turned to face Benny. "What did you have in mind?"

The redneck blinked, then shook his head. "Huh?" He wiped a hand over his face. "There's a game tonight. I thought you might want a beer." Benny obviously doubted his own motivation.

Yeah, Twist really needed to dial the bracelet back.

"Sorry, Benny," he said. "I have more work to do."

"Yeah, of course." The poor idiot looked relieved.

"Why don't you just pay me." Twist threw all his intent into his voice. "And I'll be on my way." It was usually all he needed.

Benny pulled out his wallet. "Twenty bucks, right?"

"Twenty's what you have in your wallet," he said.

"I hope twenty's all right, buddy. It's all I have." Benny handed him more than a hundred dollars.

"It'll work."

Benny took Twist's hand again as he handed the money over. "You're a good friend. The best."

Twist smiled. If the greasy redneck didn't let go of his hand, he'd send the devil rabbit after him in the night. No matter how strong he had the bracelet dialed up, it didn't work if there wasn't something receptive somewhere inside that pea brain.

"I just try to help out." He glanced at the bedroom door. "You take care of that pretty lady and that baby, now."

"Oh yeah." Benny tried to sound smooth. "I'll take care of her."

Twist escaped. He had at least two more stops he should make, but he didn't really have the ambition. Of course, he could just drop off the hokey herbs or candles or whatever bullshit was scheduled. The stuff he'd stolen from the desert witch really seemed to work, and the more he practiced with it, the more he started to think he actually understood the shit.

He'd set up a circuit of bored wives who would never try to trap him if they got pregnant. He didn't actually *need* to sex them up every time he stopped, but he'd spent so many years without so much as a girlfriend, that his newfound ability to have any woman he wanted seemed a shame to waste.

There were four other women in the trailer park carrying a child of his. He'd first tried the birth control spell the week he moved in. Unfortunately, he'd had it backwards and he planted every woman he screwed. Oops.

Five women had miscarried, but, for some reason, five had stuck. He'd tried the same "flushing" spell on all ten of them, but for some reason it didn't always work.

No matter. He'd be on the road by the time any of them came to term. Benny likely wouldn't even notice. He had the same red hair and light skin as Twist. The Moralez family would likely suspect. Oh, and the Lincolns would definitely know something was wrong. They were both dark as coal.

Twist climbed on his bike and kicked it to life. He didn't worry about helmet laws for the same reason he didn't bother wearing a shirt on his bike or worry about husbands realizing he'd screwed every woman in the trailer park. Magic fixed everything for him.

He was untouchable.

In the weeks since that fucking Van Zeeland whore had shot him to save that pretty boy son of a bitch Fox, he'd made a home for himself here in the middle of nowhere. He earned a living as a sort of medicine man who taught shooting lessons on the side, and his clients always tipped very, very generously thanks to the witch's confusion spell.

To keep in shape, he helped out on the local farms where the farmer's daughters were pretty. His skin was tan, now, and he'd built up some muscle. He'd let his hair grow out, too. The ladies never said no.

Everything was different. Everything was better.

But he couldn't stop thinking about Katy. She was the one girl he'd wanted who'd said no to him. He'd had so many women since then, more than some men had in their whole lives, but Katy was still the one he dreamed about, the one he wanted. Soon, he'd be ready to try again. Once he was a little more buff, once he'd learned a little more dancing, maybe. Once he had a little more money.

Once he was sure he could make the attraction spells last for more than a few months.

He turned off the road and made his way to the cave. He actually lived in the trailer park, but he used the cave to practice his craft. He felt the customary tingle as he passed through the barrier spells he'd set. No one without magic would notice them, but anyone who passed through would abruptly feel the need to be somewhere else. Anywhere else.

The bike ground to a stop and Twist kicked a leg over it. Silvery movement caught his attention. Mr. Bunny hopped up to him and ran ghostly circles around his feet. "What's wrong Mr. Bunny?" He'd never seen the spirit act that way.

What the hell could scare a dead rabbit?

After his initial conflict with the ghost, Twist had noticed it haunting him one day, just sort of following him around. No one else could see it, so he let it hang around the cave. It didn't do any harm and there was something sort of fun about having his own personal ghost. The books called it a familiar.

When Twist approached the mouth of the cave, Mr. Bunny screamed.

"Your rabbit doesn't seem to like me," a woman's voice echoed from inside the cave. His cave. His hideout.

He grabbed the pistol from its clip on the bike and dropped into a crouch.

"Interesting décor," the woman said, sarcasm dripping from her words. "Very. . . postmodern serial killer. I like it."

Maintaining the crouch, Twist hurried to one side of the cave entrance. How the hell had she made it past the barriers?

"For crying out loud, I'm not going to hurt you," she insisted. "If I wanted you dead, I'd have forced the rabbit to possess you and bash your brains out against a rock."

If she knew about Mr. Bunny, she had to be a witch. And her threat made him nervous. He'd actually used Mr. Bunny to kill once. He'd had the rabbit possess a bear to kill a nosy husband.

"Who are you?" He slid into the cave, gun up and ready. He lit all the candles simultaneously.

She clapped. "Pretty."

Wow. Speaking of pretty. She wore a tight black dress, slit up to her thigh, that was so formfitting it accented the curves of her petite body more than hiding anything. She wore her golden hair long and wavy. Her skin was tan and smooth. Although she was small, she radiated power. She looked to be somewhere in her mid-twenties.

When she saw him, she smiled and held her hands together. She nodded at one wall of the cave. "She's pretty, this girl you seem a touch obsessed about. What's her name?"

She seemed awfully calm about the whole thing. Twist glanced at the wall to make sure the shrine was intact. Yes, photos of Katy, icons made from her face and old clothes, mobiles of her discarded lingerie. "Her name's Katy."

"You can call me Mary," she said. "What should I call you?"

"Call me Twist." The gun felt a touch foolish considering how calm she seemed.

Maybe he should just put it away.

Wait. Was that his own thought or hers?

"That was me," she admitted. "I'm impressed you could tell."

"Why are you here?"

She crossed her arms. "As I've said, I'm not here to harm you, so—" She waved a hand and the gun was yanked out of Twist's grip. He stumbled a step forward as it drifted toward her, metal melting and twisting in midair. The piece shifted and stretched.

By the time it reached her outstretched hand, it held the shape of a perfect rose. The gunmetal of the bloom bled a dark, dark red as she raised it and sniffed.

She smiled and held it out to Twist. "Yes, David, you should be very afraid of me, but I promise I do not intend you any harm as long as you aren't so stupid as to attack me. If you do, I will rip the flesh from you bones and transform your skeleton into something creative and ironic."

Twist made no move to take the rose. The woman terrified him.

She lay the rose on the table at Katy's shrine.

"Now that I have your full attention," she said, "shall we chat?"

Twist swallowed.

"I'm here to help you," she said. "You've made a nice start, but you have a lot to learn, especially about maintaining a low profile."

Twist scoffed. "Why do that? With this kind of power, I'm untouchable."

She raised an eyebrow. "Not from the do-gooders."

"Who?"

She sighed. "You believe in witches and ghosts, now, but think that witch hunters and ghost busters are myths? Mad tales told to little demons to keep them in line?"

"Demons?"

"Focus, David." Her voice was colder now. "All magic has a price. If I noticed you already, chances are you've also drifted onto the radar of more aggressive types, types who would kill you without hesitation."

"I'd like to see them try."

She lifted a hand very casually, and Twist found himself yanked from the floor into the air. And he couldn't breathe. His hands groped at his throat.

"You got lucky with the witch in the desert," she told him while he choked. "You know nothing, Twist, nothing. You can outwit a few rednecks, screw a few of their wives and you think you're a big man. You have potential, David, you do. But if someone guts you like a fish and feeds you to the wolves, that potential will be wasted."

She waved an arm. Twist fell to the ground and sucked in a desperate breath.

"I would like to help you reach your potential."

"Why?" His throat burned.

"An old enemy of mine is gathering followers," she said. "I'd like to gather a few men of power around me." She looked down at Twist. "This enemy will one day find you and kill you if you're alone. I will protect you until you find your way. Then we can protect each other." She reached a hand down to him.

Reluctantly, he took it and let her pull him to his feet. She tugged him closer. "And if you've never fucked a powerful witch, you are missing out on one of the great delights of a lifetime."

Twist swallowed. In the flickering candlelight her beauty was overpowering.

She tapped his nose and moved away. "You're cute."

He adjusted his pants self-consciously. He was wa-ay out of his league in so many ways.

"What is your biggest question?"

He couldn't pass that one up. "Why do I stop needing the words after a while?"

She glanced at him, then held his gaze. She rubbed her delicate hands together and tilted her head to one side, turning away. "There are those who find the magic. There are those whom the magic finds. More rarely, there are those who are born to it."

"That's me?"

She turned to him. "Yes." She held up a finger. "Before you do some sophomoric happy dance, realize that being born to the magic doesn't make you good at it. I wasn't born to it. I found it myself, and look how I can play you like a puppet. Innate ability doesn't imply skill."

Twist capped his enthusiasm. He'd wanted to do exactly the happy dance she'd forbidden. He didn't speak until he knew he could contain his joy. "But being born to it makes it easier to learn?"

She considered him a long time.

His skin vibrated with excitement.

"Yes."

Twist couldn't stop his hands from closing into excited fists.

The candles flared and exploded.

Darkness flooded the cave.

Mary sighed. "It also means it's harder for you to control."

Oops.

Twist burned everything in his cave and Mary collapsed the entrance. The more he knew of her, the more she terrified him and the more he really, *really* wanted to get naked and desecrate her.

She knew it. There was no point in hiding it. All she had to do to give him a hard-on was say his name. He'd wait. Sooner or later, it would happen.

He wanted her power.

They stood a few yards from the trailer that'd been his home for two months.

She glanced at the duffle bag on the ground. "That's all you need? Really?"

It's all he'd brought with him from Dumass: the old witch's book, some herbs, some odds and ends for spell casting. For some spells, he still needed the stuff at first.

"Oh, wait." He dashed into the trailer where he'd had his first three-way, with Benny's wife and the preacher's daughter. The stuffed grackle stood in its usual place on the kitchen table. He didn't know why, but he wanted to keep it.

"You old softy," Mary said when he emerged with it under his arm.

Twist tried to avoid glancing down at Mr. Bunny. The rabbit hopped a circle around his feet. Twist didn't want to seem like a kid with a pet.

Mary smirked and watched the ghost. "Don't be embarrassed." Her sultry voice made Twist want to take her doggy style right there. "A vengeful spirit that does your bidding is actually pretty useful."

Oh, thank God. Mr. Bunny was Twist's first undead creature of the beyond, and he really did have a soft spot for the spooky thing.

"Twist?"

Twist looked up.

Benny hurried toward him wearing boxers, a threadbare wife-beater and pink bunny slippers. "You ain't leaving are you?" Something about trailer trash, they could always spot when someone was pulling up stakes.

"Afraid so, Benny."

He looked Mary up and down. "Miss." He glanced at Twist as if expecting an introduction.

Mary smiled at the redneck. "You're cute." She turned to Twist. "Friend of yours?"

Benny laughed. "You kidding? Twist here's about the best friend I ever *had*. Near about saved my wife's damn *life*, he did."

Mary laughed. She looked to Twist. "Indeed?"

Twist just shook his head.

"Twist?" Benny seemed brokenhearted.

Mary crouched down and held a hand to Mr. Bunny. "But *we're* friends now, aren't we, David?"

If friends meant someone he wanted to pound while she lay draped across a pool table, then yes. "Of course, Mary."

"See, Mr. Bunny? I'm David's friend."

Strangely, the way she said his name, it was almost sexy.

"Twist?" Benny asked. "What's she doing?" He couldn't see the rabbit.

Mr. Bunny hopped to Mary and sniffed her hand.

She pointed the hand. "Take him."

The rabbit looked up. His eyes burned red. He leapt into Benny.

Benny staggered back with a soft cry. Then he stepped forward. . . and wiggled his nose.

His eyes burned red.

Mary giggled like a girl and clapped her hands. "Let me show you how much fun this can be."

She made him strip naked and rip his own balls off with one hand. She made him eat them. She handed him a knife to cut off his dick and eat that, too. Blood poured from his crotch and from his lips, but with Mr. Bunny at the helm, Benny laughed at the destruction.

"Your eyes," she said.

Benny ripped out his eyes with the knife.

"I'm bored, Mr. Bunny. End it."

Benny used the knife to spill his guts out on the ground at his feet.

"Hold it," she said. "Hold it." She nudged Twist. "He's your best friend, Sweety. I want a photo."

So Twist ran to Benny's side a bit reluctantly and threw an arm around his shoulders while his blood soaked into the ground. Flash.

"Kiss his cheek, sweetie," she said. "That's Mr. Bunny in there. Your first ghost."

Oh, well *that* made sense. He kissed the rabbit's cheek. Flash.

"Okay," she said. "I'm bored again."

Mr. Bunny left the body, and Benny dropped to the ground in a heap, too close to death to scream. Twist dropped to his hands and knees beside the dying man. "I fucked your wife, Benny. And that baby? That baby is mine."

The life left Benny's body.

Twist rose to his feet.

Mary threw an arm around his waist and kissed his cheek. "And *that* is how you use a devil ghost rabbit."

Twist allowed his hand to caress his cheek where she'd kissed him.

He just might be in love.

The story continues in

Whiskey Tango Foxtrot
Step 2 in the *Tango Triptych*

Available now